THE CAMBRIDGE COMPANION TO AMERICAN HORROR

Opening up the warm body of American Horror – through literature, film, TV, music, video games, and a host of other mediums – this book gathers the leading scholars in the field to dissect the gruesome histories and shocking forms of American life. Through a series of accessible and informed essays, moving from the seventeenth century to the present day, *The Cambridge Companion to American Horror* explores one of the liveliest and most progressive areas of contemporary culture. From slavery to censorship, from occult forces to monstrous beings, this book is essential reading for anyone interested in America's most terrifying cultural expressions.

STEPHEN SHAPIRO is Professor of English and Comparative Literature at the University of Warwick. Author or editor of seventeen books, some of his most recent include *Pentecostal Modernism: Lovecraft, Los Angeles, and World-Systems Culture* and, as part of the Warwick Research Collective, *Combined and Uneven Development: Towards a New Theory of World-Literature*.

MARK STOREY is Associate Professor at the University of Warwick, where his teaching includes "'American Horror Story: US Gothic Cultures, 1619 to Tomorrow." He is the author of two books on American literature: *Rural Fictions, Urban Realities* (2013) and *Time and Antiquity in American Empire* (2021).

A complete list of books in the series is at the back of this book.

THE CAMBRIDGE
COMPANION TO

AMERICAN HORROR

EDITED BY
STEPHEN SHAPIRO
University of Warwick

MARK STOREY
University of Warwick

CAMBRIDGE
UNIVERSITY PRESS

University Printing House, Cambridge CB2 8BS, United Kingdom

One Liberty Plaza, 20th Floor, New York, NY 10006, USA

477 Williamstown Road, Port Melbourne, VIC 3207, Australia

314–321, 3rd Floor, Plot 3, Splendor Forum, Jasola District Centre, New Delhi – 110025, India

103 Penang Road, #05–06/07, Visioncrest Commercial, Singapore 238467

Cambridge University Press is part of the University of Cambridge.

It furthers the University's mission by disseminating knowledge in the pursuit of education, learning, and research at the highest international levels of excellence.

www.cambridge.org
Information on this title: www.cambridge.org/9781316513002
DOI: 10.1017/9781009071550

First published 2022

A catalogue record for this publication is available from the British Library.

Library of Congress Cataloging-in-Publication Data
NAMES: Shapiro, Stephen, 1964– editor. | Storey, Mark (Literature teacher) editor.
TITLE: The Cambridge companion to American horror / edited by Stephen Shapiro, University of Warwick ; Mark Storey, University of Warwick.
DESCRIPTION: Cambridge ; New York, NY : Cambridge University Press, 2022. | Series: Cambridge companions to literature | Includes bibliographical references and index.
IDENTIFIERS: LCCN 2022007096 (print) | LCCN 2022007097 (ebook) | ISBN 9781316513002 (hardback) | ISBN 9781009069892 (paperback) | ISBN 9781009071550 (epub)
SUBJECTS: LCSH: Horror tales, American–History and criticism. | Horror films–United States–History and criticism. | BISAC: LITERARY CRITICISM / American / General | LCGFT: Literary criticism. | Film criticism.
CLASSIFICATION: LCC PS374.H67 C36 2022 (print) | LCC PS374.H67 (ebook) | DDC 813/.0873809–dc23/eng/20220228
LC record available at https://lccn.loc.gov/2022007096
LC ebook record available at https://lccn.loc.gov/2022007097

ISBN 978-1-316-51300-2 Hardback
ISBN 978-1-009-06989-2 Paperback

CONTENTS

ACKNOWLEDGMENTS

We would like to thank our "American Horror Story" students at the University of Warwick, past and present, for the conversations that have formed this book. Thanks, too, to Ray Ryan, Edgar Mendez, and the entire team at Cambridge, who have been continually helpful and supportive.

We would like to dedicate this collection to Graeme Macdonald (Stephen) and Keith Nottle (Mark).

CONTRIBUTORS

XAVIER ALDANA REYES is Reader in English Literature and Film at Manchester Metropolitan University and co-lead of the Manchester Centre for Gothic Studies. He is author of *Gothic Cinema* (2020), *Spanish Gothic: National Identity, Collaboration, and Cultural Adaptation* (2017), *Horror Film and Affect: Towards a Corporeal Model of Viewership* (2016), and *Body Gothic: Corporeal Transgression in Contemporary Literature and Horror Film* (2014), and editor of *Twenty-First-Century Gothic: An Edinburgh Companion* (with Maisha Wester, 2019) and *Horror: A Literary History* (2016). Xavier is chief editor of the Horror Studies academic book series, published by the University of Wales Press.

JOHAN HÖGLUND is Professor of English at Linnaeus University and a member of the Linnaeus University Centre for Concurrences in Colonial and Postcolonial Studies. He has published extensively on imperial Gothic, horror, war, climate crisis fiction, and US, British and Nordic (neo)colonialism. He is the author of *The American Imperial Gothic: Popular Culture, Empire, Violence* (Ashgate, 2014), and the coeditor of several scholarly collections and special journal issues, including *Dark Scenes from Damaged Earth: Gothic and the Anthropocene* (Minnesota University Press, 2022), *Nordic Gothic* (Manchester University Press, 2020), "Nordic Colonialisms" for *Scandinavian Studies* (2019), *B-Movie Gothic* (Edinburgh University Press, 2018), and *Animal Horror Cinema: Genre, History and Criticism* (Palgrave Macmillan, 2015).

BETSY HUANG is Associate Provost and Dean of the College, the Klein Distinguished Professor, and Associate Professor of English at Clark University. She is the author of *Contesting Genres in Contemporary Asian American Fiction* (Palgrave, 2010) and coeditor of three essay collections: *Techno-Orientalism: Imagining Asia in Speculative Fiction, History, and Media* (Rutgers University Press, 2015), *Diversity and Inclusion in Higher Education and Societal Contexts* (Palgrave, 2018), and, most recently, *Asian American Literature in Transition, 1996–2020* (Cambridge University Press, 2021) with Victor Román Mendoza. You can find more of her work in *The Cambridge Companion to Asian American Literature*, *Journal of Asian American Studies*, and *MELUS*.

DARRYL JONES is Professor of Modern British Literature and Culture in the School of English, Trinity College Dublin. He is the author or editor of thirteen books, most recently *Horror: A Very Short Introduction* (Oxford University Press, 2021). He is the general editor of the forthcoming *New Oxford Sherlock Holmes* series, for which he has edited *The Hound of the Baskervilles*. He is currently working on Conan Doyle's *The Green Flag*, on a large-scale biography of M. R. James, and on the Irish time-travel theorist J. W. Dunne.

DAWN KEETLEY is Professor of English and Film at Lehigh University. She is author of *Making a Monster: Jesse Pomeroy, the Boy Murderer of 1870s Boston* (University of Massachusetts Press, 2017), editor of *Jordan Peele's* Get Out*: Political Horror* (Ohio State University Press, 2020), and coeditor (with Angela Tenga) of *Plant Horror: Approaches to the Monstrous Vegetal in Fiction and Film* (Palgrave, 2016) and (with Matthew Wynn Sivils) of *The Ecogothic in Nineteenth-Century American Literature* (Routledge, 2017). She has also edited a collection on *The Walking Dead* and coedited (with Elizabeth Erwin) a second. She has recently published numerous articles on folk horror and is working on an edited collection on the topic. She writes regularly for a website she cofounded, *Horror Homeroom*.

ESTHER LESLIE is Professor of Political Aesthetics at Birkbeck, University of London. Her books include various studies and translations of Walter Benjamin, as well as *Hollywood Flatlands: Animation, Critical Theory and the Avant Garde* (Verso, 2002), *Synthetic Worlds: Nature, Art and the Chemical Industry* (Reaktion, 2005), *Derelicts: Thought Worms from the Wreckage* (Unkant, 2014), *Liquid Crystals: The Science and Art of a Fluid Form* (Reaktion, 2016), and two projects on milk and dairy, *Deeper in the Pyramid* (with Melanie Jackson; Banner Repeater, 2018) and, for the Limerick Biennale 20–21, *The Inextinguishable* (with M. Jackson, 2021). She is on the editorial board of *Animation: An Interdisciplinary Journal*, for which she edited a special issue with Joel McKim on *Life Remade: Critical Animation in the Digital Age*, in 2017.

BERNICE M. MURPHY is an Associate Professor/Lecturer in Popular Literature at the School of English, Trinity College Dublin. She is the author of *The Suburban Gothic in American Popular Culture* (2009), *The Rural Gothic: Backwoods Horror and Terror in the Wilderness* (2013), and *The Highway Horror Film* (2014) as well as many book chapters on American horror and Gothic texts and topics. Her latest monograph is *The California Gothic in Fiction and Film* (Edinburgh University Press, 2022).

KENDALL R. PHILLIPS is Professor of communication and rhetorical studies at Syracuse University. He examines the rhetorical dynamics emerging at the intersection of politics and popular culture. He is author of several books, including *A Cinema of Hopelessness: The Rhetoric of Rage in 21st Century Popular Culture* (2021), *A Place of Darkness: The Rhetoric of Horror in Early American Cinema*

(2018), *Dark Directions: Romero, Craven, Carpenter and the Modern Horror Film* (2012), and *Projected Fears: Horror Films and American Culture* (2005).

CARL H. SEDERHOLM is Professor of Interdisciplinary Humanities at Brigham Young University. He is the editor of *The Journal of American Culture* and coeditor (with Jeffrey Weinstock) of *The Age of Lovecraft*. His other work includes the coedited volume *Adapting Poe: Re-imaginings in Popular Culture* (with Dennis Perry) and the coauthored book (also with Dennis Perry) *Poe, the "House of Usher," and the American Gothic*. He has also published essays on authors such as Edgar Allan Poe, H. P. Lovecraft, Stephen King, Jonathan Edwards, Lydia Maria Child, and Nathaniel Hawthorne.

STEPHEN SHAPIRO is Professor of English and Comparative Literature at the University of Warwick. Author or editor of seventeen books, some of his most recent include *Pentecostal Modernism: Lovecraft, Los Angeles, and World-Systems Culture* (2017) and, as part of the Warwick Research Collective, *Combined and Uneven Development: Towards a New Theory of World-Literature* (2015).

MARK STEVEN is the author of *Red Modernism: American Poetry and the Spirit of Communism* (Johns Hopkins University Press) and *Splatter Capital* (Repeater) and is editor of *Understanding Marx, Understanding Modernism* (Bloomsbury). He is also a Senior Lecturer in 20th and 21st Century Literature at the University of Exeter.

MARK STOREY is Associate Professor of English and Comparative Literature at the University of Warwick. He is the author of two books on American literature: *Rural Fictions, Urban Realities* (2013) and *Time and Antiquity in American Empire* (2021).

LAURA WESTENGARD is an Associate Professor of English at New York City College of Technology, City University of New York. She serves as Board Co-Chair of CLAGS: Center for LGBTQ Studies and sits on the Editorial Board for the journal *WSQ: Women's Studies Quarterly*. She coedited *The 25 Sitcoms That Changed Television: Turning Points in American Culture* and has published in journals such as *JNT: Journal of Narrative Theory* and *Steinbeck Review*. Her book *Gothic Queer Culture: Marginalized Communities and the Ghosts of Insidious Trauma*, was released in 2019 by University of Nebraska Press.

MAISHA L. WESTER is an Associate Professor of American Studies and British Academy Global Professor in English. She is author of numerous essays and articles and of *African American Gothic: Screams from Shadowed Places* (2013), and coeditor of *Twenty-First-Century Gothic* (2019). She also wrote and codirected the short film *Hegira* (2021) for the online and live exhibition *His House to*

Our Home, an exhibit she curated as part of the United Kingdom's national Being Human festival. Her research examines racial discourses in Gothic literature and horror film, counternarratives to anti-blackness in Black Diasporic Gothic literature and horror film, and sociopolitical appropriations of Gothic and horror film tropes in discussions of race.

MARK STOREY AND STEPHEN SHAPIRO

Introduction

American Horror: Genre and History

Is "American horror" a tautology? It's long been a commonplace of literary criticism to say that American writing was from the very beginning, as Leslie Fiedler put it in *Love and Death in American Novel* back in 1960, "almost essentially a gothic one" (125), one "nonrealistic and negative, sadist and melodramatic" (xxiv). (We will have more to say about the difference between "Gothic" and "horror" in a moment). In influential accounts like Fiedler's,[1] the Gothic mode established in eighteenth-century Europe migrated across the Atlantic to become an essential counternarrative to the purported triumph of enlightened republicanism and liberal pluralism represented by the American experiment. The two things overlap so often that some critics have even argued that "definitions of America and those of the gothic are . . . inseparable" (Faflak and Haslam, 2). American history is, after all, its own horror story, bloody and haunted: the conditions and legacies of Atlantic slavery, the long genocide of Indigenous peoples, white supremacy and racist murder, class struggle and conflict over immigration, imperial violence, fears of nonmale power and nonheterosexual desire, and so on. These have animated much American writing, but also film, art, theater, music, comic books, video games – the full range of cultural expressions and forms. To put it in its most familiar terms: on the other side of the American Dream was always the American Nightmare, and creators seized on Gothic language to make their critiques of the "exceptional" nation-state.

But if all American writing and culture has gothic horror in its DNA, then how can we isolate something we specifically recognize as "American horror"? Is horror a chromosome present in all culture that's aware of America's contradictions, or is it a specific genre complete with its own distinctive codes, clichés, and formulas?

The Cambridge Companion to American Horror suggests it is both. The essays gathered here share no consensus as to what horror actually is. They discuss texts that self-consciously align themselves to the horror genre, as well as texts that would not easily be found in a bookshop's horror section or a streaming services' horror movie subcategory. Yet they do share a fundamental belief that "American horror" – in all its historical and aesthetic variations – describes both a definable cultural object and a general tone or affect, a canon and also a visual and verbal language. And these essays share, too, a critical seriousness about horror's cultural place. Because while "Gothic" feels like a well-established category with a venerable critical tradition behind it (evidenced by the work of many of this companion's contributors and, for instance, the path already beaten by *The Cambridge Companion to American Gothic* edited by Jeffrey Andrew Weinstock), "horror" remains Gothic's embarrassing twin – sometimes synonymous, sometimes a subcategory, sometimes a different thing altogether. This is why we want to draw a pointed but by no means prescriptive distinction between those two keywords, "Gothic" and "horror," partly to think through how genres are invented families of ideas that disguise as much as they reveal, but also how the labels "Gothic" and "horror" have shaped the long history of criticism and popular reception of this field.

Indeed, the traditional denigration of horror turns, in part, on its apparent difference from the more respectable and somehow more "literary" notion of Gothic. This is, after all, what English novelist Ann Radcliffe established as long ago as 1826, in her frequently quoted essay "On the Supernatural in Poetry." Radcliffe's influential distinction between "horror" and "terror" is useful for us because it has tended to color and guide much of the critical work that has followed in its two-hundred-year wake. "Terror and horror," she says, "are so far opposite, that the first expands the soul, and awakens the faculties to a high degree of life; the other contracts, freezes, and nearly annihilates them." The critical industry around Gothic fiction has implicitly hung a lot on this (and similar) definitions, establishing a hierarchy of taste between the more distinguished pursuit of Gothic "terror" (as a version of Aristotelian catharsis) and the artless vulgarity of mere "horror" (as indicative of mindless shock). While the twentieth century saw Gothic establish itself as a respectable term for literary studies – evidenced by the galaxy of academic guides and handbooks available on the subject, not to mention numerous university courses and modules – horror continued to sound a note of subliterary thrills.

This elevation of Gothic's apparent sublimity over horror's crass literalism still adheres in much literary criticism today, even as horror has accrued ever more sophisticated attention.[2] Film studies have been quicker to embrace the term, and from at least Robin Wood's essays on the horror film in the 1970s there has been a rich literature of scholarly work (often geared to psychoanalytical approaches) that dares to take horror seriously: the influence of classic works such as Barbara Creed's *The Monstrous-Feminine* (1993) and

Carol J. Clover's *Men, Women, and* Chain Saws (1992) – both now three decades old – have extended beyond academia into popular culture. In fact, horror's "annihilation of the faculties" that Radcliffe recoiled from in the 1820s partly explains its trajectory toward the critical reassessment recent years have brought. The antirationalist, affective thrust of that diagnosis is precisely what has drawn some of the more sophisticated accounts of horror's political and philosophical resonances. Moreover, this revaluation has been entangled with the ongoing reappropriation of horror by women, nonwhites, and nonheterosexuals as an appropriate mode for registering the historical violence and social death forced on them by a process of cultural othering.[3]

We don't want to overstate the point. Drawing firm differences between "Gothic" and "horror" as generic categories is a game fraught with problems and typically leads to some unconvincing policing of boundaries. Our first impulse is to admit fuzziness and acknowledge that genre categories are never so distinctive as to make works easily shoehorned into one classification rather than another. Indeed, these definitions often say more about the assumptions of the moment in which they are made than they do about the works contained within them. The authors of the essays in this collection use both terms, and often make no clear distinction between "Gothic" and "horror" texts.

But let us venture a definition, some steps toward what "horror" might be and a reclaiming of sorts from Radcliffe's and critical history's sniffy dismissal. Any number of definitions of Gothic could be cited here as a counterpoint, but Fred Botting, one of the field's most distinguished critics, usefully summarizes it as a literature "depicting disturbances of sanity and security, from superstitious belief in ghosts and demons, displays of uncontrolled passion, violent emotion or flights of fancy to portrayals of perversion and obsession" (2). Similarly but even more pithily, Jeffrey Weinstock claims that "Gothic is a genre that focuses on the past and immoderate, ungovernable passions" (1). These are good places to start, especially because they open up a gap that, we suggest, horror fills. If, then, Gothic has tended to be associated with interior psychological states, uncanny forces, and – crucially – a Eurocentric history of aristocratic and religious residues and iconography, we suggest that horror points us to a more historically immediate and materially present form of experience. If Gothic's collision of strange environment and dress with psychological fugue and paranoia often tracks the persistence of the past, we see horror as the name of something more corporeal and modern-facing. If Gothic emphasizes the "terror" of anticipation, then horror highlights the moment of pain and shock. If Gothic treats the disturbed and the tense, then horror treats the slashed and the torn. If Gothic is the mind, then horror is the body. Fredric Jameson once aphoristically said that "History is what hurts"; we claim some of that same ground, and for us horror is the genre above all others that pushes beyond the hurt to the open wound. Horror is what *bleeds*.

To elaborate a bit further on these dimensions of American horror, it's worth distinguishing between two areas of focus that are prevalent throughout the essays in this book: these might be simply described as the *formal* and the *political*.

The Forms of American Horror

One of the abiding preoccupations of this book is horror's paraliterary status, that is, horror as a genre that has often occupied a marginal position within "high" culture and, as a result, the study of the humanities. This overlooked position has been integral to its taboo, even pornographic, thrills, of course. Uninvited (and so unincorporated) into polite scholarly discussion or art's institutions, horror was able to be an anteroom for those seeking out more countercultural communities and anarchic personal satisfactions. A genre with abject experience at its heart, it became an object of cultural abjection in itself. This nonrecognition within respectable culture's jurisdiction also went hand in hand with the disposability of its material transmission: from penny dreadfuls to four-color comics, from Grand Guignol to video nasties, horror's intellectual sidelining as *narrative form* was often bound up in the ephemeral nature of its *media forms*.

Indeed, some of horror's liveliest venues for innovation have come in the most maligned and dismissed forms of culture. The proliferating and collectively authored world of online "creepypasta," for instance, updates the folk traditions of urban legends and campfire storytelling through the dark recesses of message boards, blogs, and viral memes. Beginning in the 1990s, "creepypasta" is the collective name for scary or disturbing short stories, images, and video clips posted (often anonymously) to message boards and specialist sites. Here, fan fiction and professional productions have bled into one another, nowhere more so than in the development of the "Slender Man" mythos. Originally a series of doctored photographs released on message boards by "Victor Surge" (real name Eric Knudsen) in 2009, the ominous and faceless character of the Slender Man has circulated in both ambitious amateur productions – such as the YouTube–based series *Marble Hornets* – and found its Hollywood realization in *Slender Man* (dir. Sylvain White, 2018). In the world of creepypasta, the oral traditions of folklore and cautionary tales find themselves translated into and through the new digital networks of the internet. Authorial ownership and the assumed singularity of the work of art is replaced by an anonymous, evolving, ever-growing sense of communal worldmaking, cultural production happening primarily in the more unregulated territories of web-based creativity.[4]

Some of this unruly narrative energy stems from – and feeds back into – the hugely profitable video games industry. Popular horror games series such as Konami's *Silent Hill* and Capcom's *Resident Evil* (themselves evolutions of 1990s domestic and arcade video games like *Alone in the Dark* [1992] and *House of the Dead* [1996]) have taken literary and filmic horror conventions and advanced them into immersive digital experiences. Horror's generic toolbox is everywhere apparent in these games – zombies, monsters, dark and haunted houses – and while some might write them off as entirely commercialized products, in the best video games the ludic quality of game-playing meets literature and film's language of terror and becomes the site of some of horror's most innovative developments. From the mercurial and terrifying *P.T.* (the infamous *Silent Hill* teaser made by Hideo Kojima and Guillermo del Toro that takes place in a single corridor) to acclaimed independent productions such as Playdead's *Limbo* (2010) and Jon McKellan's *Stories Untold* (2017), video games can push horror's clichés and formulas into ever-richer and sometimes ever-evolving territory.

These are just two brief examples of cultural fields that have, traditionally, been given short shrift in academic commentary. But the variety of forms in which horror seems both popular and vibrantly productive speaks to the more general point about its exclusion from the venues of cultural sanctification. To put it another way, for some critics the trashiness of horror's messages is mirrored in the trashiness of its mediums. Positioned in this way – as doubly antithetical to art's role in the transmission of social capital – horror's lurid spectacles and formulas could take their apparently rightful place on the bottom rung of literary and film culture's hierarchies of prestige.

Some of horror's other fundamental characteristics further explain its exclusion from conventional cultural histories. One is its resistance to institutionalized protocols of interpretation; or, to put it more simply, horror's challenge to the seminar room's most basic question: What does it mean? Horror, on the one hand, often seems ripe for straightforward and "obvious" allegorical decoding, in ways that leave little else to say and little opportunity for a bravura display of interpretive nuance. As Jerrold E. Hogle notes, varieties of psychoanalytic, Marxist, and feminist readings still dominate Gothic (and horror) criticism, and these approaches are themselves often dismissed as lacking sufficient complexity.[5] On the other hand, it's a genre that can seem to refuse to yield any explanations at all: after all, Edgar Allan Poe opens one of his most enduring short stories, "The Man of the Crowd" (1840), with the claim that "*Es lässt sich nicht lesen*" – "It will not permit itself to be read." It's a teasing assertion of inscrutability that runs throughout American horror, from the inexplicable gathering out in the woods in Nathaniel Hawthorne's "Young Goodman Brown" (1835) to the enigmatic village ritual at the heart of Shirley Jackson's "The Lottery" (1948) to the confounding architecture of the Overlook Hotel in Stanley Kubrick's *The Shining* (1980). We see everywhere in horror a sustained confrontation with events, experiences, and forms of affect that just cannot be rationalized, cannot be explicated other than purely as what they are – pain, suffering, violence, fear; the stuff not of objective detachment and contemplation but of raw and immediate experience.

If this is what horror gives us, then it's perhaps no surprise that some of its key theorists render their object in these same elusive ways. When Julia Kristeva, in her essay *Powers of Horror* (1982), explains her concept of "abjection" (one of the central terms in horror's critical lexicon), she admits that "the twisted braid of affects and thoughts" that abjection elicits does not actually have, "properly speaking, a definable object" – it is, she says, "a 'something' that I do not recognize as a thing" (1–2). To put it in the aphoristic words of Gertrude Stein: There is no there there. And this is what Eugene Thacker, in *In the Dust of This Planet* (2011), seizes on in his account of horror and our "unthinkable" world: that horror is "a privileged site in which [the] paradoxical thought of the unthinkable takes place" (2). As critics of horror – or just as readers and watchers – we might not be able to escape the notion that part of horror's fundamental effect is the simultaneous invitation *and* refusal of our desire to interpret.

One challenge in thinking about how we interpret horror's "meanings" is that some horror tales do, in fact, consciously invite allegorical ways of reading (George Romero's *Dawn of the Dead* [1978] as critique of mindless consumerism, for instance). Consequently, readers of horror need a mechanism that *allows but does not require* the allegorical impulse to be applied, and – because of that paraliterary status – need a mechanism that does not seek to defend genre fiction through the usual categories that we've tended to invoke when venerating so-called high culture. So, we suggest a model of the valences of cultural production and consumption that can allow horror to move, as it were, outside the weight of these interpretive shackles.[6] To explain, let's separate these into three distinct approaches.

1. One aspect of many texts is that they approach a social or personal problem *thematically*. It's clear that some issue matters, but this is treated descriptively and often more at the symptomatic level of emotional concern. The thematic approach knows that something is in the air, but

does not have much more to say about it other than to notice and highlight its presence.

2. Other works come at the problem *analytically*, diagnosing it and turning it into something that requires an explanation that may help inform or educate the reader. Here is often where allegorical impulses come into play, as one (but not the only) means of analysis. Works that seem more analytical are ones that are often celebrated and canonized by academic readers, who largely see themselves as special readers due to their training and expertise in critical analysis. Generic writing is often devalued precisely because of the claim that it is not analytic enough, but this is often because (academic) criticism has devoted more time and labor to forging terms and keywords to capture analytic functions, and less on the other two listed here.
3. A third approach is when texts act *transformatively* to create a new social collective after the shared experience of reading or viewing. Examples of this process include fan communities that bond around a text's imagined world and characters, often without the actual plot or conclusion being the center of concern. This process includes practices like fan fiction, cosplay (dressing up as particular characters), and performative subcultures such as Goth or Steampunk. If generic works are considered as lacking analytic nuance, they often combine the thematic and transformative in ways that other works do less frequently.

While it may be initially compelling to see these three approaches or "valences" as forming a numerical hierarchy – where the majority of works only operate as thematic, with fewer as analytic, and only a handful as fully transformative – that would be mistaken on two accounts. First, almost no text operates in just one way; texts tend to flit through aspects of all three to greater or lesser degrees. It is almost impossible to conceive of a text that entirely lacks some analytical effort, for example, or that doesn't generate at least some social connection with others.

Second, the notion of a linear trajectory has been the cause of one longstanding difficulty in appreciating horror. The academic study of culture often tends to select and celebrate cultural productions that seem mainly analytical, since this is the ground on which the university's teachers and students are rewarded. Yet the power of "genre fiction" often comes through combining the thematic with the transformative – hence the prevalence and passion of genre fan communities, zines, forums, conventions, and so on. Academia's prejudice in favor of the analytical has been the source of much difficulty in discussing horror: unlike the analytical valence that has a large body of critical terms used to evaluate it, the thematic and the transformative (or the thematic-transformative) do not have an established set of keywords and procedures to discuss and consider them. In this way, then, the effort to look beyond allegory can be a productive search for new approaches to perceiving what makes horror more (or less!) effective.

The Politics of American Horror

Having suggested that American horror can be characterized as paraliterary narratives that require a different way of reading, we make a further and related claim: American horror's focus on the body in distress registers the faults and tensions of Western centrist liberalism.[7] While we emphasize, therefore, that "horror" is worth distinguishing from "Gothic" even as the two share much of the same ground, so too is the Americanness of our horror both distinct to a set of national conditions and yet not, finally, separate from the wider world of historical and political conditions in which the United States first took – and continues to take – shape. Part of this stems from the tumultuous conditions in which American modernity began: the widespread revolutions and rebellions of the late eighteenth century include the settler-colonial American Revolution (1765–83), the Indigenous and mestizo rebellions associated with Túpac Amaru II in the Peruvian Andes (1780–82), the French Revolution (1789–99), the Black slave uprising in the Haitian Revolution (1791–1804), the onset of the Polish-Lithuanian Commonwealth (1788–92), and conflict in Ireland (1798). The American Revolutionary flashpoint was therefore part of a broader global moment of political crisis, and this registered in all kinds of horrific tales and stories across the world. The German playwright Friedrich Maximilian Klinger's play *Sturm und Drang* (Storm and Stress) (1776), set amid the American Revolution, for instance, gave the name to an ensuing dramatic movement of antirationalist and highly emotive plays, and which in turn fed into the rise of the German *Schauerroman* (shudder-novel) that would strongly inspire both English and American Gothic writing.

Three political ideologies emerged from this moment to respond to the inevitability of constant social transformation and the new ideal of democratic rule. These ideologies were conservatism, socialism, and centrist liberalism. Conservatives emphasized the need to retain the role and sanctity of traditional formations of social "order," especially those involving the family, religious institutions, and nostalgic images of the past. Socialists favored a radical transformation against all conservative ideals and sought instead to establish a broader right to rule by social groups, especially of the laboring and lower classes. Liberals sought a position in between conservativism and socialism, and they argued that the move to nonelite rule could be managed "carefully, prudently, and above all gradually" (Wallerstein, 147). The mechanism for this moderation would be government by individuals chosen for their talent and merit, a bureaucratic management that would incrementally extend suffrage to women, nonwhites, and workers and would grant access to higher education as the mechanism that trains the individual with the social "virtue" felt necessary to handle institutional power.

Yet the more "equality" loomed as a realized social reality, the more obstacles – juridical, political, economic, and cultural – were created to prevent its actual realization. As Immanuel Wallerstein puts it, the idea of the "citizen" served to crystallize

> a long list of binary distinctions that then came to form the cultural underpinnings of the capitalist world-economy . . .: bourgeois and proletarian, man and woman, adult and minor, breadwinner and housewife, majority and minority, White and Black, European and non-European, educated and ignorant, skilled and unskilled, specialist and amateur, scientist and layman, high culture and low culture, heterosexual and homosexual, normal and abnormal, able-bodied and disabled, and of course the ur-category which all of these others imply – civilized and barbarian. (146)

If centrist liberalism paradoxically proclaimed the universality of equality while also setting up a series of binary divisions that would limit the participation in and achievement of this equality, then we can see how tales of embodied horror emerged to explore the tensions of this false promise and the fear of revenge for the denial of this ideal. If horror often lingers on the body turned inside out, it is because centrist liberalism sees the body as the container of natural human rights, even as it assumes that the individual is to be seen as a disembodied citizen. Horror's embodied violence works to make explicit the presence of exclusions based on embodied features.

So, if horror's object of consideration is the limits of liberalism we can understand why it appears globally while also having specific characteristics for each nation.[8] We can also explain why it may proliferate at certain historical moments, while always being somewhere present throughout the centuries-old duration of liberal authority. In this sense, American horror belongs to a wider family of horror across the world while also revolving around its own distinct compass points – Atlantic slavery and its residues; Native American dispossession and genocide; violent conflict (both rural and urban) over class, immigration, and rights; and matters of gender, sexuality, and ability. These distinctions, as we said earlier, have been central to the encounter between the American liberal dream and its umbilical twin, the American nightmare.

Stemming from this complex of historical, conceptual, and political questions, we can arrive in our own present moment and the new "golden age" of American horror. Against that long history of critical dismissal, horror is undoubtedly having an extraordinary renaissance in both popular culture and critical scholarship. The essays in this book therefore look back to the classic markers of nineteenth- and twentieth-century American literature and culture, but also survey the new landscapes of horror production. And here, in the evolutions of American horror both formal and political, we can end with a note of optimism for horror's future. One of the most salient aspects of this recent resurgence has been the transformation of horror's assumed creators and audience, from (young) white heterosexual men to a genre that is just as likely to be created by and for women, trans, Black, Indigenous, and people of color, and nonheterosexuals. If a truism about Gothic was that it revolved around fearful reactions to the presence of the "Other," then contemporary horror often turns the tables and indicts modern liberalism's mainstream norms as the real monster. Rather than horror simply being a topic of historical consideration, doomed to various repetitions or reiterations of what already exists, it can also be an uncompromising and visceral reimagining of the present – a present that is terrifying, but also ready for change. *The Cambridge Companion to American Horror* is haunted by the past, but also, we hope, provides a guide to the new horizons coming into our collective view.

NOTES

1. See, for instance, Teresa Goddu, *Gothic America: Narrative, History, and Nation* (Columbia University Press, 1997); Charles L. Crow, *American Gothic* (Cardiff: University of Wales Press, 2009); and Allan Lloyd-Smith, *American Gothic Fiction: An Introduction* (Continuum, 2004).
2. Kevin Corstorphine has even argued that it "can occur independently of the Gothic mode" (2) altogether.
3. "Social death" is used here to mean the exclusion of subjects from the liberal rights of self-representation, exemplified in the right to vote (suffrage), own property, make contracts, bring police charges, and testify in a court of law.
4. For more on creepypasta, see the collection of essays edited by Trevor J. Blank and Lynne S. McNeill, *Slender Man Is Coming: Creepypasta and Contemporary Legends on the Internet* (Utah State University Press, 2018).
5. Jerrold E. Hogle, "The Gothic-Theory Conversation: An Introduction," in *The Gothic and Theory: An Edinburgh Companion*, ed. Jerrold E. Hogle and Robert Miles (Edinburgh University Press, 2019), 1–30.
6. For a more detailed development of these ideas, see Stephen Shapiro, "The Cultural Fix: Capital, Genre, and the Times of American Studies," in *The Fictions of American Capitalism: Working Fictions and the Economic Novel*, ed. Vincent Dussol and Jacques-Henri Coste (Palgrave, 2020), 89–108.

7. Here we draw on Immanuel Wallerstein's argument for developments within the capitalist world-system's secular trend, or long duration, from the late eighteenth century to the period loosely from 1966 to 1970 as a corrective to Ronald Paulson's influential account of the "bloody upheavals of the French Revolution" as propelling "the popularity of Gothic fiction in the 1790s and well into the nineteenth century" (536 *ELH*, later published as *Representations of Revolution, 1789–1820* (Yale University Press, 1983)). Paulson felt that "widespread anxieties and fears in Europe aroused by the turmoil in France" found "a kind of sublimation or catharsis in tales of darkness, confusion, blood, and horror" (536). In particular, Paulson highlights the role of the crowd as "the central phenomenon of the Revolution. The crowd, with the related terms 'natural sovereignty' and 'General Will' . . . was among the most ambiguous concepts to arise from the Revolution" (540). While Paulson's description captures some of what we consider as horror's constituent elements, it remains overly fixed on the singular event of the Revolution, rather than its long cultural influence.
8. For accounts of national identity and horror and gothic traditions outside the United States, see Jonathan Rigby's *English Gothic* (Signum Books, 2015); Xavier Aldana Reyes's *Spanish Gothic* (Palgrave Macmillan, 2017); *Italian Horror Cinema*, edited by Stefano Baschiera and Russ Hunter (Edinburgh University Press, 2016); Colette Balmain's *Introduction to Japanese Horror Film* (Edinburgh University Press, 2008); Rebecca Duncan's *South African Gothic* (University of Wales Press, 2018); and Adam Lowenstein's *Shocking Representation: Historical Trauma, National Cinema, and the Modern Horror Film* (Columbia University Press, 2005).

Works Cited

Botting, Fred. *Gothic*, 2nd ed. London: Routledge, 2014.

Corstorphine, Kevin. "Introduction." In *The Palgrave Handbook to Horror Literature*, ed. Kevin Corstorphine and Laura R. Kremmel. Palgrave, 2018. 1–17.

Faflak, Joel and Jason Haslam. "Introduction." In *American Gothic Culture: An Edinburgh Companion*, ed. Joel Faflak and Jason Haslam. Edinburgh University Press, 2016.

Fiedler, Leslie. *Love and Death in the American Novel*. Criterion Books, 1960.

Kristeva, Julia. *Powers of Horror: An Essay on Abjection*. Trans. Leon S. Roudiez. New York: Columbia University Press, 1982.

Radcliffe, Ann. "On the Supernatural in Poetry." *New Monthly Magazine* 16, no. 1 (1826): 145–52.

Thacker, Eugene. *In the Dust of This Planet: Horror of Philosophy*, vol. 1. Zero Books, 2011.

Wallerstein, Immanuel. *The Modern World-System IV: Centrist Liberalism Triumphant, 1789–1914*. University of California Press, 2011.

Weinstock, Jeffrey Andrew. "Introduction." In *The Cambridge Companion to American Gothic*, ed. Jeffrey Andrew Weinstock. Cambridge University Press, 2017.

PART I

Histories

I

MAISHA L. WESTER

Slavery

Fifteen years after the United States became independent, a slave rebellion in Saint Domingue, later known as the first Haitian Revolution, shook Europe and America. While scholars readily observe the impact of the French Revolution on the development of the Gothic, the Era of Revolutions was also profoundly haunted by this slave rebellion, for it challenged political, philosophical, and racial ideologies. This was especially true in America, which was faced with a number of quandaries as a slave-holding democracy championing man's freedom and equality. Writers would address these tensions in their literature in the years to come while political intellectuals and historians would try to contain the challenges posed by the Haitian Revolution within a Gothic frame. Unsurprisingly, American horror is haunted by the Revolution and the institution that produced it, and grapples with a notable irony: "rebel slaves, excluded from dominant definitions of American identity, were actually its best exemplars of nationhood ... 'The slave, not the master, was the truer American'" (Young, 24).

African American writers were troubled not by the events in the Caribbean but by their absence in the United States. The Haitian Revolution brought into stark relief the hypocrisy of the American experiment. Thus, early slave narratives often turned to Gothic tropes to illustrate the inhumanity of white slaveholders and their failures to uphold their own ideals. Noting that they were never fully free in the United States, these early Black authors remained haunted by slavery, both as a life-threatening institution and as an ideology which underscored the (white) American way of life. Beyond the nineteenth century, slavery continues to haunt African American writers as a signifier of the social death[1] that America imposes on Blacks by necessity of the nation's ideological and structural systems. Like their ancestors, later Black authors are haunted by the incompleteness of the rebellion against slavery. Unlike Haiti, which instituted laws condemning anti-Blackness and racial oppression, slavery in the United States was largely ended in name only, followed as it was by the systemic racism that maintained socioeconomic oppression.[2]

"What has cast such a shadow upon you?"

By now, most scholars accept Toni Morrison's contention that only a writer who is an "isolato" could escape slavery's impact during the nineteenth century.[3] If, as Robert Martin and Eric Savoy have argued, the Gothic in America "may be said to be everywhere" as a genre that returns "the story generated by the national ego 'back to its source on the abominable limits from which, in order to be, the ego has broken away'" (ix, viii), then we must acknowledge the specter of slavery and (the suppression of) slave rebellion as part of this abominable source. This origin makes the American Dream a Faustian nightmare for Americans.

Numerous white American writers produced texts explicitly haunted by slavery. Consider, for instance, Alymer's "assistant" Aminidab in Nathaniel Hawthorne's "The Birth-Mark" (1843). Aminadab is described in stark contrast to Alymer's hyper-whiteness, for he is blackened by the grime of the furnace and speaks in uncouth and savage speech in contrast to Alymer's intellectual commentary and is tasked with physical labor.[4] Herman Melville explicitly meditates on the question of slavery, racial identity, and white superiority by recasting the Haitian Revolution aboard a ship in *Benito Cereno* (1856). Though the Black rebels in Melville's story fail at gaining freedom, they nonetheless succeed in troubling the boundaries of race to such an extent that whiteness, in the form of Cereno, disintegrates and dies away. Edgar Allan Poe proves most clearly illustrative of American horror's debt to slavery in a variety of his works, including but not limited to "The Gold-Bug," (1843) "The Murders in the Rue Morgue," (1841) and "Hop-Frog" (1849). Poe's *The Narrative of Arthur Gordon Pym of Nantucket* (1838) rewrites the Haitian Revolution as Pym and his friends land on an island literally marked by the signs connecting it to the US South. Encountering a population on the island that is so utterly Black that even their teeth are black, the sailors are decimated when the natives wage a surprise attack. The event is remarkably similar to Dessaline's final attack on the white French colonialist, a dissolution and exile that is sealed in Haiti's first constitution. Pym and August flee the island only to encounter a vision of whiteness that is utterly unfathomable and unsustainable, given that Pym dies at this point in recounting the narrative. Like Melville's *Cereno*, the question of slavery and rebellion confronts whiteness with its own instability in Poe's horror.

This trend appears in sociopolitical discourses and writings with unflinching regularity in the nineteenth and twentieth century. Historians and journalists used the genre in detailing momentous interracial events such as abolitionist debates and Nat Turner's rebellion. Realist nonfiction writers turned to the Gothic in their sociopolitical monographs debating racial progress and equality. This is particularly true in W. B. Seabrook's *Magic Island* (1929), the text largely responsible for popularizing the figure of the zombie in American culture. In the chapter "... Dead Men Working in Cane Fields," Seabrook explores the zombified labor that mans the US-owned HASCO sugar company. The chapter meditates on the haunting specter of slavery in US colonialist maneuvers while also implicitly reflecting on the racialized labor practices in Jim Crow America during the same era. Seabrook thus ponders how the contemporary US occupation and racial practices destabilize the nation's democratic ideals in ways similar to the destabilization offered by Haiti's very birth and critiques of slaveholding democracy.

Zombies were not the only way slavery would continue to trouble American popular culture; it also manifested in realist films that wielded Gothic tropes. This is especially evident in D. W. Griffith's 1915 film *Birth of a Nation*, which might be described as a horror film considering its various depictions of beastly Blacks brutalizing white Americans. In the film's opening, the American South appears as a pastoral region where enslaved Blacks happily work or, at worst, suffer minor scratches as a result of their own buffoonery. After Black emancipation, the South becomes blighted by disorder and chaos. Roaming bands of armed Black soldiers brutishly push genteel white families off sidewalks and lasciviously assault white women. In the North, Black servants breach their socioeconomic position to manipulate and usurp white authority. The film marks mixed-race Blacks in this region as wolves thinly veiled in human flesh. Lydia, the maid to an important politician, literally slavers at her master, ripping hungrily at her clothes and body as she plots while Lynch fiendishly threatens white men with unsolicited violence in the midst of his climb to political power. The scene in Congress epitomizes the horror of Black liberation, as the space of law becomes dominated by unruly Black "politicians" who clip their toenails at their desks, drink alcohol openly, and burst into fights among each other. The few surviving white politicians are pushed to the back of the room while white onlookers are crowded to a small corner in the balcony. The only legal proceeding this barbaric crowd of Blacks manages to complete is to legalize interracial marriage. This is a profound point of horror in the scene as the Black men in the room look with greedy eyes at the trembling, terrorized white women in the gallery.

As in Poe, the abolition of slavery and confrontation with Black authority proves the death of whiteness. This is most apparent in the fate of Flora's fate: pursued by a wanton Black man, she throws herself from a cliff. Likewise, the inspiration and resolution to the problem also testifies to slavery's abolition as the death of whiteness. The hero Ben convinces friends to dress in white sheets and hoods, pretending to be ghosts to "scare" Blacks into submission.[5] Only by reclaiming dominance and forcing Blacks back into an oppressed position can whiteness continue its corporeal, sociopolitical existence.[6] In *Birth of a Nation* white existence depends on Black social death. As fictitious and exaggerated as Griffith's recount of "history" proves, he nonetheless speaks to a sociopolitical reality in America. It is this reality that is the horror of African American fictions.

Staring Down the Barrel of 400-Plus Years

A pregnant slave woman haunts the 2020 HBO series *Lovecraft Country*. As I have noted elsewhere,[7] African American horror traces its origins back to enslaved narrators' appropriation of Gothic tropes in the early and mid-nineteenth century. For instance, in *The Bondwoman's Narrative* (2002) Hannah Crafts uses the eighteenth-century Gothic's preoccupation with darkness to portray the horrifying realities tormenting enslaved women. Slave narratives' use of the Gothic did not merely argue for Black emancipation and rename the master "monster," thereby demonizing the institution and its warping affects on white humanity (Young, 44). Rather, these narratives resist dehumanization, objectification, and social death in using horror. Slave narratives gestured toward Black interiority, complex subjectivity, and ultimately humanity, without offering up this interiority for inspection and dissection.[8] In critiquing Henry Louis Gates' willingness to read Crafts' narrative as a direct, unmediated recount of her life, Ballinger et al. importantly note that Gates "failed to recognize that the manuscript he had himself acquired and edited is perhaps the most intertextually complicated text in all of African American fiction" (209). The critique reminds us of an important but little recognized fact of slave narratives: they are profoundly intertextual, an attempt not to represent the unadulterated self but to construct a self that is stronger than that created for them. In doing so, they act as a point of resistance to the complex and insidious mechanisms of social death because the figure reduced to a monstrous fiction by racist culture seizes narrative control and tells a story themself.

Slave narratives provide an important model for twentieth- and twenty-first-century African American horror concerned with continued racist assaults in and by the United States. These texts return to the scene of slavery to reveal how the contemporary mechanisms and functions of social death reveal the lie of history as a social construct and discipline that "construes the past as dead and remote from the present" (Dubey, 789). In contrast, Black horror's determination to reveal slavery's "haunting(s) 'pulls the past into view and refuses the lie of its completion' to show that what seems to have become a matter of history still remains alive in the present" (789). Novels like Octavia Butler's *Kindred* (1979) disrupt simple readings of history as linear and forward-moving, and reveal uneasy truths about the "progressive" present's debt to historic and contemporary racial oppression. The horror of Butler's novel stems from its revelation of the fact that the horrors of slavery were necessary for the present because without it, the United States and African Americans would not exist. Hence Dana has to help Rufus rape her ancestor even as she later kills him, ending his reign of terror and will to condemn others to social death. The events, however, signal a difficult task for African Americans, who must acknowledge such violence as constitutive of a past they must remember in order to recognize it in the present, resisting its mechanisms to (it is hoped) create a different future.

Thus, we return to Hanna, the slave haunting *Lovecraft Country*, ancestor to the hero Atticus Freeman. The series repeatedly depicts Hanna's escape from her master in Atticus', and eventually his lover Letitia's, visions. In these scenes, a very-pregnant Hanna stands at an open doorway to the burning mansion, turned as if looking back before fleeing the house of horrors. She carries with her a magical text called "The Book of Names," a tome offering ultimate power to any who can read it. The scene encapsulates the concerns and themes recurrent in African American horror and is similar to Octavia Butler's *Kindred* and Phyllis Aliesha Perry's *Stigmata* (1998), among other Black horror texts, in which time travel back to slavery "make(s) possible an unmediated relation to the past as something that has not quite passed into the realm of history" (Dubey, 787). Such

> temporal doublings . . . are obviously intended to reveal the persistence of the past in the present and to ensure that their readers as well as characters feel the discomfort of straddling two time zones, of keeping one foot squarely in the present while traveling to the past. Paranormal devices of time travel are . . . calculated to make their readers as well as characters feel ill at ease in the present. (791)

In *Lovecraft Country*, Hanna's history and pregnancy recount the (sexualized) racial violence Blacks endured from America's very beginning. Like slaves who were present at the founding of a powerful country governed by white men, she too is present at the start of a powerful white group, "The Sons of Adam." Her escape while pregnant suggests a hope of escape into a different future for her descendants while also acknowledging that her enslavement and abuse will continue to haunt them. Indeed, Atticus sees her when he is positioned as a sacrifice in the midst of a ritual to give the clan's white leader immortality, thereby testifying to whiteness' continued reliance on Black death to enrich and ensure white life. The series marks this sacrifice as recurrent, for in the episode "Rewind 1921" the show centers on another group of ancestors fighting white violence in Tulsa, Oklahoma. This time they do not escape, and pregnant Letitia watches as they burn. The episode repeats the primal scene with significant variations, reminding us of the countless Black lives sacrificed to white violent hunger while also promising that African American existence will go on even in the face of such onslaught.

The vignette "Good Golly" in *Tales from the Hood 2* (dir. Rusty Cundieff and Darin Scott, 2018) shows a similar concern. Floyd, the curator of a museum of anti-Black propaganda, critically relays the history of Black objectification to Black Zoe and her white, Golly-loving friend Aubrey:

> FLOYD: Slave Masters used to brand their property with a hot iron. But as we became free men and women, America needed a new way to mark its property, a new way to control the Negro, keep him in his place. So instead of hot coals and metal, they used pen, paint and ink. NO branding iron necessary.... Lazy, shiftless, gluttonous, lying, oversexed, ugly, violent, stupid. In this way the American Nigger slash Negro became the first true corporate brand.
>
> AUDREY: Yah, this country used to be just ... really messed up.
>
> ZOE: No doubt.
>
> FLOYD: Better now, is it?
>
> AUDREY [gesturing to Zoe]: Well I mean, we're friends since grade school, sooo ...
>
> ZOE: Yahh [giggling while reaching over to affirm Audrey].

Zoe's silence is significant, given the conversation's focus on racial dynamics in contemporary America in the midst of the Black Lives Matter movement. Furthermore, shortly after this exchange Audrey inquires about purchasing a Golliwog doll within Zoe's earshot, and Zoe remains silent. Zoe fails to acknowledge the dynamics of social death in American history and in her existence. Her willingness to passively collude in its perpetuation in her current life, especially in her friendship with Aubrey and her brother Philip – who playfully lashes Zoe with a slave whip in the midst of foreplay – condemns her to actual death. A willing contributor to her undead existence, she is erased from existence altogether.

Numerous African American horror texts and media worry over the ways to best navigate the history of slavery and modern social death. Pauline

Hopkins's *Of One Blood* (1902), for example, considers the familial and gender quandaries resulting from slavery, particularly critiquing the colorism and masculinist dynamics that condemn Black women to reliving slavery's sexual manipulations and assaults. Jean Toomer and Gloria Naylor likewise meditate on the horrors of attempting to forget the history of slavery and evade social death through ascription to a dehumanizing capitalist system that particularly devalues Blackness. In *Cane* (1923), Toomer first explores the devastating impact of slavery on the US South before traveling northward to reveal the alienating stakes of trying to forget the horrors left behind. Lost, degraded people who seem mere ghosts on the ruinous landscape populate the first section, which is punctuated by a tale of a lynching called "Blood-Burning Moon." The second segment of the novel is dominated by people so distant from each other in their emotionless, soulless state that they fail to notice when their neighbor is drowning under the economic burden of the "American Dream." The final section proves a dizzying return to the South and a meditation on the difficulty of negotiating its history alongside its familial and cultural value. Similarly, in *Linden Hills* (1986) Naylor begins with the story of an enslaved man who manages to purchase his freedom. Like Hopkins, Naylor reveals the horror of reproducing slavery on the Black woman's body as the first Luther Nedeed earns the money to purchase property by selling his wife. The whole of the novel is a meditation on the costs of selling one's soul in order to achieve economic success in the hopes of disassociating the self from the history of slavery.

Jordan Peele's *Get Out* (2017) and Uche Aguh's *The House Invictus* (2018) pick up this interrogation in their depictions of the complex and nuanced ways African Americans are seduced into condemning themselves and others to social death. Peele's film repeatedly returns audiences to the scene of slavery in the wealthy white treatment of his Black protagonist, Chris. Rose only dates Chris in order to sell him to wealthy bidders in a scene reminiscent of slavery's auction blocks. The bidders' examinations of him, particularly their questions about his sexual abilities, explicitly recall the questions and examinations slave masters subjected Blacks to, while the scenes of hypnosis – as Chris, trapped in the "sunken place," views the external world as if through a television screen – worries over the ways Black psychology is actively manipulated through media. The film's repeated refrain "A mind is a terrible thing to waste" calls attention to the ways Black bodies are prized in a modern US society that nonetheless deems Black thought as detritus. As such, the film is a thorough illustration of what bell hooks called "Eating the Other":[9] as hooks notes, US culture does not consume the entirety of the Other in its appropriation of Black culture, for such appropriation always occurs on a superficial level, disdaining the sociohistorical and cultural meaning behind the artifact/practice. The thought, emotion, and, ultimately, meaning behind the consumed thing is tossed aside, expelled as so much "shit" in the consumptive process.[10]

The House Invictus proves an equally complex exploration of slavery's manifestations in modern Black existence. The plot spins around the initiation of a group of Black men into what seems to be a Black Greek Society. The men squabble among themselves, needlessly provoking each other to violence until one beats another to death as his associates look on. However, this is just one of the numerous Black and US institutions the film indicts for its racial practices. Thus in the midst of this seeming chaos, the film suddenly breaks, shifting away from the house and relocating itself in a hyper-white room with a television at the center. The camera zooms in to show the action in the house on the screen, before we are finally shown the Black butler watching. Blacks, as participants and as audiences, are indicted for both actively and passively reproducing the violence below. Notably, the very first scene of the film reveals its concern over intraracial contributions to social death. As three Black men kneel before the seeming Black butler, their eyes flash briefly blue as they utter their oath of allegiance. We later see beneath the mask of this butler once we learn the history of the location – it was a former plantation that the master burned, vowing to never liberate his slaves or any Blacks from the dynamics of slavery. This master haunts the US landscape, ensnaring unwary Blacks that wander onto his soil. Yet, as his planation is never given a location and as its mechanisms of torture are constitutive of other social groups and practices, the film argues that this master haunts the whole of the country, rather than just one unnamed wood.

The film literally reproduces the dynamics of slavery on the participants to present the grotesque, regressive nature of such active and passive participation in what proves to be (social) death. At one point, the young men are lined up naked against the wall as a Black servant in white gloves examines each, lifting the lips of one to examine his teeth, brushing his hands across the arms and chest of another, standing back to examine the genitals of yet a third. Later, a particularly rebellious participant is strapped to a post in a barn where he is brutally raped as his rapist, another Black man, recounts the ways this has been done to them all. Likewise, the film rejects socially sanctioned but nonetheless destructive methods for dealing with such assaults, for one of the primary assailants is an alcoholic while another is nearly fanatic in his religious conviction. The destructive behaviors of these two only intensifies after they (re-)experience their lynching deaths. Only the third, who finally pauses to read history – conveyed on a newspaper – manages to escape. The others are damned to repeat the cycle in what seems like an eternal, undead existence in hell. Such escapism, the film argues, only further traps you within social death.

This Is America (and Ain't It a Nightmare)

The 2017 series *American Gods* rejects traditional readings of the origins of America to place the enslavement of Blacks at the center of the nation's start. The second episode of season one begins aboard a slave ship in 1697. In a scene titled "Coming to America" Anansi appears to the praying prisoners to pronounce the future of the men and their descendants in a revealing speech:

> You all don't know you Black yet. You think you just people.... The moment these Dutch motherfuckers set foot here they decided they white and you get to be Black, and that's the nice name they call you. Let me paint a picture of what's waiting for you on the shore. You arrive in America, land of opportunity, milk and honey, and guess what? You all get to be slaves.... The only good news is the tobacco your grandkids are gonna farm for free is gonna give a shitload of these white motherfuckers cancer. And I ain't even started yet.... A hundred years after you get free you still getting fucked outta jobs and shot at by police.... You are staring down the barrel of 300 years of subjugation, racist bullshit and heart disease.... there isn't one goddamn reason you shouldn't go up there right now and ... set fire to this ship.

When a listening captive responds that if they burn the ship, they will die too, Anansi responds, "You already dead." This, the series implies, is the true start of America, second only to the initial arrival and rapid fleeing of the Vikings. America, the series time and again remarks, depends on the bloodshed of minorities.

Childish Gambino echoes this reading of the American Nightmare in his 2018 song "This Is America." In contrast to the seeming frivolity performed throughout the video, the conclusion explicitly reveals the true meaning of the performance. Gambino runs through a dark tunnel, terror clearly legible on his face as the lyrics sing:

> You just a Black man in this world
> You just a barcode, ayy
> ...
> You just a big dog yeah
> I kenneled him in the backyard
> No proper life to a dog
> For a big dog.

The concluding scene summarizes Black positionality in the United States, for, despite willingness to dance and jig, as a Black man he is nonetheless an income-generating object at best, and at worst a "dog" to amuse its owner, to be contained, and, eventually, to be run down.[11]

The song warns against Black willingness to uncritically embrace American culture and its positioning of people of color, noting that such positioning and unchallenged acceptance is apocalyptic for African Americans, reducing them to consumable objects in a ruinous country. The critique notably predicts *Lovecraft Country*, particularly the final episode, "Full Circle," in which Hanna rails against Titus for raping her to conceive a child he intends to sacrifice. Hanna's outburst alludes to how America denies Blacks inherent value, refusing to acknowledge Black existence and potential beyond its service to whiteness. Gambino's video likewise rails against such reduction and, like *The House Invictus*, criticizes Black complicity in the process. The track sings "we just want to party / party just for you / we just the money / money just for you" as Gambino jigs and jives in the foreground wearing pants reminiscent of Confederate soldiers' uniforms and making cartoonish facial expressions in a performance suggestive of Jim Crow minstrel shows. Indeed, Lori Brooks notes that some of Gambino's postures are pulled directly from an 1833 poster advertising T. D. Rice's minstrel performances (Brooks).[12] Later, in a scene focused on a singing choir, Gambino comically steals in from the hidden door behind them before catching a rifle and gunning them down. The lyrics and scenes suggest that Black performance and service to whiteness in this culture not only are profoundly destructive to Black spiritual community but earn the perpetrator no rewards, as all of the desired money is invariably for someone else.

That the video might be classed as Gothic horror is evident in the setting, background events, and discordant music. Filmed entirely in a defunct warehouse, Gambino dances around the space as chaos repeatedly erupts in the background, including fires, riots, and the appearance of a hooded rider on a pale horse. This last figure gestures both to the nightmarish assaults of the KKK and to the apocalypse alluded to in biblical Revelation. Black complicity in modern US culture therefore is not just an acceptance of social death; it also ushers in a return of a hellish, explicitly violent history threatening the end of Black populations. The jarring juxtaposition between the opening African folk song and the chords that follow after Gambino shoots the folksinger further call our attention to the disharmonies that dominate African American existence. Not only does the opening violence abruptly end the calming song; it also iterates Black ancestral disconnection as part of the sacrifice America demands. In its place, US Blacks accept janky hip-hop chords and pretensions of joy that nonetheless fail to protect them from being h(a)unted. The warehouse setting significantly suggests that such violence, chaos, and behavior is actively produced by US industry.

However, though the video ends with a dystopian scene, like many African American horror texts it does not insist that Blacks are doomed to social death. In fact, the abrupt opening shift also acts to startle and alert viewers.[13] The video begins by marking itself as a wake-up call, a task recurrent throughout the lyrics. For example, as Gambino dances with a group of South African schoolchildren against a burning background, other teens film it on their mobile phones. The lyrics for the scene are notable: "This a celly / That's a tool." The lines recall Black use of mobile phones to record anti-Black police violence, therefore reminding viewers that they are already equipped with the means to disrupt and rebel against the chaos that surrounds them. Shortly after, the song explicitly marks the will to resist the social death America offers in exchange for seeming wealth. The next stanza notes:

> Ooh-ooh-ooh-ooh-ooh, tell somebody
> (America, I just checked my following list and)
> You go tell somebody
> (You mothafuckas owe me)
> Grandma told me.

The stanza is an explicit statement of Black rage and a return to the ancestral via communication with the grandmother. The first lines signify the previous stanzas of the song, interjecting outrage into the lyrics that earlier only repeated the need to tell someone about the desire for wealth.

The song thus includes another important aspect of Black horror that forces us to confront (modern) slavery: the will to resist. Indeed, *Lovecraft Country* spins entirely around this will. The burning house and Hanna's theft of "The Book of Names" also comment on the history of Black existence as signifiers of the will to resist and the determination to guard against white despotism. If any of the white magicians were able to lay their hands on the tome, they would be invincible. Here too the series reminds us that such would-be assailants are not always wealthy white men in castles, for the most violent and antagonistic of the magicians belong to the white police force.[14] Significantly, the series questions the method of resistance, visually representing Audre Lorde's contention that "the master's tools will never dismantle the master's house. They may allow us to temporarily beat him at his own game, but they will never enable us to bring about genuine change" (112). In several visions, Atticus stands in Titus' place, screaming as flames consume his body. These visions occur at times when Atticus is determined to decipher and use Titus' magic himself. [15]

Though Atticus and family are successful at the end, claiming magic for African Americans while exiling whites from the power, it nonetheless comes at great costs. The series concludes with a shot of young Diana after she has killed Christina. In the background Atticus's Cthulhu-creature stands on a cliff, reproducing Diana's position in the foreground. The juxtaposition suggests that while Diana is now powerful, she may have also lost her humanity alongside losing her childhood. The hope that the series offers at its conclusion is therefore a grim one. The series depicts a country that is Lovecraft-like in its xenophobic will to destroy people of color and equally Lovecraftian in its nightmarish landscape. Consequently, the show offers a corrective to Lovecraft's horrors, for it is not the existence of the Other that makes the nation horrific, but the white need to oppress minorities. Lovecraft and his white (vision of) America, the series says, is the real monster.

This, then, is the hope of and warning in these texts, for in the act of writing their stories, the artists already resist a country and economy that would reduce them to happy-seeming objects of service and consumption. Through such artistic performance, African American Gothicists awaken us to the horrors of failing to resist. They urge us toward a much-needed revolution, one that will achieve the promise and ideals articulated in America's founding and that have remained a point of painful hypocrisy for numerous minority populations within the country ever since. Yet Black horror such as *Linden Hills* and *The House Invictus* also warn us against reproducing the vicious dynamics of slavery among each other in our will to individually defy social death. It is not enough, these narratives warn, to gain your freedom if you are just going to be the next master. That's not what true freedom looks like.

Filmography

Agugh, Uche, director. *The House Invictus*. 55Media, 2018.

Cundieff, Rusty, director. "Good Golly." In *Tales from the Hood 2*. 40 Acres and a Mule Filmworks, 2018.

Gambino, Childish "This Is America." *Vevo*, 2018. youtu.be/kWTBTRGfKew.

Green, Misha, director. *Lovecraft Country*. Monkey Paw Productions, 2020.

Griffith, D. W., director. *Birth of a Nation*. Epoch Producing Corp., 1915.

Peele, Jordan, director. *Get Out*. Blumhouse Productions, 2017.

Slade, David, director. "The Secret of Spoons." *American Gods*, season 1, episode 2, Freemantle, 2017.

NOTES

1. In *Slavery and Social Death: A Comparative Study* (1982), Orlando Patterson defines social death as a complete loss of identity, agency, and ultimately subjectivity; it is a violence and condition suffered by those denied recognition as a human by others in society. Patterson notes a number of social death's attributes, including natal and economic alienation, denial of stabilizing relationships such as family, withdrawal of legal protection, and the utter denial or loss of cultural capital across generations. Although Patterson particularly defined social death as the inevitable outcome of slavery, other theorists such as Henry A. Giroux and Jared Sexton have extended Patterson's theory to consider the ways African Americans and other marginalized groups remain damned to half-lives as noncitizens and not-quite-people in racist, capitalist cultures.
2. With the exception of a roughly ten-year period immediately after the Civil War, the South swiftly found other ways to return African Americans to a contained position as inferior objects. Consider, for instance, the rise of the Black Codes in various southern states, which led to Jim Crow segregation and violence as well as the beginning of a highly racialized prison industrial system.
3. See *Playing in the Dark: Whiteness and the Literary Imagination* (1992).
4. See Jennifer Fleischner, "Hawthorne and the Politics of Slavery," *Studies in the Novel* 23, no. 1 (Spring 1991): 96–106; Jay Grossman, "'A Is for Abolition?': Race, Authorship, *The Scarlet Letter*," *Textual Practice* 7 (1993): 13–20; Deborah L. Madsen, "'A Is for Abolition': Hawthorne's Bond-Servant and the Shadow of Slavery," *Journal of American Studies* 25, no. 2 (1991): 255–59; and Rita Williams, "The King's Two Bodies, and the Slave's: Diasporic History in *The Whole History of the Grandfather's Chair*," *Nathaniel Hawthorne Review* 36, no. 1 (Spring 2010): 165–85, for further discussions of race in Hawthorne.
5. This is Griffith's fantasy of the origin of the Ku Klux Klan.
6. This barely subtextual message, in addition to the grotesque depictions of Blacks, renders the film a point of horror that is difficult to digest for African Americans.
7. See, for instance, *African American Gothic: Screams from Shadowed Places* (2013) and "Slave Narratives and Slave Revolts," in *The Palgrave Handbook of Southern Gothic* (2016).
8. This is especially worth clarifying given how Black bodies were overly marked as spectacles for white consumption in medicinal, scientific, and anthropological discourses. See, for instance, the experiments on enslaved Black female bodes that led to perfecting hysterectomies or, more poignantly, Saartjie Baartman's experience in life and death.
9. See bell hooks, "Eating the Other," in *Black Looks: Race and Representation,* (Boston: South End Press, 1992).
10. For more on Peele's film, see Dawn Keetly, ed., *Jordan Peele's Get Out: Political Horror* (Columbus: Ohio State University Press, 2020).
11. Childish Gambino repeats this critique in the video for "Bonfire," a song critical of a music industry that encourages rappers to posture. In the video, Gambino plays the ghost of a camper who watches in horror as other campers tell the story of his lynching for entertainment.
12. Rice created US minstrelsy.

13. There are numerous YouTube videos of young adults watching the video with their parents, and who often watched wide-eyed after the opening scene.
14. Episodes such as "Jig-a-Bobo" explicitly connect the history of white assault on Black life from slavery to Emmett Till to the anti-Black police violence that birthed the Black Lives Matter movement.
15. Though the series later reveals that these flames are actually the manifestation of Hanna's rage, and so can be controlled, we might also consider how these flames suggest the possibility of being consumed by rage, even if it is justified.

Works Cited

Ballinger, Gill, Tim Lustig, and Dale Townshend. "Missing Intertexts: Hannah Craft's 'The Bondwoman's Narrative' and African American Literary History." *Journal of American Studies* 39, no. 2 (2005): 207–37.

Brooks, Lori. "The Hidden Meanings behind Childish Gambino's 'This Is America' Video." *Inside Edition*, youtu.be/kWTBTRGfKew. Accessed May 16, 2021.

Dubey, Madhu. "Speculative Fictions of Slavery." *American Literature* 82, no. 4 (2005): 779–805.

Hopkins, Pauline. *Of One Blood; or, The Hidden Self.* Washington Square Press, 2010.

Lorde, Audre. "The Master's Tools Will Never Dismantle the Master's House." In *Sister Outsider*. Crossing Press, 2012. 110–13.

Martin, Robert K., and Eric Savoy. "Introduction." In *American Gothic: New Interventions in a National Narrative*. University of Iowa Press, 1998. vii–xii.

Naylor, Gloria. *Linden Hills*. Penguin Books. 1986.

Poe, Edgar. *The Narrative of Arthur Gordon Pym of Nantucket*. Penguin Classics. 1999.

Seabrook, William, *The Magic Island, with Introduction by George Romero*. Dover Publications, 2016.

Toomer, Jean. *Cane*. Norton and Company. 2011.

Young, Elizabeth. *Black Frankenstein: The Making of an American Metaphor*. New York University Press. 2008.

2

MARK STEVEN

Capitalism

Capitalism is a horror story. This remains as true in the early decades of twenty-first century, when accumulation still depends on the twinned violence of expropriation and exploitation, as it was during Karl Marx's time, following the enclosure of the commons, the consolidation of the factory system, and imperial expansion into new global territories. Capitalism can be described as widespread wage dependency combined with alienable property rights and production for profit in the market, all of which is geared toward endless accumulation. From the point of origin, capitalist social relations require state violence to uproot humans from the land and feed them into industry. Accumulation is then enabled by exploitation, insofar as production consumes living labor to create value-larded commodities, which are sold for more than the bearers of that labor were reimbursed, thus realizing their surplus value in the monetary form of profit, which can finally be reinvested to engineer more and greater production processes. But exploitation is not just a matter of short-changing dispossessed workers who own nothing but their labor; it also urges the acceleration and intensification of production processes, and with that comes the crunching of bones, the rending of muscle, and the liquification of brains. Capital, in this view, is a meat grinder that crushes human lives into sellable commodities.

Working with the Marxist critique of capital, this chapter demonstrates the critical synonymy of horror and capitalism in American literary narrative. While Lenin once suggested that Marxism responds to capital using "the three main ideological currents of the 19th century" – German philosophy, English political economy, and a French revolutionary impulse – to this triumvirate we should add that Marx developed his final judgment, "that the capitalist mode of production and accumulation, and therefore capitalist private property as well, have for their fundamental condition the annihilation of that private property which rests on the labour of the individual himself," by looking away from Europe and toward America (Lenin, 8; Marx, 940). There he glimpsed the bloody and barbarous truth of capital as a short-circuit between pain and profit, in the unmediated conversion of human bodies into exchange value:

> In 1703 those sober exponents of Protestantism, the Puritans of New England, by decrees of their assembly set a premium of £40 on every Indian scalp and every captured redskin; in 1720, a premium of £100 was set on every scalp; in 1744, after Massachusetts Bay had proclaimed a certain tribe as rebels, the following prices were laid down: for a male scalp of 12 years and upwards, £100 in new currency, for a male prisoner £105, for women and children prisoners £50, for the scalps of women and children £50. Some decades later, the colonial system took its revenge on the descendants of the pious pilgrim fathers, who had grown seditious in the meantime. At English instigation, and for English money, they were tomahawked by the redskins. The British Parliament proclaimed bloodhounds and scalping as "means that God and Nature had given into its hand." (Marx, 917–18)

Beginning with colonization before accelerating into the period of exponential growth from around the Civil War through the Great Depression, during which America evolved from a leading industrial power and the world's chief banker into a state with sufficient capacity to take the helm in making capitalism global, this chapter considers the economic making of the United States and the horror contained therein. It is also concerned with the dynamics of what has been termed "racial capitalism," namely, a social relation that secures ruling class power through the manipulation of racial, ethnic, and nationalist prejudice – or, in Ruth Wilson Gilmore's description, "a death-dealing displacement of difference into hierarchies that organize relations within and between the planet's sovereign political territories" (21).

While racial capitalism perpetuates slavery's horrors into the post-emancipation era of legal rights and free markets, this chapter's intention is to demonstrate that the visceral horror of what W. E. B. Du Bois once described as the "direct barter in human flesh" (11) haunts narratives of capital no less than it does those more directly preoccupied with the plantation and its afterlives. Within this frame, the chapter looks to scenes of Indigenous dispossession, resource extraction, urban industrialization, unemployed immiseration, and finally to the reactionary suppression with which capital protects its interests. The guiding hypothesis is that horror obtains in all of these crucial areas of the economy because capitalist accumulation is, in all of its forms, a catastrophically exploitative relationship between humans that depends on sensuous creation and so requires the productive grist of blood, brains, and bodies. For this reason, the horror in which we are interested will be less the stuff of uncanny architectures and spectral hauntings, which from Shirley Jackson through Mark Z

Danielewski might offer some insight into private property, but instead our focus will be on the messily macabre and gratuitously violent: the horror of bodily obliteration, as experienced by those who are materially and viscerally terrorized by capital.

Colonial Bloodbath

Marx referred to the founding and expansion of capitalism as "primitive accumulation," a technical term that describes the confluence of dispossession, proletarianization, market formation, and the separation of agriculture from industry. But instead of using the idyllic language of political economy, which presupposed an agreeable and voluntarist entry into capitalist social relations, Marx narrated primitive accumulation using the language of horror, in sentences that chew their way through human viscera and bodily gristle. "And the history of this," he tells us of the dispossessed, "their expropriation, is written in the annals of mankind in letters of blood and fire," for that expropriation is enacted in such ways and with such force, through settler colonialism and genocidal terror, that "capital comes dripping from head to toe, from every pore, with blood and dirt" (926). If this is "the secret discovered in the new world," literary writing from the same period treats capital in precisely this way, as an open secret wherein bodily carnage and its economic determination appear as the irruptive subtext in narratives that might otherwise be coded as romance, realism, or naturalism. We encounter an early and exemplary rendition of this horror as it pertains to primitive accumulation in James Fenimore Cooper's adventure novel published in 1826 (but set in 1757), *The Last of the Mohicans*. Taking place during the colonial wars for North America as fought around Allegany County, New York – "the bloody arena, in which most of the battles for the mastery of the colonies were contested" (416) – Cooper's novel begins with conjuration of the affective comportment that might attend its telling, as would be experienced by British settlers.

If we read Cooper's novel closely, we can devise a poetics of primitive accumulation that corresponds to the hauntological aesthetic of gothic horror:

> The alarmed colonists believed that the yells of the savages mingled with every fitful gust of wind that issued from the interminable forests of the west. The terrific character of their merciless enemies increased immeasurably the natural horrors of warfare. Numberless recent massacres were still vivid in their recollections; nor was there any ear in the provinces so deaf as not to have drunk in with avidity the narrative of some fearful tale of midnight murder, in

> which the natives of the forests were the principal and barbarous actors. As the credulous and excited traveler related the hazardous chances of the wilderness, the blood of the timid curdled with terror, and mothers cast anxious glances even at those children which slumbered within the security of the largest towns. In short, the magnifying influence of fear began to set at naught the calculations of reason, and to render those who should have remembered their manhood, the slaves of the basest passions. Even the most confident and the stoutest hearts began to think the issue of the contest was becoming doubtful; and that abject class was hourly increasing in numbers, who thought they foresaw all the possessions of the English crown in America subdued by their Christian foes, or laid waste by the inroads of their relentless allies. (18)

The language of this passage reframes romance as gothic, with its "terrific" and "fearful" affects designed to curdle "the blood of the timid." But it is not just gothic. Instead, any fantastical speculation is surcharged by "the natural horrors of warfare" and so by a very real threat to life and limb. Horror, in this sense, is indexed to historical reality, to the process of colonization, which reveals itself here through style no less than narrative content. With safety found only "within the security of the largest towns," those frontier hubs of commerce and industry, the terrified colonial subject sounds like capital personified, thinking principally in terms of "class" composition and accumulated "possessions." Here, however, the resolutely bourgeois "calculations of reason" are threatened by "the magnifying influence of fear," in such a way that material reality and nightmare fantasy coalesce, just as "the yells of the savages mingled with every fitful gust of wind," so that mathematical precision gives way to the vague hyperbole of the "immeasurable," the "numberless," and the "relentless." The self-conscious departure from bourgeois calculation betrays the concealment at work in this passage. The "recent massacres" are not state-sponsored exterminations of Indigenous landowners but are instead acts of decolonial struggle, presented here as separate from an undeclared systemic violence. This is how the passage uses horror to enact something like a role reversal whereby the "natives of the forests" are rebranded as history's "principal and barbarous actors" and the militarized agents of colonial rule reimagine themselves as an "abject class" of "slaves." Horror both exposes and conceals the ideological machinery of primitive accumulation via narrative dissimulation, acknowledging the bloodshed that underwrites capitalist expansion while simultaneously displacing it onto precapitalist forms and populations.

But there is also truth to the potential doubling of agency. Horror, within primitive accumulation, reflects violent historical processes as well as full-blooded insurgency against those processes: it is both the gore-strewn mark of suppression and a return of the suppressed. Tilting toward the latter, these fearful premonitions will be repaid in full several chapters later, when a native war party of "more than two thousand raving savages" (199) ambushes the colonial army as well as the civilians under its protection after the evacuation of Fort Henry, where French-Canadian forces bombarded a British garrison into submission before their Indian allies violated the terms of surrender and attacked the retreating column. While the narrative would almost be justified in presenting this as bilateral conflict, with all the conventional heroism warfare of that sort tends to attract in literary romance, such a mode is granted only the briefest expression: "the troops threw themselves quickly into solid masses, endeavoring to awe their assailants by the imposing appearance of a military front." Beneath any such appearance of a "military front" is naught but horror. "We shall not," the narrator forewarns, "dwell on the revolting horrors that succeeded" (199). Despite this claim, which does more to intensify than inoculate, lurid description is precisely what we are given. "Death was everywhere," we read,

> and in his most terrific and disgusting aspects. Resistance only served to inflame the murderers, who inflicted their furious blows long after their victims were beyond the power of their resentment. The flow of blood might be likened to the outbreaking of a torrent; and as the natives became heated and maddened by the sight, many among them even kneeled to the earth, and drank freely, exultingly, hellishly, of the crimson tide. (199)

Here, in grotesque detail, we encounter the manipulative but incomplete disavowal of horror. As William Kelly reads this episode, even if the "chivalric conventions" of the French and British colonists "disguise the horror of warfare more effectively than the codes of Indian combat," the two are united in that horror without being equivalent. "By scalping their victims and drinking their blood," writes Kelly, "the Indians unmask the violence at the core of human identity," or more accurately the violence that inheres on the frontiers of capital (63). Horror is at once a product of the economic system but also what happens when that system strikes upon resistance.

Leviathan Gore

Once it has dispossessed and enlisted Indigenous populations, capitalism pillages the land as well as the worker, and it uses workers to pillage land. From rare earths, metals, and minerals, through agribusiness and monoculture, right down to fossil fuels and biofuels, primitive accumulation does not stop with the displacement and enslavement of local and Indigenous populations; that displacement also enables the extraction of the natural resources. This, too, is a lesson Marx takes from America. "The discovery of gold and silver in America," he writes, "the extirpation, enslavement and entombment in mines of the indigenous population of that continent, the beginnings of the conquest and plunder of India, and the conversion of Africa into a preserve for the commercial hunting of blackskins, are all things which characterize the dawn of the era of capitalist production" (915). Accompanying those inanimate and earthbound resources that are mined and the humans who perished for their extraction, animals were also colonized as resources for accumulation. And, like the entombment of Indigenous persons within mines, the conversion of native fauna into economic resources had directly genocidal consequences. To cite only the most obvious example of this, militarized bison-hunting on the Great Plains was always more than just a matter of commodity production; it was also a way of exterminating the native population by way of starvation and of rendering the survivors' dependence on American trade: "kill every buffalo you can," one member of the US Army is said to have commanded his troops. "Every buffalo dead is an Indian gone" (Phippen). It is in this way that expropriation and exploitation are fundamentally contiguous.

The literary writer most sensitive to the economics of resource extraction is Herman Melville, who in his novels made an aesthetic principle of the transformation of sperm whales into biofuel commodities: "despite the blood and the muck," C. L. R. James once described the writing, "Melville's clear strong prose without any sentimentality brings out the essential humanity of the process and the absence of any degradation," distilling from within the carnage a hard-won sense of collective being (26). Melville's best-known novel, *Moby-Dick* (1851), is as much the story of American capitalism as it is of the *Pequod*'s fated voyage, and more than allegory or fable it presents a detailed sketch of a living economy at a time when whales were hunted, and whaling became an industry, because America was fueled by whale oil. "In the late eighteenth and early nineteenth centuries," writes Heidi Scott, "whale oil was nearly as essential to a functional society as petroleum is to our own," serving as both a "leading source of lamp oil used for illumination" and "lubrication for the hulking machines of the industrial age" (5). But whaling also spoke to the emergent culture of capitalism insofar as it "cultivated the entrepreneurial spirit of early Americans, and the whale ship captured the American spirit in microcosm: it required risk, violence, individualism, bravery, and carried a sense of destiny borne on divine favor" (4). Reflecting these tendencies, *Moby-Dick* presents the business of whaling as the constitutive horror of American wealth – a hidden secret. "Whales," we learn, "must die the death and be murdered, in order to light the gay bridals and other merry-makings of men, and also to illuminate the solemn churches that preach unconditional inoffensiveness by all to all" (301). This kind of enlightenment is taken as the "profoundest homage" to the whaling industry and especially its laborers: "for almost all the tapers, lamps, and candles that burn round the globe, burn, as before so many shrines, to our glory!" (99). More economic than cultural, however, whaling is primarily a form of accumulative capital. New Bedford, Massachusetts, is described as a prosperous "land of oil," housing in opulence the beneficiaries of oceanic resource extraction. "Whence came they?" asks Ishmael of the local bourgeoisie. "Go and gaze upon the iron emblematical harpoons round yonder lofty mansion, and your question will be answered. Yes; all these brave houses and flowery gardens came from the Atlantic, Pacific, and Indian oceans. One and all, they were harpooned and dragged up hither from the bottom of the sea" (38). Before entering the market as oil, newly landed whale carcasses are repurposed by their seaborne hunters: bones are used to repair the *Pequod*; Captain Ahab has an ivory prosthesis for his severed leg; the sailors eat whale steak and fry their biscuits in its oil.

Mortified whale flesh thus becomes a useful resource that reproduces collective labor no less than it serves as the exchangeable commodity: it is both the means and the object of production. Within this, the transformation from living creature into valuable resource is a source of horror, with the labor of harpooning presented as both mortally dangerous and viscerally disgusting. "At the instant of the dart," we read of one hunt, "an ulcerous jet shot from this cruel wound, and goaded by it into more than sufferable anguish, the whale now spouting thick blood, with swift fury blindly darted at the craft, bespattering them and their glorying crews all over with showers of gore, capsizing Flask's boat and marring the bows" (301). We are given witness to this kind of horror during several hunts. In what amounts to a dialectical movement wherein quantity becomes quality, here the enormity of the whales, combining in singular form an ocean of blood with a uniquely forceful vascular system, means that when skewered the horror of their death throes becomes one with the world entire:

> The red tide now poured from all sides of the monster like brooks down a hill. His tormented body rolled not in brine but in blood, which bubbled and seethed for furlongs behind in their wake. The slanting sun playing upon this crimson pond in the sea, sent back its reflection into every face, so that they all glowed to each other like red men. (244)

And once the harpoon pierces "the innermost life of the fish," it enters into a trance-like flurry:

> And now abating in his flurry, the whale once more rolled out into view; surging from side to side; spasmodically dilating and contracting his spout-hole, with sharp, cracking, agonized respirations. At last, gush after gush of

> clotted red gore, as if it had been the purple lees of red wine, shot into the frighted air; and falling back again, ran dripping down his motionless flanks into the sea. His heart had burst! (245)

If animals are "rendered" into sellable commodities, that is because they have been valorized through the human labor of murder and butchery, and here that labor appears as horror and as a horror that extends into the natural environment as a whole. That appearance is enabled by the verbal and metaphoric consistencies in this passage, which blend the torrential outpouring of gore with oceanic movement: the flowing ichor is a "red tide" that pours and surges and gushes, transforming the sea into a scene of omnipresent carnage, which reflects in crimson on everything and everyone. Indeed, the language of horror extends beyond the hunt to shade the vessel's passage at large, so that "when the ivory-tusked Pequod sharply bowed to the blast" she also "gored the dark waves in her madness, till, like showers of silver chips," as though shattering ivory bone, "the foam-flakes flew over her bulwarks" (201). That the violence of harpooning is inflicted upon the sea itself is more than just hyperbole; it is, moreover, a sign of America's economic expansion. "From the ports of New England," writes Scott, "American whaling ships of that era would compete on remote oceans with the great global powers of the day – among them England, France, and Japan – and emerge victorious, hulls riding low in the water with a burden of spermaceti" (5). It is an early sign of what George Washington descried as "the rising empire," a geopolitical form that built territorial expansion into its state structure no less than its colonial aspirations.

Nightmare Factories

With the horror of resource extraction socially adjoined to the experience of labor, we can now look to horrors specific to work itself – and, in particular, to the kinds of labor that took place in the mills and factories that served the largest domestic market in the world and which elevated American industry to its world-systemic primacy. "If you could go into this mill," wrote Rebecca Harding Davis in 1861, "and drag out from the hearts of these men the terrible tragedy of their lives, taking it as a symptom of the disease of their class, no ghost Horror would terrify you more. A reality of soul-starvation, of living death, that meets you every day under the besotted faces on the street" (47). Exemplary of this horror, Upton Sinclair's muckraking novel *The Jungle* was published serially in 1904 and as a book in 1906. Researched by undercover work in the stockyards and meatpacking plants, this novel narrates the plight of a Lithuanian family fighting for survival in

Chicago, which is to the United States what the *Pequod* is to New Bedford: a disavowed zone of profitable violence.

In Sinclair's narrative, the forces of production, that combination of industrial machinery and living labor, are portrayed in as much technical detail as Melville afforded the butchery of whales. The industry, connected by galleries and railroads, is described as "the greatest aggregation of labor and capital ever gathered in one place. It employed thirty thousand men; it supported directly two hundred and fifty thousand people in its neighbourhood, and indirectly it supported half a million" (42). But, whereas Melville was committed to the ennoblement of work, wherein humans are granted an elevated status separate from the beast in whose entrails they wallow, Sinclair systematically erases the distinction between human and animal, so that the treatment of pig carcasses is also a vision of human exploitation. "It was porkmaking by machinery, porkmaking by applied mathematics," we read of the slaughterhouse.

> And yet somehow the most matter-of-fact person could not help thinking of the hogs; they were so innocent, they came so very trustingly; and they were so very human in their protests – and so perfectly within their rights! They had done nothing to deserve it; and it was adding insult to injury, as the thing was done here, swinging them up in this cold-blooded, impersonal way, without a pretense of apology, without the homage of a tear. (37).

Less a secret than a disavowed truth, the abattoirs continue to function irrespective of common knowledge of their operations. "Now and then a visitor wept, to be sure; but this slaughtering machine ran on, visitors or no visitors. It was like some horrible crime committed in a dungeon, all unseen and unheeded, buried out of sight and of memory" (37).

If humans and hogs are of apiece – "each of them had an individuality of his own, a will of his own, a hope and a heart's desire; each was full of self-confidence, of self-importance, and a sense of dignity," we read of the slaughtered animals – the ruinously inhuman force is that of capital. "Relentless, remorseless, it was; all his protests, his screams, were nothing to it – it did its cruel will with him, as if his wishes, his feelings, had simply no existence at all; it cut his throat and watched him gasp out his life" (37). When the narrative turns to labor, to the human experience of work, it undertakes a seasonal narrative of exploitation, an industrial georgic, wherein weather conditions horror. "There was no heat upon the killing beds," we learn of winter: "you were apt to be covered with blood, and it would freeze solid; if you leaned against a pillar, you would freeze to that, and if you put your hand upon the blade of your knife, you would run a chance of leaving your skin on it," and here

> the air would be full of steam, from the hot water and the hot blood, so that you could not see five feet before you; and then, with men rushing about at the speed they kept up on the killing beds, and all with butcher knives, like razors, in their hands – well, it was to be counted as a wonder that there were not more men slaughtered than cattle. (80)

Summer yields entirely different horrors, when thaw means stench,

> with the stifling heat, when the dingy killing beds of Durham's became a very purgatory; one time, in a single day, three men fell dead from sunstroke. All day long the rivers of hot blood poured forth, until, with the sun beating down, and the air motionless, the stench was enough to knock a man over; all the old smells of a generation would be drawn out by this heat – for there was never any washing of the walls and rafters and pillars, and they were caked with the filth of a lifetime. (100)

Of the family around which the book's narrative constellates, all but the patriarch, Jurgis, fall victim to the impersonal and inescapable violence of capital: Jurgis' father dies from respiratory infection; one of his children dies of food poisoning and another drowns in the muddy street; his teenage wife, Ona, is forced into prostitution and then dies in childbirth because the family cannot afford a doctor. In its accumulating body count, this novel is a story of industrialized social murder.

It is only after Jurgis breaks his ankle and is forced from the meatpacking plant without compensation that he takes on employment in the fertilizer works, where bones are made into phosphate and blood into albumen. Whereas the killing floor allowed for some division between the working day and nonwork, between wage and domestic labor, this next job is a kind of labor whose horror pollutes every aspect of his being and which carries murder within itself. To labor in the fertilizer works is to read one's own death sentence: "here they dried out the bones, – and in suffocating cellars where the daylight never came you might see men and women and children bending over whirling machines and sawing bits of bone into all sorts of shapes, breathing their lungs full of the fine dust, and doomed to die, every one of them, within a certain definite time" (125). If the prose here is oppressive, with its layered hypotaxis and interlocking conjunctions, that is because we have entered the inescapable inferno to the killing beds' transitional purgatory. "Few visitors ever saw them," we read, "and the few who did would come out looking like Dante, of whom the peasants declared that he had been into hell" (125). Tasked with shoveling compost, Jurgis is confronted with a "a great brown river" of gore, "with a spray of the finest dust flung forth in clouds," and is set to work against this coalface of tankage in a way that condemns him to psychical no less than physical ruin, devolving the worker into "a brown ghost at twilight," a shambolic, gore-caked monstrosity:

> The stuff was half an inch deep in his skin – his whole system was full of it, and it would have taken a week not merely of scrubbing, but of vigorous exercise, to get it out of him. As it was, he could be compared with nothing known to men, save that newest discovery of the savants, a substance which emits energy for an unlimited time, without being itself in the least diminished in power. He smelled so that he made all the food at the table taste, and set the whole family to vomiting; for himself it was three days before he could keep anything upon his stomach – he might wash his hands, and use a knife and fork, but were not his mouth and throat filled with the poison? (127)

This book famously led to the passage of the Meat Inspection Act and the Pure Food and Drug Act of 1906 – what it failed to inspire, however, is the social revolution against capitalism its author had in mind when descrying morbid working conditions. The novel depicts, with its horror, "the inferno of exploitation," but only served as catalyst for change, in its author's words, "not because the public cared anything about the workers, but simply because the public did not want to eat tubercular beef" (Sullivan, 222–23). Of the many horrors this book relates, central are the emulsification of workers fallen into vats of lard, the severed limbs and digits that make their way into sellable foodstuffs, and the sheer amount of human blood, sweat, and effluvium on which America dines. The meatpacking factory, we are told, "sent its products to every country in the civilized world, and it furnished the food for no less than thirty million people!" (42). In the fertilizer plant, we also see the inverse of workers being rendered into comestibles: here the disgusting comestible substance, the putrescence of foul marrow, is embedded within the exploited worker, who will carry that horror to their grave.

People of the Abyss

As the old saying goes, "the only thing worse than being exploited under capitalism is not being exploited under capitalism," to which we should add that the proper form of "not being exploited" – namely, unemployment – is precisely constitutive to exploitation and accumulation. What Marx and Engels would call the "relative surplus population" is a floating mass of humans that fluctuates in size and shape relative to the boom and bust cycles of capitalism, growing in negative correlation with capital's capacity or willingness to absorb labor, and whose immiseration presents an altogether different horror than that of the exploited worker. While naturalist writing as exemplified by Émile Zola and Thomas Hardy has traditionally depicted this group as a gulf into which the downwardly mobile might descend, in American literature the relative surplus population performs double-duty as the gruesome embodiment of inchoate yet antisystemic violence. That is what we see in Jack London's descriptions of what he terms "the people of the abyss," a phrase used for the title of a journalistic study of homelessness in London but also for a chapter of his anticapitalist dystopia, *The Iron Heel* (1908), which imagines the surplus population as a deus ex machina, a "rushing stream of human lava" intervening in a conflict between the oligarchic establishment and the insurgent socialists:

> It was not a column, but a mob, an awful river that filled the street, the people of the abyss, mad with drink and wrong, up at last and roaring for the blood of their masters. I had seen the people of the abyss before, gone through its ghettos, and thought I knew it; but I found that I was now looking on it for the first time. Dumb apathy had vanished. It was now dynamic – a fascinating spectacle of dread. It surged past my vision in concrete waves of wrath, snarling and growling, carnivorous, drunk with whiskey from pillaged warehouses, drunk with hatred, drunk with lust for blood – men, women, and children, in rags and tatters, dim ferocious intelligences with all the godlike blotted from their features and all the fiendlike stamped in, apes and tigers, anaemic consumptives and great hairy beasts of burden, wan faces from which vampire society had sucked the juice of life, bloated forms swollen with physical grossness and corruption, withered hags and death's-heads bearded like patriarchs, festering youth and festering age, faces of fiends, crooked, twisted, misshapen monsters blasted with the ravages of disease and all the horrors of chronic innutrition – the refuse and the scum of life, a raging, screaming, screeching, demoniacal horde. (232–33)

This prose echoes Edgar Allan Poe's "The Man of the Crowd" (1840), in which an unnamed narrator observes the daily commute in extraordinary detail, recording a long catalogue of particulars rendered in a parataxis, before he trains his focus on "a decrepit old man, some sixty-five or seventy years of age," who, unlike the obviously classed types surrounding him, wears an "absolute idiosyncrasy of expression," which is eventually said to conceal "the type and genius of deep crime" (396). This man is the affective center to Poe's story and, in that capacity, he is a source of an unspeakable horror, carrying with him the "worst heart of the world." By absolute contrast, in London's novel that horror, the seething monster of social reproduction, is on full display, for it is not one subject but the immiserated masses, excluded from wage labor and so from the basic means of subsistence, here devolved into the zombified beast of collective retribution: they are the human bioproduct abjected by capital, unaffirmable and ununifiable, as much a hazard to the socialists as to the oligarchs, the negative image of class solidarity.

Imperial Steamroller

Though we have looked to only a limited sampling of literary works, it will nevertheless be worth observing that these narratives, all of which represent capital as synonymous with horror, also contain the suggestion of alternative modes of production or, at least, signs of anticapitalist insurrection, from Indigenous insurgency through ever-present threats of mutiny to socialist organization and communist futures. This is why all of the novels are also engaged with reactionary suppression, with the violence employed by capital to shut down alternative ways of living. American history runs bloody with examples of this violence, but here we will turn in closing to the interwar years, when capitalist hegemony was threatened as never before, by a revolutionary socialism that had seized for itself a state in Russia and which was setting out to foster a communist international. Against this backdrop and on the eve of the Great Depression, it was in 1926 that modernist author John Dos Passos met two immigrant anarchists, Nicola Sacco and Bartolomeo Vanzetti, who had been arrested for armed robbery and were sentenced to execution after a highly politicized and still controversial trial. Forging an immediate friendship with them, Dos Passos published open letters in their favor, was arrested for protesting their imminent execution, and composed a pamphlet on the case. The night of their execution – August 22, 1927 – would provide the affective motivation for his U.S.A. Trilogy. "It is up to the writers now to see to it that American does not forget Sacco and Vanzetti," he wrote for *New Masses* soon after. In the face of capitalist society's "idiot lack of memory," he says, laying out something of a literary program, "we must have writing so fiery and accurate that it will sear through the pall of numb imbecility that we are again swaddled in after the few moments of the sane awakening that followed the shock of the executions" (25). Dos Passos' literary writing would thus be an attempt to present that violent interaction between the anticapitalist left and the instruments of American capitalism. The trilogy constructs its dense narrative weave around the first three decades of the twentieth century, positioning a multitude of characters in front of what Dos Passos calls "the great imperial steamroller of American finance" (Denning, 172).

The book's most horrific individual "steamrolling" is an episode dedicated to World War I veteran and sharpshooter Wesley Everest, who returns to his parents' home on the outskirts of Tennessee. Having resumed work as a lumberjack in an increasingly exploitative because monopolized logging industry, Everest joins the Industrial Workers of the World. He hopes that organized labor will lead not necessarily to the overthrow of capitalism but to payment "in real money instead of in company scrip," "a decent place to dry his clothes, wet from the sweat of a day's work in zero weather and snow, an eight hour day, clean bunkhouses, wholesome grub," and that is all: not revolution but fair remuneration. But, as we are told, "the wobblies are reds," and "to be a red in the summer of 1919 was worse than being a hun or a pacifist in the summer of 1917" (457). Before Armistice Day, 1919, the sawmill owners plan an armed attack on the union hall with the objective of lynching its leaders. After putting up a fight, Everest is taken to jail; that night, "the city lights were turned off," and he is handed over to the mob:

> They took him off in a limousine to the Chehalis River bridge. As Wesley Everest lay stunned in the bottom of the car a Centralia business man cut his penis and testicles off with a razor. Wesley Everest gave a great scream of pain. Somebody has remembered that after a while he whispered, "For God's sake, men, shoot me . . . don't let me suffer like this." Then they hanged him from the bridge in the glare of the headlights. The coroner at his inquest thought it was a great joke. He reported that Wesley Everest had broken out of jail and run to the Chehalis River bridge and tied a rope around his neck and jumped off, finding the rope too short he'd climbed back and fastened on a longer one, had jumped off again, broke his neck and shot himself full of holes. They jammed the mangled wreckage into a packing box and buried it. (460–61)

Figured here is the invisible hand of capital – metonymized by limousines, businessmen, and corrupt coroners – now stained with workers' blood. The sadism on full display shares a family resemblance to the "bloody transactions" witnessed by Frederick Douglass and Harriet Jacobs, spectacles of horror enacted in the name of discipline no less than punishment. Like slaves whipped and hanged to death, this martyrdom is sadistic, shocking, and undignified. Dos Passos' narrative remembers all of it – not just his pleas for mercy – and remembers all of it as horror, in such a way to jolt a "sane awakening" from the nightmare of systemic violence faced by all who would oppose the beneficiaries of capital.

And yet, bringing this chapter full circle, capitalism persists in the United States even as American economic hegemony now lurches through its death throes. Here is how one critic describes the economic recovery after the financial crisis that began around 2007: "Conjure, if you will, a primal sequence encountered in B-grade horror films, where the celluloid protagonist suffers a terrifying encounter with doom, yet on the cusp of disaster abruptly wakes to a different world, which initially seems normal, but eventually is revealed to be a second nightmare more ghastly than the first"

(Mirowski, 2). While the horrors of that persistence might belong to screen media more so than written narrative, we nevertheless glimpse the entrails of a wounded empire in the novels of Octavia E. Butler, Mira Grant, Stephen King, Victor Lavalle, and Colson Whitehead, where horror obtains in the reproduction of intergenerational traumas up and down the rural hinterlands, in the deindustrialized immiseration of rustbelt cities and urban ghettoes, in the molecular plasticity unleashed by pharmaceuticals and biotech, and in a zombified slavery reanimate within racial capitalism's prison-industrial complex. In American fiction, the undeath of capital finds form with the undead. "We're not survivors," announces one of the contemporary moment's signal works of literary fiction. "We're the walking dead in a horror film." (McCarthy, 47)

Works Cited

Cooper, James Fenimore. *The Last of the Mohicans*. 1826. Oxford: Oxford University Press, 2008.

Davis, Rebecca Harding. *Life in the Iron Mills*. New York: Bedford, 1861.

Denning, Michael. *The Cultural Front: The Laboring of American Culture in the Twentieth Century*. London: Verso, 1997.

Dos Passos, John. "Sacco and Vanzetti." *The New Masses*, November 25, 1927.

U. S. A. New York: Modern Library, 1930.

Du Bois, W. E. B. *Black Reconstruction: An Essay toward a History of the Part Which Black Folk Played in the Attempt to Reconstruct Democracy in America 1860–1880*. New York: Harcourt, Brace, and Co., 1935.

Gilmore, Ruth Wilson. "Fatal Couplings of Power and Difference: Notes on Racism and Geography." *The Professional Geographer* 54, no. 1 (2002): 15–24.

James, C. L. R. *Mariners, Renegades, and Castaways: The Story of Herman Melville and the World We Live In*. Hanover, NH: University Press of New England, 1953.

Kelly, P. William. *Plotting America's Past: Fenimore Cooper and The Leatherstocking Tales*. Carbondale: Southern Illinois University Press, 1983.

Lenin, Vladimir. *Karl Marx: A Brief Biographical Sketch with an Exposition of Marxism*. Peking: Foreign Language Press, 1967.

London, Jack. *The Iron Heel*. London: Penguin, 2006.

Marx, Karl. *Capital: A Critique of Political Economy*, vol. 1. Trans. Ben Fowkes. London: Penguin, 1990.

McCarthy, Cormac. *The Road*. London: Picador, 2006.

Melville, Herman. *Moby-Dick*. 1851. New York: Norton, 1967.

Mirowski, Philip. *Never Let a Serious Crisis Go to Waste: How Neoliberalism Survived the Financial Meltdown*. London: Verso, 2013.

Phippen, J. Weston. "'Kill Every Buffalo You Can! Every Buffalo Dead Is an Indian Gone.'" *The Atlantic*, May 13, 2016. www.theatlantic.com/national/archive/2016/05/the-buffalo-killers/482349/.

Poe, Edgar Allan. *Poetry and Tales*. New York: Library of America, 1994.

Scott, Heidi. "Whale Oil Culture, Consumerism, and Modern Conservation." In *Oil Culture*, ed. Ross Barrett and Daniel Worden. Minneapolis: University of Minnesota Press. 2004. 3–18.

Sinclair, Upton. *The Jungle*. Oxford: Oxford University Press, 2010.

Sullivan, Mark. *Our Times: America at the Birth of the Twentieth Century*. New York: Scribner, 1996.

3

CARL H. SEDERHOLM

Religion and Spirituality

American horror is braided with religion so often that it would be nearly impossible to pull the strands apart without missing all the important social, cultural, and individual ways they are plaited together. Although they do not always have the same ultimate goals, religion and horror nevertheless do share an interest in the same kinds of questions pertaining to human experience, particularly on the subjects of human purpose, place, and destination. However, even if many of the critical attempts to make sense of these shared questions recognize those connections, they do not always explore why they matter or why they should warrant further investigation. Some critics even prefer to ignore religion altogether, believing that any connections to horror are easily dismissed as simple thematic coincidences, cultural conveniences, or ideological influences. This approach has sometimes succeeded because religion itself has been frequently defined against its apparent opposites, as in the differences between sacred and profane, religious and secular, faith and doubt, conversion and disbelief (Jakobsen, 215). But these once-helpful binaries may not be as obvious (or as useful) as they once were. Analyzing anything in terms of religion also requires an understanding of how it impacts human experience generally (217). As Robert Orsi explains, "Religions are lived, and it is in their living, in the full and tragic necessity of people's circumstances, that we encounter them, study and write about them, and compare them, in the full and tragic necessity of our circumstances" (13).

Exploring the intersection of horror and religion can benefit from a similar approach, one that recognizes how both wrestle with what happens when human experience goes sideways, how people attempt to understand things beyond their experience, and how they address questions pertaining to why they are here and where they think they are going. While both clearly confront such key questions of human existence, religion frequently addresses them within expectations tied to core doctrines, beliefs, and practices, while horror more often reaches beyond those limits. Moreover, readers do not necessarily expect to find explicitly religious teachings about sin and salvation in novels like *The Shining* or *The Exorcist*, at least not in ways presented exactly like those in sacred writings or formal religious settings. And yet there are moments in which both kinds of texts overlap in that they share an interest in the kinds of overwhelming questions people ask in times of concern or crisis. As Douglas Cowan writes, horror intersects with religion often enough that it could be considered "religion's conceptual and cultural sibling" because it is "often asking the same questions as religion while challenging religion's answers to them" (5).

Similarly, Eugene Thacker argues that in a world that is "increasingly unthinkable," tragic, and relentless, horror provides an important "*non-philosophical attempt to think about the world-without-us philosophically*" (1, 9, emphasis in the original). Thacker refers to nonphilosophical thinking as "negative philosophy," or an inversion of traditional philosophy built on the better-known "negative theology," or an approach to thinking about theology (and religion) without assuming the existence of God (9). Whatever we call it, the point is that horror, like religion, is strongly attuned to T. S. Eliot's sobering point that "human kind / Cannot bear very much reality" (118). There is simply too much suffering and too much tragedy to go through life unaware that eventually the other shoe drops and trouble finds its way into our lives. Perhaps that is also why horror shares with religion an interest in confronting life's inevitable monsters and, perhaps, even (temporarily) defeating them. As Stephen King writes about *The Shining*, "That our better angels sometimes – often! – win instead, in spite of all odds, is another truth of *The Shining*. And thank God it is" (xvii). There is, perhaps, something approaching a glimmer of hope in darkness and grace in tragedy. The ways the intersection between horror and religion can shed light on that possibility of hope we will now, briefly, address.

According to Charles Crow, "some of the best and most revealing of our literary works have been Gothic, and many of America's finest authors have worked within this tradition" (1). A similar case can be made about many of the same authors and the ways they have also interlaced horror tropes with religious questions, themes, and ideas. To begin, we turn to some examples from New England Puritanism to illustrate what Faye Ringel calls its "double vision," or the striking and overwhelming ways it imagines a future just as full of fear as it is of hope (16–17). American Puritanism was haunted by a peculiar – and insurmountable – tension between certainty and doubt, salvation and damnation, security and insecurity, complacency and action (Morgan, 70). This tension was generally understood as necessary because it worked against pride and presumption. If all human beings are understood to be depraved, they can focus on improvement and on how God might work in their lives (70–71). Added to that was the distinctive way the American Puritans drew significant parallels between their own experiences and those of the Old Testament's wandering Israelites. And, like those ancient Israelites, Puritans were sometimes guilty of inconsistency, worshipping false gods, and seeking inappropriate kinds of comfort and security. To help them stay on the right path, they turned to faithful leaders who could warn them about the devastating consequences of straying from the path (Bercovitch, 40). Lurking behind all these teachings was a powerful assumption of looming failure and ultimate destruction – after all, God will not help a people that fall behind in their commitments and covenants. John Winthrop's famous lay sermon, "A Model of Christian Charity" (1630), is particularly noteworthy for the way it juxtaposes the biblical image of an exemplary "city on the hill" with a clear threat of divine punishment if the people turn away from their main purposes. According to Winthrop, failure to live up to divine commands meant that "the Lord will surely break out in wrath against us, [and] be revenged of such a perjured people, and make us know the price of the breach of such a covenant" (83).

Similarly, Michael Wigglesworth's poem "The Day of Doom" (1662) takes up the prospect of God's wrath, only it imagines a people who have already lapsed in their faith because of their ease and prosperity. The poem begins with the people of the world sleeping peacefully, calm and comfortable in their expectation that day will follow night and that life will go on as it always has: "Still was the night, Serene and Bright, when all Men sleeping lay; / Calm was the season, and carnal reason / thought so 'twould last for ay" (55). Implicit in that last line (and then expanded in great detail throughout the poem) is the belief that all human hopes and expectations will change forever and that they cannot be reversed. For Wigglesworth, that means the return of Jesus Christ and the pouring out of his judgments on the wicked. Though Wigglesworth plainly believed that God's elect would be saved, he is unsparing in laying out the everlasting punishments everyone else will receive. In perhaps one of his most challenging passages, Wigglesworth articulates why even helpless, stillborn children will be damned; fortunately, his God recognizes their lack of a mortal life and so grants them the small mercy of "the easiest room in Hell" (102).

Though once widely popular, "The Day of Doom" has long since been dismissed as the worst caricature of Puritanism because of its confident sense of correctness, its relentless attempts to frighten, and its ultimate condemnation of those outside the faith. Wigglesworth underscores the point by representing the saved as watching from a safe distance, secure in their wide-eyed "thankful wonderment, / To see all those that were their foes / thus sent to punishment" (112). But Wigglesworth's triumphal ending masks an otherwise daunting sense of anxiety over the problem of human weakness itself. In his mind, the human race is largely ultimately responsible for their own destruction; God may bring the destruction, but human action prompted the need for it in the first place.

Jonathan Edwards's infamous sermon, "Sinners in the Hands of an Angry God" (1741), also draws on the prospect of divine anger to motivate his listeners to greater action. However, his opening text, "their foot shall slide in due time" (taken from Deuteronomy 32:35), clearly argues that people will ultimately fail to live up to expectations (89). As Edwards elaborates, humans have already merited damnation and so it is only a temporary mercy that keeps God from destroying them. To illustrate, Edwards develops a series of strikingly dramatic passages that employ images of people suspended just outside a fiery doom, their bodies held up only by a spider web:

> Your wickedness makes you as it were heavy as lead, and to tend downwards with great weight and pressure towards hell; and if God should let you go, you would immediately sink and swiftly descend and plunge into the bottomless gulf, and your healthy constitution, and your own care and prudence, and best contrivance, and all your righteousness, would have no more influence to uphold you and keep you out of hell, than a spider's web would have to stop a falling rock. (96)

God spares individuals from falling not because of who they are but because he has not dropped them yet. All humans are equally guilty of sin and so must face the prospect of suffering for them. Perhaps that is why Perry Miller concluded that Edwards' sermon is ultimately "a monstrous accusation against mankind" (145). Unsparing and overwhelming, "Sinners" warns the young and old alike to consider their ways. It also undermines any possibility of permanent health, ease, comfort, or salvation based on human effort alone. Although God is omnipotent, his favor cannot be curried and he is more often angry with people than he is pleased: "his wrath towards you burns like fire; he looks upon you as worthy of nothing else, but to be cast into the fire" (Edwards, 97). Edwards concludes with a sobering warning that some of his hearers will find themselves in hell "before this year is out" and, worse, that those who feel "quiet and secure" about themselves and their circumstances may even die and face damnation that very night (103).

For Edwards, human beings are never completely safe and never completely secure and so they live out their days expecting doom. But instead of having it come, Wigglesworth-like, in a single dramatic moment, Edwards suggests that "*every* day is potentially the Day of Judgment" (Lloyd-Smith, 110, emphasis in the original). This is what makes Edwards' sermon so important; beyond the fiery images and stern warnings, it is also an unforgettable reminder about the ways human actions and human hopes tend toward failure and, perhaps, even toward damnation. As Edwards explains, "Sin is the ruin and misery of the soul; it is destructive in its nature; and if God should leave it without restraint, there would need nothing else to make the soul perfectly miserable" (92). Without any source of divine help, all human hopes and aspirations crumble.

Nathaniel Hawthorne's own interests in the problems related to sin and salvation, punishment and redemption, and reform and regret drive some of his best – and most frightening – tales. Like Edwards before him, Hawthorne brooded over the problem of the human tendency to "slide," only he did so with the understanding that fiction would allow him to do so without having to draw any particular theological conclusion. Hawthorne was especially fascinated with the metaphor of the human heart and how its steady beating masked a propensity to waver into inexplicable, unexpected, or all-too-human actions. In stories like "Earth's Holocaust" (1844), "The Ambitious Guest" (1835), and "Young Goodman Brown" (1835), Hawthorne worked over this problem from a variety of perspectives, but consistently held out the frightening prospect that people are always their own worst enemies. In "Earth's Holocaust," for instance, Hawthorne imagines a world "so over-burthened" that people created a "general bonfire" on which they threw everything from trash to books to implements of war, torture, and punishment (336). Ever the allegorist, Hawthorne worked his fantasy not simply into a reflection on what humans stand to lose in the name of general reform but also into a stern warning that human life can never be completely cleansed so long as the human heart continues to beat. A scarcely disguised demonic figure makes this point in his snickering confidence that "it will be the old world yet!" because the fire burns only the material objects and not the drives that brought them into existence (357). The real problem, the devil-figure explains, is the ongoing existence of the human heart. As the narrator finally suggests, "The Heart – the Heart – there was the little, yet boundless sphere, wherein existed the original wrong, of which the crime and misery of this outward world were merely types" (357).

In "The Ambitious Guest" (1835), Hawthorne echoes Jonathan Edwards' "Sinners" in the ways it dramatically illustrates that "it is no security to wicked men for one moment, that there are no *visible means of death* at hand" (Edwards, 93, emphasis in original; Colacurcio, 510). The story, inspired by a real-life tragic mudslide in the White Mountains, gave Hawthorne a means of reflecting on the ironies inherent in human ambition. The story opens with images familiar to readers of Michael Wigglesworth or Jonathan Edwards in that they suggest a family enjoying a "sure place of ease" in a modest cottage even though they live just below a looming, restless, and unpredictable mountain (164). When the unnamed "ambitious guest" stops at the cottage for a brief rest, he and the family converse about their hopes, dreams, and memories in ways that resonate with familiar questions such as: What is the purpose of life? Why must we die? What makes a life worth living? As the discussion continues, the young man declares that his ambitions are such that they should outweigh any immediate prospect of death: "I cannot die till I have achieved my destiny. Then, let Death come! I shall have built my monument!" (166). But these claims are soon dashed by the inevitable sounds of a landslide making its way toward the cottage. Hawthorne suggests that the sounds were so awful and the shaking so bad that it was as if "the foundations of the earth seemed to be shaken, as if this awful sound were the peal of the last trump" (170). Unfortunately, instead of sheltering in place, the characters flee the cottage in the hopes of finding safety outside, but as Hawthorne explains, "Alas! they had quitted their security and fled right into the pathway of destruction" (170). With shouts of "The Slide! The Slide," each character quickly falls prey to the falling rock and debris, their words echoing with Edwards' own sense that "their foot shall slide in due time" (170; Edwards, 89). In a particularly devastating sentence, Hawthorne sums up the tragedy: "the simplest words must intimate, but not portray, the unutterable horror of the catastrophe" (170). Although the ambitious guest never created a monument focused on his accomplishments, his tragic death nevertheless marks the vanity of human accomplishment.

A similar gloom hangs over "Young Goodman Brown" (1835), only Hawthorne now incorporates his melancholy mood into profound reflection on human hypocrisy, secret sins, and the collective weight of human guilt. He also plays with the potential connections between one's civic, religious, and marital responsibilities by naming Brown's wife "Faith" and never steps away from puns about the ways Brown might leave or lose his "faith." In the story, Brown leaves on an urgent, but unspecified, errand into the woods where he encounters a devil-like figure and then follows him into its deepest recesses. Eventually, Brown discovers that the people in his community, the wise and responsible people who taught him in all precepts of his faith, are guilty of secret sins – lust, murder, greed, envy, and so on. While struggling with that realization, Brown also learns that he and Faith are the unwitting guests at a secret ceremony that will bring them both into a "worshipping assembly" founded on the depth and degree of human sin (145). Knowing Brown's hope in human virtue, the devil-figure proclaims, "Now are ye undeceived! Evil is the nature of mankind. Evil must be your only happiness. Welcome, again, my children to the communion of your race!" (146). As everyone joins in the welcoming cry, Brown appeals to Faith, yet once more, to resist "the Wicked One" and to find some glimmer of hope in the human

(146). But he never knows what path she chose. Instead, he is left with a hazy sense of uncertainty. Was it just a dream? Perhaps, but Hawthorne withholds easy answers. Instead, he shows that Brown lives out his days unable to shake off his gloom and his elevated sense of human sin. Though he lives to old age and maintains some outward sense of family and religious responsibilities, he cannot let go of what he might have witnessed in the forest. As Hawthorne concludes, there was "no hopeful verse upon his tomb-stone; for his dying hour was gloom" (148).

Hawthorne wrote "Young Goodman Brown" at a time when debates over slavery intensified in ways that would ultimately divide the nation and lead to the Civil War. Nat Turner's bloody revolt on August 21, 1831, the largest slave uprising in American history, was especially galvanizing due to its shocking violence and its explicitly religious underpinnings. Turner's actions led directly to the deaths of almost sixty people in Southampton County, Virginia, and terrified whites throughout the South so much that it quickly led to increased suspicion, violence, and oppression toward Blacks, especially those who, like Turner, were literate, somewhat independent, and deeply spiritual (Johnson, 180). Turner's rebellion also led to increased panic, perhaps even paranoia, over the revolutionary possibilities that many whites feared were inherent within African American religious practices in general (23).

Turner's religious convictions began from an early age when he heard family members suggesting that the birthmarks on his body were portents of a prophetic destiny. Throughout his life, Turner experienced a wide variety of other spiritual signs and omens, including voices and visions that persuaded him not only that the end of the world was imminent but that he would play a significant, messianic role in it. One of Turner's visions depicted a climactic battle between whites and Blacks and indicated that divine, retributive justice for African American slaves was coming and that Turner himself would take up a Messianic role: "Christ had laid down the yoke he had borne for the sins of men, and that I should take it on and fight against the Serpent for the time was fast approaching when the first should be last and the last should be first" (Greenberg, 47–48).

Unlike Nat Turner, Edgar Allan Poe was more interested in exploring his protagonists' disturbed minds than in wondering about the state of their souls. Even his notion of "perverseness," as developed in "The Black Cat" and "The Imp of the Perverse," attempts to explain the worst of human action in a strictly rational sense, without any recourse to religious concepts like sin, judgment, or damnation. But his definition of perverseness can also be read as a variation on the problem of sin, or of the ways humans behave in such inconsistent, unkind, or violent ways. The narrator of "The Black

Cat" ruminates on this topic after he has tortured and hung the family cat – and experiences the awful horrors that ensued. As he attempts to understand his actions, he can only conclude that he fell victim to perverseness, or "the unfathomable longing of the soul to *vex itself* – to offer violence to its own nature – to do wrong for the wrong's sake only" (350, emphasis in original). But these conclusions only trip him up. Knowing that there is no simple way to link cause and effect neatly, the narrator simply indicates that he will focus only on a "chain of facts" that fly in the face of reason and logic (351). Now, facing a death sentence, he finally appeals to the idea that he can somehow "unburthen [his] soul" and find his way back from stepping "beyond the reach of the infinite mercy of the Most Merciful and Most Terrible God" (350).

"The Tell-Tale Heart" also reads like a confession, only this time there is even less clarity about the narrator's audience or purpose. Instead of reflecting on God's mercy and judgment, however, the narrator focuses on the apparent chain of reasoning that should transform his murderous acts into reasonable and smart conclusions. But his account quickly begins to unravel as every claim to reason takes on an increasingly deranged cast. In one of the most chilling passages, the narrator explains how he spied on the old man at night and once heard his victim groaning in bed, certain that his life was about to end. As the old man stares desperately into the dark, sensing that someone (or something) is looming, the narrator holds back, quietly listening and waiting. As the narrator explains the rest, "Presently I heard a slight groan, and I knew it was the groan of mortal terror. It was not a groan of pain or of grief – oh, no! – it was the low stifled sound that arises from the bottom of the soul when overcharged with awe" (318). He then explains that the old man's attempts to find comfort in that moment were fruitless. He was no longer safe, and his groaning came from his understanding that hope was "*All in vain*; because Death, in approaching him had stalked with his black shadow before him, and enveloped the victim" (318, emphasis in original).

"The Black Cat" and "The Tell-Tale Heart" both suggest that human motivation frequently works beyond reason and is mostly a matter of impulse, faulty thinking, or self-destructive tendencies. Even in a formal religious or legal setting, the rhetorical demands of confession can still mask true understanding. Poe tests understanding even further in "The Facts in the Case of M. Valdemar," a story that explores the boundaries of death by appealing to the pseudo-scientific methods of mesmerism. In the story, M. Valdemar agrees to be placed in a mesmeric trance to arrest the process of death and, perhaps, to help provide some kind of insight into death – or what comes after death. But as the study drags, the narrator and his assistants make very little progress in their understanding. As things develop, they are able to communicate with Valdemar, whose vibrating tongue somehow conveys a sense of mortal expression. With the words "I am dead," Valdemar grows increasingly desperate to be released from his suspended state. But in the attempt to awaken Valdemar, the narrator can only step back in horror as he witnesses Valdemar's body as it "shrunk – crumbled – absolutely *rotted* away beneath my hands" (414, emphasis in original). All that remained was "a nearly liquid mass of loathsome – of detestable putrescence" (414). The story began with a clear interest in crossing the fixed boundaries of life and death, but it ends up crashing into them violently, leaving behind a gory and indescribable mess. As Fred Botting explains, Poe's story leaves us cold by showing how everything "dissolves rather than resolves" (98).

"Valdemar" represents death as the worst possible horror, a fixed barrier, one that cannot be crossed without experiencing the same kinds of visceral, oozing, and decaying awfulness that Poe describes. But those barriers began to break down with the rise of Spiritualism. Spiritualists rejected Poe-like horrors in favor of an open-ended perspective on death, one that allowed for the immortality of the soul – and for a relatively stable means of communicating with the dead. Though lacking formal doctrines and organized houses of worship, Spiritualism initially seemed wild and untamed, opposed to convention, but its larger promises of ongoing communication between the living and the dead gave it a semblance of order that helped make it popular.

Spiritualists did not invent the idea that humans could potentially communicate with the dead, but they did formalize it in ways that remain influential. Although the movement had several lines of influence, it is commonly said to have begun in Hydesville, New York, in March 1848 when the Fox sisters (Katherine and Margaret) claimed they were actively communicating with a disembodied being they called "Mr. Splitfoot" (Ahlstrom, 488). They did so through a series of rappings, or rhythmic knocking and clicking (488). These communications drew the attention of friends and neighbors and quickly led to public performances sponsored by none other than P. T. Barnum. They also led to increasing claims of supernatural gifts, the rise of more mediums, and the demand for ever more elaborate and dramatic demonstrations of otherworldly communications. Given Spiritualism's rapid growth and ties to the entertainment industry, it also led to an intractable suspicion that it was nothing but a sham, a type of theater that preyed on the gullible or the vulnerable. Nevertheless, Spiritualism genuinely appealed to those looking for spiritual experiences outside the formal structures of organized religion. As Ahlstrom explains, "Spiritualism was not a 'sect' in the usual sense of the term, yet it became a component in many kinds of sectarian revolt from the more traditional churches" (490). What Spiritualism lacked in doctrinal structure and complexity it made up for in the accessibility and flexibility of its ideas and practices. It could even be paired with other spiritual interests ranging from traditional Christianity to Occultism.

Jack London, for example, wrote a handful of stories that blend the supernatural with overtones of horror in ways that echo Spiritualism's ongoing influence in the early twentieth century. London denounced any rumors of a personal interest in Spiritualism, perhaps as a means of distancing himself from his mother's own passion for seances and from the discovery that his biological father was not the man who raised him but was an itinerant astrologer. Nevertheless, London had a strong interest in "nonrational experience" and "actively explored such alternative psychic phenomena as mystical transcendence, creative inspiration, and subconscious motivation" in his fiction (Watson, 193–94). These interests appear in early stories such as "A Ghostly Chess Game" (1897) and "The Mahatma's Little Joke" (1897), but they were much more developed in "Planchette" (1906), a story that introduces elements of Spiritualism to complicate London's otherwise straightforward account of two lovers, Chris Dunbar and Lute Story, who are puzzled over Dunbar's recent spate of strange – and nearly deadly – riding accidents. Given that Chris' accidents began shortly after revealing that he cannot marry Lute but refuses to offer any explanation, the accidents seem oddly suspicious. Later, while participating in a series of planchette demonstrations led by the medium Mrs. Grantley, they receive very specific warnings, purportedly from Lute's deceased father, that he is actively trying to murder Chris, presumably out of spite for the way Chris refuses to marry Lute. Even though the supernatural warnings continue, Chris remains skeptical of them and eventually tempts fate by going out for another ride. Not surprisingly, Chris is thrown from his horse and falls to his death, leaving Lute to assume that the supernatural has prevailed over Chris' lack of belief. To some extent, "Planchette" illustrates what Charles Watson calls London's "double vision" when it comes to the kinds of ideas embraced by Spiritualism (199). Though publicly resistant to Spiritualism, London nevertheless struggled to let go of its general appeal to a belief in real supernatural forces.

Spiritualism brought forward the voices of the dead and suggested that, perhaps, there was more to life than the span of mortality. But there were other, even more revolutionary, voices coming forward in the early years of the twentieth century. In the same year that London published "Planchette," the Pentecostal movement dramatically brought forward the practice of speaking in tongues and other charismatic gifts into the popular consciousness in new and unprecedented ways. The origins of Pentecostalism are beyond the scope of this chapter, but scholars typically point to the ways Holy Ghost power manifested itself at the Azuza Street revivals (1906–9) in Los Angeles, California, as a major turning moment in its modern development. Azuza's success was partly due to the ways it brought together a relatively unified body of vulnerable and displaced persons who cast aside racial and class divisions in the spirit of worship. As Paul Conkin writes, Azuza Street represents "one of the few times in American history [when] blacks and whites, men and women, joined in complete equality in exhilarating and exhausting religious services" (299). Central to the Azuza revivals was the distinctive practice of speaking in tongues, which highlighted the power of voice in ways that suggested not only increased spiritual power, but also a keen awareness that spiritual change does not necessarily reflect secular change. As Shapiro and Barnard argue, speaking in tongues may serve as a "sign of aspirational frustration" or of the bringing forward of revolutionary drives, desires, and powers that presage the possibility of real change even if it occurs slowly (58, 86). Significantly, for our purposes, an analogy between charismatic gifts such as speaking in tongues and seeking to overcome human limitations can be read into the horror tradition, including in the ways Lovecraft introduced strange and otherworldly voices brought forward with the same kind of emotional and ecstatic depth (73).

Similarly, texts such as *The Exorcist* (1971) and *The Amityville Horror* (1977) depend, to a large extent, on the kinds of questions, objects, persons, and practices connected with hearing otherworldly voices. Some of these things were distantly connected to Spiritualism, but they also appealed to a more broadly popular sense of the supernatural as manifested by mediumistic gifts, spirit manifestations, spirit boards or Ouija boards, and other similar objects and practices. In *The Exorcist*, for instance, William Peter Blatty first hints at the demon Pazuzu's terrible presence in the MacNeil house by suggesting that Chris MacNeil, mother to the soon-to-be-possessed Regan MacNeil, hears a series of "tapping sounds" that she thinks of as "Odd. Muffled. Profound. Rhythmically clustered. Alien code tapped out by a dead man" (12). Although Chris tries diligently to dismiss the tapping as nothing more than evidence of rats in her walls, she is also quick to assume that the tapping patterns suggest something more than just animal sounds. Things also take a stranger turn when Chris discovers that Regan has been playing with a Ouija board and has befriended a spirit named "Captain Howdy," an entity Regan believes to be friendly (40–42). But, unlike the story of Mr. Splitfoot and the Fox Sisters, Captain Howdy has a different purpose than simply establishing communication. His hopes are set on battling the Jesuit priest Father Merrin, who will soon enter the fray in his efforts to rescue an innocent, but possessed, girl.

Though it clearly owes something to Spiritualism, *The Exorcist* quickly outstrips those seemingly antiquated trappings and focuses, instead, on the question of theodicy, or the larger problem of explaining evil, suffering, and sin. As David F. Ford writes, the world is everywhere full of clear evidence of human evil, injustice, and suffering: "Every relationship and activity can be distorted or corrupted. The natural world can be polluted, spoiled or destroyed. Evil can be part of our deepest friendships, our marriages, and our family life, and its effects can accumulate year after year" (69). Blatty underscores the point not only in representing the suffering of a possessed girl but also in his multiple epigraphs that juxtapose the ancient biblical story of Legion and the Gadarene Swine with brief mentions of twentieth-century atrocities that range from contract killings to wartime atrocities to the Holocaust. In fact, the epigraphs conclude with the words "Dachau," "Auschwitz," and "Buchenwald" listed without additional commentary. Blatty's point is clear: evil takes on various forms and has never disappeared completely from the world.

Blatty emphasizes the point in the closing conversation between Chris MacNeil and Father Dyer, a priest who hopes to understand just what happened to Father Merrin and Father Karras. Chris explains to Father Dyer that she has come to believe that it is easier to believe in the devil than in God:

> Well, like you say . . . as far as God goes, I *am* a nonbeliever. Still am. But when it comes to a devil – well, that's something else. I could buy that. I do, in fact. I do. And it isn't just what happened to Rags [Regan]. I mean, generally.. . . You come to God and you have to figure if there is one, then he must need a million years' sleep every night or else he tends to get irritable. Know what I mean? He never talks. But the devil keeps advertising, Father. The devil does lots of commercials. (382, emphasis in original)

Chris's closing metaphor is apt. Her experiences as an actress have taught her the value of keeping oneself – or one's product – in front of the camera. For her, evil is similarly aggressive and relentless, something alluring, but not always necessary. Her daughter's experiences also helped her accept the possibility that the devil somehow exists in the modern world. The devil is not merely in the details but in the actions that make those details possible. Worse, he was presumably the center of a battle of wills over her daughter's life. After hearing Chris talk, Father Blatty asks her a surprising question, one that turns the traditional problem of theodicy on its head: Assuming that there is a literal devil, how, then, can we "account for all the *good* in the world"? (382). Chris has no answer. Instead, she simply offers up a noncommittal "yeah" and "that's a point" (382). There may be hope in that concession, but it is weighed down by her fear that evil will always be with us.

In both religion and horror salvation appears to be an uneasy prospect, something that we cannot simply take for granted. But, as the horrors of the twentieth century transform into the escalating challenges of the twenty-first century, religion remains a significant part of American horror, if only because it, too, shares an interest in the difficult questions pertaining to human life, purpose, and destiny. To be sure, horror has its fair share of clichéd figures – wicked priests, violent fanatics, and right-wing ideologues – but beyond that are the questions that we ask to make sense of why, as Eugene Thacker writes, "it is increasingly difficult to comprehend the world in which we live and of which we are a part" (1). As Stephen King writes in the afterword to *The Colorado Kid*:

> I ask you to consider the fact that we live in a *web* of mystery, and have simply gotten so used to the fact that we have crossed out the word and replaced it with one we like better, that one being *reality*. Where do we come from? Where were we before we were here? Don't know. Where are we going. Don't know. A lot of churches have what they assure us are the answers, but most of us have a sneaking suspicion all that might be a con-job laid down to fill the collection plates. In the meantime, we're in a kind of compulsory dodgeball game as we free-fall from Wherever to Ain't Got a Clue. (183–84, emphasis in original)

King's commentary did not exactly endear readers to *The Colorado Kid* – the novel infamously ended without real closure – but his move to making it all about life's mysteries nevertheless resonates with the all-too-human wish to find hope in a world otherwise saturated in nightmares.

Works Cited

Ahlstrom, Sydney E. *A Religious History of the American People*. 1972. New Haven, CT: Yale University Press, 2004.

Bercovitch, Sacvan. *The American Jeremiad*. Madison: University of Wisconsin Press, 1978.

Blatty, William Peter. *The Exorcist*. New York: Harper, 1971.

Botting, Fred. "Poe, Voice and the Origin of Horror Fiction." In *Sound Effects: The Object Voice in Fiction*, ed. Jorge Sacido-Romero and Sylvia Mieszkowski. Leiden: Brill, 2015. 73–100.

Colacurcio, Michael J. *The Province of Piety: Moral History in Hawthorne's Early Tales*. Durham, NC: Duke University Press, 1995.

Conkin, Paul K. *American Originals: Homemade Varieties of Christianity*. Chapel Hill: University of North Carolina Press, 1997.

Cowan, Douglas E. *America's Dark Theologian: The Religious Imagination of Stephen King*. New York: New York University Press, 2018.

Crow, Charles L. *American Gothic*. Cardiff: University of Wales Press, 2009.

Edwards, Jonathan. "Sinners in the Hands of an Angry God." In *A Jonathan Edwards Reader*, ed. John E. Smith, Harry S. Stout, and Kenneth P. Minkema. New Haven, CT: Yale University Press, 1995. 89–105.
Eliot, T. S. "Burnt Norton." In *T. S. Eliot: The Complete Poems and Plays, 1909–1950*. New York: Harcourt, 1952. 117–22.
Ford, David F. *Theology: A Very Short Introduction*. Oxford: Oxford University Press, 1999.
Greenberg, Kenneth S. *The Confessions of Nat Turner and Related Documents*. New York: Bedford, 1996.
Hawthorne, Nathaniel. "The Ambitious Guest." In *Selected Tales and Sketches*. New York: Penguin, 1987. 162–71.
"Earth's Holocaust." In *Selected Tales and Sketches*. New York: Penguin, 1987. 336–57.
"Young Goodman Brown." In *Selected Tales and Sketches*. New York: Penguin, 1987. 133–48.
Jakobsen, Janet R. "Religion." In *Keywords for American Cultural Studies*, 2nd ed., ed. Bruce Burgett and Glenn Handler. New York: New York University Press, 2014. 215–17.
Johnson, Curtis D. *Redeemer Nation: Evangelicals and the Road to Civil War*. Chicago: Ivan R. Dee, 1993.
King, Stephen. *The Colorado Kid*. New York: Hard Case Crime, 2005.
"Introduction." In *The Shining*. New York: Pocket, 1977. xv–xvii.
Morgan, Edmund. *Visible Saints: The History of a Puritan Idea*. Ithaca, NY: Cornell University Press, 1963.
Lloyd-Smith, Allan. "Nineteenth-Century American Gothic." In *A Companion to the Gothic*, ed. David Punter. Malden, MA: Blackwell, 2000. 109–21.
London, Jack. "Planchette." In *The Complete Short Stories of Jack London*, ed. Earle Labor, Robert C. Leitz, and Milo Shepard. Stanford, CA: Stanford University Press, 1993. 1035–72.
Miller, Perry. *Jonathan Edwards*. Lincoln: University of Nebraska Press, 2005.
Noll, Mark A. *America's God: From Jonathan Edwards to Abraham Lincoln*. Oxford: Oxford University Press, 2002.
Orsi, Robert A. "Introduction." In *The Cambridge Companion to Religious Studies*, ed. Robert A. Orsi. Cambridge: Cambridge University Press, 2012. 1–13.
Poe, Edgar Allan. "The Black Cat." In *The Selected Writings of Edgar Allan Poe*, ed. G. R. Thompson. New York: W. W. Norton, 2004. 348–55.
"Facts in the Case of M. Valdemar." In *The Selected Writings of Edgar Allan Poe*, ed. G. R. Thompson. New York: W. W. Norton, 2004. 407–14.
"The Tell-Tale Heart." In *The Selected Writings of Edgar Allan Poe*, ed. G. R. Thompson. New York: W. W. Norton, 2004. 316–21.
Ringel, Faye. "Early American Gothic (Puritan and New Republic)." In *The Cambridge Companion to American Gothic*, ed. Jeffrey Andrew Weinstock. Cambridge: Cambridge University Press, 2017. 15–30.
Shapiro, Stephen, and Philip Barnard. *Pentecostal Modernism: Lovecraft, Los Angeles, and World-Systems Culture*. New York: Bloomsbury, 2017.
Thacker, Eugene. *In the Dust of This Planet: Horror of Philosophy*, vol. 1. Winchester: Zero Books, 2011.

Ward, Graham. "Deconstructive Theology." In *The Cambridge Companion to Postmodern Theology*, ed. Kevin J. Vanhoozer. Cambridge: Cambridge University Press, 2003. 76–91.

Watson, Charles N. "Jack London: Up from Spiritualism." In *The Haunted Dusk: American Supernatural Fiction, 1820–1920*, ed. Howard Kerr, John W. Crowley, and Charles L Crow. Athens: University of Georgia Press, 1983. 193–207.

Wigglesworth, Michael. "The Day of Doom." In *America Poetry of the Seventeenth Century*, ed. Harrison T. Meserole. University Park: Penn State University Press, 1985. 55–113.

Winthrop, Jonathan. "A Model of Christian Charity." In *The American Puritans: Their Prose and Poetry*, ed. Perry Miller. New York: Columbia University Press, 1956. 78–84.

4

JOHAN HÖGLUND

Settlement and Imperialism

The history of settler colonialism in North America and of the imperial ambitions of the United States cannot be told without the register that horror provides. Horror emerges in relation to the physical violence that takes place on the frontier as land is settled and Indigenous people eliminated, and also out of the realization that the necropolitics that generates violence in the settler colony is built into settler culture. Horror is furthermore generated by capitalism's actions of extraction that transform land and people into property and resource, that destroy precarious ecosystems and produce ecological crisis. This chapter proposes that these dark histories of death and ongoing planetary devastation are primary sources for American horror, from the earliest accounts of contact between colonizers and Indigenous people to twenty-first-century narratives that explore the attempt to maintain US global hegemony.

While previous studies of the relationship between settler colonialism and American horror have focused primarily on the frontier (Mogen et al.), this chapter shifts attention away from this disappearing line and toward the land itself. Indigenous and decolonial studies have made the important observation that settler colonialism is primarily about the occupation of land, and the treatment of this land as resource. Patrick Wolfe has argued in "Settler Colonialism" that a "logic of elimination" guides the expropriation and occupation of Indigenous land. This logic performs its insidious work not just on the frontier at specific moments in time, but across occupied space and over centuries. Taking the settlement of land as the starting point thus enables a focus on the horrors that arise out of maintained occupation of land, and on the process of extraction taking place on the slavery plantations, in the reservations, in the quickly growing American megacities and their suburbs, and across borders to Latin America, to Asia, and to the Middle East. The focus on land also makes it possible to consider how horror narrates settler colonialism's understanding of land and people as extractable "cheap nature" (Moore, *Capitalism*) and to discuss how this understanding has contributed to the slow yet violent erosion of the planetary ecosystem.

American horror, as I will argue in this chapter, has both participated in and opposed this history of appropriation and extraction. As I have argued elsewhere (Höglund, *American Imperial Gothic*, "Imperial Horror and Terrorism"), the genre is dominated by often racist and anthropocentric "imperial" narratives produced by and for the settler community. In this type of narrative, white settler society is depicted as desperately fending off various threats (Indigenous people, prehistoric or supernatural monsters, even the land itself) to its self-mythology of peaceful existence. By casting settler-colonial violence as self-defense, imperial horror inverts the actual power relationship that exists between the settler and Indigenous and marginalized people and land. At the same time, as Stephen Shapiro has argued, this type of horror directs attention away from the recurrent violence inherent in the capitalist project itself. Thus, just like the British imperial gothic that emerges during what Brantlinger in *Rule of Darkness* calls the "Dusk" of the British Empire, American settler horror is most insidious and popular at times when the settler state is exposed to stress from international military and economic competition and when the capitalist system is forced to adapt to new challenges.

However, American horror needs to be understood not only as a cultural form automatically produced by capitalist anxieties but also as a type of intellectual and critical indictment of the violence and epistemologies these anxieties produce. That horror has the potential to critique settler violence becomes increasingly visible and central as people marginalized by settler culture acquire access to the means of cultural production and start to produce horror stories of their own, and as settler culture itself begins to become aware of the logic of elimination that has fueled the settlement of the American continent and beyond. This progressive type of American horror is also a reaction to the systemic violence of capitalist settler colonialism, but it is mediated by agents who have historized, rather than internalized, this violence and who are able to constructively criticize it.

Horror in the Early Republic

Before the attempt to settle land in America began, European imperial ambition manifested in America in the form of smallpox, measles, influenza, and the bubonic plague. The lack of antibodies in the Indigenous population brought on what has been called the Great Dying, reducing the population of the continent by an estimated 55 million people by the year 1600 (Koch et al.). As part of this Columbian exchange, European livestock, rodents, birds, insects, and seeds engaged in their own destructive settlement of the continent. Some of these species were introduced in an attempt to refashion the American continent into an Anglo European ecology (Dunlap).

This aggressive "ecological imperialism" (Crosby) was accompanied from the very beginning by an extractive relationship where species and land were understood as commodifiable resources. The central mechanism used to make the new continent available for extraction was the privatization and enclosure of land. This transformation of common land began in Britain in the late feudal period and made it possible to control resource extraction from the land (see Neeson; Yelling) and to police and punish those seen to violate the new boundaries (Vitale). Settler colonialism can be understood as the extension of this project into land outside formal national borders, where it could transform the energy of new people, animals, and land into extractable resources. In a related move, as observed by Moore, the status of humanity was granted only to those people who were deemed capable of owning land ("The Rise of Cheap Nature," 79). Those outside this privileging category were either eliminated or imagined as part of the land so they could be conquered, extracted, or used to extract.

This rethinking of common land into private and enclosed space is, as Robert Marzec and Stephen Shapiro have observed, essential to how settler colonialism and the world in which it existed were imagined. As Marzec has noted, Daniel Defoe's Robinson Crusoe is so frightened by the sight of the Caribbean island on which he will make his home that he "codes the land as 'more frightful than the Sea'" (130). Yet this unenclosed land is also full of potential to Robinson, who assumes with "a secret kind of pleasure" that if he can enclose its wild geography, he will be elevated to a "king and lord" with a "right of possession" (Defoe, 98). This tension between land imagined either as wild and open to exploitation or as safe and enclosed crucially informs early American horror.

Charles Brockden Brown's *Edgar Huntly* (1799), one of the first American horror novels, exemplifies this tension. In his foreword, Brown promises to replace the "[p]uerile superstition and exploded manners, Gothic castles and chimeras" common to the European Gothic, with "incidents of Indian hostility, and the perils of the Western wilderness" (4). In the novel, the eponymous Huntly tries to solve the strange murder of a close friend and first blames it on another settler, the Irish Clithero. However, Huntly eventually realizes that horror in America is produced by the wildness of the land itself and by the Indigenous people who occupy its unenclosed spaces. This realization prompts Huntly to embark on a long sequence of brutal violence against the Indigenous community. Unlike the ghosts haunting the British

Gothic novels, Indigenous uprising is a threat that can be resolved through massive violence.

It can be argued that Huntly's thirst for blood is so excessive that the true savages of the novel are not the Indigenous people but "the so-called civilized Europeans who are bestially invading and devouring aboriginal people's lands" (Barnard and Shapiro, xlii). Indeed, the extreme violence that Huntly exercises vies for the reader's attention with its racist portrayal of Indigenous people. This turns the narrative into a fundamentally ambiguous chronicle of the encounter between settlers and Indigenous people in eighteenth-century America. Written and published at a time when settler society had become so firmly entrenched on the East Coast that Indigenous people could not hope to shift it, *Edgar Huntly* does indeed remind the reader of the history of bestial settler violence that paved the way for white hegemony. However, the narrative never clearly guides the reader toward condemnation of this violence. The Indigenous assailants are termed savages and likened to dogs; they do not present as people out to reclaim stolen land. Thus, the text's extreme violence can be read as a legitimate resolution to Indigenous resistance. In this way, *Edgar Huntly* appears both as furtive critique of the settler project and as a text assisting in the creation of an imaginary that made it possible to cast the 100 years of westward expansion that followed the novel's publication as a violent yet regenerative attempt to civilize an imagined wilderness.

Expansion and the Plantation

The model for (mis)understanding settler violence that *Edgar Huntly* makes possible became a staple first in the novels of James Fenimore Cooper and then in the cheap and widely circulated dime Westerns that appeared at the middle of the nineteenth century. Even more than in Brown's text, settler violence is cast by this fiction as a performative, masculine, and regenerative response to Indigenous sexualities and spaces. Indeed, as Leslie Fiedler and Renée Bergland argue, miscegenation haunts the early American novel. This fear of racial mixing, often stronger in British colonies than in the French and Spanish (see Hodes), parallels the relationship between settler society and the land itself. Just like the sexual union of different peoples threatens the imagined homogeneity of whiteness, the entry into unenclosed, Indigenous, and often feminized land risks disturbing the perceived homogeneity of white settler identity. As Donald Worster has influentially argued, capitalism encouraged settlers to imagine land as something to be busted and broken as a preliminary to extraction (4–9). Thus, to steer clear of the risk of contamination, settler entry into new land was accompanied by severe and self-confident violence, by the attempt to break both Indigenous resistance and the land itself.

The first generation of horror writers born in the US republic were not unaware of the violence practiced on the Indigenous community, but they still expressed great unease at the notion of unbroken land. From the vantage point of Massachusetts, Nathaniel Hawthorne interrogated the motifs of the Puritan community that helped colonize New England. His fiction deviates from much earlier writing by casting Puritan society as dishonest and corrupted and settler violence as fundamentally destructive. His short story "Young Goodman Brown" (1835) describes how a young Puritan ventures into the forest to rendezvous with the devil. As the night proceeds, Goodman Brown discovers that all members of his community are friends of the devil, and when the devil tells him that "it was I that brought your father a pitch-pine knot, kindled at my own hearth, to set fire to an Indian village, in King Philip's War" (113), the protagonist understands that settler violence is an intrinsic part of his own family history.

This description of settler-Indigenous relations is both reminiscent of and notably different from the one proposed by Brown in *Edgar Huntly*. The burning of Indigenous communities is here clearly spelled out as a horror. Even so, Indigeneity and the land itself remain sources of enormous anxiety. Hurrying toward the meeting, the road on which Goodman Brown travels grows "wilder and drearier, and more faintly traced, and vanished at length, leaving him in the heart of the dark wilderness" (118) where "the creaking of the trees, the howling of wild beasts," are accompanied by "the yell of Indians" (119). Thus, while "Young Goodman Brown" importantly problematizes settler history, unbroken land and the people of this land remain sources of uncanny horror. Refusing to join his depraved yet virile community, Goodman Brown exits the wilderness in an emasculated state and his dying hour is "gloom" (124).

If the still unenclosed land is one central signifier of anxiety in American nineteenth-century horror, the plantation is the other. One of the foremost reasons for enclosing land was to enable the plantations that became central to the settler community's extraction of resources. The establishment of the American slave plantation is a crucial stage of what Donna Haraway has termed the Plantationocene, marked by a "devastating transformation of diverse kinds of human-tended farms, pastures, and forests into extractive and enclosed plantations" (162).[1] As a site of unsustainable extraction of land and of human and nonhuman labor, the plantation was thus part of a systemic, geological shift that organizes ecology, energy, and capital. In this way, plantation violence is simultaneously the product of a certain racist order enacted at a specific time in history and the effect of an extractive, long-term, and capitalist relationship to ecology. As a racist order, the plantation extracted and obliterated both American Indigenous and Black African American lives. The Indian Removal Act of 1830 and the Trail of Tears that followed eliminated Indigenous communities from the fertile lands of the Deep South, making these lands increasingly available for the white plantation complex and the already predominant slave system. As extractive, capitalist order, the plantation helped produce an exceedingly liberal paradigm that allowed the white settler community to use and exhaust the land itself.

In much American horror of the nineteenth century, the horror of the plantation is obscured by the privileging of whiteness and the erasure of the destruction of Black bodies. In several of his stories, Edgar Allan Poe assists in the construction of an abject Blackness against which a normative whiteness can emerge. In *The Narrative of Arthur Gordon Pym of Nantucket* (1838), a young man sneaks aboard a whaling ship to experience the world outside the now thoroughly settled Massachusetts. An increasingly dreamlike journey eventually brings him close to the South Pole, where he and his ship encounter an island inhabited by Black people who first appear friendly, but that later slaughter all except Pym and a fellow traveler. In an effort to escape the island, Pym sails further south into a territory where the sea and the animals are white, and where a white ash-like powder falls from the sky. Confronted with this whiteness a Black islander who has been forced to accompany Pym expires. Pym's narrative then ends with an encounter with an enormous, shrouded figure whose skin "was of the perfect whiteness of the snow" (243).

As Tony Morrison and Teresa Goddu have observed, Poe's writing tends to confirm the contemporary construction of Blackness as the negation of whiteness. In Poe's *The Narrative*, this construction informs the understanding of land and sea as racially coded sites of extraction. The black island that Pym arrives at thus takes shape through the resources that are available for extraction. Before being slaughtered, the white explorers have "established a regular market on shore, just under the guns of the schooner," where local fauna are exchanged for "brass trinkets, nails, knives, and pieces of red cloth" (207). In this way, the black island is fundamentally different from the geography of whiteness that Pym reaches after the natives have killed his fellow travelers. What emanates out of this ultimate land is a whiteness so potent that it cannot be broken and enclosed. This reduces Pym from Crusoean adventurer to awed witness. If (imperial) settler horror is about how Indigenous people and land are transformed into resources, this white land cannot be storied. It is logical that Pym's narrative ends abruptly at this encounter.

Breaking New Land

In his influential essay "The Significance of the Frontier in American History" (1893), Fredrick Jackson Turner laments the disappearance of the "free land" that he fears will halt the progress of "American development" (1). Now that the continent has been formally settled, American history appears to Turner to have ended. But Turner sees the potential of a revival driven by "a vigorous foreign policy" enabling "the extension of American influence to outlying islands and adjoining countries" (1). Turner's hope of a continuation of the settlement project and thus of capitalist development were realized, but it takes somewhat different forms in the century that follows. A growing economy and an ever-stronger command of the Western Hemisphere did make it possible for the United States to annex a number of formerly Spanish colonies. Securing access to cheap land and cheap labor was still the issue, as when the United States entered the confrontation that was World War I, but the increasingly globalized world enabled a shift in the strategies used to counter the periodical challenges that the settler state faced. Rather than forcibly colonizing the Global South, the United States moved toward a system of informal control that allowed cheap labor and resources to be extracted across national borders.

American horror of this era is informed by these expansive phases, as well as by the related and ongoing physical and epistemological violence used to supress nonwhite communities. In the early American film industry, the search for new and unbroken land combined with the already existing tropes of the white female as hapless captive and Indigenous and Black peoples as primitive and violent. A particularly vivid example is Merian C. Cooper and Ernest B. Schoedsack's *King Kong* (1933), shot during the middle of the Depression. In the film, a group of actors and film makers escape New York in search of a mysterious island located in the Western Pacific. On this island, they discover the impossibly large Kong, whose colossal body symbolizes both the threat of Black hypervirile sexuality but also the wild and unbroken land itself. Acting out the old settler-colonial horror trope, Kong captures Ann in a gesture redolent of rape and the threat of miscegenation. After retrieving Ann, the party extracts Kong from the island with the intention of commodifying his enormous body as Broadway spectacle. When Kong escapes the chains with which he has been fettered and again seizes Ann, he has turned from commodity to invasive species. To contain the threat he constitutes, the white settler community "seizes upon war technology" (Rony, 188) and guns Kong to death in a prolonged, public, and bloody sequence strongly reminiscent of the lynching violence practiced to intimidate the Black community at this point in time (see, e.g., Jackson).

The enormous and enduring success of the film testifies to the economic potential of this particular horror narrative.

In the 1930s when *King Kong* premiered, the land had begun to visibly react to the extractive practices used by the rapidly growing settler community. The mining of ore and minerals all over the United States, and particularly of gold in California, with the help of explosives and chemicals had succeeded in literally breaking the land, destroying it in radical ways. The most striking example from the period is the ecological crisis in the Southern Plains known as the Dust Bowl. In this region, extractive farming of the land in combination with droughts caused the soil to erode into fine dust that could not be farmed and that rose into the air during severe storms. The arid lands and the storms added to the depravations of the Indigenous people, now reduced to some 330,000 individuals, and to the local multispecies ecology. At the same time, it aggravated the capitalist crisis that the Depression constituted and caused the first climate migration in the settler community.[2]

The suffering of a busted and broken land became a discernible theme in settler horror. The tentacular, and obsessively racist, horror of H. P. Lovecraft is anthropocentric in its valorization of (white) settler humanity, but Lovecraft's insistance that this humanity is folded into a malignant and organic cosmology still enables an oblique investigation of the relationship between settlers and land. His widely read story "The Colour Out of Space" (1927) is set on a farm that borders a primeval ecology with "deep woods that no axe has ever cut" (9). This liminal territory is suddenly energized by a meteorite that crashes to the earth and seeps into the soil, producing enormous, prismatic plants that never ought to have sprouted "in a healthy world" (18). Insects and animals are also warped and enlarged by this posioned land until they shrivel uncannily. Shortly after, the humans on the farm begin turn brittle and disintegrate, gray flakes falling off their bodies, the cosmic horror visited upon the community attempts to return to space. But a part of it remains behind, and the building of a water reservoir that will drown the now abandoned farm will allow this contaminated region to pollute the drinking water for the foreseeable future. Lovecraft's weird horror may be firmly aligned with the white settler perspective, yet this story describes a land that has clearly lost its patience and is turning on the settler community. The modernization and exploitation of this area through the building of the reservoir will only accelerate and spread this destructive impatience.

When American settler society discovered the devastating powers inherent in atomic energy and in certain chemical compounds, this enabled a staggering acceleration of the violence used break land. At the end of World War II and in Vietnam, war was conducted not only against people but against the land itself. The atomic bombs detonated over Hiroshima and Nagasaki and the defoliation of entire forests in Vietnam dramatically testify to this geologic and atmospheric turn. When narratives appear that describe how horror rises out of the very land itself, or out of the sea or the atmosphere, these narratives respond most immediately to this new stage in the relationship between settler society and land, and in doing so they also continue a tradition of imperial settler horror that posits (unenclosed) land as something dangerous that must be constantly broken and checked. This is most clearly seen in a series of American horror films produced in the 1950s and 1960s, where enormous creatures rise out of oceans or land damaged by nuclear explosions. In *The Beast from 20,000 Fathoms* (1952), a prehistoric dinosaur is melted out of the Arctic ice by radiation and attacks New York. In *Them!* (1954), gigantic ants crawl out of the New Mexico desert where the first atomic bomb was detonated. These films indirectly recognize that devastating violence to land generates horror, but the solution to the ecological crises they portray is ultimately to increase the amount of violence. The dangers that a depleted, radiated ecology poses are thus addressed with the help of soldiers, tanks, and even more atomic weapons. To retreat before these monsters would be to abdicate the dominance of the (settler) human and to symbolically abandon capitalism's need to move toward an ever-expanding frontier. In the 1950s and 1960s, the Arctic, the ocean floor, or the deserts of New Mexico cannot be left alone any more than Korea or the Moon.

Freedom Movements, Neoliberalism, and Horror

The 1950s was never the age of prosperity nostalgically rehearsed by popular culture. It can, however, be described as the final era during which mainstream settler culture could comfortably ignore the violence with which it had settled the continent. In the 1960s, a certain awareness of the violence and (ecological) injustice built into settler society was produced by the civil rights movement, the American Indian movement, second wave feminism, the gay liberation movement, and early environmentalism. The war in Vietnam, mediated by often uncensored newspapers and television, brought images of excruciating horror into the living rooms of privileged settler communities, making it more difficult to ignore the violence being practiced on their behalf.

The growing awareness of the historical and contemporary violence that US settler culture generated became an important starting point for a number of iconoclastic American horror narratives. Cormac McCarthy began writing *Blood Meridian* (1985) at the end of the Vietnam War. The novel follows a young man known as “the kid” as he drifts west from Tennessee in the mid-1840s and joins up with a group of “Indian hunters” who collect Apache scalps that can be traded for gold. Turning the traditional Western on its head, *Blood Meridian* is one long and horribly violent description of how this paramilitary unit slaughters Indigenous tribes, Mexicans, women, and children. The indiscriminate violence seems haphazard to the reader, but Judge Holden, a character whose immense cruelty is matched only by his strange erudition, theorizes the constant slaughter as an extractive and eliminatory Enlightenment practice that makes the wilderness known, regulated, and privatized. From Holden’s perspective, killing is an attempt to rein in all the “autonomous life” that, by its very existence, threatens the settler order he sees himself producing: “In order for it to be mine nothing must be permitted to occur upon it save by my dispensation” (209). Few narratives of frontier violence have described with such clarity how the breaking of Indigenous land also entailed the appropriation and commodification and extraction of all that was on it.

While members of the white settler community who wrote American horror became increasingly aware of the violence done to Indigenous and Black people, to nonhuman animals, and to land, they also began to respond to the dismantling of white privileges. The 1960s and 1970s experienced a series of capitalist crises that primarily affected vulnerable Black and Indigenous people, but also changed the prospects of the socially stratified white settler community. Many members of this group had grown up partially protected by the New Deal’s labor legislation, and they had been elevated economically by the roaring postwar economy. With the advent of neoliberalism, responsibility for a person’s health and social welfare was again shifted from the state to the individual. This shift produced a crucial new strand in American settler horror. If fear before this era had been generated primarily by the very existence of unenclosed space, by Indigenous resistance, or by (creatures of) the land rising to protest the violence of extraction, horror was now clearly described as emerging also out of white extractivist society.

A number of influential and often independently produced films, including Wes Craven’s *The Hills Have Eyes* (1977) and Tobe Hooper’s *The Texas Chain Saw Massacre* (1974), exemplify this trend by resisting the temptation to displace structural capitalist violence. Instead, it is white settler culture that appears as the vortex of horror. In Hooper’s film, five white people travel through Texas farmland in a minivan. Looking out the window, one of them observes that the killing of livestock has now been industrialized, thus noting how capitalism has reorganized human-animal relationships. Eventually stranded at the abandoned family house, they walk over to an adjacent farm where they encounter Leatherface, a white killer wearing another white man's face as a dried-up mask, who proceeds to murder them one by one, like livestock, with the help of a sledgehammer and a chainsaw. Leatherface and his dysfunctional family of cannibals are best understood as the settlers that the "Indian hunters" of McCarthy's novel paved the way for. As farmers and as employees of the slaughterhouse and the local gas station, they fulfill essential roles in the extractive economy made possible through the obliteration of Indigenous populations and the breaking of the land. However, the film critically reveals this economy's own extractive logic. It matters little if you are white or Black, or an animal. Even the white urban population that the extractive economy is supposedly designed to privilege and protect gets eaten by the system. The innocent young white woman, once the captive victim of Indigenous or Black violence, is beset by white perpetrators, and in the film's final scene, Leatherface dances with his chainsaw dressed in a business suit. As the century draws to a close and neoliberalism further erodes society, the figure of horror is increasingly separated from the working class tasked with extraction. As Annalee Newitz has observed, texts such as *American Psycho* or *The Silence of the Lambs* feature killers that belong, like the suit Leatherface is wearing, to the moneyed, ruling class that manipulates extraction and that operates the neoliberal economy.

9/11 Settler Horror

In *Battle: Los Angeles* (2006), aliens from outer space have landed on the Western Seaboard and have begun to pull water from its surface. Water is apparently a scarce resource in the universe, and the effort to extract the ocean water is accompanied by a large-scale military effort that is at the same time visually overwhelming and strangely conventional. A group of US Marines who resist the alien war effort are informed of the stakes of the conflict by a television broadcast: "[T]hey are here for our resources. When you invade a place for its resources, you wipe out the indigenous population. Those are the rules for any colonization." This statement clearly references the logic of elimination that Wolfe argues guides settler colonialism, but this logic is not introduced ironically as a critique of the long history of US settler colonialism or of the increasingly bloody occupation of Iraq that coincides with its release. Instead, it informs an imaginary where current geopolitics have been upended so that the United States is cast as occupied territory rather than as invading imperialist power.

Battle: Los Angeles is only one of a great number of similar invasion narratives to appear at this moment in time. Many of these directly reference

British invasion horror, such as H. G. Wells' *The War of the Worlds* (1897) or Bram Stoker's *Dracula* (1897), and just like these original texts, *Battle: Los Angeles* is involved in a project of reactionary occlusion. What generates this narrative of reverse colonization is not the fear of interstellar colonization, but rather the crisis for American settler society brought on most immediately by 9/11 and the invasions of Afghanistan and Iraq, and by the general sense that the opportunity that the end of the Cold War constituted for American capitalism had been lost. Facing growing competition from China and India, the United States' control of cheap nature and labor in the global south was slipping, and the invasions of the Middle East, as argued by Immanuel Wallerstein, were accelerating rather than slowing its decline. Against this material history, and with funding from the US Department of Defense (Löfflmann), *Battle: Los Angeles* asks its audience to embrace the military ethos that its protagonists rehearse ad infinitum and to internalize the notion that the militarized settler state is the only institution capable of securing citizens from the horror and chaos that lurk beyond the reach of this state.

Horror in the post-9/11 era is marked by a series of such reactionary narratives but also by a number of texts that interrogate the sense of insecurity that 9/11 brought and that critically problematize the bid to seize control over the Middle East's supply of fossil fuels. Few novels describe the extractive necropolitics that functioned as the framework for the invasion of Iraq as vividly as Ahmed Saadawi's *Frankenstein in Baghdad* (2018). The narrative centers on a junk dealer by the name of Hadi, who creates a body out human parts torn off during suicide bombings. The body becomes animated when the soul of yet another bombing victim enters it. In order to remain animated, the body must find and kill the people who perpetrated the violence that produced the bodies. When those deeds have been completed, body parts belonging to these people shrivel up and disappear. This forces this new Frankenstein to continue killing, extracting new body parts from its victims so it can remain in its undead state. In this way, as argued by Rebecca Duncan and Rebekah Cumpsty, the pieced-together walking corpse embodies the "lived reality" of supremely violent extractive capitalism at work in the Middle East, where precarity "inheres in the fabric of the day-to-day as an omnipresent, unpredictable and immediate threat to body and life" (598). Thus, Saadawi's novel responds both to the permanent War on Terror and to the global neoliberal order that is stimulated by, and stimulates, this war.

Conclusion: *The Walking Dead* and Future Ecologies

Imperial projects, Ann Stoler reminds us, "are processes of ongoing ruination" (195). The extractive practices imperial projects pursue ruin people and land equally, until settler society, the land itself, and the epistemologies that have shielded the project cave in on themselves. It can be argued that the American settler project has reached precisely this particular stage. The depression that followed the invasion of Afghanistan and Iraq accelerated the deregulation of labor and environmental laws, especially during the Trump presidency. When the COVID-19 pandemic arrived in the United States as a strange retort from a history that began with the arrival of European plagues, it encountered a settler state that took little responsibility for the health and well-being of its citizens. The disregard evident at this moment, for Indigenous and Black lives, for the white working class, and for life itself, as evidenced by the relentless and ongoing destruction of the planetary ecology, makes America appear literally as a ruined land, stripped of the imagined glories that once accompanied its imperial project.

The most widely circulated signifier of this ruination in American horror is the zombie. Its current incarnation builds on the figure invented by George Romero, but extends his vision to encompass an America where "we are all infected," as the long-running AMC TV series *The Walking Dead* puts it (Keetley). The few who have not yet succumbed to zombification, who are infected but still walk the planet as living humans, typically fail to rebuild settler society in these narratives. A life stripped of comforts continues in hostile and poisoned wildernesses, and constant military-grade violence is the only way to remain alive. While this vision of the future rhymes well with the militant rhetoric of supremacist prepper organizations such as the Proud Boys, the zombie narrative abandons such militant subjects in a world where their vision of a racially pure and utopian society can never be realized. As food for the now dominant, undead species, the champions of white settler masculinity have to scavenge the ruins with everyone else.

Yet in the midst of these post-apocalyptic horror visions, Black and Indigenous counterculture horror imagines alternative endings. In *Lovecraft Country* (2016), Matt Ruff calls out the racism inherent in H. P. Lovecraft and in US society generally by renaming American land as a space effectively organized around this author's Manichean views on race. Unlike in Lovecraft's stories, the protagonists manage not only to stay sane but to wrest occult power from white racist society. In First Nation director Jeff Barnaby's zombie narrative *Blood Quantum* (2019) and in Indigenous writer Louise Erdrich's *Future Home of the Living God* (2017), evolution is reversing. In *Blood Quantum*, civilization collapses to a zombie pandemic that affects only white people. Battling the mindless yet still voracious white settlers, Indigenous survivors observe how the planet, sick of the ecological violence done by settler capitalism, turns "these stupid fucking white men into something she can use again: fertilizer." In Erdrich's novel, creatures from previous geological eras invade suburban gardens and children are born strange, no longer fully human. As in many other dystopian stories, settler society responds by incarcerating women's bodies, thus inverting the old captivity trope. Yet, as society breaks down, Indigenous communities in America are able to organize and reclaim stolen land. The settler project begins to unravel. It was never sustainable. Its slow and, in the novel, incomplete demise is not an accident, but a geological inevitability. At the same time, the novel does not describe a genocide in reverse. Settlers remain on the land, but the policing and extraction of this land by settler authorities grind to a halt. Barnaby's film and Erdrich's novel are dark and frightening visions of Indigeneity and ecology protesting a long history of violence. At the same time, these texts conjure, out of ruination and ecological crisis, the image of a land and an Indigeneity that shake off the paralyzing and extractive hold of settler colonialism. That momentous shrug offers up a hope of decolonization not as metaphor but as an actual practice.

NOTES

1. The Plantationocene, in turn, can be said to mark a specific sequence or aspect of what Jason W. Moore has termed the "Capitalocene."
2. See McLeman and Smit for a discussion of the relationship between climate change and migration.

Works Cited

Barnard, Philip, and Stephen Shapiro. "Introduction." In Charles Brockden Brown, *Edgar Huntly; or, Memoirs of a Sleep-Walker: With Related Texts*. New York: Hackett Publishing, 2006. ix–xlii.

Bergland, Renée L. *The National Uncanny: Indian Ghosts and American Subjects*. Hanover, NH: University Press of New England, 2000.

Brantlinger, Patrick. *Rule of Darkness: British Literature and Imperialism, 1830–1914*. Ithaca, NY: Cornell University Press, 1988.

Brown, Charles Brockden. *Edgar Huntly; or, Memoirs of a Sleep-Walker: With Related Texts*. 1799. Indianapolis, IN: Hackett Publishing, 2006.

Crosby, Alfred W. *Ecological Imperialism: The Biological Expansion of Europe, 900–1900*, 2nd ed. Cambridge: Cambridge University Press, 2004.

Defoe, Daniel. *The Adventures of Robinson Crusoe*. 1719. London: Henry Lea, 1850.

Duncan, Rebecca, and Rebekah Cumpsty. "Introduction: The Body in Postcolonial Fiction after the Millennium." *Interventions: International Journal of Postcolonial Studies* 22, no. 5 (2020): 587–605.

Dunlap, Thomas R. "Remaking the Land: The Acclimatization Movement and Anglo Ideas of Nature." *Journal of World History* 8, no. 2 (1997): 303–19.

Fiedler, Leslie A. *Love and Death in the American Novel*. New York: Stein and Day, 1960.

Goddu, Teresa A. *Gothic America: Narrative, History, and Nation*. New York: Columbia University Press, 1997.

Haraway, Donna. "Anthropocene, Capitalocene, Plantationocene, Chthulucene: Making Kin." *Environmental Humanities* 6, no. 1 (2015): 159–65.

Hawthorne, Nathaniel. *Young Goodman Brown and Other Tales*. 1835. Oxford: Oxford University Press, 1998.

Hodes, Martha. *Sex, Love, Race: Crossing Boundaries in North American History*. New York: New York University Press, 1999.

Höglund, Johan. *The American Imperial Gothic: Popular Culture, Empire, Violence*. Farnham: Ashgate, 2014.

"Imperial Horror and Terrorism." In *The Palgrave Handbook to Horror Literature*, ed. Kevin Corstorphine and Laura R. Kremmel. London: Palgrave Macmillan, 2018. 327–37.

Jackson, Robert. "A Southern Sublimation: Lynching Film and the Reconstruction of American Memory." *The Southern Literary Journal* 40, no. 2 (2008): 102–20.

Keetley, Dawn. *"We're All Infected": Essays on AMC's the Walking Dead and the Fate of the Human*. Jefferson, NC: McFarland, 2014.

Koch, Alexander, et al. "Earth System Impacts of the European Arrival and Great Dying in the Americas after 1492." *Quaternary Science Reviews* 207 (2019): 13–36.

Löfflmann, Georg. "Hollywood, the Pentagon, and the Cinematic Production of National Security." *Critical Studies on Security* 1, no. 3 (2013): 280–94.

Lovecraft, H. P. *The Colour Out of Space*. 1927. London: Read & Co., 2020.

Marzec, Robert P. "Enclosures, Colonization, and the *Robinson Crusoe* Syndrome: A Genealogy of Land in a Global Context." *boundary 2* 29, no. 2 (2002): 129–56.

McCarthy, Cormac. *Blood Meridian, or The Evening Redness in the West*. 1885. London: Picador Classic, 215.

McLeman, Robert, and Barry Smit. "Migration as an Adaptation to Climate Change." *Climatic Change* 76, nos. 1–2 (2006): 31–53.

Mogen, David, Scott Patrick Sanders, and Joanne B. Karpinski. *Frontier Gothic: Terror and Wonder at the Frontier in American Literature*, ed. David Mogen, Scott P. Sanders, and Joanne B. Karpinski. Rutherford, NJ: Fairleigh Dickinson University Press, 1992.

Moore, Jason W. *Capitalism in the Web of Life: Ecology and the Accumulation of Capital*. London and New York: Verso, 2015.

"The Rise of Cheap Nature." In *Anthropocene or Capitalocene?: Nature, History, and the Crisis of Capitalism*, ed. Jason W. Moore. Oakland, CA: PM Press, 2016. 78–115.

Morrison, Toni. *Playing in the Dark*. Cambridge, MA: Harvard University Press, 1992.

Neeson, Jeanette M. *Commoners: Common Right, Enclosure and Social Change in England, 1700–1820*. Cambridge: Cambridge University Press, 1993.

Newitz, Annalee. *Pretend We're Dead: Capitalist Monsters in American Pop Culture*. Durham, NC: Duke University Press, 2006.

Poe, Edgar Allan. *The Narrative of Arthur Gordon Pym of Nantucket*. 1838. Peterborough, Ontario: Broadview Press, 2010.
Rony, Fatimah Tobing. *The Third Eye: Race, Cinema, and Ethnographic Spectacle*. Durham, NC: Duke University Press, 1996.
Shapiro, Stephen. "Transvaal, Transylvania: Dracula's World-System and Gothic Periodicity." *Gothic Studies* 10, no. 1 (2008): 29–47.
Stoler, Ann Laura. "Imperial Debris: Reflections on Ruins and Ruination." *Cultural Anthropology* 23, no. 2 (2008): 191–219.
Turner, Frederick Jackson. "The Significance of the Frontier in American History." 1893. In *The Frontier in American History*. New York: Henry Holt, 1920. 1–38.
Vitale, Alex S. *The End of Policing*. London: Verso, 2017.
Wallerstein, Immanuel. *The Decline of American Power: The US in a Chaotic World*. New York: New Press, 2003.
Wolfe, Patrick. "Settler Colonialism and the Elimination of the Native." *Journal of Genocide Research* 8, no. 4 (2006): 387–409.
Worster, Donald. *Dust Bowl: The Southern Plains in the 1930s*. 1979. Oxford: Oxford University Press, 2004.
Yelling, James Alfred. *Common Field and Enclosure in England 1450–1850*. Basingstoke: Macmillan Press, 1977.

5

KENDALL R. PHILLIPS

Censorship and State Regulation

In his *Republic*, Plato argues that maintaining good civic virtues requires that society "oversee the work of the story-writers" (377c). Plato warns against stories that might detract from society, including stories "designed to make everyone who hears them shudder" (386c). Terrifying tales of the underworld risked damaging society by promoting inappropriate feelings of fear and timidity. Something like Plato's logic of censorship has operated in Western civilization since that initial writing. The arts have been consistently portrayed as having the capacity both to instill virtues and to promote dangerous vices. While the means of guarding public sentiment has changed over time, from Julius Caesar's *famosi libeli* to the Church's *Index liborum prohibitorum*, there has been a consistent concern that the ideas and images circulating within the public be regulated, and throughout this history stories of the horrific have been viewed with particular apprehension.

Americans have long valued some sense of freedom of expression, even instantiating it into the US Constitution in the First Amendment. Yet, in spite of this stated value, censorship has a long and rich history in the country. This censorship has, at times, taken the form of explicit legal restrictions, but, more often, efforts to restrict the public circulation of texts have been made by civic organizations or the very corporate entities that produce such texts. Indeed, it is notable that while horror narratives were, at times, embroiled in restrictions related to blasphemy or obscenity, there have been relatively few laws directed explicitly at the concept or images of horror. Regulation of horror has more often been enacted through public pressure put on the companies who produced these narratives.

Together these entities – governmental, corporate, public – have engaged in a complex and dynamic dialogue about the limits of social acceptance. Horror, a genre in part defined by its capacity to transgress social boundaries and shock its audience, has naturally been a key topic in these conversations and controversies as various actors have worried about the effects of horrific stories and the feelings they might evoke. And yet audiences are continually drawn to stories that are seen as shocking and horrifying. Herein lies one of the most puzzling aspects of horror: its capacity to both attract and repel audiences and, indeed, to attract audiences by its promise to be repellant. Exploring the regulatory rhetorics and controversies that have circulated around horror narratives provides useful insights into the ways American society has sought to answer the question of how much transgression is too much, when does horror go too far in its capacity to horrify. In what follows, I trace the history of efforts to regulate horror in American culture by focusing on four of its most prominent media: literature, comic books, motion pictures, and radio and television.

Literature

The history of literature in America is replete with instances of censorship, ranging from high-profile court cases around classics like *Tropic of Cancer* and *Ulysses* to threats to boycott publishers and efforts to remove certain titles from schools and libraries. As Miles Tittle notes, "It is hardly surprising that horror novels have often met with strong opposition, contempt, and censorship" (182), and, indeed, horror novels have consistently provoked outrage and concern within the legal, corporate, and public spheres.

The legal travails of horror novels can be traced back to one of the foundational novels in the Gothic tradition, Matthew Lewis' *The Monk* (1796), which provoked controversy and threats of legal action. As Michael Gamer notes, "beginning with *The Monk*, social conservatives began attempting to apply the law to the tradition of gothic writing that we now characterize as 'horror gothic'" (80). Indeed, a broad public campaign was staged to limit the availability of Gothic novels in the newly established free circulating libraries. The anonymous writer of the 1797 essay "Terrorist Novel Writing" criticized "the great quantity of novels with which our circulating libraries are filled" that had made "terror the order of the day, by confining the heroes and heroines in old gloomy castles, full of spectres, apparitions, ghosts, and dead men's bones" (227). The combination of increasing literacy and the expanding availability of works of literature led to the growing concern about the contents of these fictional tales and the deployment of a three-pronged attack against the increasingly popular Gothic novels: legal threats, pressure on authors and publishers, and restrictions on public circulation.

The American tradition of Gothic and, later, horror novels was heavily influenced by its English predecessors. So too was the legal notion of obscenity. In the United States, British common law was reframed in relation to the Constitution and its prohibition of legal restrictions on "freedom of speech, or of the press." Yet, despite this foundational protection for free expression, US laws soon appeared designed to curtail the circulation of obscene material. Massachusetts enacted a law forbidding obscenity or blasphemy in the eighteenth century, but even without formal legal parameters, courts regularly recognized the doctrine of obscene libel (see Dennis, 382). The impetus to expand prohibitions on obscene literature was led by civic organizations. In the United States, the New York Society for the Suppression of Vice sprang out of the city's YMCA in 1873. Based on concerns for the moral upbringing of children in the city, the Society's case was pressed by Anthony Comstock, who in 1873 traveled to Washington, DC, with an exhibition of obscene materials, mainly sexual, he labeled "The Chamber of Horrors" (McGarry, 8). Comstock's efforts were successful and led to what would become widely known as the "Comstock Laws," including Section 211 of the Federal Criminal Code, which criminalized posting any "obscene, lewd, or lascivious, and every filthy book, pamphlet, picture, paper, letter, writing print or other publication" through the mail. The introduction of this federal legislation led to an avalanche of "little Comstock laws" passed by states across the country (McGarry, 19).

While horror novels were often criticized as shocking, they rarely featured in the high-profile legal battles over the question of censoring literature. This did not mean, however, that the questions of obscenity and censorship were not applied to horror fiction. H. P. Lovecraft, as an example, was reportedly told that one of his stories could not be published because "its extreme gruesomeness would not pass Indiana's censorship" (Joshi and Schultz, 125). More common in the American experience was the practice of publicly shaming book authors, publishers, and sellers with the language of obscenity. These moves often entailed calls for boycotting publishers or sellers in an effort often termed "corporate censorship." The tendency to focus outrage on the publishers and booksellers, rather than the government, has marked many of the controversies over horror literature in the twentieth century.

Illustrative of this tendency was the public outcry around the publication of Bret Easton Ellis' novel *American Psycho* in 1991. Originally contracted to Simon & Schuster, with a $300,000 advance to the author, the novel tells the graphic story of a Wall Street investment banker who recalls committing horrible murders, primarily of young women. The horrific novel met with heavy public condemnation after extracts from the novel appeared in *Time* and *Spy* magazines, and the resulting negative publicity led Simon & Schuster to withdraw the book from publication. Ellis kept his advance and the rights were picked up by Alfred A. Knopf, who published it amid widespread public concern. The debate roiled through American culture, ultimately providing invaluable publicity for the book and author. The

Authors Guild, National Writers Union, and PEN American Center all expressed concern over the corporate nature of the decision to withdraw the book. On the other side of the dispute, the National Organization for Women condemned the novel and called for a boycott of Knopf and its parent company Random House. The ensuing controversy raised questions of the novel's literary merit, its capacity to inspire violence against women, and the role of corporations in shaping the public's taste. As Rosa Eberly notes, "regardless of how painful Ellis's book is ... [it] at least temporarily resulted in communication in public by journalists, booksellers, libraries, and a few citizen critics about issues of common concern" (130). In the end, the book went on to some success and has subsequently become a staple of American literature of the 1990s, its literary merit assured by numerous critical treatments and a thoughtful film adaptation directed by Mary Harron in 2000.

Controversies over horror novels rarely reach the level of national attention afforded *American Psycho*. More commonly, efforts at regulating horror literature occur at local levels through efforts to remove books from school curricula or from library shelves. Book banning has a long history and in the United States has often taken the form of pushing for the removal of titles from places where they might be accessible, especially to the young. Sara Zeigler notes that "between 1990 and 2000, most challenges seeking the removal of books from libraries involved school districts" (n.p.). Stephen King is one of the authors often targeted for removal from school curricula and libraries (see Power et al.). Similarly, R. L. Stine's *Goosebumps* series of children's horror novels was seen, according to Perry Nodelman, by "many parents, teachers, and librarians ... as a monstrous intrusion into the well-intentioned world of children's publishing" (118) and subsequently became one of the most commonly banned/challenged series of books in American libraries. Indeed, horror novels appear regularly in the American Library Association's annual report on challenged or banned books, with young adult series such as *Twilight* and *House of Night* often featured.

Comic Books

Literary horror has always enjoyed two interrelated forms of protection from censorship. On one level, there is the assumption that the value of "literary merit" might outweigh a work's offensiveness. On another level, the literary merit serves to restrict those who can read it. Not surprisingly, media designed to be more accessible has been more likely to provoke the censors, legal and social, and this is also true in relation to horror. Horror comics, in particular, faced remarkable levels of legal and social scrutiny and routine calls for censorship.

The impetus to censor horror comics arose from the same social organizations that targeted obscene novels; as early as the 1870s, they were also targeting magazines that depicted criminal activities in lurid and graphic detail. In 1879, for example, Boston's Ward and Watch Society, an organization parallel to the New York Society for the Suppression of Vice, called for a ban on magazines like the *Police Gazette*. Charging these magazines with "manifestly tending to corrupt the morals of youth," the Watch and Ward pushed through a bill that would ban their sale or even display (qtd. in Boyer, 11). As Paul Boyer notes, by 1892 at least seven booksellers had been convicted under the statute.

Illustrated magazines were soon combined with the increasingly popular comic strips running in newspapers, and as early as 1911 there was a booklet of Mutt and Jeff strips followed in the late 1920s by publications like *The Funnies* devoted entirely to comic strips. In 1937, *Detective Comics* debuted and with it more sophisticated stories of crime and adventure. While some may associate comics with heroes in capes, superheroes were not the only genre available to comic book purchasers in the 1940s and 1950s. Among the crime, romance, and Western comics a new genre emerged in 1948, the horror comic. American Comics Group began publishing *Adventures into the Unknown*, which featured stories of ghosts and monsters. The title was, according to William Schoell, "an immediate hit with readers" (5), and its success led other companies to begin producing horror comics, including Entertaining Comics (EC), which produced titles like *Tales from the Crypt*, *Vault of Horror*, and *Shock SuspenStories*. In the 1950s, EC became infamous for pushing social boundaries with graphically illustrated stories featuring murder, necrophilia, cannibalism, and torture.

By the mid-1950s, John E. Twomey declared, "No other medium of American popular culture has been subjected to such widespread, vehement, and continuing attack as the so-called comic-books" (621). Much of this furor centered around a series of highly publicized congressional hearings. As early as 1952, the House Select Committee on Current Pornographic Materials turned its attention to comic books and, in particular, those titles featuring crime and horror. David C. Cook, a publisher of religious material, testified before the committee about the dangers of horror comics and included numerous illustrations, including "heads cut off by guillotine," "piles of skulls and human bones," a "woman being eaten alive by worms," and a "scaly vampire (slimy variety) sucking blood" (US Congress, *Report of the Select Committee*, 251).

The most widely publicized congressional inquiry into comics came with the Senate Subcommittee to Investigate Juvenile Delinquency in 1954 and 1955. Driven, in part, by reports of rising levels of juvenile crime, the Subcommittee sought to determine what role comic books might play in corrupting the youth of the nation. Dr. Frederic Wertham, a New York City psychiatrist who spent several years with the New York City Department of Hospitals, made a cottage industry of criticizing the comics for their role in corrupting America's youth, including in his popular 1954 book, *Seduction of the Innocent.* Appearing before the Subcommittee, Wertham recounted the horrific images in comics, including "a baseball game where they play baseball with a man's head; where the man's intestines are the baselines. All his organs have some part to play ... there is nothing left to the morbid imagination" (US Congress, Committee on the Judiciary, 83).

Several states enacted legislation specific to horror in comics. Alaska, for example, made it "unlawful for a person to knowingly display, sell, offer for sale, distribute, lend or give away or otherwise make available to a person a horror comic book" (Wallace, 49) and Connecticut made disseminating comic books "which are devoted to or principally made up of pictures of accounts of physical torture or brutality, horror or terror" a Class A misdemeanor (Wallace, 77).

These legal restrictions were the result of public campaigns against the comic book industry by various organizations. The Catholic Church's National Organization for Decent Literature, for example, established a code in 1956 objecting to publications that "exploit horror, cruelty or violence" (qtd. in O'Connor, 400). In Chicago, the Citizen's Committee for Better Literature arose out of the Police Department's Censor Bureau and established a network of voluntary readers to scan comic books for objectionable materials, including plots or illustrations of horror or the gruesome (Twomey, 627).

Fearing even greater public pressure and the possibility of sweeping federal laws, the comics industry sought to self-regulate. On September 4, 1954, the Comic Magazine Association of America incorporated and within a few weeks had established the Comics Code Authority to enforce a voluntary industry code of ethics. The Comics Code forbade the use of terms like "horror" or "terror" in comic titles and prohibited "scenes dealing with, or instruments associated with walking dead, torture, vampires and vampirism, ghouls, cannibalism, and werewolfism" (qtd. in Nyberg, 165). The Comics Code effectively ended horror comics as a genre for decades.

The Comics Code was slowly eroded by changing cultural norms and the industry's desire to remain relevant to new readers. By 1971, the Code was amended to allow some of the prohibited monsters and additional criminal actions. Additionally, the rise of new independent comics publishers undermined the moral and economic pressure the Comics Code Authority could hold over creators. Even mainstream comic book publishers began to abandon the Code, and in January 2011 Archie Comics, the last publisher subscribing to the Code, withdrew, effectively ending the Comics Code.

Motion Pictures

If the easy accessibility of comics provoked anxiety in guardians of American values and morality, motion pictures provoked outright panic. The rise of motion picture popularity led to a moral outcry that saw calls for legislation and legal restrictions, the formation of public pressure groups seeking to discourage immoral pictures, and a delicate balancing act by movie producers who wanted to feed the public's interest in the immoral and shocking while not provoking public outcry or legal penalties. As with other mediums, horror in motion pictures has been profoundly shaped by the complex terrain of government, public, and industrial anxieties.

A decade after the first publicly projected motion pictures in 1895, the first small theaters dedicated to showing motion pictures appeared with a clientele largely made up of children and the working class. As with concerns over literature and comic books, fear of cinema was motivated by its perceived capacity to influence and potentially corrupt those seen by the elites as impressionable: youth, immigrants, working classes, and those who were uneducated (see Grieveson; Phillips). As early as 1908, New York City's mayor, George McLellan, sought to close down the movie theaters out of concern for their physical condition as well as their capacity "to degrade or injure the morals of the community" ("Picture Shows," 1). By 1911, the state of Pennsylvania established the first state board of censorship focused on motion pictures and was soon followed by boards in Ohio and Kansas and, shortly thereafter, virtually every state in the union.

State boards wielded enormous and disjointed power over motion pictures, as legal exhibition of a picture required a state seal of approval. Kansas, as perhaps the most notorious example, routinely insisted on changes to films ranging from elimination of dialogue to the removal of entire scenes or, at times, barred the screening of films altogether. During the silent era, the Kansas Board of Review, for example, insisted that the 1917 film *The Haunted House* eliminate scenes detailing a bank robbery and required the 1920 version of *Dr. Jekyll and Mr. Hyde* to cut a scene with Hyde "placing hands on bare shoulders" of a young woman ("The Haunted House"; "Dr. Jekyll"). Such concerns only intensified as motion pictures entered the sound era and horror films emerged as a recognizable genre.

The 1932 version of *Dr. Jekyll and Mr. Hyde* was again cut by the Kansas censors. This time the Board focused on the use of close-ups during a scene of strangulation (see Butters).

The legality of this system of prior restraint was challenged shortly after the first board appeared in a court battle between Mutual Film Corporation and the Industrial Commission of Ohio, which served as the official censorship board for the state. In a unanimous decision in 1915, the US Supreme Court ruled that motion pictures were not covered by the constitutional guarantee of free speech, and, indeed, in their decision in *Mutual v. Ohio*, the Court argued that the state has not only the legal right to censor motion pictures but a responsibility to guard the public from the uniquely persuasive power of moving pictures. This decision set the legal groundwork for the network of state censorship boards until the Court reversed the decision in 1952 with *Burstyn v. Wilson*, which recognized free speech protection for moving pictures.

During the decades of legalized state censorship, American film producers had to navigate a complex system of uneven state interpretations and create different versions of their films to suit the tastes of different regions of the nation. Their real concern, however, was about the prospect of a federal censorship board. Driven by fear of this possibility, Hollywood established its own system of self-regulation. Former Postmaster General William H. Hays was enlisted in 1922 to head the Motion Picture Producers and Distributors of America, and this group began crafting various codes for movie producers. Eventually, these restrictions would give rise to the Production Code and the Production Code Administration (PCA). The "codes" of the first decade were loose and informally applied, but after 1934, the PCA required all films to be approved and receive a PCA certificate of approval before release. This gave the PCA absolute power over the selection of source material, scripts, scenes, dialogue, and final cuts of all films legally screened in the United States.

Horror as a recognizable genre within American film emerged around 1931 with the release of both *Dracula* and *Frankenstein*. The initial reaction of the PCA to the shift toward more gruesome and macabre tales focused on the explicitly supernatural was mild. After screening Tod Browning's *Dracula*, Jason S. Joy commented that "it is quite satisfactory from the standpoint of the CODE" and predicted few problems with censors (n.p.). However, as horror films gained in popularity, the PCA became increasingly critical of depictions of horror. *The Mask of Fu Manchu* (1932) was charged with being "too long on horror elements" (Wingate). Responding to the script for the 1934 film *The Black Cat*, the PCA cautioned Universal to avoid becoming "too gruesome or revolting" (Hays). This concern increased around 1936 as the PCA pushed studios to abandon the genre altogether. Following the introduction of the H rating for "horror" by the British Board of Film Censorship, the PCA actively dissuaded studios from producing horror films (see Naylor). Tod Browning's 1936 *The Devil Doll*, for example, was originally written as a tale of voodoo, but a PCA official wrote to MGM that "black magic associated with religious rites [is] definitely prohibited" and urged the studio to change the narrative to one of science gone wrong instead of supernatural magic (Blum, n.p.). In 1937, the Code was amended to reflect this new stance with a dictate that "scenes of excessive brutality and gruesomeness must be cut to an absolute minimum" (qtd. in Towlson, 141).

The moral strictures of the Code would eventually give way to changing American tastes and the competition from television. In 1954, for example, Warner Brothers was specifically informed that the PCA was taking a "very definite stand" that the popular Broadway play *The Bad Seed* could not be made into a Code-compliant film (qtd. in Simmons, 4). Warner Brothers defied the stand and not only produced the film but advertised it as "THE BIG SHOCKER" and "recommended for ADULTS ONLY." The film was a major box office success for the studio. Studios would continue to push and defy the strictures of the Production Code throughout the 1950s and 1960s, and the era would see increasingly macabre and exploitative films produced independently by filmmakers like William Castle and Herschell Gordon Lewis.

The Code officially ended in 1968, opening up a remarkably productive space for the production of increasingly graphic, brutal, and inventive horror films, which some have characterized as the genre's "second golden age." The Motion Picture Association of America (MPAA) replaced the formal Code with a ratings system administered by the Classification and Ratings Administration (CARA). Anonymous members of CARA watched and reviewed films and classified them as G for General Audience, M for mature audiences with parental discretion advised, R for restricted to those over sixteen unless accompanied by parent or adult guardian, and X, which prohibited viewers under sixteen. The system was soon altered to raise the age from sixteen to seventeen and shifting M to PG for "parental guidance." Horror films released in the early years of the CARA system were forced either to accept the rating given, edit their film to meet CARA expectations, or release their film unrated. George Romero, for example, chose to release his 1978 *Dawn of the Dead* unrated rather than receive an X-rating, which was culturally associated with hard-core pornography. The film's poster listed the film as unrated but also noted that this was not due to sexual content.

Horror films were also involved in two significant changes to the ratings system. First, in 1984, CARA created a new rating of PG-13, or parental guidance recommended for those under thirteen. The new rating was created, in part, as a response to Tobe Hooper's *Poltergeist* (1982) and Joe Dante's *Gremlins* (1984). The second major change came in 1990 after of a series of controversies related to the pornography-associated X-rating. Legal challenges to the X-rating for John McNaughton's *Henry: Portrait of a Serial Killer* (1986) and other protests led CARA in 1990 to introduce NC-17 as an alternative to the stigmatized X-rating, though the new rating has not proven successful in allowing gruesome or adult-oriented films a place in major cineplexes, which still largely refuse to screen them.

Radio and Television

Unlike the other mediums considered here, radio and television operated on a different legal ground. Since the public airwaves for broadcast signals were understood to be public resources, they were viewed as within governmental purview. The 1927 Radio Act, which established the Federal Radio Commission, later the Federal Communications Commission, provided the industry with a clear legal regulator from the outset and reduced the number of legal challenges to the regulatory system (see Levi).

Horror programming on radio emerged in the 1930s, shortly after the genre appeared on the silver screen, with numerous series offering anthologies of spooky and macabre tales, including: *The Witch's Tale* (1931–38), *Inner Sanctum* (1941–45), and *Suspense* (1940–62). These shows were popular among young listeners, and as early as 1936, there was a growing concern among parents. In that year, a Columbia University study found that while parents approved of more than 3,000 radio programs, they objected to "791, largely of the 'horror' type" ("Listening to Radio," 11). These concerns were not limited to New York. A Michigan radio programmer defended the value of children's radio programming but insisted, "Every right-thinking parent agrees that horror and gruesome details should never appear in children's programs" ("Defends Children's," 3).

Drawing on this public concern, in 1937, Senator Clyde Herring of Iowa proposed legislation that would establish a new federal board for program review, and one of the key provisions was aimed at "horror tales." Senator Herring would even publicly target a reading of Edgar Allan Poe's "The Evil Eye" by Boris Karloff on the popular *Chase & Sanborn Hour* ("C&S Again on the Spot," 1). This legislative movement led FCC Commissioner George Henry Payne to launch a campaign in November of that year to "clean up" children's radio, and horror was one of the prime targets ("Payne Launching Drive," 1).

The cultural panic provoked by Orson Welles and his Mercury Theater players' 1938 broadcast of a radio play based on H. G. Wells' *War of the Worlds* led some to call for more restrictions on the medium. As is now infamous, thousands of Americans mistook the broadcast for an actual alien invasion and mass hysteria followed. Americans fled their homes, armed themselves, and even shot at a local water tower, fearing it was an invading alien craft. In the aftermath of the public panic, there were indeed many calls for more regulation of radio programming, but there was also a growing concern that government control over the powerful medium of radio might be used for propaganda purposes (see Schwartz). In the end, the FCC largely ignored the public reaction to the Welles performance. As the *New York Times* reported, "there were fairly definite indications that no action would be taken," with Commissioner Payne shifting focus back to the broader problem of "radio terror programs [which] are frightening children" ("No FCC Action," 26).

Concerned about potential future federal regulations, the National Association of Broadcasters adopted a "code of standards for self-regulation" in July 1939. Not surprisingly, children's programming was a substantial part of the code and included instructions to "not contain sequences involving horror or torture or use of the supernatural or superstitious or any other material which might reasonably be regarded as likely to over-stimulate the child listener" ("Teeth Pulled," 2, 3). While horror programs remained popular throughout the 1940s, several networks shifted their schedules to keep them away from children's listening hours (see Pondillo).

After World War II, television expanded rapidly across the United States and would soon become the dominant media in the country. In 1952, the National Association of Broadcasters adopted the TV Code, which included numerous provisions aimed specifically at depictions of the horrific and supernatural, such as: "the use of horror for its own sake will be eliminated." The TV Code also instructed broadcasters to avoid material that "would create morbid suspense, or other undesirable reactions in children," and to depict "fortune-telling, astrology, phrenology, palm reading, and numerology" only in ways that do not "foster superstition or excite interest or belief in these subjects." Indeed, this last provision virtually eliminated a popular genre of astrology television show in the early 1950s (see Jamarillo).

Perhaps not surprisingly, the Television Code did not quell all controversy surrounding television horror. Public concerns over television continued and the early 1960s saw a 300–400 percent increase in complaints to the FCC. One of the Commission's largest categories for these complaints was "crime, violence, horror" ("FCC Staffers," 103). In 1962, Representative William Randall of Missouri introduced legislation to add to the FCC's powers a specific provision allowing it to "revoke the license of any station which broadcasts programs emphasizing sex, crime, horror or violence" ("Rep. Randall," 58). While the legislation did not move forward, it was further evidence of public concern about horror on the small screen.

The 1970s, which Lorna Jowett and Stacey Abbott characterize as a "golden age" for TV horror, was also a period of increasing censorship by the FCC. The Commission became more active in policing obscenity and reducing the number of hours for network "prime time" programming. Among the new developments was stricter control over programming prior to late night shows, which were granted more latitude. The producers of popular horror series of the time, such as *Dark Shadows* (1966–71) and *Kolchak: The Night Stalker* (1974–75), became adept at mitigating their horror and violence with other elements like fantasy or humor in order to avoid too many audience complaints. Made-for-television horror movies were also carefully crafted to avoid the increasingly conservative views of the FCC, often using titles that suggested more horror and gruesomeness than they would deliver, such as *Weekend of Terror* (1970) or *Vacation in Hell* (1979) (see Reyes).

The 1980s saw diversification in the ways that television programming entered the home, with the introduction of satellite dishes and cable and with them a range of options beyond traditional broadcast programming, including subscription channels and pay-per-view. This, in turn, helped to create opportunities for more niche programming, including horror. Programs such as HBO's *The Hitchhiker* (1983–91) or *True Blood* (2008–14) were freed from FCC restrictions and therefore could be, as Bridgit Cherry puts it, "unafraid to be confrontational in their writing or in their explicit visuals" (7). This trend has continued to the present day with horror series proliferating on cable television and becoming some of the most popular in the country. While shows like *The Walking Dead* (2010–) and *American Horror Story* (2011–) regularly receive complaints from viewers, the FCC has largely avoided fining or formally notifying these cable series.

The availability of horror on television has reached a new "golden age" with the increasing number of streaming services that cater to horror fans. At this point, such services lie outside the regulatory parameters of the FCC, and there have been virtually no efforts to expand governmental regulatory power over these new modes of dissemination. In part because of this lack of formal regulation, streaming services like Netflix, Amazon Prime, and the horror specialty service Shudder have begun providing a wide variety of horror programming, ranging from classic films to extreme subgenres to international films and series.

Conclusion

The preceding offers only a broad sketch of the regulatory rhetorics surrounding horror in the United States. This summary is also limited by the mediums it did not include, such as live theater, music, or video games. But, in considering the rough outline of efforts to regulate horror, a few consistent patterns are worth noting. First, in the United States, efforts to censor horror have consistently involved a complex interplay of governmental, industrial, and public organizations. Second, while most censorship efforts in the United States have focused on sex and, to a lesser extent, violence, there has been a consistent strain of regulatory rhetoric that seeks to restrict the affective dimensions of horror narrative through prohibitions on programs designed to elicit feelings of horror or shock. These first two patterns may be derived, in part, from the fluid and dynamic nature of the horror genre, which is not easily defined by specific elements or motifs. Third, horror was most likely to be targeted for regulation when it was more accessible, especially to those considered more "vulnerable" to influence.

At the beginning of the 2020s, horror seems to have entered a third golden age with intriguing and provocative narratives of terror gaining popularity in almost all mediums. At the moment, there are relatively few broad, national efforts by public or governmental organizations to regulate the proliferation of popular horror narratives, although the consolidation of entertainment industries does raise the ongoing concern that publication, exhibition, and broadcast decisions are driven by profits more than by artistic inclinations. If the history of regulation of horror suggests anything, it is that this tension between provocation and profit will boil over into controversies and lead to future calls for regulating those stories that give us chills.

Works Cited

Blum, D. Telegram to Samuel Marx, September 12, 1935. Motion Picture Association of America, Production Code Files, Margaret Herrick Library, Academy of Motion Picture Arts and Science, Beverly Hills, CA.

Boyer, Paul S. *Purity in Print: The Vice-Society Movement and Book Censorship in America*, 2nd ed. Madison: University of Wisconsin Press, 2002.

Butters, Gerald R. *Banned in Kansas: Motion Picture Censorship, 1915–1966.* Columbia: University of Missouri Press, 2007.

"C&S Again on the Spot." *Radio Daily* (February 4, 1938), 1.

Cherry, Bridgit. *True Blood: Investigating Vampires and Southern Gothic*. London: I. B. Tauris, 2012.

"Defends Children's Shows." *Radio Daily* (November 12, 1937), 3.

Dennis, Donna. "Obscenity Law and the Conditions of Freedom in Nineteenth-Century United States." *Law & Social Inquiry* 27, no. 2 (2002): 369–99.

"Dr. Jekyll and Mr. Hyde," November 9, 1920. Censorship file from the Kansas Board of Review. Kansas Historical Society. Box No. 35-06-06-06. Topeka, KS.

Eberly, Rosa A. *Citizen Critics: Literary Public Spheres*. Urbana: University of Illinois Press, 2000.

"FCC Staffers Become Licensee Pen Pals." *Broadcasting* (February 19, 1962), 102–3.

Gamer, Michael. *Romanticism and the Gothic: Genre, Reception, and Canon Formation*. Cambridge: Cambridge University Press, 2000.

Grieveson, Lee. *Policing Cinema: Movies and Censorship in Early Twentieth-Century America*. Berkeley: University of California Press, 2004.

"The Haunted House." November 11, 1917. Censorship file from the Kansas Board of Review. Kansas Historical Society. Box Number 35-06-06-09. Topeka, KS.

Hays, Will H. Letter to Harry Zehnder, February 26, 1934. Production Code Administration Correspondence, Margaret Herrick Library, Academy of Motion Picture Arts and Sciences, Beverly Hills, CA.

Jamarillo, Deborah L. "Astrological TV: The Creation and Destruction of a Genre." *Communication, Culture & Critique* 8 (2015): 309–26.

Joshi, Sunand Tryambak, and David E. Schultz. *An HP Lovecraft Encyclopedia*. Westport, CT: Greenwood Publishing Group, 2001.

Jowett, L., and Stacey Abbott. *TV Horror: Investigating the Dark Side of the Small Screen*. London: Bloomsbury Press, 2013.

Joy, Jason S. Letter to Will H. Hays, December 5, 1931. Production Code Administration Correspondence, Margaret Herrick Library, Academy of Motion Picture Arts and Sciences, Beverly Hills, CA.

Levi, Lili. "The FCC's Regulation of Indecency." *First Reports* 7, no. 1 (2008): 1–98.

"Listening to Radio Is Third Principal Activity of Child." *Broadcast* (June 1, 1936), 11.

McGarry, Molly. "Spectral Sexualities: Nineteenth-Century Spiritualism, Moral Panics, and the Making of U.S. Obscenity Law." *Journal of Women's History* 12, no. 2 (2000): 8–29.

Naylor, Alex. "'A horror picture at this time is a very hazardous undertaking': Did British or American Censorship End the 1930s Horror Cycle?" *Irish Journal of Gothic and Horror Studies* 9 (2011): 44–59.

"No FCC Action Due in Radio 'War' Case." *New York Times* (November 2, 1938), 26.

Nodelman, Perry. "Ordinary Monstrosity: The World of *Goosebumps*." *Children's Literature Association Quarterly* 22, no. 3: (1997): 118–25.

Nyberg, Amy Kiste. *Seal of Approval: The History of the Comics Code*. Jackson: University Press of Mississippi, 1998.

O'Connor, Thomas F. "The National Organization for Decent Literature: A Phase in American Catholic Censorship." *The Library Quarterly* 65, no. 4: (1995): 386–414.

"Payne Launching Drive on Juvenile Programs." *Radio Daily* (November 12, 1937), 1.

Phillips, Kendall R. "Fear of Film: Cinema and Affective Entanglements." In *Philosophy, Film and the Dark Side of Interdependence*, ed. Jonathan Beever. New York: Rowan & Littlefield, 2020.

"Picture Shows All Put Out of Business." *New York Times* (December 25, 1908), 1.

Plato. *Republic*. Trans. Robin Waterfield. Oxford: Oxford University Press, 1993.

Pondillo, Robert. *America's First Network TV Censor: The Work of NBC's Stockton Helffrich*. Carbondale: Southern Illinois University Press, 2010.

Power, Brenda M., Jeffrey Wilhelm, and Kelly Chandler, eds. *Reading Stephen King: Issues of Censorship, Student Choice, and Popular Literature*. Urbana, IL: NCTE, 1997.

"Rep. Randall Asks for Sex-Violence TV Curbs." *Broadcasting* (April 20, 1962), 58.

Reyes, Amanda. *Are You in the House Alone?* Truro, MA: Headpress, 2017.

Schoell, William. *The Horror Comics: Fiends, Freaks and Fantastic Creatures, 1940s–1980s*. Jefferson, NC: McFarland Press, 2014.

Schwartz, A. Brad. *Broadcast Hysteria: Orson Welles's War of the Worlds and the Art of Fake News*. New York: Hill and Wang, 2015.

Simmons, Jerold. "The Production Code under New Management: Geoffrey Shurlock, The Bad Seed, and Tea and Sympathy." *Journal of Popular Film and Television* 22, no. 1 (Spring 1994): 2–10.

"Teeth Pulled from Code Adopted by NAB." *Heinl Radio Business Letter* (July 14, 1939), 2–3.

"Terrorist Novel Writing." In *Spirit of the Public Journals for 1797*, vol. 1. London: James Ridgway, 1802.

Tittle, Miles. "'Inside … Doesn't Matter': Responding to *American Psycho* and Its Dantean Agenda." In *Fear and Learning: Essays on the Pedagogy of Horror*, ed. Aalya Ahmad and Sean Moreland. Jefferson, NC: McFarland. 2013. 179–99.

Towlson, Jon. *The Turn to Gruesomeness in American Horror Films, 1931–1936*. Jefferson, NC: McFarland, 2016.

Twomey, John E. "The Citizens' Committee and Comic-Boook Control: A Study of Extragovernmental Restraint." *Law & Contemporary Problems* 20, no. 4 (1955): 621–29.

US Congress, House of Representatives. Report of the Select Committee on Current Pornographic Materials, Pursuant to H. Res. 596. 82nd Cong., 1952.

US Congress, Senate, Committee on the Judiciary, Juvenile Delinquency. 84th Cong., 1st sess., 1955, S. Res. 62.

US Criminal Code §211.

Wallace, Paul S. *Regulation of Obscenity: A Compilation of Federal and State Statues and Analysis of Selected Supreme Court Opinions*. Washington, DC: Congressional Research Service, 1976.

Wingate, James. Letter to Will H. Hays, October 28, 1936. Production Code Administration Correspondence, Margaret Herrick Library, Academy of Motion Picture Arts and Sciences, Beverly Hills, CA.

Zeigler, Sara. "Book Banning." In *The Encyclopedia of Civil Liberties in America*, ed. David Schultz and John R. Vile. New York: Routledge, 2005.

6

ESTHER LESLIE

Schlock, Kitsch, and Camp

Schlock horror is a type of horror that, even within the realms of what horror normally offers, appears excessive, too much. Its horror may be extremely graphic, gore-filled, aiming for great effects and the provocation of intense emotions, and yet, like kitsch, it fails, because something rings untrue, even for the false word of film or pulp fiction – the acting, the scriptwriting, the sets, the too-bright red blood. Camp horror paints its themes bright and large, pretending to be deadly serious, when it is really not, either intentionally or unintentionally. These modes of horror have long been a part of the genre, but they wax and wane across time, victims of technological demands within the culture industry or vagaries of fashion. Artworks that were designed more or less earnestly might come to be seen as schlocky, and artworks designed to become cult objects of bad taste might find themselves elevated into the zone of high art. It is pertinent to look at the longer history of the terms – schlock, kitsch, and camp – and to consider how various cultural critics have derived meaning from often disdained productions.

Starting with etymologies, definitions, first usages, and so on is sometimes useful. The etymological origins of "schlock" are as uncertain as those of its companion concept, "kitsch," and the first usage of "camp" to indicate exaggerated, artificial gestures is likewise difficult to locate with any certainty. It derives possibly from the French *campagne* or from *se camper*, to strike a pose, or maybe from British Polari gay slang, or from military cant, or from the Scots. Schlock and kitsch – both, apparently, in the linguistic realm of Yiddish or German – are words whose hard *k*s and compacted *sch*s sound less like proper terms, aesthetic categories, or philosophical adjectives and more like uncontrolled ejaculations – *sch*, *kkk*. These words onomatopoeically eject something from the mouth a little violently, like an improper gobbet of gloopy sick or a sudden spray of crimson blood, but there may also be some joy in articulating the unfamiliar, words that linger in their sibilance and entertain the mouth, lips, teeth. The very sound seems to resonate with expressions of disapproval. The words seem vulgar – but also funny. Camp has a different quality. It sounds simple, recognized, and yet, conceptually, cannot be quickly described and, indeed, goes only in the illusory guise of transparency, while being actually opaque.

All three of the words are fuzzy in their origins and signify something that is itself indistinct, indefinable, or in-between. With certainty, though, it can be said that the words "schlock," "kitsch," and "camp" are descriptors for sloppily put together cultural entities – films most predominantly in the case of schlock, various visual or musical forms in the case of kitsch, theatrical productions when it comes to camp. Pulp fiction books, with covers as schlocky as the contents, are kitsch, and take their cue from films. These descriptors – pulp, camp, kitsch, schlock – name artworks that are as stupid as they are captivating, as repulsive as they are funny, as superficial as they are deep. They aim for one thing and achieve something else. Schlock, for one, might promise bloodcurdling shivers and horror – but delivers, along with those effects, ludicrousness and crassness. Kitsch and camp dangle before audiences a promise of experiences of extreme intense emotion, only to serve up banality, cliché, laughter, and derision, when the excessiveness of their scenarios and gestures marries with the inadequacy of the realization and – in the case of film – when the strings are visible, the corpse still breathes, the grotesquery is so over the top that the narrative is suspended and only groans echo around the auditorium. Audiences might, at best, in watching these low-rent efforts marvel at what special effects can wring into being and simultaneously negate – and through the agency of just how sick or cynical an imagination. The adjectives or nouns describing these works – schlock, kitsch, camp – sound alien, suggesting something odd, off the track of the known, and yet a space can be found for this weirdness, and it will be one in which the unfamiliar becomes familiar, or groaningly predictable. These artworks will live up to the low expectations, or they will simply be forgotten.

The pleasures that schlocky films and gory literature, kitschy overblown paintings or mawkish music provide are multiple and erratic: thrills and terrors, farcicality and heart tugs. Fear can be dissipated in a moment, laughs pivoted rapidly to a chill. It is, as the clichéd blurb on some video packaging or back of the pulp book might say, a rollercoaster experience. The viewer might, at first, take what is presented seriously, only to be ejected suddenly into the realms of the absurd and implausible. The sensibility cultivated in audiences is as rickety as the props and settings in a schlocky film. The pleasures derived from enjoying this substandard fare might be called vulgar – and to be vulgar means to have a failure of taste, in the tenets of bourgeois aesthetics from David Hume and Immanuel Kant onward; that is to say, to possess bad taste is to know that something, in the realm of art or design, is poor quality, but to indulge in it anyway. Where can these confections sit in any canon formation? Or are they condemned to hover at the margins, not welcomed into academic literary, cultural or film studies, which have themselves had to fight for serious attention, or for attention to their objects as serious forms, artworks worthy of analysis. These shoddy products of schlock and kitsch, overblown but underfinanced, excessive in their gestures, but falling short of their ambitions, detract from the claims to legitimacy of the serious partakers in the cultural field. These grotesque products evidence a mismatch between the means or the acting ability or storytelling capacity and its realization. The lack, the failure to achieve what it thinks it could do opens up a chasm between the artwork-as-is and the imagined artwork. Out of this chasm, hollow laughter echoes. Outliers, they threaten to unmask all cultural analysis as a pretentious game, in which the throwaway – and it is all throwaway – gets taken far too seriously. Or they exist as markers of what not to loiter on, the depraved relative that exists to let the good ones shine all the more brightly. What can be done with these kitschy, schlocky, camp things? And what were the beginnings of the trash aesthetic?

Kitsch

While the origins of the words "kitsch" and "schlock" are murky, it can be said with confidence that these words are somehow bound up with developments within industrial production. Most sources declare the origins of "kitsch" to lie in German and Germany and that "kitsch" means, variously, something that is chucked together hurriedly, gathered up from the streets, or constructed cheaply. Its derivation has also been supposed from the English word "sketch," signifying a relationship to inexpensive and mass-produced tourist art in the later nineteenth century. It may be a metathesis of the French word "chic," as well as related to a Russian word for the state of being puffed up and haughty. Some commentators argue that the term first appears in the 1860s and 1870s among Munich art dealers to describe paintings that are aesthetically worthless. Kitsch, in any case, whatever its origins, is that which is gaudy, sentimental, and tasteless. Tastelessness is significant, because it signals a failure to play by the rules of aesthetics. To partake in the realm of aesthetics is to share an understanding of what is tasteful. To be tasteful is to remain within boundaries – not to spill across lines of what ought or ought not be seen or thought, not to let bodies spill from their flesh bags or allow the lesser senses of smell and touch to overwhelm the body, in contrast to the more abstracted senses of hearing and sight. In kitsch, an audience of the industrial age is produced, one that allows itself to respond to what is seen with an automatic emotional reactivity, rather than critical aesthetic reflection. Kitsch, according to the most vocal commentators, signals a lack, in either the artwork or the viewer, though over time, kitsch achieves ironic appreciation by viewers "in the know." Scholarship on kitsch remained a German-language concern until the 1970s – after which significant contributions to its analysis appeared, notably in the United States, as in the work of Eve Kosofsky Sedgwick. Attempts to make more precise the distinctions between kitsch and other trash aesthetic categories was often in dialogue with the key text from 1964 by Susan Sontag, "Notes on Camp." The word "kitsch," however, had already made its way to various countries and languages – appearing in English in 1920, which makes it contemporaneous with the establishing of film as a cultural form in the process of becoming industrialized and which will play into burgeoning arguments about cultural value.

Schlock

The word "schlock" may have been borrowed from Yiddish, from a word that means dross, first used in the fourteenth century and itself derived from Middle Low German. Or it may stem from a word that means to strike or a stroke, which designates in some way a calamity. This is probably unlikely, according to the *OED*. "Schlock" is negative, in any case. It crops up as a term in the United States, with various spellings from the start of the twentieth century – schlag, slock, schlock – and it means cheap, shoddy goods or material, such as inferior-quality suits, picked up for a dollar downtown. It takes sixty-odd years for "schlock" to be applied to films, which is where it really comes into its own, but arguably many films in the early years were schlocky, by any measure that valued quality: acting in the silent era was exaggerated, stories were simplified, sentimentality was rife, implausibility and lapses in continuity were prevalent. When Universal Pictures produced the monster movies that made Boris Karloff and Bela Lugosi household names at the beginning of the 1930s, with *Dracula* (1931), *Frankenstein* (1931), *The Mummy* (1932), *The Invisible Man* (1933), and *Bride of Frankenstein* (1935), they invented also a genre of horror film, a "Universal Horror" that already established the characteristics of schlock and camp: creaking staircases, spooky castles, and mobs of incensed peasants.

It could be argued that the propensity toward a rather exaggerated and ultimately brittle terror aesthetic was particularly pronounced in the United States – and that schlock is a peculiarly American form. If so, its roots could be traced to the epoch of bourgeois revolution and burgeoning industrial capitalism. Karl Marx wrote, in 1852, in his *Eighteenth Brumaire of Louis Bonaparte*, that, owing to the youthfulness of the nation, there was a different quality of existence in the United States, one that was too busy acting, building, eradicating, and settling to spend time dealing with the past. As a result, that past lingered like a pile of rubbish that no one bothered to throw out – thematically it will take on filmic form in haunted house movies, including comedically, as early as 1932 in James Whale's *The Old Dark House*, with its exploration of class tensions and other hangovers of the past. Marx's conception of the United States was a place

> where, though classes already exist, they have not yet become fixed, but continually change and interchange their elements in constant flux, where the modern means of production, instead of coinciding with a stagnant surplus population, rather compensate for the relative deficiency of heads and hands, and where, finally, the feverish, youthful movement of material production, which has to make a new world of its own, has neither time nor opportunity left for abolishing the old world of ghosts. (Marx, 195)

In the United States, spiritualist movements proliferated with table-knockers and aura photographers. Marx's collaborator Friedrich Engels contributed some thoughts in a letter to F. A. Sorge in 1886, addressing the consequences of a fervent world of spirits, in which various extraordinary events were unmasked as frauds and hoaxes:

> [T]he Americans are worlds behind in all theoretical things, and while they did not bring over any medieval institutions from Europe they did bring over masses of medieval traditions, religion, English common (feudal) law, superstition, spiritualism, in short every kind of imbecility which was not directly harmful to business and which is now very serviceable for making the masses stupid. (Marx and Engels, 451)

European popular culture, with its superstitions and subjection to folkloric illogic, arrived in the baggage of immigrants on the *Mayflower* and all the other ships. The US masses are made stupid, are made vulnerable to an imbecility that does not impede business, indeed might even champion it. The coalescence of duped masses, shoddy culture, and burgeoning capitalist activity is a theme that will recur again and again in relation to critical theories of schlock culture and kitsch entertainment.

Camp

The word "camp" appears in print in the first decade of the twentieth century. It refers to exaggerated gestures and mannerisms and came to be associated with gay male subculture. The first theorist proper of camp is said to be the novelist Christopher Isherwood, whose episodic novel *Goodbye to Berlin* (1939), on which the film *Cabaret* (1972) was based, contained depictions of Weimar culture at its campest. The hero, with his non-judgmental camera-eye, trails through the demimonde of queer Berlin and finds in Sally Bowles a campy tragic heroine. She is a performer. For the camp sensibility, life is the playing of a role. She is decadent, living life intensely, and in the moment, vulnerable and resilient at once. When all the campiness, all the queerness – as it is played out in cabarets and in bars and studied sympathetically at Magnus Hirschfeld's Berlin Institute of Sexology – is eradicated by the Nazis, there remains only death and deadly seriousness. Isherwood's narrator, Christopher, gives a sense of that, as he says goodbye to Berlin and speculates on the awful fate of his friends and their worlds. Camp thrives on tragic gestures, on lament at the transience of life, on an excess of sentiment, an ironic sensibility that art and artifice is preferable to nature and health, in a Wildean sense.

In camp, the enemy is the straight world, the suburban ordinariness that may turn out to be unmasked as a cover for dangerously perverse or brutal practices. Camp cannot survive when the deathliness becomes all too real. Isherwood flees Berlin, escaping to the United States, from where he reflects on camp in the novel *The World in the Evening* (1954). Isherwood's character insists on a serious core to camp: "True High Camp always has an underlying seriousness. You can't camp about something you don't take seriously. You're not making fun of it; you're making fun out of it. You're expressing what's basically serious to you in terms of fun and artifice and elegance." Camp is a stance, a disguise under which what is core appears only as a surface, an irrelevancy – all the better to parade it, under the nose of those who might outlaw it. His character's insistence that there is a serious, critical core to camp is what emboldens Susan Sontag to write her much-cited *Notes on Camp* in 1964. A quotable line is: "Camp asserts that good taste is not simply good taste; that there exists, indeed, a good taste of bad taste" (291). This is the "so bad it is good idea" that occurs in both kitsch and schlock, the pleasure taken in excessive stupidity and ludicrousness. That which delegitimates the cultural proposal for it transgressing the boundaries of taste becomes that which legitimizes it, according to another set of evaluations: knowing pleasure, ironic appreciation, critically aware enjoyment. In film history, this idea of "so good it is bad" can lead back to Berlin, to Isherwood's location in the years between the wars and to battles around the status of film in relation to art. An example serves to show an early example of schlocky, kitschy, camp horror film replete with the attitude that is prepared to receive badness as part of what makes it so good. One evening in 1927, the expressive dancers Anita Berber and Henri

(Châtin-Hoffman) perform nude prior to a screening of a film version of Dante's *Divine Comedy*, which film critic Leo Hirsch describes as "So dire it was truly magnificent." The film is dire – which means it is schlocky, kitschy; the film technologies of the time – of any time? – cannot contain the immensity that is Dante's vision of Hell. But furthermore, in this place where camp is born and will die, only to die a thousand deaths in the fascist repression, the high culture of Dante meets film along with the decadent Weimar culture of expressive cocaine-fueled dance. It is excessive – more excessive than a depiction of Hell, in a strange way. It is over the top and bound for tragedy, a tragedy that will indeed soon befall Berber and guarantee her place in the pantheon of camp heroines.

Kitsch things are rapidly used up. No canon conserves it, and yet it appealed to the Dadaists and Surrealists, who found spurs therein for their urban poetry and their dismissals of modern rationality and the compulsions to be up-to-date, because that contemporaneity is what powers economy: buy today, buy again tomorrow. The Surrealists polemicize against good taste, speak in favor of bad taste – for example, Louis Aragon in *Le libertinage*, from 1924. Objects of bad taste, in Walter Benjamin's interpretation, require less sublimation and provide a more immediate vector to desire and pleasure. He observes that what really matters is "the undisturbed unfolding of the most banal, most fleeting, most sentimental weakest hour" in a life (238). Kitsch reminds us of childhood. Kitsch has not kept up with the technical and aesthetic standards of the time. Kitsch has ambition but poor means. Kitsch fails to achieve what it sets out to do – to terrify, to affect greatly, to be art – and so becomes pathetic.

Kitsch was a key concept for Benjamin. Kitsch, he argues, is "art with 100 percent, absolute and instantaneous availability for consumption" (Benjamin, *Arcades Project*, 395). In its absoluteness, sheer effect, excessive sentiment, imperfections and decaying nature, and lack of requirement for sublimation, it signals much about desire, fantasy, social shifts, historical obsolescence, and transient ideology. For Benjamin, experience is something linked to tradition, bodily apperception, and unconscious desires. One of its vessels was religious ritual, which is displaced in the modern world, as existence is organized around fragmentary and disrupting events, momentary distractions, incoherent partial glimpses, perceptual worlds rapidly obliterated by new techniques. There is no collective language – in place of traditional religion, it will dream up new cults: cult fashions, cult novels, cult films (Menninghaus, 46).

If Weimar and its progressive theorists could perceive in trash culture hints of desire and longing, this case was not transferred unequivocally to the United States. In 1939, art critic Clement Greenberg wrote *Avant Garde and*

Kitsch. Coming out of super-modern New York, Greenberg was writing in a setting plagued by anxiety about Old World values and whether the New World could compete on this ground when its cultural contributions were not, apparently, drawn from centuries of high art practices but drawn instead from jazz and cartoons and "the funnies." It was an environment in which a spat arose over something called "middlebrow" culture – a parochial, conservative form promulgated by enterprises such as the Book-of-the-Month Club, classical recordings, or the *Reader's Digest*. For anyone interested in so-called high culture, such stuff was simply an embarrassment – culture for those who knew nothing about culture or, worse, for those who knew but did not care, did not care about the development of culture into new forms, following avant-garde progression according to art's own immanent necessity. Its antithesis was, in short, kitsch. For Greenberg, the dross produced for the industrialized masses was ersatz culture. Kitsch, for Greenberg, is that which is instantly and vividly recognizable. Kitsch is an enhanced reality made dramatic, absorbed effortlessly. It is an effects-driven form, providing a short-cut to the pleasure of art. Kitsch steals from genuine culture and makes a meaningless facsimile of it. Its results are forgettable, because there is always more to replace it. Who remembers the popular, commercially successful poems of Eddie Guest or *Indian Love Lyrics*, two of Clement Greenberg's examples of US kitsch?

What Greenberg brings out in his essay, though, is that the most kitschy, most schlocky of modern industrialized culture is that approved and championed by the totalitarian states of Germany and the Soviet Union, under the rule of Nazis and Stalinists. Far from camp and kitsch being expunged in Nazi Germany or Fascist Italy or Stalinist Russia, it colonizes all culture, if it is to be understood as that which is cheap, inauthentic, worthless. Greenberg stresses that the choices in cultural policy derive not from the philistine predilections of the rulers, but rather because "kitsch is the culture of the masses in these countries, as it is everywhere else" (154). It is obeisance to mass industrialized taste. Expediently for the totalitarian leaders, Greenberg notes, kitsch culture was a far more efficient vehicle of propaganda, with sugar-coated stories of homeland and heroes, and it provided a low-cost way to tug the heartstrings of the masses. In the United States, kitsch culture sold well and was forgettable enough to sell well day after day.

Greenberg's critical take on products of US culture parallels debates on the value of mass culture as conducted in the 1940s by Theodor Adorno and Max Horkheimer. These German theorists had relocated to the United States and were confronted by a lively, popular culture that they called, famously, the "Culture Industry." Culture is an industry, like shoe making or steel, produced for profit and without even a semblance of artistic integrity. Indeed, where there is a pretension to artistic integrity, it is even worse, according to Adorno and Horkheimer, because it falls short and thus is kitsch. Cinema is the prime example of culture made industrially and, like any other industrial product, made for profit. Film exists merely with an eye to its exchange value: "Cultural entities typical of the culture industry are no longer *also* commodities, they are commodities through and through" (Adorno, *Culture Industry*, 86).

Involved in market machinations, film tends toward standardization and typecasting and, in the process, creates audiences in its image, who are subjected to easily interpretable messages. It turns its audience into spoon-fed passive children and draws on their sadistic and negative impulses. It attunes people to the monotonous cruelties of life under capitalism, in a training for what Adorno calls the "life in the false," that is, a life survived in an over-technologized, pitiless, machine-driven, alienating environment, which resembles the one depicted in film:

> People give their approval to mass culture because they know or suspect that this is where they are taught the mores they will surely need as their passport in a monopolised life. This passport is only valid if paid for in blood, with the surrender of life as a whole and the impassioned obedience to a hated compulsion. ("Schema of Mass Culture," 80)

The imagery is itself horror-laden – payment in blood, compulsion to go on in this blighted life, asymmetric power, cruelty. But could it be that horror – the most exaggerated horror – teaches us something about our hellish existence, by laying out so explicitly the violence, the often unpredictable, unjust brutality of the system? In a line in *Minima Moralia*, written for rhetorical effect, Adorno notes, "In psychoanalysis nothing is true except the exaggerations" (29). Might the exaggerated reality of schlock horror hint at social truth? Not absent from the artwork, the existing world is there in its exaggerations. In "Commitment" (1962), Adorno points out how Kafka's disturbing novels or Samuel Beckett's absurdist drama, which refuse and distort empirical reality, provoke a fear, or a "shudder" – a term Adorno uses again and again, and which is intrinsic to many analyses of the aesthetics of horror. This shudder exists in a pact with the bleak truth of our existence ("Commitment," 190). As Adorno phrases it: "He over whom Kafka's wheels have passed, has lost for ever both any peace with the world and any chance of consoling himself with the judgement that the way of the world is bad; the element of ratification which lurks in the resigned admission of the dominance of evil is burnt away" (191).

Evil's domination in the world can be dislodged by the exaggerated and irreal depictions in Kafka's stories. Is it only these Old World, higher art contributions that achieve this?

In "Transparencies on Film" (1966), which to some extent revises his extremely negative thinking on film, in light of new developments in 1960s German cinema, Adorno adheres to the criticism that there is something potentially fascistic about film, which consists of "mimetic impulses which, prior to all content and meaning, incite the viewers and listeners to fall into step as if in a parade" (*Culture Industry*, 158). Through ostensibly photocopying the world, film confirms and reaffirms the world as it endures. No modification is imaginable. But might there be a chink here that allows for the grand guignol of horror films, especially tacky ones, to escape the mimetic drive? Adorno's negative aesthetics logs a space for a connection to the world that is not guided by the constraint to emulate the surface of reality.

But Adorno did not see the uses of schlocky horror for a dialectical enlightenment or, if he did, he kept it quiet. It took the urbane and critical producers of something akin to, if not identical with, popular culture to articulate the ways in which something could surface from even the most kitschy and rubbishy of mass culture's outputs. The epoch of schlock arises only with the emergence of postwar mass culture, a culture industry that had upped its production and, to extend it even further, had manufactured new consumers, notably teenagers. These teenagers needed a plentiful supply of entertaining stuff to fill evenings at the movies, drive-in, or grindhouse. B-movies, lower budget, slightly shorter films existed to draw youth to the cinema, be exposed to adverts, consume more. In the 1960s, a number of subgenres developed, owing to a more lax regime of censorship. What came to be known as exploitation films moved toward the mainstream, drawing from the type of film that pruriently presented cautionary tales for moral educational purposes. Their pleasure lay in the transgressing of taboos, rather than in the commitment to them. The lurid nature of these films was taken up in various subgenres and scored a success in Alfred Hitchcock's psychologizing drama *Psycho* (1960), which was comparatively low budget and did not rely on the glamour of Hollywood stars. Others emulated the film's tense and nasty shock-aesthetic as slasher and gore or splatter films pushed the dark side of human nature further along the line. The films advertised themselves as tests of endurance and stamina, offering sick bags or declaring themselves to be the most terrifying film ever made. Jack Curtis' *The Flesh Eaters* (1964), Herschell Gordon Lewis' *A Taste of Blood* (1967), and George Romero's *Night of the Living Dead* (1968) are three prominent examples from the period. In this last, amid the defining template of zombie shuffling, the period's emergent racial and social politics were focused dramatically.

This was this period that saw the efflorescence of films made on a low budget with excessive gore and lots of erotic content, put out by production companies such as Roger Corman's New World Pictures or New Line Cinema. They cost little and made a lot – some of them, at least. Such successful industrializing of trashiness, but in its own way now rather slick and competent, left some nostalgic for an earlier epoch, where the blood looked more like ketchup and the plainly plastic monsters moved through wobbly sets. Amid the shadows cast by the well-oiled and well-financed machinery of studio Hollywood and an equally efficient emerging genre cinema of sexploitation and blaxploitation, which the major studios were also beginning to produce, something else, something from the detritus emerges. A cult cinema develops, one that venerates a failed culture, holds up, in a most knowing way, the kitschy, schlocky, and campy low-budget films of the immediate postwar B-movie culture. *The Rocky Horror Picture Show*, a stage production in 1973, made into a film in 1975, is the most prominent transgressive tribute to the glorious tackiness of low-budget science fiction and horror films from the 1930s to the 1960s. The turn to cult is tracked in Frank Zappa's critical look at US culture in a song on his 1974 album *Roxy and Elsewhere*. "Cheepnis" begins with a two-minute monologue about the film *It Conquered the World*. Zappa praises the exigencies forced on filmmakers by low budgets: "true cheepnis is exemplified by visible nylon strings attached to the jaw of a giant spider." He describes the monster in Corman's film:

> The monster looks sort of like an inverted ice-cream cone with teeth around the bottom. It looks like a (phew!), like a teepee or . . . sort of a rounded off pup-tent affair, and, uh, it's got fangs on the base of it, I don't know why but it's a very threatening sight, and then he's got a frown and, you know, ugly mouth and everything, and there's this one scene where the, uh, monster is coming out of a cave, see? There's always a scene where they come out of a cave, at least once, and the rest of the cast . . . it musta been made around the 1950s, the lapels are about like that wide, the ties are about that wide and about this short, and they always have a little revolver that they're gonna shoot the monster with, and there is always a girl who falls down and twists her ankle . . . heh-hey!

The scenarios are predictable – as might be discerned from the fact that sets were reused in days won back from already punishing production schedules. The roles are stereotypical. The things that should be scary fail to scare or scare only in surprisingly stupid ways. Zappa goes on to observe that the filmmakers are loathe to reshoot, despite the fact that the monster's wooden base is wrongly in view: "and then obviously off-camera somebody's goin': 'NO! GET IT BACK!' And they drag it back just a little bit as the guy is goin': 'KCH! KCH!' Now that's cheepnis." The band then launches into a song that evokes all the clichés of trashy film making and ends up blending images of napalm assaults in Vietnam with attacks on oversized poodles. Like Adorno's critique of the violence underpinning the glossy outputs of the US culture industry, crummy films draw together the most throwaway items of the culture and the imperialist domination of the US state and military. That it is poorly thrown together, shoddy goods means that the joins can be seen not just between the monster and the transportation wooden frame but also between the culture industry and the military industrial complex. The truth was in plain sight: It conquered the world.

It could be said that kitsch, schlock, and camp, far from being naive products of a rampantly capitalist enterprise or the immature outputs of an insufficiently cultured set of producers made for an ignorant and work-weary audience, are, rather, outputs of the revenge of mass culture. This cheaply made but affective culture of the masses refuses marginalization by gatekeepers of cultural value and sets itself against the self-seriousness of art that is really just the knowledge of some codes that are themselves banalized and conventional. Every mass market pulp paperback with a garish cover and a screamingly obvious name – like James Herbert's *The Rats* (1974) or *The Fog* (1975) or Shaun Hutson's *Slugs* (1982) or *Spawn* (1983) – hopes to affirm a delight in over-the-top excess. The energies of Romantic aesthetics, with their tasteful evocation of sentiment and reined-in provocation of emotion, are long depleted – or themselves kitsch – in an age of commodity capitalism (Marcinkiewicz). There is an honesty displayed in gore – the false life is shown in its falseness. Things are pushed so far, become so ludicrous, it can no longer be believed, as when in a thousand films, such as *Sleep Away Camp* from 1983, the deaths come thick and fast, but importantly they come stupidly – bee stings, death by curling tongs. This is how stupid the violence in our world is, how cruel and apparently arbitrary. It is a life lesson. Kitsch and camp horror is in and not in our world – its realism is compromised, there but not there. Therein lies a considerable power – because it may evoke things buried deep within, fantasies from childhood, the reality that contorts in dreams – and Benjamin notes that dreams are kitsch, for they are unseemly, infantile, effort-saving, clichéd, improbable (Benjamin, 3). Schlock draws on the half-remembered and deeply feared truths of the world that elude us in daylight. Or, to take another stance, could it be that kitschy, campy products such as the TV series *The Addams Family* or *The Munsters* (both airing from 1964 to 1966) have meaning because they cast a light on how that Old World Gothic came over to the New World as an unreflected form, a bit of stuff left in an old suitcase and never dealt with – but only imperfectly, stupidly mobilized, a kitsch version, not serious, but also not really itself? Maybe those titles that named so many schlock horror movies – *It Came from ...*, *The Thing from ...*, *The Return of ...*, *Plan 9 from ...*, *Killer Klowns from ...* – are hints at this transposition from the past to the present, from out there to over here.

Schlock becomes a genre for itself, rather than a by-product of low-budget production methods. In 1973, a film with *Schlock* as its title appears, featuring a prehistoric ape-man on the rampage in Southern Californian suburbs. Schlock dies – like King Kong dies before him. Of course, he has a son. The next hastily put-together movie is already storyboarding. Such is schlock – which has its glory days in the 1970s and is tied up with the specific economics of the film industry of the time, with the existence of B-movies or the requirements for speedy, shorter products, with drive-in movies for American teens, with the shift to video rental stores and the desire for content. These are the years of grindhouse – low-rent cinemas devoted to exploitation movies. Spawning uncontrollably like something in a horror film, the genres multiply from the early nudies, roughies, and gore: shocksploitation, teensploitation, blaxploitation, hixsploitation, mondo, zombies, slashers, and more. John Waters begins his "Trash Trilogy" with *Pink Flamingos* in 1972, whose tagline is "An exercise in poor taste." His lead actor, Divine, appears in the sequel *Female Trouble* (1974), but is replaced in *Desperate Living* (1977) by another cult entertainer, Liz Renay. Waters' setting is suburban Baltimore, his childhood home. The suburbs are the proper home of kitschy campy schlock. Tim Burton's *Edward Scissorhands* (1990), for one, takes place in a world of stifling normalcy – Avon ladies, pastel-colored houses, lonesome housewives, tidy lawns, a kind of ever-time 1950s. In the normals' rejection of creative strangeness, they reveal themselves in truth to be inhabitants of the weird home of scary consumer conformity.

Kitsch and camp and schlock horror does not ever stop being made, but it is now, as it tangentially was since the 1970s, at least, something to be regarded nostalgically, or through a twice- or third-time removed nostalgia for an age of paradoxically innocent cynicism or unintentional badness. Some things become camp and kitsch. Others are made to be so. Some things become cult. Others aim at that status from the start. Schlock and kitsch horror becomes a quality or set of styles to be evoked in art, as, for example, in Ryan Trecartin's *A Family Finds Entertainment* (2004), with its garish colors, excessive makeup, and zombie-like behaviors of confusion and broken language – a homage to the homage to gory films made by first-year students in art college. The slasher films of the 1980s are revisited as camped-up camp in *Final Girls* (2015), *The Cabin in the Woods* (2012), the TV series *Scream Queens* (2015–16). "Not blood, red," stated Jean-Luc Godard in response to an interviewer observing the gory violence in *Pierrot Le Fou* (1972) (Godard, 217). This garish color is not real blood, not a sign of actual violence, but a trace of artifice, as is all film. This is pleasure and terror and all that is sublime and ridiculous, scary and funny, all at once.

Works Cited

Adorno, T. W. "Commitment" (1962). In *Aesthetics and Politics: Debates between Bloch, Lukács, Brecht, Benjamin, Adorno*, edited by Ronald Taylor. London: NLB, 1977.

The Culture Industry. London: Routledge, 1991.

"The Culture Industry Reconsidered" (1963). In *The Culture Industry*. London: Routledge, 1991. 86.

Minima Moralia: Reflections from Damaged Life. London: Verso, 2005.

"The Schema of Mass Culture" (1942). In *The Culture Industry*. London: Routledge, 1991. 80.

Aragon, Louis. *Le libertinage*. Paris: Gallimard, 1977.

Benjamin, Walter. *The Arcades Project*. Cambridge, MA: Harvard University Press, 2000.

Selected Writings, vol. 2. Cambridge, MA: Harvard University Press, 1999.

Godard, Jean-Luc. *Godard on Godard*. Trans. Tom Milne. London: Secker and Warburg, 1972.

Greenberg, Clement. *The New York Intellectuals Reader*. Ed. Neil Jumonville. New York: Routledge, 2007.

Isherwood, Christopher. *Goodbye to Berlin*. London: Hogarth Press, 1939.

The World in the Evening. New York: Random House, 1954.

Kosofsky Sedgwick, Eve. *Epistemology of the Closet*. Berkeley: University of California Press, 1990.

Marcinkiewicz, Pawel. "Contemporary Anglo-American Poetry and the Rhetorical Bomb." In *Redefining Kitsch and Camp in Literature and Culture*, ed. Justyna Stępień. Newcastle: Cambridge Scholars Press, 2014.

Marx, Karl. *Selected Writings*. Indianapolis, IN: Hackett Publishing, 2004.

Marx, Karl, and Friedrich Engels. *The Selected Correspondence of Karl Marx and Frederick Engels 1846–1895 with Explanatory Notes*. Marxist Library Volume 29, translated by Dona Torr. New York: International Publishers, 1942.

Menninghaus, Wilfried. "On the 'Vital Significance' of Kitsch: Walter Benjamin's Politics of Bad Taste." In *Walter Benjamin and the Architecture of Modernity*, ed. Andrew Benjamin and Charles Rice. Melbourne: re.press, 2009.

Sontag, Susan. "Notes on Camp." *Against Interpretation and Other Essays*. New York: Farrar, Straus and Giroux, 1966.

PART II
Genres

7

XAVIER ALDANA REYES

Body Horror

All horror fiction is "body horror," insofar as the experience of reading this literary genre is premised on the foregrounding of its intended effects on readers. Horror aims to scare, create suspense and dread, gross out, and scandalize. In short, it is preoccupied with the general mechanics of "fear," which becomes localized through the identification of specific sources of threat that may lead to injury or death. Since some of these sources may well be socially constructed and even time-specific (Bourke, 1–9), this means that horror fiction itself is ever changing and adapting. Unlike other genres like the Western or science fiction, horror is therefore not as strongly marked by specific settings and characters as by the emotion it seeks to generate and by the fragility of the human body (Aldana Reyes, "Introduction," 7–10). In fact, it is hard to think of the horror genre without thinking about the body's messy and intimate materiality – its blood and guts, its painful vulnerabilities, its inevitable rot and decay – and the forces that threaten to exceed and transform the apparently inviolable cohesion of our physical state: the monstrous, the freakish, the parasitic, the hybrid.[1] Despite this corporeal basis, the term "body horror" is generally used to describe a particular type of horror subgenre concerned with the total or partial destruction, mutilation, deformation, transformation, or (evolutionary) degeneration of the human body. These changes may sometimes be rendered subtly or in passing; however, since the 1980s, the term has been associated with a certain exploitative approach that relishes detailed description and may even indulge in what could be perceived as a sadistic gaze. The victims in body horror are not merely maimed, killed, or metamorphosed, but brutally and usually irrevocably so. This chapter looks at some of the more queasy manifestations of horror culture, the ones that foreground questions of the body's – and the reader's or viewer's – limits.

Body horror has been associated with modern cinema – the films of Sam Raimi, David Cronenberg, Tom Six, or Eli Roth, for example – but I want to argue here for a longer and more diverse lineage. An attention to embodied experience and its grotesque transformations can indeed be found in early US fiction, from Charles Brockden Brown's spontaneous combustion in *Wieland; or, The Transformation* (1798) and the viral hemorrhagic ravages of yellow fever in *Arthur Mervyn; or, Memoirs of the Year 1793* (1799) to the apparent blood-choking curse visited upon the males of the Pyncheon family in Nathaniel Hawthorne's *The House of the Seven Gables* (1851). The short stories of Edgar Allan Poe, perhaps the most significant and influential of nineteenth-century American Gothic writers, return time and again to the body, to its unruliness and destruction through cruel and painful means. For example, gruesome death punishments by razor-sharp pendulum and immurement are devised for the victims in "The Pit and the Pendulum" (1842) and "The Cask of Amontillado" (1846). The ending of "The Facts in the Case of M. Valdemar" (1845), in which a man left in a mesmeric state at the point of death for several months is suddenly awakened, must surely be one of the most shocking ever written. As Valdemar "crumble[s]" and "absolutely rot[s] away beneath [the narrator's] hands," all that is left on his bed is "a nearly liquid mass of loathsome – of detestable putridity" (842). In some cases, as in "William Wilson" (1839) and "The Tell-Tale Heart" (1843), motifs like the double or the beating heart of a murdered man can act as the primary catalyst for Poe's unique strand of psychological horror; whether supernatural events are real or hallucinated by a perturbed mind remains ambiguous. Later nineteenth- and twentieth-century writers, from Charlotte Perkins Gilman to Shirley Jackson, Robert Bloch, or Stephen King, would recuperate and update this macabre formula.

Naturally, as the spectacles of British revenge tragedy and the French Grand Guignol or the many novels and stories by writers like Mary Shelley, Robert Louis Stevenson, H. G. Wells, Shaun Hutson, James Herbert, and Clive Barker demonstrate, body horror is not necessarily nation-specific or an American creation. In this chapter, I focus exclusively on US manifestations of the genre because many of them have been the most foundational to the history of body horror. "Body horror" is a useful conglomerate term, but the workings of H. P. Lovecraft's "The Shadow Over Innsmouth" (1936), a novella about the horror inherent in the discovery of a hybrid fish-human race, are not exactly the same as those of Katherine Dunn's novel *Geek Love* (1989), about a group of circus freaks seeking to challenge the othering of nonnormative bodies. In what follows, I will center on five main types of body horror and the differences that exist between them: hybrid corporeality and the taxonomic crisis it engenders; parasitism, typically connected to nightmares about animal or alien invasion; abjection and disgust, that is, the normative policing of the "clean" body; the similar, but less supernaturally inclined, grotesque body;

and, finally, body horror built around gore and the explicit rendering of violence. This classification does not intend to propose that body horror may not, in places, operate across categories. For example, the zombie novels I turn to at the end tend to resort to gore, abjection, and the grotesque while simultaneously inviting considerations about what constitutes the "human."

In her influential book on the Gothic of the British fin de siecle, Kelly Hurley defines the "abhuman," a term borrowed from the fiction of weird writer William Hope Hodgson, as "a subject" that "is a not-quite-human subject, characterized by its morphic variability, continually in danger of becoming not-itself, becoming other" (3–4). For Hurley, the use of the prefix "ab" indicates "a loss," "a movement away from a site or condition" and toward a different and "unspecified one" (2); this process is both threatening and promising. It is threatening because it veers toward the unknown and unfamiliar, and promising because that transformation need not end in tragedy, but can involve acceptance and even the widening of given conceptual horizons. The interstitiality of the abhuman can be best illustrated through the Beast Folk in H. G. Wells' *The Island of Doctor Moreau* (1896).[2] Their appearance is referred to repeatedly as "ugly"(27), "grotesque" (28), "unnatural" (37), and "inhuman" (41) by the protagonist, Prendick, who feels almost unexplainably threatened by these characteristics.[3] The strangeness of the bodies of Dr. Moreau's experimental creatures reveals deeper anxieties about atavism (or evolutionary regression), a literary response to Charles Darwin's transformational work on evolutionary science. As is the case with the uncanny (*unheimlich*), Sigmund Freud's notion of the strangely familiar or the familiar estranged, the abhuman body instills a categorical crisis: human attempts to piece apart the natural world collapse in the presence of figures that either blur or directly defy our definitions and delimitations of the animal and the human. The abhuman is horrific because it upends the scientific laws we follow in order to make sense of earthly life, its history, and the position of our own bodies within nature. This is certainly the premise behind horrible mutation stories such as George Langelaan's "The Fly" (1957), where a scientist studying matter transference accidentally splices his DNA with that of a housefly. The two resulting hybrids, a man with the head and arm of a fly and a fly with the head of man, are equally aberrant as creatures that cross and contaminate discrete animal groups.

The oeuvre of H. P. Lovecraft stands as one of the greatest explorations of the abhuman in US fiction. Without seeking to homogenize what is an incredibly varied set of short stories, novellas, and novels, it is safe to suggest that Lovecraft's better known tales – those that belong to the Cthulhu Mythos shared universe – rely on the mind-shattering revelation of alien bodies for horrific effect. The Great Old Ones in "Dagon" (1919), "The Whisperer in Darkness" (1931), and "At the Mountains of Madness" (1936), among others, form a pantheon of deities who predate humans and, with some exceptions, live outside of our space-time continuum. The encounters between narrators and these beings usually catapult the former into existential crises that challenge not just the parameters of the human psyche but also anthropocentrism. Crucial to the workings of "cosmic horror" is the struggle to define what are perceived as abominations that exceed the boundaries of known living organisms and can be linguistically approximated only through comparison and analogy. In "The Call of Cthulhu" (1928), which introduced Lovecraft's most famous creature, Cthulhu is defined as a confusing mélange, as a "monster of vaguely anthropoid outline, but with an octopus-like head whose face was a mass of feelers, a scaly, rubbery-looking body, prodigious claws on hind and fore feet, and long, narrow wings behind" (148). Importantly, this description is of a stone statue and thus involves a dual process of (re)presentation. As becomes apparent, the real "Thing" goes beyond all that is thinkable: "there is no language for such abysms of shrieking and immemorial lunacy, such eldritch contradictions of all matter, force, and cosmic order" (167). Unnamable, fluid corporealities are a source of anxiety, so it follows that miscegenation, specifically the mingling of the human species with aliens or ape-like creatures, in "Facts Concerning the Late Arthur Jermyn and His Family" (1921), "The Colour Out of Space" (1927), and "The Dunwich Horror" (1929) gives birth to related taxonomic nightmares. As Allan Lloyd-Smith once noted, it is possible to identify the origin of these abhuman and hybrid horrors in Lovecraft's revulsion for the urban "other," in "his own racial prejudice" (115). Contemporary writers have actually drawn from his writings to confront the racist demons at the heart of twentieth-century America. For example, Matt Ruff's *Lovecraft Country* (2016) presents white supremacy during the era of Jim Crow laws as more dangerous than esoteric "shoggoths," and Victor LaValle rethinks and fills in the gaps of Lovecraft's infamous "The Horror at Red Hook" (1927) to great effect in *The Ballad of Black Tom* (2016). The discriminatory misgivings latent in the abhuman can also be turned on their head for social commentary.

Parasitic horror is closely linked to the abhuman because it foregrounds physiological disarray, but primarily revels in infection phobias and tells stories about the gradual domination of one body (the human) by another (a foreign and sometimes supernatural one). In body horror that develops this thematic strand, the emphasis is as firmly placed in the body of the invader as interstitial locus of doubt – who and what is it? – as it is in the potential obliteration of the former body, either that of an individual or of all humanity. Parasitic panic forms the basis of many medical thrillers about viral or bacterial infection, or "outbreak narratives" (Wald), which contemplate possible containment processes and survival scenarios. In body horror, parasitism is more gruesome and underscores questions of moral integrity and helplessness. Naturally, there is some slippage, especially of the generic type, and many of the best American parasitic body horrors could be considered science fiction/horror/medical thriller crossovers. Richard Matheson's post-apocalyptic *I Am Legend* (1954), about the struggles of the last man, Robert Neville, in a world now populated by vampires, rethinks these supernatural creatures as the result of a bacterial strain that is capable of infecting both living and dead bodies. Much of the novel revolves around bio-horror, with Neville killing his way through hordes of vampires as he tries to figure out the workings of the disease. Its famous ending disturbs the invader/invaded dyad. A dying Neville suddenly realizes that he has been feared too, that to the vampires "he was some terrible scourge they had never seen," "an invisible specter who had left for evidence the existence of the bloodless bodies of their loved ones" (159), and that this makes him so much "black anathema and black terror to be destroyed" (160). This type of undecidability is also apparent in John W. Campbell's *Who Goes There?* (1938), the novella that inspired Christian Nyby's monster epic *The Thing from Another World* (1951) and, in turn, John Carpenter's body horror remake, *The Thing* (1982). Its alien being has cells made of "protoplasm" (29) that study and reshape themselves to imitate those of the subjects it ingests: an Alaskan husky in the first instance and, later, the humans who make up the research expedition. Far from the alien doppelgängers in Jack Finney's body horror classic *The Body Snatchers* (1955), who are ultimately imperfect and appear to have "something *missing*" (15, emphasis in original), the parasite in *Who Goes There?* is seamless in its assimilation of humans. The novella's climax involves a test where the blood of the survivors is exposed to a hot wire. Since the "thing" is itself a living organism, the only way to tell it apart from the other men is by forcing it to crawl away from the source of heat. Anxieties about duplication run through parasitic horror, which, since the 1950s, has also mediated Cold War hysteria.

The double, at least since Robert Louis Stevenson's *Strange Case of Dr Jekyll and Mr Hyde* (1886), operates as the unbridled negative of our psyche, as the expression of the ungovernable unconscious. This "other" engages in forbidden behaviors and indulges in all the pleasures frowned on by society. The figure of the "abject," the object or subject which transgresses conventional notions of the clean and the pure and must be cast out in order to reestablish the normative, operates in a similar way. Rather than express duality or hedonism, the abject serves as an excremental mirror, a narrative surface that returns an image of that which is considered unacceptable or baleful (Aldana Reyes, "Abjection"). In the field of horror studies, abjection has been most productively utilized as a theoretical concept through which to study the institutionalization of corporeal discourses that exceptionalize and control the bodies of women, especially their perceived sexual excesses. Abjection is interested in the ways in which religion and ritual and, by extension, the socializing operations that underlie the ideological regulatory systems of patriarchy, continue to police and punish certain manifestations of femininity considered inappropriate or dangerous (Douglas; Kristeva). Barbara Creed has referred to this archetype as the "monstrous-feminine" or the "woman-as-monster" (*Monstrous-Feminine*, 1). Like disgust, which can be underpinned by biological primers (the avoidance of infectious pathogens that lie in tainted meat, feces, or other substances) but is largely culture-specific, abjection constructs certain bodies and functions as loathsome. In Stephen King's *Carrie* (1974), the eponymous heroine develops telekinetic powers upon experiencing her first period in a school shower, a traumatic experience that casts her as unclean. The novel then effectively turns Carrie into a menstrual leviathan. After being announced prom queen, she is covered in pig blood by popular girl Chris, and this moment sparks a series of psychic phenomena that ends in the death of many of Carrie's classmates and teachers. Like the female abject she represents, Carrie must be destroyed, the threat she poses defused. Similar horrific scenarios are played out in William Peter Blatty's *The Exorcist* (1971), via the trope of demonic possession, and in Charles Burns' *Black Hole* comic series (1995–2005), in which a sexually transmitted disease causes gross mutations to the bodies of teenagers. In these texts, body horror does more than act as a metaphor for the hormonal changes of puberty; it also establishes sexual awakening as a formative phase in the institutionalization of abjection.

Abjection can be homogenous with the "grotesque"; as Mary Russo notes, Mikhail Bakhtin, the literary critic most closely associated with the latter term, at one point connects it to the bodies of old hags, with the corresponding "fear and loathing around the biological processes of reproduction and of aging" (63) that have already been established as key to body horror. The grotesque, in my reading, is less interested in the fantastic and often supernatural rethinkings of the abhuman and the abject, and more preoccupied with the exclusion and "othering" of actual (rather than outright fantastic) human bodies. The grotesque can be productively separated from other manifestations of body horror because its "monstrous" bodies are intelligibly human, their "otherness" a gross extension or exaggeration of the normative body. In this respect, I follow Justin D. Edwards and Rune

Graulund's understanding of the grotesque as combining the horrific and the comic in its portrayal of the "[p]eculiar, odd, absurd, bizarre, macabre, depraved, degenerate [and] perverse" body (1). Crucially, this literary mode is not predestined to the reproduction of ideological codes that continue to "other" and "uglify" (even "monsterize") certain bodies, but can offer "a creative force for conceptualizing the indeterminate that is produced by distortion, and reflecting on the significance of the uncertainty that is thereby produced" (Edwards and Graulund, 3). Grotesques can become more than reverse images of oppression based on corporeal canons tainted by ableist, racist, gendered, and sexist biases. Their playfulness allows them to question and subvert the very registers used to "otherize."

In American body horror, the grotesque has primarily materialized in the Southern Gothic. In texts such as William Faulkner's "A Rose for Emily" (1930), Flannery O'Connor's *Wise Blood* (1952), and Cormac McCarthy's *Child of God* (1973), exceptional bodies (a mummified dwarf, a self-blinding preacher) and aberrant behaviors (necrophilia) are used to comment on the particular history of the South, especially how it has been shaped by religion, isolation, and the legacy of slavery.[4] Dunn's aforementioned *Geek Love*, whose traveling carnival members ruminate on their nature as "freaks," offers one of the most nuanced investigations of the grotesque outside this tradition. It is also worth exploring in some detail because it epitomizes a problematic double-bind at play in horror texts that sensationalize unusual bodies, such as Tod Browning's controversial film *Freaks* (1932). *Geek Love* follows the lives and struggles of Arturo ("Arty"), Electra ("Elly"), Iphigenia ("Iphy"), Olympia ("Oly"), and Fortunato ("Chick"), all of whom are born with genetic alterations that manifest either physically or psychically. They are the result of drug experimentations and the consumption of radioactive material on the part of their parents, who deliberately attempted to create their own "freak show" once their initial business began to dry out. The novel follows their evolution into either acceptance or rejection of their own individual situations. For example, Arty evolves into a tyrannical messianic figure bent on revenge against the "norms" (nonfreaks) who have tyrannized him, but Oly has a child, Miranda, to whom she teaches self-acceptance. A metafictional passage where Arty explains to his sister why he finds horror and ghost stories edifying encapsulates the novel's self-reflective mood:

> "Those are written by norms to scare norms. And do you know what the monsters and rancid spirits are? Us, that's what. You and me. We are the things that come to norms in nightmares. The thing that lurks in the bell tower and bites out the throats of the choirboys – that's you, Oly. And the thing in the closet that makes the babies scream in the dark before it sucks their last

> breath – that's me. And the rustling in the brush and the strange piping cries that chill the spine on a deserted road at twilight – that's the twins singing practice scales while they look for berries.
>
> "Don't shake your head at me! These books teach me a lot. They don't scare me because they are about me." (52–53)

Geek Love raises important questions about the limits of body horror. Horror that exploits the grotesque necessarily imbricates itself within the oppressive corporeal regimes that produce particular bodies as undesirable, pitiable, or detestable. Dunn makes it difficult to imagine how it might be possible to produce any kind of critique of such pernicious socializing systems unless the grotesque itself is revealed to be constructed and problematically marginalizing. *Geek Love* ultimately reverses the operations of body horror: the freaks are not the monsters but those who have profited by parading the differently abled (the parents) or who have subjugated others due to jealousy (Miss Lick, a woman who purportedly sets other women free by mutilating them and thus liberating them from the constraints imposed by their beauty).[5] These amoral fetishists are the real nightmares attendant on the reader, as are the social and medical codes that prioritize and privilege certain bodies over others.

Finally, body horror can foreground the depiction of grievous bodily harm, spectacularizing brutal attacks on characters and presenting the effects of violence aesthetically or in minute detail. This type of visceral horror is the one usually described by the term "body horror" in popular culture, especially in the cinematic context. The term gained momentum in the field of film studies after the publication of a special issue of *Screen* in 1986 that contained a reprinting of a 1983 article in which Philip Brophy attempted to situate the specificity of contemporary horror and identified "the destruction of the Body" (8) as a prolific trend in the genre in the late 1970s and early 1980s. The issue also contained ground-breaking writings on body horror by Pete Boss and Barbara Creed ("Horror and the Monstrous-Feminine") that went some way toward legitimizing its value. According to John McCarty, one of the first critics to dedicate an entire book to "splatter movies," these films did not aim "to scare their audiences, necessarily, nor to drive them to the edge of their seats with suspense, but to *mortify* them with scenes of explicit gore" (8).[6] For him, films fixated on mutilation originated in the nightmares of the theater of the Grand Guignol, crystallized as discernible cinematic product through the oeuvre of American director Herschell Gordon Lewis, and were then popularized by the commercial success of *Night of the Living Dead* (1968). Medium differences aside, McCarty's definition applies quite comfortably to body horror novels. In them, the organizing principle is the prioritization of graphic descriptions of torture and death, with expository downtimes stringing along moments of carnage often told from the perspective of those being attacked. Characters act as literary proxies, describing what is happening to them in a manner that creates a shared sense of corporeal vulnerability and which can be compared to camera alignment with the victim in horror cinema. The shocking content of the splatter films of the late 1970s and early 1980s found an imaginative counterpart in certain novels of the 1980s horror boom. If body horror films were marked by innovative special effects, both realistic and histrionic, body horror novels emphasized innovative and elaborate accounts of pain and destruction.

The best exponent of the gore-filled end of body horror was "splatterpunk," a short-lived movement that could be said to have stretched from the publication of Clive Barker's *Books of Blood* in the United States in 1986, also the year the term was coined by author David J. Schow at the Twelfth World Fantasy Convention, to the mid-1990s, when the paperback horror market ground to a halt. Splatterpunk came to designate an intense and hyperviolent form of horror fiction that prioritized gross-out and humor. In his introduction to *Splatterpunks: Extreme Horror*, editor Paul M. Sammon described the stories in the anthology as "know[ing] no restraints, bow[ing] to no god, recogniz[ing] no boundaries" (xv). Despite this pledge to out-of-bounds freedom and its celebration of "schlock" (the book is dedicated "to bad taste"), Sammon was also careful to emphasize that splatterpunk could move beyond initial "shock value" and was capable of offering "harrowing insights into our own sick and shining twentieth century" (xv). The inclusive or progressive nature of the novels of its associated acts – Schow, John Skipp, Craig Spector, Joe R. Lansdale, or Ray Garton – has since been called into question (Hendrix, 197), but the writers' provocative, playful, and anarchic spirit seems incontrovertible. In novels such as *The Scream* (1987) and *The Kill Riff* (1988), the "punk" attitude of the movement is literalized, with members of rock-and-roll bands as the protagonists. However, the lack of thematic specificity or any other common aspects beyond explicitness means that it is actually quite difficult to separate self-avowed splatterpunk from other extreme offerings of the period. For example, Gregory A. Douglas' *The Nest* (1980) is as radical and outlandish in its description of people being eaten alive by gigantic mutated cockroaches as Joe R. Lansdale's *The Nightrunners* (1987), a novel about gang rape and home invasion linked to splatterpunk in 1988 by Lawrence Pearson. Yet *The Nest* clearly belongs to the "animal attack" subgenre popularized in the previous decade by James Herbert's *The Rats* (1974) and Peter Benchley's *Jaws* (1974).

In the 1990s, some literary and crossover writers, like Bret Easton Ellis, Joyce Carol Oates, Dennis Cooper, and Poppy Z. Brite, would indulge in similar scenarios of gruesome violence through the figure of the serial killer, whose tell-tale egotism, sadism, and inhumanity acted as a mouthpiece for the injustices of late capitalism and modern America. *American Psycho* (1991) is a powerful indictment of late 1980s yuppie culture, its Wall Street investment banker Patrick Bateman, who may be either really or only imagining the murders of prostitutes and colleagues, an avatar of the self-centered free market entrepreneur consumed by brands and power. Novels such as Cooper's *Frisk* (1991), Oates' *Zombie* (1995), and Brite's *Exquisite Corpse* (1996) are also more than mere explorations of troubled psychologies and the depravity of which humans are capable. In these texts, the lobotomies, tortures, and dismemberments practiced on gay lovers stand as a curious study of the difficulty of establishing fulfilling sexual relationships and queer intimacy in an overwhelmingly heterosexual world. Serial killer texts had dramatically changed with the publication of Thomas Harris' Hannibal Lecter novels, especially with *The Silence of the Lambs* (1988), which won two major horror prizes and whose significance only grew after its 1991 film adaptation won five Academy Awards.[7] The gritty, bottom-feeder sociopath would be replaced by the refined intellectual who plots complex revenge schemes and whose sympathy could be articulated by virtue of his often being pitted against more morally objectionable individuals.[8] In fact, as Philip L. Simpson has argued, it is possible to read serial killers as the monster du jour of the 1980s and 1990s (2) and as a recognizable American product that illustrates the country's obsession with, in Mark Seltzer's words, "shock, trauma, and the wound" (1). Naturally, not all serial killer texts propose postmodern ethical reflections or provide radical national self-assessments, but many have indeed taken issue with the perceived irregularity of the psychopath's mind and blurred the boundaries between reality and fiction.[9]

In recent years, the zombie has competed with the serial killer for the spot of body horror's most prevalent and consistent manifestation. In the 1980s and 1990s, a number of authors had already taken their cues from George A. Romero's *Night of the Living Dead* and foregrounded the violent cannibalistic spectacle of its brain-munching monsters (Boon). Yet the publication of Robert Kirkman's *The Walking Dead* (2013–19) comics certainly bookended a period of intensive production that saw even a big stalwart like Stephen King pen his own zombie effort, *Cell* (2006). Some of the novels published during this period, such as Max Brooks' *World War Z: An Oral History of the Zombie War* (2006) and M. R. Carey's *The Girl with All the Gifts* (2014), crossed into the mainstream and were also adapted into major films. A syncretic reading of the very dispersed texts that constitute this contemporary phenomenon must encompass other media, like television and video games, but the ubiquity of zombies is necessarily connected to their capacity to channel a plurality of cultural anxieties. Some of these include marginalization, in novels like Daniel Waters' *Generation Dead* (2008), S. G. Browne's *Breathers: A Zombie Lament* (2009), and Corey Redekop's *Husk* (2012); outbreak panic, in Z. A. Recht's *Plague of the Dead* (2006) and Mira Grant's *Feed* (2010); and post-apocalyptic civilizational breakdown (and sometimes reconstruction), in Alden Bell's *The Reapers Are the Angels* (2010) and Colson Whitehead's *Zone One* (2011). The abject corporeality of zombies, always decomposing and potentially contagious, makes them ideal figures through which to explore the fears covered in this chapter (invasion, infection, the grotesque), but also other more positive concepts like compassion and tolerance. This is especially the case with "sympathetic" zombies, who are mournfully sentient and can sometimes be loved back to life (Aldana Reyes, "Contemporary Zombies," 95–100). Through these mindless hive monsters and shuffling memento mori, contemporary body horror continues to explore some of its most persistent areas of interest: the body's social inscription, its vulnerability to attack, and its position in an increasingly commodified age that privileges surface and immediacy. The subgenre's concerns are sure to become ever more relevant in a post–COVID world traumatized by speedy contagion, human contact, and crowd control.

NOTES

1. My point is that, even when the horror subgenre might not be particularly corporeal, as in occult horror or the ghost story, the safety of the characters and the body's vulnerability remain a constant.
2. Another great source of the type of categorical horror channeled by the abhuman is the shape-shifting corporeality of the monster in Richard Marsh's *The Beetle: A Mystery* (1897), which amalgamates insect and human, male and female.
3. It could be argued that, since the Beast Folk are animals, Prendick's apprehension is simply instinctive: his body is responding to predatory threat. Given the novel's emphasis on atavism, however, it is also necessary to read this hostility as inherently attached to notions of the normative body. The abhuman is horrific because it questions the purity, primacy, and uniqueness of the human as conceptual construct.
4. For more on all these aspects of the Southern Gothic, see the various chapters in Castillo Street and Crow.
5. Miss Lick's real intent is revealed to be a lot more selfish and cruel.
6. I use the terms "splatter" and "gore" indistinctively, although I want to acknowledge that, for some, the latter term may indicate an even more explicit type of body horror.
7. It has even been argued that Harris' novel and its adaptation are responsible for a shift in the marketing of some horror novels, which began to be sold as thrillers (Hendrix, 210).

8. This is especially the case in Jeff Lindsay's "Dexter Morgan" novels (2004–15), whose main serial killer follows the "Code of Harry," a series of rules that morally justify his actions.
9. Bret Easton Ellis purportedly researched real murders when writing *American Psycho*; *Zombie* is based on the life of Jeffrey Dahmer; and *Exquisite Corpse* was inspired by Dahmer and Dennis Nilsen.

Works Cited

Aldana Reyes, Xavier. "Abjection and Body Horror." In *The Palgrave Handbook of Contemporary Gothic*, ed. Clive Bloom. Basingstoke: Palgrave Macmillan, 2020. 393–410.

"Contemporary Zombies." In *Twenty-First-Century Gothic: An Edinburgh Companion*, ed. Maisha Wester and Xavier Aldana Reyes. Edinburgh: Edinburgh University Press, 2019. 89–10.

"Introduction: What, Why and When Is Horror Fiction?" In *Horror: A Literary History*, ed. Xavier Aldana Reyes. London: British Library Publishing, 2016. 7–17.

Boon, Kevin Alexander. "Trailing the Zombie through Modern and Contemporary Anglophone Literature." In *The Written Dead: Essays on the Literary Zombie*, ed. Kyle William Bishop and Angela Tenga. Jefferson, NC: McFarland, 2017. 15–26.

Boss, Pete. "Vile Bodies and Bad Medicine." *Screen* 27, no. 1 (1986): 14–25.

Bourke, Joanna. *Fear: A Cultural History*. London: Virago Press, 2005.

Brophy, Philip. "Horrality – The Textuality of Contemporary Horror Films." *Screen* 27, no. 1 (1986): 2–13.

Campbell, John W. *Who Goes There?* London: Gollancz, 2011.

Castillo Street, Susan, and Charles L. Crow, eds. *The Palgrave Handbook of the Southern Gothic*. Basingstoke: Palgrave Macmillan, 2016.

Creed, Barbara. "Horror and the Monstrous-Feminine – An Imaginary Abjection." *Screen* 27, no. 1 (1986): 44–70.

The Monstrous-Feminine: Film, Feminism, Psychoanalysis. London: Routledge, 1993.

Douglas, Mary. *Purity and Danger: An Analysis of Concepts of Pollution and Taboo*. London: Routledge and Kegan Paul, 1966.

Dunn, Katherine. *Geek Love*. London: Abacus, 2012.

Edwards, Justin D., and Rune Graulund. *Grotesque*. Abingdon: Routledge, 2013.

Finney, Jack. *The Body Snatchers*. London: Gollancz, 2010.

Hendrix, Grady. *Paperbacks from Hell: The Twisted History of '70s and '80s Horror Fiction*. Philadelphia: Quirk Books, 2017.

Hurley, Kelly. *The Gothic Body: Sexuality, Materialism, and Degeneration at the* fin de siecle. Cambridge: Cambridge University Press, 1996.

Kristeva, Julia. *Powers of Horror: An Essay on Abjection*, trans. Leon S. Roudiez. New York: Columbia University Press, 1982.

Lloyd-Smith, Allan. *American Gothic Fiction: An Introduction*. London: Continuum, 2004.

Lovecraft, H. P. *The Call of Cthulhu and Other Weird Stories*. London: Penguin, 2002.

Matheson, Richard. *I Am Legend*. London: Gollancz, 2010.
McCarty, John. *Splatter Movies: Breaking the Last Taboo*. New York: Fantaco Enterprises, 1981.
Pearson, Lawrence. "The Splatterpunks: The Young Turks at Horror's Cutting Edge." *Nova Express* 2, no. 1 (1988): n.p. Available at RobertMcCammon.com, www.robertmccammon.com/splatterpunks/splatter-2.html. Accessed January 21, 2020.
Poe, Edgar Allan. *Poetry, Tales, and Selected Essays*. New York: Library of America, 1996.
Russo, Mary. *The Female Grotesque: Risk, Excess and Modernity*. Abingdon: Routledge, 1994.
Sammon, Paul M. "Introduction." In *Splatterpunks: Extreme Horror*, ed. Paul M. Sammon. London: Xanadu Publications, 1990. xv–xvi.
Seltzer, Mark. *Serial Killers: Death and Life in America's Wound Culture*. New York: Routledge, 1998.
Simpson, Philip L. *Psycho Paths: Tracking the Serial Killer through Contemporary American Film and Fiction*. Carbondale: Southern Illinois University Press, 2000.
Wald, Priscilla. *Contagious: Cultures, Carriers, and the Outbreak Narrative*. Durham, NC: Duke University Press, 2008.
Wells, H. G. *The Island of Doctor Moreau*. London: Penguin, 2005.

8

LAURA WESTENGARD

Queer Horror

In "On the Supernatural in Poetry" (1826), Gothic author Ann Radcliffe established a famous binary by distinguishing between terror and horror. "Terror and horror are so far opposite," she writes, "that the first expands the soul, and awakens the faculties to a high degree of life; the other contracts, freezes, and nearly annihilates them" (149). Horror confuses and confounds while terror leaves something to the imagination, remains mysterious and obscure, and thereby lends itself to the experience of the Burkean sublime, a "tranquility tinged with terror" (Radcliffe, 149). In the centuries following Radcliffe's musings, horror has come to be associated with those works penned by men, and terror with those penned by women. This was in part due to the influence of Radcliffe herself as a writer of Gothic romances such as *The Mysteries of Udolpho* (1794) and *The Italian* (1797), which deploy the restraint of terror via a series of apparently supernatural events that are explained away by the end of the novel. Conversely, Matthew Lewis' Gothic novel, *The Monk* (1796), creates the annihilating spectacle of horror via demonic manipulations, sadistic and sexual violence, and scenes of bodily suffering and decay. American Gothic author Charles Brockden Brown reinforces the presumptive superiority of the "terrific style," for which Radcliffe set a standard of "true genius" while her "ordinary" imitators "endeavour to keep the reader in a constant state of tumult and *horror*, by the powerful engines of trap-doors, back stairs, black robes, and pale faces" (288; my emphasis). However, Gothic fiction, the genre to which Radcliffe's binary has most frequently been applied, is characterized in part by its very disruption of binaries.

Contemporary horror connoisseurs will recognize both of the experiences that Radcliffe describes – shocking, visceral confusion and cautious, imaginative intrigue – as features of the horror genre as well. The horror/terror divide is, perhaps, not as distinct a polarity as Radcliffe implies since both often appear in the same text and work synergistically to create heightened responses that cannot be clearly parsed. Similarly, the gender binary established in relation to the horror/terror divide does not hold, since creators and consumers of the Gothic occupy complex subject positions that cannot be contained by an oversimplified gender schema not accounting for queerness, race, class, or any other number of intersecting categories. In *Queer Gothic*, George Haggerty explains that the Gothic emerged at a time in which "gender and sexuality were beginning to be codified for modern culture" and functioned as a "testing ground for many unauthorized genders and sexualities" (2). "Transgressive social-sexual relations," he explains, "are the most basic common denominator" of Gothic texts and metaphors, marking the genre as queer (2). Max Fincher extends the reading of Gothic queerness to its form, explaining that "we can read Gothic writing at the level of narrative as intimately related to the 'perverse' or 'wayward.' Gothic stories never follow a 'straight' course, a fact that in itself makes them queer" (4).

Once a derogatory term for homosexuality, "queer" has shifted in meaning since the 1990s when, in response to the AIDS crisis, some in the lesbian, gay, bisexual, and transgender (LGBT) communities began reappropriating the term "queer" as an umbrella term indicating membership in the LGBT community as well as a "range of nonnormative sexual practices and gender identifications beyond gay and lesbian" (Love, 172). In addition to more well-defined genders or sexual orientations, "queer" offers a term to represent those with fluid and expansive relationships to gender and/or sexuality not fully represented by the LGBT moniker. Further, the term's roots in politicized reappropriation also hold a valence as "resistance to regimes of the normal" more broadly (Warner, 16). Nonnormative genders and sexualities circulate throughout the Gothic, but the mere existence of formal and sexual transgression does not mean that the Gothic always condones queerness. In fact, the use of Gothic horror metaphors such as monsters, vampires, ghosts, and the undead to represent queer ways of being has long been a conservative strategy for marginalizing those who do not conform to the norm.

Gothic fiction was a popular genre that emerged in eighteenth-century England with the publication of Horace Walpole's *The Castle of Otranto* (1764), a novel that included the supernatural, monstrosity, haunting, familial curses, paranoia, subterranean passages, medieval Catholicism, and sexualized power dynamics represented by a vulnerable woman being victimized by a rapacious patriarch. By the nineteenth century, Gothic novels such as Mary Shelley's *Frankenstein* (1818) and Robert Louis Stevenson's *The Strange Case of Dr. Jekyll and Mr. Hyde* (1886) became more concerned with the potential horrors of science and technology, while novels such as Bram Stoker's *Dracula* (1897), through the figure of the atavistic vampire who threatens to seduce and taint British womanhood, address anxieties around immigration and modern gender roles. At its core, the Gothic "may be loosely defined as the rhetorical style and narrative structure designed to produce fear and desire within the reader" by metaphorically representing anxieties and the fantasies, often simultaneously (Halberstam, 2). In the United States, for example, the Gothic emerges from the fears and anxieties arising out of the "frontier experience, with its inherent solitude and potential violence; the Puritan inheritance; fear of European subversion and anxieties about popular democracy which was then a new experiment; the relative absence of developed 'society'; and very significantly, racial issues concerning both slavery and the Native Americans" (Lloyd-Smith, 4). In other words, the Gothic is inherently shape-shifting, meaning that Gothic "metaphors and aesthetics can offer each generation of readers means for negotiating the complexities of anxiety and desire" in their own time and place (Westengard, 8).

This foundational indeterminacy, "structured so as to heighten this multiplicity of interpretive possibilities" (Haggerty, *Gothic Fiction*, 10), is a characteristic that often creates the affective experience of "a state of thrilling suspense and uncertainty" (Kilgour, *Rise of the Gothic Novel*, 6), a state with which horror consumers are certainly familiar. Indeed, the forms and functions of the Gothic map onto the horror genre in generative ways. For example, Ellen Moers describes the "female Gothic" as a narrative in which the "central figure is a young woman who is simultaneously persecuted victim and courageous heroine" (91). Carol Clover names a similar dynamic "the final girl" motif, a feature of many horror films that conclude with a surviving "female victim-hero" (4). Unlike Moers, however, Clover emphasizes the disruption of gendered semiotics in horror, asserting that male audience members identify with the combination of "suffering victim and avenging hero" epitomized by the final girl (17). In other words, while Gothic tropes may have originated in the eighteenth and nineteenth centuries, Gothicism is not tied to any specific historical location or literary time period. The Gothic tropes, aesthetics, and metaphors that entered into the popular consciousness during a certain time period continue to function in similar and divergent ways in contemporary texts, including literature, popular culture, and visual media. While critics such as Radcliffe and Moers have set up binary distinctions such as horror/terror, male/female, victim/perpetrator, and mind/body, these distinctions seldom hold when it comes to both horror and the Gothic. This chapter will take as its foundational assumption that it is the very fluidity of distinction and the disruption of binary frameworks that characterizes queer horror. This is partially due to the fact that the Gothic – as well as its tropes, aesthetics, and metaphors that make their way into horror texts – is inherently queer. This chapter will examine the queer Gothicism of American horror to consider the ways in which marginalized genders and sexualities have either been condemned or covertly endorsed through horror's textual and visual mediums.

In mainstream cis-heteronormative society, queer genders and sexualities have been an abjectified, "horrific" presence, and these mainstream investments represented via horror, as a mode of expression devoted to irruptions of the body, mean that the presence of queerness is often registered as an a priori spoliation of bodily norms. Indeed, the narrative trajectory of most horror texts involves monstrous creatures threatening the status quo with their very existence before finally being destroyed. Horror, then, and its Gothic rhetoric and aesthetics, is a tautology – queer and horror collapse into each other in the public imagination. Monstrous figures become a representation of anything that is "other" – "deviant subjectivities opposite which the normal, the healthy, and the pure can be known" – and as such can stand in for anxieties around race, class, and ability in addition to gender and sexuality (Halberstam, 2). In Gothic horror, this othering often means that the monstrous figure is usually the antagonist, a villain who disrupts the norms established at the beginning of the narrative, terrorizes the protagonist, threatens their way of life (and often their life itself), and who is ultimately conquered for the sake of the "restoration of a norm, which after the experience of terror, now seems immensely desirable" (Kilgour, *Rise of the Gothic Novel*, 8). This general trajectory implies that any disruption of norms by social and cultural outsiders is a horrifying, threatening nightmare that must be destroyed for the sake of reinforcing the status quo.

This conservative mode, however, has always existed in tandem with queer counterstrategies of content creation and viewer identification. Horror and its subcultures have frequently been a means for these "villainous" identities to be represented as a form of resistant or alternative sociality. In *The Celluloid Closet* Vito Russo describes the counter-identificatory strategies of queer viewers of twentieth-century cinema, explaining that even though queerness was often coded as insanity, predation, and monstrosity, queers recognized and gravitated toward representation in film despite its consistent association with villainy and death. This is certainly true in the context of horror in which conservative Gothic metaphors represent queer "others" for the sake of marginalization and destruction, but queer consumers are still able to read queer coding, or the subtextual evocation of queerness that is generally used to signal danger or perversion, and thereby access representation despite its negative connotations.[1] Indeed, like the term "queer" itself, audiences have often reappropriated the Gothic figures that appear in horror, and some queer creators have intentionally deployed such

Gothicisms for the sake of representing queerness – from the ghostliness, monstrosity, and high camp in James Whale's *The Old Dark House* (1932) and *The Bride of Frankenstein* (1935) to the queer beefcake horror of David DeCoteau.[2] In the remainder of the chapter, I will explore the conflicting purposes of horror's depiction of queerness by reviewing several Gothic tropes as they appear in American horror texts, focusing specifically on monstrosity, vampirism, the asylum, medical body horror, and haunting.

Monstrosity, a Gothic trope that arguably originated with the entrance of a deadly giant knight in the first pages of *The Castle of Otranto*, figures prominently in horror, often with queer connotations. As a hybrid creature pieced together in a laboratory from both human and animal remains and birthed from the mind of an obsessive genius, Frankenstein's creature queers the concept of heteronormative reproduction as well as binary gender and the human/other divide. In *The Strange Case of Dr. Jekyll and Mr. Hyde*, Mr. Hyde's physiognomy is described as "troglodytic" and his nocturnal pleasures, never to be explicitly described, range from "undignified" to "monstrous" but are consistently aligned with the Victorian conflation of homosexuality with the unspeakable.[3] Vampires entered the popular consciousness with the publication of John Polidori's *The Vampyre* (1819), in which the "protagonist's 'coded' interest in a mysterious older man echoes the discursive production of 'homosexuality'" (Rigby, para. 3). Later, Sheridan Le Fanu's *Carmilla* (1872) would bring a lesbian valence to the vampire through Carmilla, a strange visitor who develops intense romantic connections with lonely and unsuspecting young women by sneaking into their rooms at night in the form of "a monstrous cat" to suck from their breasts. Directly influenced by the publication of *Carmilla*, Bram Stoker crafted the quintessential and perhaps most influential vampire in 1897.[4] Count Dracula, a powerfully wealthy, primitively feudal, and inscrutably foreign figure, threatens the norms of British sexuality when he decides to immigrate to England. His very presence is an unwanted and improper colonial penetration as he brings his "boxes of earth" from Transylvania into the center of the British Empire (Stoker, 81). Further, his desire to penetrate Jonathan Harker, Lucy, and Mina is a queer one, in terms of both their varied genders and his creation of new, unorthodox holes through which to consume their blood. Many theorists over the years have discussed Count Dracula's queer semiotics, often arguing as Carol Snef does that "his thirst for blood and the manner in which he satisfies this thirst can be interpreted as sexual desire which fails to observe any of society's attempts to control it – prohibitions against polygamy, promiscuity, and homosexuality" (428).[5] There is a long history of queer coding in monster and vampire figures, and that association continues into the American horror texts emerging in the twentieth and twenty-first centuries.

The Frankensteinian monster frequently stands in for transgender embodiment in the horror genre, and because of its widespread use to marginalize transgender characters for the sake of shoring up binary gender norms, monstrosity serves "widely divergent narratives of transphobic insult and trans* resistance alike" (Koch-Rein, 134). In films such as Alfred Hitchcock's *Psycho* (1960), Tobe Hooper's *The Texas Chain Saw Massacre* (1974), and Jonathan Demme's *The Silence of the Lambs* (1991), maniacally homicidal killers don the clothing and skin of dead women as a means of accessing alternate modes of gender expression. These films imply that gender transgression is not only motivation for violence but is itself an act so monstrous that it often supersedes the horror of the murders themselves. However, trans and gender nonconforming viewers can also potentially identify with the attribution of monstrosity in complex and redemptive ways. Anson Koch-Rein explains the tension between critique of monstrosity as a transgender signifier and the reclamation of the monstrous figure for trans uses:

> In a world where the monster is circulating as metaphoric violence against trans* people, reclaiming such a figure faces the difficulty of formulating resistance in the same metaphorical language as the transphobic attack. Moreover, as a figure of difference, the monster appears in racist, ableist, homophobic, and sexist discourses, making its use especially fraught. Still, we cannot simply dismiss the monster for its history or injurious potential. It is precisely the monster's ambivalent ability to speak to oppression and negative affect that appeals to trans* people reclaiming the monster for their own voices. (134)

In this sense, the monstrosity that resonates with trans audiences stems in part from the horrors of compulsory gender norms and the violence of their social, medical, and legal policing. Transgender studies scholar Susan Stryker theorizes the power of the monster as both identity and tool, explaining, "I want to lay claim to the dark power of my monstrous identity without using it as a weapon against others or being wounded by it myself." By "embracing and accepting" words such as "creature," "monster," and "unnatural," she continues, "we may dispel their ability to harm us" (240).

Jim Sharman's *The Rocky Horror Picture Show* (1975) (based on Richard O'Brien's stage cabaret) recirculates Frankensteinian monstrosity with a decidedly queer and campy bent. The film follows the sexual awakening of Brad and Janet, just-married virgins from the Midwest, as they find themselves in a Gothic castle inhabited by Dr. Frank-N-Furter, a scientist who has created a creature named Rocky to serve as a sexual plaything. The film advances an intentionally topsy-turvy worldview in which all that was normative in 1970s culture is cast as disdainful, and the subversive, the strange, and the queer rule the day. In their study on the sociology of cult films, Kinkade and Katovich explain that the film "offers a pessimistic world view that appeals to postmodern sensibilities in the nuclear age. Its vilification of institutions, degradation of heterosexual romance, and its reflexive critique of its own production (in which the audience participates) make Rocky Horror a unique document" (203). Beyond simply unique, I would add, the upending of norms marks the film's overall value system as decidedly queer. Dr. Frank-N-Furter's relationship with his creation exemplifies this since Rocky is not the hideous wretch of Shelley's *Frankenstein* but a gloriously sexy beefcake, and Dr. Frank-N-Furter himself, as he reveals his penchant for women's lingerie and explains that he is "a sweet transvestite from Transexual, Transylvania," aligns with the common horror trope figuring gender nonconformity as monstrosity.[6] Of course, in this context the monstrosity of gender transgression is desirable rather than horrifying, and queer fans have identified with and embodied Frank-N-Furter in midnight showings around the world by dressing as him (and other characters) and pantomiming scenes as they occur on the screen. The problematic transgender/monstrous affiliation still stands – especially since Frank-N-Furter turns out to be (spoiler alert) a homicidal cannibal alien and is destroyed in the end – but that has not stopped queer audiences from seeing representation, empowerment, and community in his depiction and in the film as a whole. As Judith Peraino explains, "at the height of the movie's cult popularity in the early 1980s, city dwellers and suburbanites, gays and straights, participated together in a ritualistic celebration of unfettered and undefined sexuality" (234). *Rocky Horror*'s brand of participatory Gothic queer horror has been a touchstone of queer community building.

In a more recent take on monstrosity and gender nonconformity, Ari Aster's 2018 film *Hereditary* depicts a young girl named Charlie who is a host to the spirit of a demon named Paimon. However, Paimon's gendered essence aligns more with the physiological markers of masculinity than with those associated with Charlie's body. As a result, Charlie is decapitated early in the film so that Paimon may systematically inhabit a more appropriate body, that of Charlie's brother Peter. Sasha Geffen argues that this film represents anxieties around narratives of transgender transition in which cisgender folks feel threatened by the gender-affirming measures taken by trans folks. "*Hereditary*'s transition allegory," Geffen explains, "involves not only the violent death of a girl, but also the torture and eventual evacuation of a cis male body. Charlie does not merely change, but steals something that belongs to a man," and in this way, the film "employ[s] in reverse, a formula used by *Silence of the Lambs* and *Psycho*: One gender swirled up into another creates a monster" (paras. 9, 3). However, Geffen argues, some trans and gender nonconforming viewers also see their own experiences of gender dysphoria in the narrative of Paimon's deeply "gendered spirit" searching for a physical body that feels more appropriate (para. 12). Like the ambiguous portrayal of gender transgression in *Rocky Horror*, the demonic monstrosity of *Hereditary* can be read both as a transphobic narrative of body theft and as an affirmation of gender that exists beyond its physical manifestation. In her examination of the intersection of queer desire, trans embodiment, and monstrosity, Ana Valens explains the attraction of monstrosity: "we see our queer selves in monsters. We see the queer bodies we desire in their beautiful grotesqueness. We see the narratives that define our queer lives. There's no better role model for the transgressive queer than the fantastical beasts of our collective imaginations" (para. 5). The expansiveness that monstrosity represents – around concepts of gender, sexuality, and humanity – makes it a Gothic trope that resonates with horror fans for contradictory reasons, eliciting simultaneous fear and desire as well as imaginative possibility.

As a specific type of monster, the vampire also appears in horror texts as a representation of sexual and gendered others. Unlike Frankensteinian monsters, however, the vampire has become an increasingly glamourous figure of sexualized power and freedom; Anne Rice's *Vampire Chronicles* (1976–2018), Stephenie Meyer's *Twilight Saga* (2005–20), and Charlaine Harris' *The Southern Vampire Mysteries* (2001–13) circulate around individualistic identity within a neoliberal worldview in which the discovery and eventual acceptance of one's vampire lifestyle – coming "out of the coffin" – represents "liberation from the fear and terror generated by ignorance or outdated notions of sexuality" (Harris, 1; Day, 31). However, the fear and desire that vampires elicit relate to their taboo meal of choice – blood – as well as their method of consumption – penetration. The ingestion of blood from living humans means that vampires are cannibalistic monsters whose diet both threatens and challenges distinctions since cannibalism "depends upon and enforces an absolute division between inside and outside; but in the act itself that opposition disappears, dissolving the structure it appears to produce" (Kilgour, *From Communion*, 4). In other words, both cannibalism and vampirism demand and then collapse the distinction between eater and eaten as the ingested creature becomes part of the eater. This dizzying disruption of categories is both fascinating and repulsive, an experience of abjection that is familiar to horror connoisseurs.

The spectacle of the penetrated, oozing body is also one of the terrors of horror – often in the form of body horror that grotesquely disrupts distinctions between self and other, inside and outside. Partly because of the term's ability to elicit disgust, cannibalism has been a tool of power. Colonizers often labeled indigenous people as cannibals in order to justify territorial occupation and genocide, and they also used the label "sodomite" for the same purpose.[7] Jonathan Goldberg explains that sodomy, like cannibalism, "names something otherwise unnameable, something that goes beyond the evidentiary and the logical; it is a category of a violation that violates categories" (196–97). The unnatural penetration that constitutes the vampire's bite stands in for queer sexualities, making vampires, like cannibals and sodomites, aligned with the violation of taboos and norms. Kelly Hurley describes the Gothic fixation with the ruination of the human body, or the "abhuman subject" which is a "not-quite-human subject, characterized by its morphic variability, continually in danger of becoming not-itself, becoming other" (*Gothic Body*, 3–4). The dual nature of this fascination reflects the conflicting purposes of queer Gothic horror more broadly: "The prefix 'ab-' signals a movement away from a site or condition, and thus a loss. But a movement away from is also a movement towards – towards a site or condition as yet unspecified – and thus entails both a threat and a promise" (4). Shape-shifting vampires, as well as their victims, are always in danger of uncanny corporeal collapse or eruption. Bram Stoker's Count Dracula is among these abhuman "interstitial creatures" because he is "Nosferatu, or Undead: living and not living, aglow with a horrible ruddy vitality, and yet stinking of the charnel house" (Hurley, *Gothic Body*, 24). As with the Frankensteinian monster, the vampiric, cannibalistic, sodomical monster queers normativity in a spectacle of nauseating corporeal decay paired with a "certain gleefulness at the prospect of a world in which no fixity remains, only an endless series of monstrous becomings" (28).

In her later exploration of body horror films such as *Alien* (1979) and *Rabid* (1977), Hurley explains that the "narrative told by body horror again and again is of a human subject dismantled and demolished: a human body whose integrity is violated, a human identity whose boundaries are breached from all sides" ("Reading like an Alien," 205). Where perverse, violating appetites are concerned, queer horror can be found, whether it is in vampire texts such as Tony Scott's *The Hunger* (1983) or those that more explicitly merge vampirism with cannibalism, such as Antonia Bird's *Ravenous* (1999). In *The Hunger*, queerness in the form of bisexuality constitutes an explicit element of the plot. The opening sequence introduces Miriam and John, an apparently heterosexual couple lurking in an underground Manhattan club to the tune of Bauhaus' "Bela Lugosi's Dead." Once they stalk, seduce, and consume their victims in a deadly *ménage á quatre*, however, their queerness and vampirism come into focus. Later, Miriam seduces young gerontologist Dr. Sarah Roberts in order to replace the rapidly aging John with Sarah as Miriam's new eternal (lesbian) partner. The erotic encounter not only challenges Sarah's apparent heterosexuality, but breaches her body and identity from within as we watch her frantically grapple with her drastically shifting appetites. From its opening scene to its casting of David Bowie as John to its spectacular treatment of decaying opulence, *The Hunger* celebrates Goth(ic) subculture, queer sex, and alternate ways of living and dying while centering the "dismantled and demolished" body ravished by vampiric penetration.

Ravenous, however, is a story of homosocial normativity gone awry, less of a queer celebration than a cautionary tale. A tongue-in-cheek Western horror film, *Ravenous* is set in a remote California fort in the 1840s whose inhabitants encounter a desperate man and his story of Donner party–esque survival cannibalism. The film indulges in gory depictions of cannibalistic incorporation as the characters become increasingly tempted by the power and energy they gain from consuming the bodies of others. Simultaneously, the homosociality of the film slips increasingly into queer-coded tableaus of sexuality, romance, and kinship. In a scene of homosexual panic, a search party sets out to rescue the remaining members of the stranded survival cannibals, and the soft-spoken Private Toffler, who had earlier sustained a deep wound on his abdomen, awakens screaming, "He was licking me ... sick man outside!" to which the assailant replies, "It's not what you think. I was having a nightmare.... I awoke. I was on top of him ... my lips were on his wound." It is unclear whether Toffler's greater horror lies with the act of cannibalism or the erotic implications of having his oozing and bloody wound licked by another man. The cannibal is revealed as Colonel Ives, a man who has discovered that cannibalism provides him with a kind of vampiristic quality – the ability to incorporate the vitality of those he consumes and to heal from mortal wounds. He decides to create a new kind of family, a queer kinship structure in which several of the men at the fort would join him in his uncontrollable cannibalistic appetites while establishing a sustainable and reliable vampire lifestyle at the fort. Captain John Boyd gives in to Ives' plan for a while but later resists, and we watch as they fight to the death. The film concludes with an unmistakably romantic tableau as Ives and Boyd are caught together face to face in a bear trap, mutually perishing in an eternal embrace. From homosexual panic to queer alternate lifestyles, *Ravenous* uses the collapse of cannibalism and vampirism to figure the threat of masculine homosociality collapsing into queer ways of being. The film's poster proclaims, "You are who you eat," and it is this very disruption that rests at the heart of the horrors of cannibalism, vampirism, and the queerness they imply.

Another Gothic trope that frequently appears in contemporary horror involves the threat of institutionalization in an asylum and the culturally contingent definitions of sanity deployed to pathologize difference. Eighteenth-century Gothic fiction introduced the threat of involuntary institutionalization within the walls of the convent where one was subject to the rules and (often sadistic) caprices of those in power. With the rise in scientific and medical discourse in the nineteenth and early twentieth centuries, the locus of institutional, top-down control shifted from the convent to the asylum. Hurley argues that nineteenth-century medical discourse itself was indebted to the Gothic that came before it, meaning "scientific disciplines like sexology, which sought to fix the meanings of human identity" contained Gothicism, and Gothic fiction incorporated new discourses emerging from science and medicine in a reciprocal relationship (*Gothic Body*, 9). The "province of the nineteenth-century human sciences," Hurley explains, "was after all very like that of the earlier Gothic novel: the pre-Victorian Gothic provided a space wherein to explore phenomena at the borders of human identity and culture – insanity, criminality, barbarity, sexual perversion – precisely those phenomena that would come under the purview of social medicine in later decades" (5–6). The resulting cultural productions such as Edgar Allan Poe's "The System of Doctor Tarr and Professor Fether" (1845) incorporate a kind of medicalized Gothic horror depicting the vulnerable body under institutional control as well as the dehumanizing bureaucracies that can arise out of scientific and medical theories.

Two contemporary examples of medical queer horror can be found in Ryan Murphy's Netflix series *Ratched* (2020) and Tina Horn's queer dystopian comic book series *SfSx (Safe Sex)* (2019–21). *Ratched* is the backstory to Nurse Mildred Ratched's character from Ken Kesey's novel *One Flew over the Cuckoo's Nest* (1962) in which she serves as the face of the mental institution where McMurphy is committed. After an extended battle for power – and McMurphy might argue the battle for his humanity in a context designed to erase individuality and nonconformity – Ratched wields her institutional power to have McMurphy lobotomized. Sarah Paulson's 2020 version of Nurse Ratched is cold, manipulative, and monstrous, fitting perfectly in the vein of those sadistic monks and abbesses of eighteenth-century Gothic convents. Notably, Nurse Ratched is also a lesbian. In a nod to the cinematic history of the treatment of lesbians as unhinged, obsessive, (often vampiric) fiends, Nurse Ratched's queerness paired with her icy, calculating demeanor certainly evokes queer-coded figures such as Countess Marya Zaleska in Lambert Hillyer's *Dracula's Daughter* (1936), Mrs.

Danvers in Alfred Hitchcock's *Rebecca* (1940), Miss Holloway in Lewis Allen's *The Uninvited* (1944), and of course Miriam in *The Hunger*. The controlled and withholding demeanor of these characters is distinctly at odds with their unorthodox and uncontrollable appetites, making them uncanny figures. Sigmund Freud writes that the uncanny is an uneasy feeling that occurs when something that "ought to have remained secret ... has come to light," creating a sense that something once familiar and knowable has become strange (225). Uncanny figures in horror are perhaps the most frightening because they seem familiar and are even invited into the narrative, but eventually their hidden desires come to light, shifting our understanding and giving us "that weird feeling," to quote a promotional poster for *Dracula's Daughter*. Like its Gothic predecessors, the appearance and eventual destruction of the uncanny lesbian figure in twentieth-century horror cinema "generally titillates audiences with transgression and then returns to the comfort of normative values in the end" (Westengard, 13).

The queer coding of the uncanny lesbian comes together in *Ratched* with a specifically medical form of institutional power and the horror of the vulnerable body, penetrated and desecrated either intentionally or by indifference or human error. As in the finale of Kesey's novel, Nurse Ratched is fond of the lobotomy as a tool to further her purposes. The "Ice Pick" episode features several scenes of experimental lobotomies being demonstrated in the medical theater for the "cure" of conditions such as "juvenile distraction, mania, memory loss, [and] lesbianism." While Nurse Ratched eventually realizes that she, as a lesbian herself, could be subject to this inhumane procedure, she is immediately fascinated by the ease of erasing both memory and personality by inserting an ice pick through the orbital cavity to scramble the brain's frontal lobe. We see her apply this skill with a hotel room ice pick upon a person whom she wishes to silence. This scene combines the horror of a medical procedure developed to erase all forms of nonnormativity with the queasy crunch of its misapplication in the hands of one using it as a tool to access unfettered power and control. Nurse Ratched's explicit lesbianism provides some dimensionality to a classically evil character and has the potential to disrupt the historic queer coding of lesbians as perverse and uncanny. However, adding an explicit lesbian backstory in order to explain Nurse Ratched's heartless acts while still reveling in their institutional and corporeal horrors does more to replicate than to disrupt the association of queerness with depravity and sadistic appetites.

The comic book series *SfSx (Safe Sex)* integrates the themes of institutional Gothic horror with intersectional complexity and nuance and provides an example of how contemporary horror might utilize the queerness inherent in

Gothic tropes to challenge and remix their potentially problematic and conservative histories. The dystopian series includes elements of horror – torture, gore, frantic pursuit – set in a near-future "draconian America where sexuality is strictly bureaucratized and policed" following an "ongoing takeover of American civil life by the ultra-conservative religious organization known as the Party" (Horn, back cover, 1). The creators tellingly define dystopia as "institutional horror," characterized by oppression and control via tedium, surveillance, and red tape so that its depiction is simultaneously "vivid and upsetting and mundane" (Hickman, 24).[8] For example, the Party gives citizens a "purity score" maintained by filing paperwork every time they have sex, and all sex toys, pornography, and kink-related materials are strictly prohibited. Notably, the series flips traditional Gothic horror tropes by framing the members of the sexual and racial underclass – queer people, sex workers, and members of the kink and leather communities – as heroes rather than villains. These characters employ superhero-level power merely by turning to their subcultural skill sets as they fight for their right to express nonnormative genders and sexualities as well as to form communities and friendships around those queer preferences. Like Nurse Ratched, Party leader Judy Boreman self-righteously and cold-heartedly pursues her agenda in the form of the "reformation program," which kidnaps and tortures those who commit "self-objectification, deviance, exploitation, pandering, and perverting others against God's law" (Horn, issue 1, 3). Rather than lobotomies, however, Boreman's program has developed a variety of technologies to mutilate and reprogram queer bodies and desires, including tattoo removal, genital electrocution, urethral sounding, and device implantation. The series depicts these medicalized torture tactics in all of their gory, visceral detail, driving home the materially destructive power of repressive regimes and giving readers a taste of body horror along with the bureaucratic horrors of its dystopian world.

In addition to the violation of vulnerable bodies by a sadistic agent of an all-powerful, government-sanctioned institution, another particularly Gothic element of this series is its depiction of ghostly, subterranean spaces as both subcultural location and site of physical reclamation. The heroes of the story work and play at an underground collective and sex club called The Dirty Mind. After the Party raids The Dirty Mind, it turns the club's space into the center of its operations, and the underground club goes more deeply (and literally) underground, relocating to the cavernous, abandoned underground chambers of a "blighted bathhouse" (Horn, issue 2, 4). Bathhouses, it should be noted, are historic sites of queer cruising and public sex that were largely shut down during the panic around HIV in the 1980s.[9] While ghosts in Gothic novels such as *The Castle of Otranto* are often ancestral ghosts of the patriarchy emerging to warn of the effects of impropriety and to reestablish order, the superhero sex workers of *SfSx* function as the ghosts of past freedom haunting and disrupting the machinery of fascism. The Party colonizes the club's old space, but the ghosts of The Dirty Mind linger, haunting both the subterranean "blighted bathhouse" and the halls of their past home, now a site of surveillance, torture, and control, as they use their queer ancestral knowledge of the building and its new inhabitants to infiltrate its underground passages and rescue those being tortured there. Paulina Palmer notes that the "spectre and phantom," as "key signifiers of the uncanny, carry connotations of 'excess' since their appearance exceeds the material, and this is another concept that connects the uncanny with 'queer'" (7). In the horrifically mundane world of *SfSx*, the surface houses the state-sanctioned corrective torture of queer bodies, and in the subterranean passages and corridors, the queer heroes are sites of excess because they linger beyond their "appropriate" time, becoming powerful specters, making the space they haunt uncanny, and promoting the messiness of antinormativity by attacking the machinery of oppression and control.

Ghosts also appear in less institutional settings, most famously in the domestic sphere of the haunted house. Shirley Jackson's Gothic horror novel *The Haunting of Hill House* (1959) tells the story of Eleanor Vance, a woman who is prone to fantasy and magical thinking and whose sickly and demanding mother has just passed away, leaving her to find her way in the world now that she is no longer occupied by her all-encompassing role as caretaker. Unlike the institutional setting of the asylum or hospital, Eleanor's journey of haunting seems to begin once she steps away from the medicalized space of long-term care. However, Dr. John Montague invites Eleanor and a handful of others to participate in an experiment at a stately old mansion that is said to be haunted. In other words, Eleanor moves from the medicalized space of domestic caregiving and into another medicalized domestic space in which she is now the experimental subject. Eleanor quickly forms a bond with the modern, independent, probably psychic, and possibly lesbian Theodora. As the novel progresses, Eleanor's fascination with Theodora grows along with escalating paranormal occurrences that all seem to center around Eleanor. The confusion around her unacknowledged queer desires and the guilt around her mother's death seem to swirl together and erupt as externalized hauntings. As her grasp on reality loosens, collapse and confusion run rampant, and Eleanor's desire for Theodora becomes inextricable from her desire for her lost mother as well as the urge not simply to *have* Theodora but to *become* her. Additionally, her psyche becomes increasingly enmeshed with the house as a suffocating maternal entity, slowly enveloping Eleanor in its sticky folds.

Though the house does not, ultimately, collapse, there is an atmospheric nod to Poe's "The Fall of the House of Usher" (1839) as Eleanor, who is no longer in control of her own mind and actions, psychologically collapses under the weight of unspoken desires. In this text, the very concept of haunting is queered as the reader is left to question if it is the house or Eleanor herself who is haunted. If Eleanor is the true cause of the occurrences, then she epitomizes what Terry Castle calls the "ghost effect" of lesbian depiction in literature and culture (2). "The lesbian," she explains, "is never with us, it seems, but always somewhere else: in the shadows, in the margins, hidden from history, out of sight, out of mind, a wanderer in the dusk, a lost soul, a tragic mistake, a pale denizen of the night" (2). Eleanor seems to be there at times, but as the lesbian subtext develops, she shifts out of view, blending and melting away from subjecthood and merging with that which surrounds her – a fantasy, a friend, a lost mother, and ultimately Hill House itself.

Queer horror has seen many permutations across media and across centuries and its treatment of queerness has been variable, from the dehumanizing use of gender and sexual nonconformity as marks of deviance and monstrosity to more nuanced and empowering depictions and the murky spaces between. Regardless of the intention or mainstream reception of queer content and queer coding in horror, queer creators and consumers have often identified and embraced the presence of queerness through a kind of reclamatory, knowing, and empowered lens. This chapter has focused specifically on the use of tropes, metaphors, and aesthetics arising from eighteenth- and nineteenth-century Gothic fiction as they appear in American horror texts. I have argued that the Gothic is inherently queer, and because of this, much of the queer content in horror is conveyed through Gothic tropes. Starting with Radcliffe's early attempt to establish the binary distinction between horror and terror, people have attempted to parse notoriously complex and slippery genres into clear binaries. The Gothic, however, disrupts such neat distinctions, and in its queer "resistance to regimes of the normal" Gothicism circulates throughout American horror texts addressing sexual and gender nonnormativity.

NOTES

1. Scholar Heather Petrocelli is currently completing the "largest ever qualitative/quantitative study of the habits, tastes, and experiences of queer fans of horror film" and presented this research at the Gothic Manchester Festival Conference in 2019. The preliminary results indicate that 44.3 percent of queer viewers identify with both the monster and the victim in horror films.

2. The *Jeepers Creepers* films, as well as other horror films by gay director Victor Salva, are an example of a queer director's deployment of monstrosity to stand in for homoeroticism. However, Salva's documented history of child abuse shifts the reading of monstrous predation from one of potential reclamation to an eerie repetition of the conservative conflation of queerness with pedophilia. For more on DeCoteau and Salva, see Benshoff.
3. See Cocks.
4. Stoker's working papers indicate that he originally placed the Count in Styria, the same location in which *Carmilla* was set (see Frayling).
5. The *Norton Critical Edition of Dracula* includes several critical essays exploring the nonnormative sexuality and gender at work in the novel, including Christopher Craft's "'Kiss Me with Those Red Lips': Gender and Inversion in Bram Stoker's *Dracula*" and Talia Schaffer's "'A Wilde Desire Took Me': The Homoerotic History of *Dracula*."
6. While the LGBTQ+ community has largely moved away from the terms "transsexual" and "transvestite" in part due to their association with pathologizing medical discourse of the twentieth century, they were in wider circulation the 1970s when the movie was written and released. For more on these terms, see *TSQ: Transgender Studies Quarterly*'s issue on Postposttranssexual Key Concepts for a Twenty-First-Century Transgender Studies.
7. See Berglund; McClintock.
8. Horn and Hickman have also collaborated on a short story in the queer horror comic anthology, *Theater of Terror: Revenge of the Queers*.
9. For more on the "misguided witch hunts of AIDS hysteria," see Rubin (226).

Works Cited

Benshoff, Harry M. "'Way Too Gay to Be Ignored': The Production and Reception of Queer Horror Cinema in the Twenty-First Century." In *Speaking of Monsters: A Teratological Anthology*, ed. Caroline Joan S. Picart and John Edgar Browning. Palgrave Macmillan, 2012. 131–44.

Berglund, Jeff. *Cannibal Fictions: American Explorations of Colonialism, Race, Gender, and Sexuality*. University of Wisconsin Press, 2006.

Brown, Charles Brockden. "Terrific Novels." *The Literary Magazine, and American Register* 3, no. 19 (April 1805): 288–89.

Clover, Carol J. *Men, Women, and Chainsaws: Gender in the Modern Horror Film*. Princeton University Press, 1992.

Cocks, H. G. *Nameless Offences: Homosexual Desire in the Nineteenth Century*. I. B. Taurus, 2003.

Craft, Christopher. "'Kiss Me with Those Red Lips': Gender and Inversion in Bram Stoker's *Dracula*." In *Dracula: Norton Critical Edition*, ed. Nina Auerbach and David J. Skal. Norton, 1997. 444–59.

Currah, Paisley, and Susan Stryker, eds. Postposttranssexual Key Concepts for a Twenty-First-Century Transgender Studies, special issue of *TSQ: Transgender Studies Quarterly* 1, nos. 1–2 (2014).

Day, William Patrick. *Vampire Legends in Contemporary American Culture*. Lexington: University Press of Kentucky, 2002.

Dracula's Daughter. Directed by Lambert Hillyer. Universal Pictures, 1936.

Fincher, Max. *Queering Gothic in the Romantic Age: The Penetrating Eye*. Palgrave Macmillan, 2007.

Frayling, Christopher. "Bram Stoker's Working Papers for Dracula." In *Dracula: Norton Critical Edition*, ed. Nina Auerbach and David J. Skal. Norton, 1997. 339–50.

Freud, Sigmund. "The Uncanny." 1919. In *The Standard Edition of the Complete Psychological Works of Sigmund Freud*, vol. 17, ed. and trans. James Strachey. Hogarth Press, 1955. 219–56.

Geffen, Sasha. "Trans Horror Stories and Society's Fear of the Transmasculine Body." *Them*, August 21, 2018, www.them.us/story/transmasculine-horror-stories.

Goldberg, Jonathan. *Sodometries: Renaissance Texts, Modern Sexualities*. Fordham University Press, 2010.

Haggerty, George E. *Gothic Fiction/Gothic Form*. Pennsylvania State University Press, 1989.

Queer Gothic. University of Illinois Press, 2006.

Halberstam, Jack. *Skin Shows: Gothic Horror and the Technology of Monsters*. Duke University Press, 1995.

Hall, Justin, and William Tyler, eds. *Theater of Terror: Revenge of the Queers*. Northwest Press, 2019.

Harris, Charlaine. *Dead until Dark*. Ace Books, 2001.

Hickman, Jen. "Backpages." Interview by Tina Horn. In *SfSx (Safe Sex): Protection Arc*, vol. 1, no. 4. Image Comics, 2019. 24–25.

Horn, Tina, et al. *SfSx (Safe Sex): Protection Arc*, vol. 1, nos. 1–7. Image Comics, 2020.

The Hunger. Directed by Tony Scott. Metro-Goldwyn-Mayer, 1983.

Hurley, Kelly. *The Gothic Body: Sexuality, Materialism, and Degeneration at the Fin de Siècle*. Cambridge University Press, 1996.

"Reading like an Alien: Posthuman Identity in Ridley Scott's *Alien* and David Cronenberg's *Rabid*." In *Posthuman Bodies*, ed. Jack Halberstam and Ira Livingston. Indiana University Press, 1995. 203–24.

"Ice Pick." Season 1, episode 2, of *Ratched*, created by Ryan Murphy and Evan Romansky. Netflix, September 18, 2020.

Jackson, Shirley. *The Haunting of Hill House*. 1959. Penguin, 2013.

Kesey, Ken. *One Flew over the Cuckoo's Nest*. Viking Press, 1962.

Kilgour, Maggie. *From Communion to Cannibalism: An Anatomy of Metaphors of Incorporation*. Princeton University Press, 1990.

The Rise of the Gothic Novel. Routledge, 1995.

Kinkade, Patrick T., and Michael A. Katovich. "Toward a Sociology of Cult Films: Reading 'Rocky Horror.'" *The Sociological Quarterly* 33, no. 2 (1992): 191–209.

Koch-Rein, Anson. "Monster." *TSQ: Transgender Studies Quarterly* 1, nos. 1–2 (2014): 134–35.

Le Fanu, J. Sheridan. *Carmilla*, 1872. Project Gutenberg, 2003, www.gutenberg.org/files/10007/10007-h/10007-h.htm.

Lewis, Matthew. *The Monk: A Romance*. 1796. Penguin Books, 1998.

Lloyd-Smith, Allan. *American Gothic Fiction: An Introduction*. Continuum, 2004.

Love, Heather. "Queer." *TSQ: Transgender Studies Quarterly* 1, nos. 1–2 (2014): 172–76.
McClintock, Anne. *Imperial Leather: Race, Gender and Sexuality in the Colonial Contest.* Routledge, 1995.
Meyer, Stephenie. *The Twilight Saga.* Little, Brown, 2005–20.
Moers, Ellen. *Literary Women.* Doubleday, 1976.
The Old Dark House. Directed by James Whale. Universal Pictures, 1932.
Palmer, Paulina. *The Queer Uncanny: New Perspectives on the Gothic.* University of Wales Press, 2012.
Peraino, Judith. *Listening to the Sirens: Musical Technologies of Queer Identity from Homer to Hedwig.* University of California Press, 2005.
Petrocelli, Heather. "From Subtext to Text: Queered Gothic & Horror Film through Time." Gothic Manchester Festival Conference. Manchester Centre for Gothic Studies, Manchester Metropolitan University, October 26, 2019, www.youtube .com/watch?v=NCNwAJe6voo&feature=youtu.be.
Poe, Edgar Allan. "The Fall of the House of Usher." 1839. In *The Works of Edgar Allan Poe*, vol. 2. Project Gutenberg, www.gutenberg.org/files/2148/2148.-h/ 2148-h.htm.
"The System of Doctor Tarr and Professor Fether." 1845. In *The Works of Edgar Allan Poe*, vol. 4. Project Gutenberg, www.gutenberg.org/files/2150/2150-h/ 2150-h.htm.
Polidori, John. *The Vampyre; A Tale*, 1819. Project Gutenberg, www.gutenberg.org/ files/6087/6087-h/6087-h.htm.
Psycho. Directed by Alfred Hitchcock. Shamley Productions, 1960.
Radcliffe, Ann. *The Italian.* 1797. Oxford University Press, 2008.
The Mysteries of Udolpho, a Romance Interspersed with Some Pieces of Poetry. 1794. Penguin Books, 2001.
"On the Supernatural in Poetry." *New Monthly Magazine* 16, no. 1 (1826): 145–52.
Ravenous. Directed by Antonia Bird. Fox 2000, 1999.
Rebecca. Directed by Alfred Hitchcock. Selznick International Pictures, 1940.
Rice, Anne. *The Vampire Chronicles.* Knopf, 1976–2018.
Rigby, Mair. "'Prey to Some Cureless Disquiet': Polidori's Queer Vampyre at the Margins of Romanticism." *Romanticism on the Net*, nos. 36–37, 2004, www .erudit.org/fr/revues/ron/2004-n36-37-ron947/011135ar/.
Rubin, Gayle. "The Catacombs: A Temple of the Butthole." In *Deviations: A Gayle Rubin Reader.* Duke University Press, 2011. 224–40.
Russo, Vito. *The Celluloid Closet: Homosexuality in the Movies.* Harper & Row, 1981.
Schaffer, Talia. "'A Wilde Desire Took Me': The Homoerotic History of *Dracula.*" In *Dracula: Norton Critical Edition*, ed. Nina Auerbach and David J. Skal. Norton, 1997. 470–82.
Shelley, Mary. *Frankenstein; or, The Modern Prometheus.* 1818. The Penguin Group, 1992.
The Silence of the Lambs. Directed by Jonathan Demme. Strong Heart, 1991.
Snef, Carol A. "*Dracula*: The Unseen Face in the Mirror." In *Dracula: Norton Critical Edition*, ed. Nina Auerbach and David J. Skal. Norton. 1997. 421–31.

Stevenson, Robert Louis. *The Strange Case of Dr. Jekyll and Mr. Hyde*. 1886. Project Gutenberg, www.gutenberg.org/files/43/43-h/43-h.htm.

Stoker, Bram. *Dracula*. 1897. Norton, 1997.

Stryker, Susan. "My Words to Victor Frankenstein above the Village of Chamounix: Performing Transgender Rage." *GL/Q: A Journal of Lesbian and Gay Studies*, no. 1 (1994): 237–54.

The Texas Chain Saw Massacre. Directed by Tobe Hooper. Vortex, 1974.

The Uninvited. Directed by Lewis Allen. Paramount Pictures, 1944.

Valens, Ana. "Trans/Sex: On Queer Desire, Fantasy Porn, and Monsters." *Daily Dot*, February 11, 2020, www.dailydot.com/irl/trans-sex-fantasy-porn-queer-monsters/.

Warner, Michael. "Introduction: Fear of a Queer Planet." *Social Text*, no. 29 (1991): 3–17.

Westengard, Laura. *Gothic Queer Culture: Marginalized Communities and the Ghosts of Insidious Trauma*. University of Nebraska Press, 2019.

9

BERNICE M. MURPHY

Folk Horror

Although initially most associated with English forms of horror and gothic culture, as interest in folk horror has intensified over the course of the past decade it has become apparent that the subgenre's scope transcends national boundaries. It has also become obvious that there is a distinctive – and evolving – North American folk horror tradition.

As is the case with the often closely related "rural gothic" subgenre, the most prominent strand of American folk horror (which also frequently focuses on isolated, tradition-bound, and white agricultural communities) tends to negatively depict characteristics of rural and/or backwoods life that would, in less-menacing contexts, be considered positive.[1] Here, the rustic community's closeness to the land, self-reliance, and determination to preserve "traditional" belief systems invariably elicits terror rather than admiration. As Adam Scovell notes, "Folk Horror regularly builds its sense of the horrific around societies and groups of people that have very specific ways of life, and it is not by sheer chance that these often happen to be rural rather than urban.... Folk Horror uses the otherness that can be attributed to rural life to warp the very reality of its narrative worlds and often for its own explicit means" (81). Paul Cowdell similarly observes that a well-defined sense of place and of rural authenticity is key: "The superstitious peasantry, in all their muddy reality, move from background to foreground in Folk Horror. Farming is an actual practice in Folk Horror rather than a pretextual backdrop" (301).

As well as sharing an overlapping interest in rural and backwoods places and the peoples who inhabit them, American folk horror, like the American rural gothic, also often dramatizes "mainstream" abhorrence toward the kinds of beliefs that may take hold in "backward" regions when urban and suburban modernity either fail to take hold or have been decisively rejected by the local population. There is a sense that when they are left to their own devices, "these kinds of places" become the ideal breeding ground for barbaric and outlandish rituals and behaviors that would never take hold in a "civilized" settlement. Yet at the same time, these extreme practices also evoke a degree of fascination by dint of their apparent "authenticity" and willingness to resist the expectations of a society that is otherwise defined by the conventions of capitalist modernity.

This chapter will have three strands. The first will establish that this powerful suspicion of the community in the wilderness owes much to anxieties spawned during the English colonization of North America, as is underlined by Robert Egger's 2015 film *The Witch: A New-England Folk Tale*. In the second section I will briefly survey some of the most prominent post–World War II American folk horror texts. Finally, I will discuss several recent folk horror texts in which the recent feminization of American folk horror is placed at the forefront, concluding with a discussion of Ari Aster's *Midsommar* (2019).

9.1 *The Witch* and the Colonial Origins of American Folk Horror

The Witch is of interest not just for writer/director Egger's well-publicized efforts to convey historical and folkloric authenticity, but because in its depiction of the New England forest as a source of moral and physical danger, it also illuminates the colonial origins of one of the most important American folk horror strands: that of the community (or household) that falls under the spell of arcane influences that thrive in the shadows cast by wilderness.[2] As Roderick Nash observed in *Wilderness and the American Mind* (1967), for early Puritan settlers in New England, "wilderness was metaphor as well as actuality. On the frontier, the two meanings reinforced each other, multiplying horrors" (36). As we shall see, these dual meanings certainly hold true in *The Witch*.

The film opens in the month of March, sometime in the 1630s, as William (Ralph Ineson), an English farmer, his pregnant wife Katherine (Kate Dickie), and their children, teenagers Thomasin (Anya Taylor-Joy) and Caleb (Harvey Scrimshaw), and young twins Jonas (Lucas Dawson) and Mercy (Ellie Granger), attend a tense gathering in the Salem Meeting House (Eggers, 1).[3] William's stubbornness has led to an insurmountable theological falling-out with the community's leaders. The film's opening lines underline the sense of religious mission central to the Puritan errand into the wilderness, as well as William's estrangement from his fellow colonists: "What went we out into this wilderness to find? Leaving our country, kindred, our father's houses? We have traveled a vast ocean.... For what? For what?"

William and his family are banished from Salem and must leave the safety and the security – both moral and physical – of the settlement behind. After a journey of a day or more they find themselves in what Egger's screenplay describes as a "beautiful, idyllic natural clearing of rolling hills" (4). However, as both the brooding cinematography and the screenplay suggest, the omens are not good: "the clearing is surrounded by a forest – a dark and ancient wood. Its enormous pines stand like giants above the family. The presence of the wood is profound, disturbing, ominous" (4). After the family arrives at the site of their new home, the film moves forward in time a few months. Although a rough cabin has been built for shelter, livestock enclosures have been erected, and corn has been planted, they are barely eking out a meager existence. When baby Samuel is abducted by something from the forest, it marks the onset of a terrifying sequence of events that confirm that evil forces have targeted the family.

Like Hawthorne's eponymous Puritan Young Goodman Brown (1835), who has a nocturnal appointment in the forest outside Salem, William does not bring his family to the midst of the forest by accident (Hawthorne, 111). His stubborn refusal to bow down to the elders of the church has brought about their perilous exile. In addition to the rapid undermining of William's role as patriarch/protector, the film's formal and narrative framing leave us in no doubt that teenager Thomasin is, even from the start, at odds with the rest of the family.

The film's sustained focus on Thomasin is interesting because within the wider North American rural gothic tradition the wilderness has in the past more frequently been a place in which male crises of conscience are played out (as in Charles Brockden Brown's *Edgar Huntly* [1799], James Dickey's 1970 novel *Deliverance*, and Stephen King's *The Shining* [1977]). Indeed, the plot trajectory of *The Witch* is indicative of the trend in recent American folk horror whereby a female protagonist chafes against the rigid belief system of her family and her community.

Thomasin's increasing alienation from her family, her longing for a life beyond her grim, preordained lot, and, crucially, the targeted cruelty of the malevolent forces that inhabit the forest all inform her climactic transformation into that most suggestive of Puritan supernatural threats: the witch. The moral and psychological state of "bewilderment" into which the family has been thrust following their expulsion from Salem has resulted in the eradication of all but the most discontented – and, ultimately, the most adaptable – family member.[4] In this depiction of the forest beyond the settlement as a location where dangerous but potentially tempting alternate belief systems can find fertile ground, and its bracingly literal dramatization of seventeenth-century folk belief, *The Witch* underlines the extent to which foundational (English) perceptions of the North American wilderness have continued to inform the most prominent strand of the contemporary American folk horror tradition. The film also underlines the strong relationship between anxieties rooted in white settler colonialism and folk horror that is also a major focus of the recent documentary *Woodlands Dark and Days Bewitched: A History of Folk Horror* (2021), written and directed by Keir-La Janisse.

9.2 Lotteries, Harvests, and Cannibals

As I have outlined elsewhere, Shirley Jackson's 1948 short story "The Lottery" is a foundational text within modern American folk horror.[5] It is a lucid, exquisitely controlled tale of a rural village that meets once a year (on June 27) to carry out a communal ritual that is believed to ensure a successful harvest. A ritual drawing of lots – carried out in the town square and organized with unfussy competence by the civically minded Mr. Summers – decides which of the villagers will be the one chosen that year (Jackson, 226). One of the things that helps the story retain its considerable power to disturb is the fact that for everyone concerned (except the villager chosen), this is an entirely unremarkable annual event. What's more, there is also a tantalizing reference to the fact that lotteries happen in other communities, such as the "north village" (although the rumor is that they may be thinking of ending theirs [Jackson, 230]). Even Tessie Hutchinson, the housewife whose ballot is drawn, appears to go along with the tradition right up to the moment that her own name is announced. Her futile attempt to evade what happens next means that "The Lottery" anticipates the focus on female protagonists at odds with their community frequently found in more recent American folk horror narratives of the "community in the wilderness" kind.

The fact that so many of Jackson's readers assumed that the setting for "The Lottery" was rural New England (even though, as is generally the case in her fiction, the exact location is never explicitly mentioned) underlines a more long-standing association between that region and folk horror practices (as also acknowledged in the full title of *The Witch*, which is explicitly presented as "A New-England Folk Tale").[6]

Of course, Jackson was by no means the only twentieth-century American horror author to see macabre possibility in New England's more isolated rural communities. In stories such as "The Dunwich Horror" (1929), "The Shadow over Innsmouth" (1936), and "The Picture in the House" (1921),

H. P. Lovecraft anticipated this association, although the horrific rites practiced by his backwoods communities are invariably associated with nefarious "foreign" influences and/or miscegenation.[7] "The Picture in the House" underlines the frequency with which the horror in Lovecraft's tales often comes from a combination of Old Yankee degeneration and racial mixing. We are told of the Puritans that "[d]ivorced from the enlightenment of civilisation, the strength of these Puritans turned in to singular channels; and in their isolation, morbid self-repression, and struggle for life with relentless Nature, there came to them dark furtive traits" (Lovecraft, 373).

Ritual cannibalism associated with foreign locales – and carried out by the inhabitants of an isolated New England community – also features in Richard Matheson's 1957 story "The Children of Noah," which is set in a Maine fishing village founded by a whaler who brought home from the South Seas a taste for human flesh passed on to his present-day descendants (Matheson, n.p.). Coincidentally, the 1978 story "Sons of Noah" by Jack Cady initially features a broadly similar premise: yet again, a cocky city-dweller falls foul of an isolated and insular rural community, this time one located in a mountain valley in the Pacific Northwest – but this is in fact an elegiac, poetic, and ecologically minded tale of a community doing its best to preserve their idyllic way of life, and which are ultimately able to fend off rapacious modernity (for now at least) by ritualistically calling on the primal power of the flood.

Several of the most notable folk horror narratives to follow in Jackson's wake also have strong New England associations. Actor-turned-author Thomas Tryon's 1973 bestseller *Harvest Home* features a rather typical American folk horror setup: the arrival in a long-established rural community of naive urbanites who fail to appreciate that their new town's adherence to the "old ways" goes rather further than they could ever have suspected. Newcomer Ned Constantine eventually finds out the hard way that the charming village of Cornwall Coombe is in fact a matriarchal cult that, like the village in "The Lottery," carries out rituals drawn straight from Sir James Frazer's *The Golden Bough* on contemporary American soil.[8]

Ken Greenhall's 1982 novel *Childgrave* also pits a naive city dweller against a community that strictly adheres to the old ways. A New York photographer named Jonathan Brewster, who declares himself to have "always [been] devoted to moderation and the inexplicable," finds himself falling for Sara, a mysterious young woman from the ominously named Upstate New York village of Childgrave (Greenhall, 5). It gradually becomes clear that like the residents of most of the isolated rural communities previously mentioned in this chapter, *Childgrave*'s inhabitants hold fast to certain niche religious beliefs that have been taking place for centuries, and that they see absolutely nothing wrong with these rites, even though they are horrifying to outsiders. As the local police chief warns Jonathan:

> It's dangerous to make light of someone's faith. You probably don't believe that, living in a big city. I imagine you worry about someone coming up in back of you on a subway platform, or you fear that when you get home, the door will be ajar, a panel punched out of the wood you thought was so strong. You don't worry about someone interfering with your grace or your rituals. (218).

We also find here yet again another connection with the earliest days of European settlement. In the local meeting hall, Jonathan, who is a typically snoopy urban outsider, finds a leather-bound account written in 1660 by Josiah Golightly, the town's founding father. Golightly explains that he was banished from the Massachusetts Bay Colony, but just when we and his family were on the verge of starving to death in the snow, an "Angel" appeared to him and told him that if he ate his daughter, little "Colony," he would be saved. Golightly did so, and survived, as had been promised. To ensure that God's "grace" was preserved, Golightly convinced his fellow townsfolk to make an annual commemorative ceremony the centerpiece of their new community's spiritual beliefs. Each year, a little girl under the age of six is chosen by lottery (another probable nod to Jackson) from among the local children, lavished with care and attention, and sacrificially murdered so that her blood and flesh can be consumed by the congregation, with her memory revered thereafter.[9]

Childgrave represents an overlooked but fascinating example of the strong connection American folk horror of this kind makes between the pursuit of religious freedom and the accompanying fear of what might happen if that freedom is taken too far. Greenhall's New England villagers, like those discussed previously, practice their own twisted form of Christianity that has taken root in geographically obscure American soil and mutated into something much darker, with dire consequences that every family in the community nevertheless willingly accepts. As Jonathan, who has a young daughter, Joanne, who would be eligible to participate in the lottery if he moves to the village before Easter (when the ceremony is held), is told, "to be a Childgravean means that you are willing to make that sacrifice" (235). Although the novel ends as Jonathan vows to end the lottery once and for all for the sake of his and Sara's unborn child, he has already secured acceptance to the village by allowing Joanne to participate. Another girl is chosen, but he has still gambled with the life of his own flesh and blood for the sake of his new family and the wider community and, in doing so, has proven himself to be a true Childgravean.

9.3 "Everything Just Mechanically Doing Its Part": Twenty-First-Century American Folk Horror

Twenty-first century American folk horror has continued to prominently feature isolated rural communities that stubbornly cling to their own ways in the face of external disapproval or indifference. In 2006, writer/director Neil LaBute adapted the most famous British folk horror film of them all, *The Wicker Man* (1973), changing the setting from an island off the coast of Scotland to one in the Pacific Northwest. Hardy's original focused on the fascinating clash of worldviews between its naive outsider, the devoutly Christian Sergeant Howie (Edward Woodward), and the free-spirited, carousing islanders who cheerfully lure him into their titular death trap. Here, the original film's free-spirited neo-pagans are reconceived as a matriarchal colony of honey producers who scheme to entrap a decidedly non-religious out-of-state policeman named Edward Malus (Nicolas Cage).

Malus' bumbling investigation of the island community is so boorishly executed that, in stark contrast to the genuine dread evoked by the infamous climax of the original, here, viewers may well find themselves cheering on the cultists. It is, ultimately, a film that suggests that the most paranoid fears men may have about the women in their lives are sometimes true. The women of Summersisle really do need men only to help them procreate (and to do the heavy lifting), and be they young or old, they will use their feminine wiles to get their way at all costs. Malus' desire to protect the daughter he didn't even know he had before arriving on the island is ultimately his undoing.

In M. Night Shyamalan's 2004 film *The Village*, the inhabitants of an otherwise-idyllic village in what appears to be the late nineteenth century must appease the mysterious creatures that inhabit the forest surrounding their settlement – "those we don't speak of." They avoid the color that is said to attract the creatures (red), patrol the boundaries of their settlement, and provide offerings during the ominously titled "Ceremony of Meat." The youngsters of the village live happy and safe lives, but as they come of age, some begin to wonder what really lies in the forest beyond.

Shyamalan's typically audacious twist reveals this to be a film about the ways in which ritual and myth can be self-consciously manipulated for the purposes of binding a community together. Unbeknownst to the young people of the village (who have only ever known this life), their community is a simulacrum of sorts, and a relatively modern construct at that: a "back to basics" rural community established in the 1970s by a support group of grieving family members who lost loved ones to urban crime and decided to turn their backs on modernity. Although the film still presents its community as a much more wholesome, loving place than the outside world, it is therefore nonetheless founded on a conspiracy that prevents the children of the founders from knowing the truth about their circumstances. Yet again, family ties and community bonds appear to be inextricable.

Although no ritual human sacrifice per se is practiced here (benign community events are a major focus of village life), the violent death of Noah (Adrian Brody), the most disruptive and uncontainable member of the younger generation, ensures that the communal status quo will be maintained, at least for another few years. The film's setting – the Pennsylvania woods – also recalls the fact that the state historically has been associated with religious groups who sought freedom from persecution, most particularly, Quakers such as Willian Penn, founder of the Pennsylvania Colony, which rapidly attracted religious dissenters from all over Europe.[10]

An increasingly isolated and disenchanted young woman is the focus of the 2019 film *The Other Lamb* (dir. Malgorzata Szumowska). It is about a small group of women living off the grid who worship a charismatic and manipulative male cult leader known as "Shepherd" (Michiel Huisman). As is the case with many of the backwoods villages mentioned earlier, this tiny community in the wilderness again seems to somehow exist outside conventional time and space. Indeed, it takes some time before it is established that the film is set in the contemporary United States. This sense of regional nonspecificity is enhanced by the fact that the rugged green landscape through which the group wearily trudges is decidedly Hibernian looking: much of the film was shot in Ireland.

Shepherd is a Manson-like figure who treats his female flock like livestock. As with several of the other fundamentalist settlements discussed in this chapter, he appears to preach a perverted form of Christianity (one in which ovine metaphors abound, as the film's title suggests). Selah (Raffery Cassidy) is a teenager on the verge of being chosen as one of Shepherd's new wives (even though it seems likely that he is also her father). Early in the film, Shepherd is warned by a local police officer that the time has come for the community to move on (so there is some external awareness that this community on the margins exists, but a lack of will to investigate or interfere with its workings). As they embark on a grueling journey, on foot, to an alleged new "Eden," Selah is exposed to the heretical ideas of an older woman shunned by the rest of the community, and gradually begins to question the authority of their leader. Selah is eventually able to turn the rest of the women against Shepherd by spinning her own narrative, one in which the women are in charge. Her recurrent visions of a woman naked in the forest echoes the association between the natural world and female liberation/empowerment found in the ecstatic final moments of *The Witch*.

However, it is only after Shepherd has brutally murdered the older women so that they can be replaced in his roster of bedmates/breeders by their own daughters that his control is definitively rejected. "You are not our Shepherd. I don't want your grace," Selah ultimately declares. The film concludes on an image of righteous female vengeance – the false prophet is crucified by his rebellious flock, a crown of ram's horns mockingly placed upon his bloody head. The bewildered local cops sum things up nicely: "Well, this is fucked." Meanwhile, the young women journey on in the wilderness to an unknown destination, this time under their own direction, with Selah carrying a black lamb in her arms (a visual detail that is perhaps a little *too* on the nose).

Young women also turn the tables on those around them in *The Curse of Audrey Earnshaw* (dir. Thomas Robert Lee, 2020), yet another recent example of folk horror clearly influenced by Eggers' film. This time, the insular community concerned is made up of descendants of a rogue sect of Church of Ireland settlers who came to the United States in 1873. The film is unusual in that the community is of Irish rather than explicitly English/Puritan descent, like those in *Childgrave* and *Harvest Home*: they even still have Irish accents, and stereotypically Irish Catholic names such as Brigid, Seamus, and Colm. Nevertheless, the desire to keep alive religious and communal beliefs overtly associated with Europe within the very different geographical and cultural context of the "New World" is again to the forefront.

We are told that in 1956, a terrible blight began to kill off the crops, with only the farmstead belonging to one local woman, Agatha Earnshaw (Catherine Walker), remaining unaffected. As a result, the community decided that she must be a witch. The film takes place a generation later, in 1973, initially focusing on Agatha and Audrey (Jessica Reynolds), the daughter she has raised in absolute secrecy, hidden from all except the all-female members of the (possibly) Satanic coven in the woods to which she belongs.

Audrey begins to reveal her malevolent true nature after her mother is assaulted by a grieving local father. Seeking revenge, Audrey inserts herself into the man's home and uses her uncanny abilities to destroy his life. It gradually becomes clear that Audrey is not entirely human and that, indeed, she may be the daughter of Satan himself. Ultimately, Agatha herself falls victim to the anger of her now uncontrollable offspring, and in what is a rare development for the subgenre, the film ends with the female protagonist leaving the backwoods settlement behind entirely. Though the film treads familiar ground in some respects, then, the mash-up between satanic panic tropes (the spawn of the devil wreaks havoc) and folk horror elements featured here ultimately makes this a relatively original contribution to the subgenre.

The most notable recent American folk horror text happens to be set largely outside the United States. Ari Aster's *Midsommar* effectively combines many of the most notable themes we have seen explored in earlier folk horror narratives – particularly the tendency to use the "ritual human sacrifice for the good of the crops" theme seen in both Jackson's "The Lottery" and *The Wicker Man* – with a uniquely disturbing take on the increasingly prominent "female outsider in an insular community" theme. *Midsommar* also further underlines the extent to which narrative inevitability is an important part of many of these stories. In fact, the entire plot arc of the film is revealed in the opening seconds, which feature a colorful mural depicting (almost) everything that is about to occur. The rituals held dear by the community in question ultimately unfold exactly as their organizers would have wished and escape yet again proves impossible – in the end, there is only death or assimilation for outsiders.

As my analysis thus far has suggested, American folk horror narratives revolving around rural communities tend to have two basic starting points. Either they are about an insider – a preexisting member of the community – who, for whatever reason, begins to question the beliefs they have grown up with (as in "The Lottery," *The Other Lamb*, and *The Curse of Audrey Earnshaw*) or they are about a naive and/or vulnerable outsider who gradually finds themself becoming dangerously involved with terrifying folk rites they (initially at least) find to be barbaric and unforgivable (as is the case with Burt and Vicki in Stephen King's 1977 story "Children of the Corn," Ned in *Harvest Home*, Jonathan in *Childgrave*, and Malus in *The Wicker Man* [2006]). *Midsommar* belongs to this latter category.

Midsommar opens as Dani Ardor (Florence Pugh), a twenty-something graduate student in psychology, receives news from home that shatters her already delicate emotional equilibrium: her mentally unstable sister has murdered their parents and taken her own life. Dani's shallow, cowardly boyfriend Christian (Jack Reynor) had been on the verge of breaking up with her, but now feels unable to do so. As a result, Dani ends up tagging along with Christian and his resentful fellow anthropology students as they head to Hälsingland, Sweden, to visit a community known as the Hårga at the invitation of their amiable classmate Pelle (Vilhelm Blomgren). Pelle is going "home" to participate in his village's annual Midsummer celebrations, which take on enhanced significance every ninety years (as is the case now). Pelle's "family" – which consists of everyone in the community – is very welcoming and they seem delighted that he has managed to bring so many outsiders home with him.

Anyone who has even basic familiarity with *The Wicker Man* will immediately suspect the cheerful affect and cordial hospitality of the Hårga. As I have already noted, this is in some respects a deeply predictable film that plays out exactly as one might expect (as Pelle says of the workings of the natural world a little later, "Everything just mechanically doing its part"). It comes as little surprise to learn that the community practices ritual scapegoating and human sacrifice (to symbolically banish evil and ensure the safety of the community). In the final moments, as in Jackson's most famous story and Ken Greenhall's novel, a ritual drawing of lots takes place to decide who will be the final person sacrificed for the sake of the wider community. As a result, Christian is burned alive in an elaborate wooden structure, alongside the bodies of his fellow visitors, two "euthanized" elders who took their own lives in dramatic fashion earlier in the film, and some willing Hårga volunteers. Here, it is a sacred wooden building, rather than a Wicker Man, that goes up in flames, and the final body count (nine) is much higher than in Jackson's story or Robin Hardy's film, but the core premise is certainly one we have seen before.

However, *Midsommar* distinguishes itself by foregrounding from the very outset Dani's emotional and psychological vulnerability. Close-ups of Pugh's expressive face are a key visual trope. For much of the film, Dani is desperately trying to conceal the extent of her anxiety and grief from Christian and the others, and we often see her break down in private, when she can no longer successfully hide her deep emotional turmoil. The film therefore continues the focus on an isolated and troubled young woman seen in other recent American folk horror narratives.[11] Although Dani is, like the other visitors, sickened early on by the discovery that the Hårga practice a particularly violent form of ritualized euthanasia, as her already fraying bonds with Christian begin to break entirely, she finds herself becoming more and more enmeshed within the community. Her disappointing boyfriend's name is of course a clue in itself: Dani will ultimately find herself rejecting both Christian *and* Christianity.

In the Hårga, Dani eventually finds a family to replace the one she has lost. She is also finally able to openly express her overwhelming pain in front of an attentive and empathetic audience that genuinely tunes in to her emotional state (and even seem to share it). But while the Hårga do seem to have a genuine interest in and appreciation of Dani – particularly once she is crowned their May Queen – they also ruthlessly exploit her obvious vulnerability for their own long-term goal: that of bringing "new blood" into their insular, select community.

During several key scenes, Dani is under the influence of a powerful natural hallucinogenic doled out by her hosts, and it is they who aggressively push Christian toward the climactic act of infidelity that ultimately ends their relationship – in fact, it could well be argued that he is a victim of all-out sexual assault here. Importantly, too, Dani clearly has the "right" kind of racial heritage to make her a viable member of the community: as a white woman with blonde hair and green eyes, she is the visitor who physically most resembles their decidedly Aryan-looking hosts, whose telling fondness for runes also evokes the Nazi fascination with a hyper-idealized, white supremacist, Nordic past. Indeed, an academic volume brought to Sweden by Christian's academic rival Josh (William Jackson Harper), who is himself African American, underlines this connection: the title is *The Secret Nazi Language of the Utbark* (the runic language that recurs throughout the film).[12]

Whereas the other recent films mentioned that focused on young women ended with them trying (not always successfully) to evade their seemingly preordained fate, here it is strongly implied that Dani ends the film as the newest member of the cult that has just burned her boyfriend alive and brutally murdered her travel companions. *Midsommar* concludes by showing how seductive this kind of all-encompassing communal solidarity can be for someone who has lost everything (and everyone) else. The Hårga, although close-knit and insular, are notably cosmopolitan. Their young people are encouraged to travel, and, like Pelle, they appear to be urbane, warm and well educated. The community members are also clean, attractively costumed, physically appealing, and (outwardly) welcoming to outsiders. The idyllic music festival–style site of their nine-day ritual is initially presented to us a kind of pastoral paradise into which the outsiders stride open-mouthed. Indeed, the frequency with which mild-altering substances are consumed and the prominence afforded communal feasts underlines this sense that Dani is a kind of anxiety-ravaged Alice who has fallen into a beguiling but deeply sinister Wonderland. This subtle sense of *wrongness*, however, is convened though the subtly off-kilter, rune-inscribed architecture. In making Hälsingland, with its lush meadows, flowers, feasts, and costumes, appear to be pretty on the surface, Aster underlines the sense that for his emotionally unmoored protagonist, it is a toxic paradise, a place where she will find a new home, but at the probable cost of her sanity.

During *Midsommar*'s remarkable denouement, Dani collapses in apparent shock and revulsion as she watches the building Christian and the other "sacrifices" are in go up in flames. Her horror is even more striking given that it is Dani herself, in her role as May Queen, who has "selected" Christian rather than a Hårga volunteer for this fate. Then, as the score swells to a tremulous climax, she slowly smiles though her tears, as though finally letting go of the grief, uncertainty, and loneliness that has dogged her since the horrific tragedy that unfolded during the opening sequence. As we have seen, American folk horror often relies on the notion that the arcane rituals carried out by its backwoods folk are derived from traditions or belief systems initially brought over from the Old World of Europe. Here, however, there is something of a narrative reversal: events that took place many months before, back in the United States, have made Dani's fate here in Sweden seem inescapable.

Of course, it was there for us to pick up on all along. "You are the family now, yes?" one of the Hårga says to Dani late in the film, reminding us that the word "family" – previously an anxiety-spawning emotional trigger for her – has been repeated throughout the film. The American outsider has become a European (and a specifically *Nordic*) insider. It's a development anticipated by a subtle geographical reference mentioned in Aster's screenplay: Dani's birth family live in Minnesota, one of the Midwestern states most associated with Swedish immigration to the United States, meaning that her trip to Hälsingland is arguably a kind of genetic "homecoming" for her as well.

Midsommar's conclusion – both cathartic and horrific – also provides an indication of the ways in which some recent American folk horror narratives – among them also *The Witch* and *The Other Lamb* – have contributed to a fascinating reconfiguration of Carol J. Clover's immensely influential concept of the iconic "Final Girl" – the traumatized survivor who somehow remains standing after her friends have been murdered one by one. Hannah Holway persuasively contrasts Dani's facial expression in the final seconds of *Midsommar* to that of the lone survivor whose hysteria pervades the iconic closing seconds of Tobe Hooper's *The Texas Chain Saw Massacre* (1974):

> Where Sally Hardesty maniacally laughed in Texas's final shot, supposedly driven to insanity through the torture she's endured, Dani placidly smiles, because like these other modern Final Girls, she knows she can't return to what came before; and nor does she want to. While her decisions have ultimately left her unable to leave this new community, despite their violence and Pelle's questionable behaviour, she appears at peace in the knowledge that she has found her people. (Holway).

To an even greater extent than Christian's ghastly death, or the gruesome murders of their traveling companions, Dani's climactic assimilation into the Hårga collective is therefore the ultimate horror in *Midsommar*. The desperately isolated protagonist is now part of a brutally utilitarian and exclusive community for whom the collective "good" will always take precedence over individual agency, and white supremacy is a foundational principle.[13]

Yet again, the worst has inevitably come to pass in an American folk horror narrative, but this time, the grim narrative climax is all the more disturbing because we can understand why this might, even for a moment, seem like a happy ending to the vulnerable young woman whose devastating personal losses have made her the perfect new addition to the Hårga "family."

NOTES

1. For more on "Rural Gothic," see Murphy.
2. This discussion of *The Witch* originated in a paper I gave at the "Gothic Nature: New Directions in Ecohorror and EcoGothic" conference held at Trinity College Dublin in November 2017.
3. The decade in which the film is set and the ages of the children are mentioned in Eggers' script, rather than referenced in the film.
4. As Nash puts it, "The wilderness was conceived as a region where a person was likely to get into a disordered, confused or 'wild' condition" (2).
5. See my essay "Black Boxes and Corn: Backwoods Horror and Human Sacrifice in Rural American Folk Horror," in *Folk Horror: New Global Pathways*, ed. Dawn Keetley and Ruth Heholt (University of Wales Press, forthcoming).
6. Jackson discussed the extreme reactions the story generated in her 1960 essay, "Biography of a Story," published in *Come along with Me*, 211–24.
7. I also discuss these stories in Murphy, 135.
8. This aspect of *Harvest Home* is considered in more detail in "Black Boxes and Corn."
9. A similar origin story – ritualized cannibalism in the present day prompted by survival cannibalism in the colonial past – features in Jim Mickle's 2013 film *We Are What We Are*.
10. I discuss this and other aspects of *The Village* briefly mentioned here in more detail in *The Rural Gothic*, chapter 2.
11. I would also add Chad Crawford Kinkle's fascinating 2013 film *Jug Face* (aka *The Pit*) to this lineup; I discuss the film in my "Black Boxes" essay.
12. The book is discussed during a scene that features in Aster's extended director's cut of the film. See also Robert Spadoni, "*Midsommar*: Thing Theory," *Quarterly Review of Film and Video* 37, no. 7 (2020): 711–26.
13. See Lea Anderson's article "So, We're Just Going to Ignore the Sunlight Then? Aesthetic Whiteness in *Midsommar*" for an in-depth reading of the film's critique of white supremacy (*Horror Homeroom*, May 30, 2020). Noor Al-Sibai argues that the film is essentially a "satire of the neo-pagan and anti-immigrant teachings employed by some on the far-right" in her piece "In *Midsommar*, Silent White Supremacy Shrieks Volumes," Truthdig.Com, August 2, 2019, accessed November 16, 2020.

Works Cited

Cady, Jack. "The Sons of Noah." In *The Sons of Noah and Other Stories*. Broken Moon Press, 1992.

Clover, Carol J. *Men, Women and Chainsaws: Gender in the Modern Horror Film*. BFI, 2004.
Cowdell, Paul. "'Practicing Witchcraft Myself during the Filming': Folk Horror, Folklore, and the Folkloresque." *Western Folklore* 78, no. 4 (2019): 295–326. www.jstor.org/stable/26864166. Accessed July 20, 2021.
The Curse of Audrey Earnshaw. Directed by Thomas Robert Lee. A71 Entertainment, 2020.
Eggers, Robert. *The Witch: A New-England Folk Tale*. October 11, 2013, draft.
Greenhall, Ken. *Childgrave*. 1982. Valancourt Books, 2017.
Hawthorne, Nathaniel. "Young Goodman Brown." In *Young Goodman Brown and Other Tales*. Oxford University Press, 2008. 111–23.
Holway, Hannah. "Beyond the Final Girl: *Midsommar*, Family and the Final Girl Smile." *Talk Film Society*, https://talkfilmsociety.com/columns/beyond-the-final-girl-midsommar-family-and-the-final-girl-smile/.
Jackson, Shirley. "The Lottery." In *Come along with Me: Part of a Novel, Sixteen Stories and Three Lectures*. Penguin, 1995. 225–33.
Lovecraft, H. P. *Lovecraft Omnibus 3: The Haunter in the Dark*. HarperCollins, 2000.
Matheson, Richard. "The Children of Noah." In *Shock! Thirteen Tales of Sheer Terror*. Dell, 1961.
Midsommar. Directed by Ari Aster. A24, 2019.
Murphy, Bernice M. *The Rural Gothic in American Popular Culture*. Palgrave Macmillan, 2013.
Nash, Roderick. *Wilderness and the American Mind*, 3rd ed. Yale University Press, 1982. *The Other Lamb*. Directed by Malgorzata Szumowska. IFC Midnight, 2019.
Scovell, Adam, *Folk Horror: Hours Dreadful and Things Strange*. Auteur, 2017.
The Village. Directed by M. Night Shyamalan. Buena Vista Pictures, 2004.
The Wicker Man. Directed by Robin Hardy. British Lion Films, 1973.
The Wicker Man. Directed by Neil LaBute. Warner Bros. Pictures, 2006.
The Witch: A New England Folk Tale. Directed by Robert Eggers. A24, Elevation Pictures, Universal Pictures, 2015.
Woodlands Dark and Days Bewitched: A History of Folk Horror. Directed by Keir-La Janisse. Severin Films, 2021.

10

DARRYL JONES

Occult Horror

"The Occult World," or *occulture*, is a term that has developed a very wide meaning in modern academic discourse. In 1974, the occult scholar James Webb formulated what is still the most widely accepted definition of his subject: "The occult is *rejected knowledge*" (191; see also Hanegraaff). The academy, it is argued, might be said to maintain a discursive monopoly on knowledge, whose boundaries it polices rigorously. The occult could be defined as that which falls outside these boundaries. It includes, for example, serious investigations into the real existence of subjects such as the supernatural and the paranormal, hermetic and esoteric philosophy and the practice of magic, Satanism and demonology, astrology, tarot reading and other forms of divination, theosophy and spiritualism, UFO visits and abductions, psychical research, and much else besides (see the essays collected in Partridge).

While investigation into these subjects as praxis and reality falls outside the boundaries of academic knowledge, they have a vivid popular existence. They form a real part of the lives of billions of people worldwide. My own university, for example, has a large and successful School of Psychology, but no parapsychologists – and yet the academic parapsychologist or paranormal investigator is a recurring figure in popular culture. This division between academic and popular forms of knowledge has its modern origins in nineteenth-century scientific materialism, or "scientific naturalism" (a term coined by T. H. Huxley in opposition to "supernaturalism").[1] Scientific naturalism provided the intellectual structure for J. G. Frazer's monumental work of anthropology and mythography, *The Golden Bough* (1890), where it served as an influential explanatory model for the analysis of culture. Magic, Frazer suggested, is the oldest human form of knowledge; with the coming of organized urban civilization, it was superseded by religion; modernity, in turn, has seen religion superseded by science: "It is therefore a truism, almost a tautology," Frazer wrote, "to say that all magic is necessarily false and barren; for if it were ever to become true, it would no longer be magic but science" (46). But some modern theorists of magic, while maintaining Frazer's tripartite structure of magic-religion-science, insist on a relationship of continuity rather than hierarchy: "Human history as a whole," writes Chris Gosden, "is made up of a triple helix of magic, religion and science, the boundaries between which are fuzzy and changing, but their mutual tension is creative" (12).

By the hospitable definition of occulture, the full panoply of occult thinking is enormous and encompasses the subject matter of most if not all of the essays in this collection. While always mindful of this broader definition of my subject, this essay is largely limited to what I think would be an acceptable vernacular definition of the occult as essentially referring to black magic, and most especially to the satanic. This has been a subject with enormous resonance for American history and culture. My argument in this chapter is that Satan has played, and continues to play, a central – and on occasion a decisive – role in American cultural and political life. He is a figure deeply in the American grain, a vivid and personal presence in the lives of many millions of Americans, and given powerful and recurring embodiment in American popular culture, in particular. But he is also a presence centrally informing some of the classic works of American literature – and this is where I shall begin.

***

"America is not a young land: it is old and dirty and evil before the settlers, before the Indians. The evil is there waiting" (Burroughs, 12). These famous words from William S. Burroughs' *The Naked Lunch* (1959) are highly suggestive. Obviously, they speak to, and from, Burroughs' own unique sensibility, a bleak and dark rejection of the characteristically optimistic and progressivist official discourse of 1950s America. But Burroughs' act of refutation and negation is also an utterance powerfully in the American grain. The American experience defines itself as embodying enlightened and progressive modernity; yet it also contains regressive, paranoid, and secret histories. America is a Christian country, and yet also a satanic one.

These contradictions inform the American tendency for saying what the critic Leslie Fiedler called, in the title of one of his best books, *No! in Thunder* (1960). American cultural expression, Fiedler thought, was at its most characteristic, and most powerful, when at its most "Demonic, terrible and negative" (6): when it recognized and embraced the waiting evil. The book's title is a phrase Fiedler borrowed from Herman Melville's Gothic account of the work of his friend Nathaniel Hawthorne: "There is the grand truth about Nathaniel Hawthorne. He says No! in thunder; but the Devil himself cannot make him say yes. For all men who say *yes*, lie" (letter to Nathaniel Hawthorne, April 16, 1851, in Melville, *Letters*, 125).

There is an argument to be made that the greatest of all American novels is in fact a satanic book. Indeed, that is precisely how its author understood it. For Melville, *Moby-Dick* (1851) was a novel enmeshed in a web of occult meanings, rituals, and beliefs. He claimed that the key to the meaning of *Moby-Dick* was Captain Ahab's blasphemous asseveration, "Ego non baptizo te in nominee patris, sed in nomina diaboli" ("I baptise thee not in the name of the Father, but in the name of the Devil") (Fiedler, 6; Melville, *Moby-Dick*, 1315). This was, Melville maintained in a letter to Hawthorne, "the book's motto (the secret one)"; it was a book "broiled" in "hell-fire" (letter to Nathaniel Hawthorne, June 29, 1851, in Melville, *Letters*, 133).

In the winter of 1933–34, the poet Charles Olson examined Melville's own seven-volume set of Shakespeare, which was in the possession of Melville's granddaughter, Frances Osborne. This was part of the research that was to lead in due course to the publication of Olson's major critical study of Melville, *Call Me Ishmael* (1947). On the last leaf of the final volume, in Melville's own hand, Olson discovered something truly startling:

> It is better to laugh & not sin than to weep & be
> wicked. – Ten loads of coal to burn him. –
> Brought to the stake – warmed himself by the
> fire.
> Ego non baptize te in nominee Patris et
> Filii et Spiritus Sancti – sed in nomine
> Diaboli. – Madness is undefinable –
> It & right reasons extremes of one.
> – Not the (black art) Goetic but Theurgic
> magic –
> seeks converse with the Intelligence, Power, the
> Angel. (Sanborn, 212)

It is difficult to say with certainty what Melville actually means in an utterance as gnomic and private as this, but it undoubtedly comes from a place of some familiarity with occult and magical discourse. "Goetic … magic" is, as Melville rightly contends, the "black art." The *Goetia*, or the *Lesser Key*, is the most influential of the three books of Solomonic magic – it is the one concerned with the summoning of demons. The nineteenth-century magus Éliphas Lévi, who uses the term frequently, defines "Göetia" as "the Magic of darkness" or "sorcery" (89). Melville's distinction between "Theurgic" and "Goetic" magic derives from the Ancient Greeks. Georg Luck's *Arcana Mundi* (1985), the classic work on magic in the Greek and Roman world, describes theurgy as "a glorified kind of magic practiced by a highly respected priestlike figure, not some obscure magician" (20). The *Goētes*, conversely, were necromancers: they were a variety of Persian magi who were "experts at manipulating the dead" (Stratton, 95). The fact that Melville wrote his incantation on the flyleaf at the end of the last volume of Shakespeare seems to suggest that he had been reading and thinking about *The Tempest*, often counted as Shakespeare's last play, in which the magus Prospero uses "Theurgic magic – [which] seeks converse with the Intelligence, Power, the Angel" to summon and command the spirit Ariel. The great historian of hermetic philosophy Frances Yates argued that, in his last plays, Shakespeare's interest in magic, never far from the surface, becomes serious and profound. Melville seems to share that intuition here, and counterpoints the "Theurgic" magic of Prospero, which summons Angels, with the "Goetic" magic of Ahab, which makes deals with the Devil.

For Leslie Fiedler, the phrase "No! in thunder" unites Melville and Hawthorne in their artistic commitment to a distinctively American "Demonic, terrible and negative" art. But where Melville's account of the informing principles of *Moby-Dick* hints at a sophisticated and learned occultism, Hawthorne's Devil is a more populist figure and, as such, a more representatively American one.

"The Devil himself," Melville thought, might converse with Nathaniel Hawthorne. Some of Hawthorne's best stories offer a complex perception of the sense that the "Devil himself" was waiting out there, just beyond the lights of precarious human settlements, in the wilderness or the woods. As Bernice M. Murphy has suggested, the motif of the "cabin in the woods," an isolated outpost of settler society menaced on all sides by terrors, many of which are supernatural, is "the true starting-point of American horror" (15). This is certainly the anxiety explored in "Young Goodman Brown" (1835), one of the landmark works of American short fiction. The protagonist, a young Massachusetts Puritan, meets the Devil while walking through the woods near his home. He is led to a clearing in the forest where, around a stone altar, the entire community is celebrating a Black Mass:

> [H]e recognized a score of the church-members of Salem village famous for their especial sanctity. Good old Deacon Gookin had arrived, and waited at the skirts of that venerable saint, his reverend pastor. But, irreverently consorting with these grave, reputable, and pious people, these elders of the church, these chaste dames and dewy virgins, there were men of dissolute lives and women of spotted fame, wretches given over to all mean and filthy vice, and suspected even of horrid crimes. (Hawthorne, 285)

Among the satanic congregation, Brown also sees "the Indian priests, or pow-wows, who had often scared their native forest with more hideous incantations than any known in English witchcraft" (285).

The anxieties hinted at by Burroughs and explored in "Young Goodman Brown" are very self-consciously in keeping with the beliefs of emerging vernacular American religion. In pre-Revolutionary America, the Puritan divine Henry Alline recalled a teenage encounter in the New England woods with "thousands of devils and damned spirits" (Poole, 39). Cotton Mather believed that the New World was a world over which Satan held sway and that the Native Americans were therefore "the children of the devil" (Poole, 15–16). This belief was developed by Joseph Smith and the Mormons, who used it as the basis for a larger cosmology: in *The Book of Mormon*, it is revealed that Christ visited America in the time between his resurrection and his ascension, only to face rejection from the indigenous Lamanites. The Native Americans are the descendants of these Christ-denying Lamanites. Smith thought that their dark skin was the sign of God's curse upon them (Poole, 52–53).

Hawthorne's story is a nuanced and complex one. Ostensibly, like much of his most distinctive work, "Young Goodman Brown" offers a critique of Puritan religious bigotry, hypocrisy, and violence. In this, it closely resembles, for example, "The May-Pole of Merry Mount" (1836), in which Puritan townsfolk brutally oppress and drive out a pagan community living in the nearby woods, whom they can understand only as a collection of "Gothic monsters" (Hawthorne, 361). This violent confrontation has decisive implications for the American character: "The future complexion of New England was involved in this important quarrel" (Hawthorne, 366). In "Young Goodman Brown," the Devil makes direct reference to a history of Puritan atrocities: "it was I that brought your father a pitch-pine knot, kindled in my own hearth, to set fire to an Indian village" (278). But Devil-worship, "Young Goodman Brown" suggests, goes deeper than this. It is part of an authentic American religious experience, one that unites Native Americans and Puritan settlers. Furthermore, the Devil is not only an old friend of the Brown family, long established in Salem society, but the physical double of Goodman Brown himself. *All* Americans, the story seems to suggest, worship the Devil, and this is what makes them American.

The Devil in "Young Goodman Brown" stands near the beginning of an authentic American tradition of folksy, down-home, demotic Satans. These figures are perhaps slightly more sophisticated that the rural Americans they aim to entrap, but generally not by much – a difference of degree, seemingly, rather than kind, for they are certainly the types of figures who don't seem radically out of place in the neighborhood. This is the Devil who can often be found in American popular music, whether waiting at the crossroads with a contract to buy Robert Johnson's soul in exchange for making him a blues guitarist of genius, or in Charlie Daniels' 1979 song "The Devil Went Down to Georgia," in the guise of a fiddle-playing Devil who is "lookin' for a soul to steal." (Daniels took the line "Hell's broke loose in Georgia" from Stephen Vincent Benét's "The Mountain Whippoorwill," a poem about a fiddle-playing competition; Benét, *Poems*, 376–79.) In other popular cultural forms, he is Randall Flagg, who arises from the ashes of a global pandemic to rebuild a totalitarian America in Las Vegas in Stephen King's *The Stand* (1978); or he is Bob, the double-denim-clad Devil who snarls back at you out of the mirror in Mark Frost and David Lynch's cult TV series *Twin Peaks* (1990–91). In Mark Twain's *The Mysterious Stranger* (1916), he is "No. 44," ostensibly an orphan boy who turns up in an Austrian schloss during the Reformation, but who has been to America "in the past, in the present, in the future," and has developed a particular fondness for American food, especially Arkansas corn pone and Alabama fried chicken: "Try it, and grieve for the angels, for they have it not!" (Twain, 896, 912). In Stephen Vincent Benét's short story "The Devil and Daniel Webster" (1936), he is Mr. Scratch, "a soft-spoken, dark-dressed stranger ... in a handsome buggy" (Benét, *Prose*, 33), who makes a deal with a luckless New Hampshire farmer whose crops won't grow. Pressed by the lawyer Daniel Webster, Mr. Scratch proudly claims American citizenship:

> "And who with better right," said the stranger, with one of his terrible smiles. "When the first wrong was done to the first Indian, I was there. When the first slaver put out for the Congo, I stood on her deck. Am I not in your books and stories and beliefs, from the first settlements on? Am I not spoken of still, in every church in New England? 'Tis true the North claims me for a Southerner and the South for a Northerner, but I am neither. I am merely an honest American like yourself – and of the best descent – for, to tell the truth, Mr. Webster, though I don't like to boast of it, my name is older in this country than yours." (Benét, *Prose*, 39)

Like Hawthorne's Devil, Mr. Scratch gives the lie to the virtuous pieties of American history and insists that the history of America is a history of atrocity, brutality, and exploitation. This is, in fact, a shadow form of American historiography that has long underwritten radical histories of the nation, in influential books such as Howard Zinn's *A People's History of the United States* (1980; see also Poole).

This folksy tempter is, as W. Scott Poole smartly puts it in his critical study *Satan in America*, "The Devil We Know." He is imagined simultaneously as an "evil cosmic warlord," the immortal adversary of God Himself, and as "a close and personal devil" (42), a small-scale local and individual antagonist who looks like one of your neighbors and is out to get *you*, personally. This vernacular American Satan is a figure arising out of Puritanism, as we have seen, and also out of the nineteenth-century American Religious Revival: he is an *evangelical* Devil. As such, he embodies an exaggerated version of what his greatest historian, Jeffrey Burton Russell, defined as the characteristic relationship of humanity to the Devil under Protestantism: "it was you versus the Devil; you alone, the individual, who had the responsibility for fending him off" (Russell, *Mephistopheles,* 31).

This should not surprise us. The Devil is, as his biographer Peter Stanford has argued, fundamentally "a popular figure, not a dogmatic abstraction, and has come alive not in learned tomes or seminary debates, but in the lives of the faithful, terrifying, omnipresent and grotesque, evil incarnate" (95). The existential and cosmological questions posed by theodicy (the branch of theology that deals most directly with the nature of evil) are, in the words of the theologian Marilyn McCord Adams, "the deepest of religious problems" (Oldridge, 3). But they are also notoriously unanswerable, or answerable only by slippery evasions, which is why mainstream or official theology tends to avoid the subject of the nature and existence of evil and its relationship to divine grace in a monotheistic creation. In the words of another contemporary theologian, Charles T. Mathewes, lived reality often "seems cruelly inappropriate to the sort of account Christianity proposes ... In this situation, to say that 'God is love' can seem like handing daisies to a psychopath" (Oldridge, 4). In the face of this, much of the territory of what Russell terms "radical evil" has been ceded to popular culture, a tendency both he and Poole view as a mark of American failure to take evil seriously (Russell, *Devil*; Poole, xvi).

The historian of religion Karen Armstrong has argued that fundamentalism has since the late twentieth century been the signal religious mode of the contemporary world, a development seen across "all major religions" and whose "manifestations are sometimes shocking" (ix). In its distinctively American form, as dispensationalist evangelical Protestantism, twentieth-century fundamentalism was given early articulation in a widely circulated series of pamphlets published between 1910 and 1915, collectively entitled *The Fundamentals: A Testimony to the Truth*. The farthest-reaching assertion of the pamphlets was their insistence on "the literal truth of the Bible" (Morone, 335). The message of *The Fundamentals* spread rapidly across America, and in the words of James A. Morone, "a loose alliance of orthodox traditions found a common name – fundamentalists" (335).

American fundamentalism and the evangelical American Devil are deeply culturally embedded within – are representative products of – American anti-intellectualism, the structure of feeling that the historian Richard Hofstadter famously analyzed as a central fact of American life:

> The case against intellect is founded upon a set of fictional and wholly abstract antagonisms. Intellect is pitted against feeling, on the ground that it is somehow inconsistent with warm emotion. It is pitted against character, because it is widely believed that intellect stands for mere cleverness, which transmutes easily into the sly or the diabolical.... It is to certain peculiarities of American religious life – above all to its lack of firm institutional establishments hospitable to intellectuals and to the competitive sectarianism of its evangelical denominations – that American anti-intellectualism owes much of its strength and pervasiveness. (Hofstadter, *Anti-Intellectualism*, 45–46, 53)

In the words of Billy Sunday, the influential fundamentalist preacher of the 1910s, "When the word of God says one thing and scholarship says another, scholarship can go to hell" (Morone, 335). Rooted in biblical literalism, fundamentalism also has a distinctly millenarian strain, a sense of realized eschatology that amounts to an obsession with the end-time, the imminent apocalypse, and the predetermined role of Satan and his agents in these foretold events.

Popular cultural representations of the fundamentalist Devil sometimes present him as a highly sophisticated, intellectual member of the cultural, social, and political elite. That is, he is a product of anti-intellectualism by inversion, the embodiment of everything American anti-intellectualism defines itself against. Thus, in *The Omen* (1976) and its sequels, he is Damien Thorn, adopted son of the American Ambassador to the United Kingdom, who is revealed to be the Antichrist – and, by the third leg of the trilogy, *The Final Conflict* (1981), the adult Damien has himself been appointed American Ambassador to the United Kingdom. Through the influence of its religious consultants, the fundamentalist pastors Robert Munger and Don Williams, *The Omen* propounds a covert ideological agenda that is very much in tune with the apocalypticism of the religious right, given popular articulation for the 1970s by Hal Lindsay's megaseller *The Late, Great Planet Earth* (1970).

More influential still is Tim LaHaye and Jerry B. Jenkins' *Left Behind* series of evangelical apocalyptic thrillers (1995–2007), selling in the high tens of millions, one of the true publishing phenomena of the modern age. The evangelical pastor Tim LaHaye, who was responsible for *Left Behind*'s theology, was a veteran Moral Majoritarian and culture warrior of the Christian right. *Left Behind*'s Antichrist is Nicolae Carpathia, a cultured and polyglot Romanian diplomat who becomes Secretary General of the United Nations. The series' female lead, Chloe Williams, undergoes a religious conversion at the beginning of the first book, when she abandons her Stanford education in favor of evangelical homeschooling: "You can go to college right here," her pastor tells her, "Every night at eight" (LaHaye and Jenkins, 31). At the height of the series' success, polls showed that 71 percent of *Left Behind*'s readers were from the American South and Midwest, compared with just 6 percent from the traditionally more liberal Northeast. *Left Behind*'s "core buyer," according to David Gates, was "a 44-year-old born-again Christian woman, living in the South" (44). It should not surprise us that a religion that rejects mainstream or majoritarian forms of knowledge should be drawn to the occult and the supernatural as explanatory models for lived experience. The political scientist Michael Barkun has taken up James Webb's formulation of "rejected knowledge" – which he further defines as "ideas outside the academy's definition of respectable knowledge" (12) – for his own account of the animating ideologies of the American extreme right.

"Young Goodman Brown" inaugurated an important recurring trope of American horror: the realization that one's seemingly benign and kindly neighbors are in league with the Devil, whom they worship in secret, or even that whole communities are in fact satanic cults. Twentieth-century American modernity gave the trope a distinctively urban, or even metropolitan, articulation, for example, in *The Seventh Victim* (1943), set in Greenwich Village, or Ira Levin's *Rosemary's Baby* (1967, and filmed by Roman Polanski in 1968), set in Manhattan's affluent Upper West Side. Twenty-first-century American horror films have continued to deploy this trope in rural and regional settings, as seen in films such as *The Last Exorcism* (2010) or *Hereditary* (2018). Much modern popular cultural theodicy is keen to explore the possibility of large-scale political satanic conspiracies, and *Rosemary's Baby*, in particular, provides an important literary and cinematic example of this major preoccupation with what the theologian Douglas E. Cowan has termed "the naziresis of evil": "the possibility of a satanic legacy, of a child dedicated in some way to the Devil ... In the cinematic horror inversion of naziresis, a variety of ritual preparations seek to ensure the birth of a satanic savior who will deliver the world *from* the power of God" (*Sacred Terror*, 37, 188). In the wake of *Rosemary's Baby*, contemporary American popular culture has produced a number of high-profile narratives of the naziresis of evil: *The Omen*, *Left Behind*, *Hereditary*.

The existence of satanic cults nurturing and protecting the Antichrist has clear links with what Hofstadter famously called "The Paranoid Style in American Politics," a recurring political discourse characterized by "heated exaggeration, suspiciousness, and conspiratorial fantasy." For Hofstadter, the "paranoid style," which had informed American politics for as long as there had been a nation, grew out of a feeling of dispossession, the sense among some that "America has been largely taken away from them and their kind ... by cosmopolitans and intellectuals" ("Paranoid Style"). In the late 2010s and 2020s, many conservative and nonmetropolitan Americans, feeling themselves economically dispossessed and culturally disenfranchised, turned to the paranoid populism of Donald Trump and to the paranoid conspiracies of QAnon, at the center of which was a Satan-worshipping cabal of high-ranking Democrats and their Jewish backers.

Not all modern American occultism, however, has its origins in the populist political and religious right. Together, William Peter Blatty's novel *The Exorcist* (1972) and William Friedkin's subsequent 1973 film adaptation comprise what may be the most celebrated and important cultural example of twentieth-century American satanic Gothic. To "the Jesuits, for teaching me to think": so reads the close of Blatty's acknowledgments in *The Exorcist*. A series of epigraphs, beginning with the Gospel of St. Luke's account of the Gadarene swine through to a transcript of an FBI wiretap of a conversation about a brutal Mafia torture and murder to an account of atrocities committed against Catholic priests in Maoist China, and closing with the words "Dachau Auschwitz Buchenwald," make clear by juxtaposition the novel's belief in the direct relationship between demonic possession and modern evil.

Written in the wake of the modernizing doctrinal shock of the Second Vatican Council (1962–65) – the process its instigator, Pope John XXIII, called *aggiornamento*, "bringing up to date" – *The Exorcist* amounts to a highly conservative institutional restatement of traditional Catholic authority and values (see O'Malley). Both the film and, particularly, the book go out of their way to raise and discuss every conceivable psychological and somatic explanation available to modern medicine as an explanation for young Regan MacNeil's apparent case of possession. All are eventually rejected in the face of the overwhelming evidence for the fact of demonic possession. *The Exorcist*'s Father Damien Karras is the archetype of the post–Vatican II priesthood, someone who has built a career on modern, secular forms of knowledge: he is a distinguished psychiatrist, Georgetown University's foremost practitioner, who trained at Harvard, Johns Hopkins, and Bellevue, and the film tells us that he is the author of a study of witchcraft "from the psychiatric end." *The Exorcist* charts his rejection of religious modernism as theologically empty and powerless, a capitulation to the Devil.

Karras is one of a number of modernizing Catholic priests in 1970s American horror who find their training completely inadequate in the fight against embodied, supernatural, radical evil. Stephen King engages with the relationship between Catholicism and modernity in one of his landmark novels of the 1970s, *'Salem's Lot* (1976), through the representative figure of a Catholic priest, Father Callahan, troubled by the contemporary sociological orientation of his vocation in the wake of Vatican II: "he was being forced into the conclusion that there was no EVIL in the world at all but only evil – or perhaps (evil)" (164). The novel forces Father Callahan into a confrontation with old-school, pre–Vatican II, European EVIL in the person of the vampire Mr. Barlow – a confrontation he loses decisively, as, no longer undergirded by faith, sanctity, or metaphysics, the trappings of his vocation are empty symbols in his hands. Father Callahan closes the novel wandering the earth anathematized, the Mark of Cain placed upon his forehead by Barlow, unable to cross the threshold of a church. In the 1979 film version of Jay Anson's bestseller *The Amityville Horror* (1977), Father Delaney (Rod Steiger) is "a trained psychotherapist" who comes to realize far too late the real presence of radical evil in the modern world and, worse, realizes that the Church is institutionally incapable of dealing with it. He also loses his battle with evil decisively, and closes the film a blind, mute hermit.

Friedkin's film shocked and horrified many viewers when it was first released in 1973. The Reverend Billy Graham, for one, condemned it, declaring that there was "an evil embodied in the very celluloid of the film" (Kermode, 45). The film was banned in the United Kingdom and Ireland in the wake of the "video nasties" scandal of the early 1980s, and not subsequently given a video or DVD release until the late 1990s. *The Exorcist* was also banned elsewhere, including Tunisia, where it was seen as "unjustified propaganda in favour of Christianity" (Kermode, 87). If anything, the Tunisian government's response seems more rational than that of its British counterpart. The film did divide critics on release, and some Catholic commentators were admittedly skeptical about its sensationalism or worried about the potentially damaging effects of its extreme images and language on a vulnerable audience (Cuneo, 28). Nevertheless, this notorious film was made with the full blessing and assistance of the Catholic Church, and featured a number of Jesuit priests as actors, playing versions of themselves – one of whom, Father Thomas Bermingham, who played the president of Georgetown University, was an old professor of Blatty's (he was professor of classics at Georgetown and then at Fordham) and "Vice-Provincial for Formation of the New York Province of the Society of Jesus." He was thanked in the novel's acknowledgments "for suggesting the subject matter of this novel" and also served as the film's technical advisor on matters of religion. Some viewers of the film were so disturbed and terrified that they dashed out of the cinema and ran to the nearest church, convinced of the literal physical existence of the Devil and therefore with a newly rejuvenated faith in Christianity. The increase in applications for the priesthood in the 1970s is directly attributable to *The Exorcist*; it was, in the words of the film critic Mark Kermode, the foremost authority on the making of the film, "the greatest advert for Catholicism that the world had ever seen" (*Fear of God*). Looking back on the making of the film in 1998, Father William O'Malley, who played Father Dyer, could even justify the film's most notorious image, that of Regan MacNeil masturbating with a crucifix: "It *was* merited.... It served a purpose" (*Fear of God*). In spite of the film's controversial history with, for example, the British Board of Film Classification and the American religious right, the Catholic Church has continued firm in its support of *The Exorcist*.

Finally, an important strand of American occultism, and American horror, has its philosophical origins – whether consciously or not – in one of the classic works of American high-intellectual discourse, William James' *Varieties of Religious Experience* (1902). At the beginning of his chapter on "The Reality of the Unseen," James writes: "Were one asked to characterize the life of religion in the broadest and most general terms possible, one might say that it consists of the belief that there is an unseen order, and that our supreme good lies in harmoniously adjusting ourselves thereunto" (James, 55).

This certainly seems to be the guiding principle animating much of the writing of Stephen King, for example – a writer who is, as Cowan has written, habitually given to raising (though not necessarily to resolving) profound theological issues (Cowan, *America's Dark Theologian*). King is certainly a populist writer, but he is also an implacable opponent of the American political and religious right: one of the reasons why he was such a powerful and trenchant critic of Donald Trump's America is because he understood it all too well: growing out of an authentically American vernacular theology, evangelicalism's illiberalism is a dark mirror to King's own democratic, liberal beliefs, which are equally folksy and down-home. King practices, as Cowan puts it, "the people's theology" (*America's Dark Theologian*, 70).

In King's cosmology, however, traditional Christian issues of morality, of personal salvation, of a loving God, or of the One True Faith seem to be secondary, if not irrelevant. As with William James, there is "an unseen order," and if we know what's good for us we need to stay on the right side of it. The unanswerable questions of theodicy are simply not operative here, since God is definitely not love, and quite likely not God at all. Like the American folk-Satan (and, as I have suggested, *The Stand*'s Randall Flagg is one manifestation of this figure), King's godlike, transdimensional, or destructive entities and forces tend to be proudly demotic: Tommyknockers, Leatherheads, Pennywise, Mister Yummy, Captain Trips.

Over a long and prolific career, King has ranged across a wide and varying landscape of rejected knowledge and marginal identities, taking in telekinesis and other psychic powers, vampirism, psychopathy, doppelgängers, and much else besides. Leland Gaunt, the junk shop proprietor of *Needful Things* (1991), is perhaps the nearest King has come to writing a straightforward Satan, though again very much in the American grain: he claims to be from Akron, Ohio. King has suggested that he intended Gaunt to be in part a political caricature, "the archetypal Ronald Reagan: charismatic, a little bit elderly, selling nothing but junk, but it looks bright and shiny" (Cowan, *America's Dark Theologian*, 109–10).

Elsewhere, the origins of King's occult threats are more inchoate. Pennywise, the malevolent entity of *IT* (1986), seems to have existed "[b]-efore the universe ... forever" (965). The fact that this immortal cosmological force spends its time preying on children from the drains of a small town in Maine might seem bathetic, if not pathetic, typical of the American failure to take evil seriously, as diagnosed by Russell and Poole. But it is also, as we have seen, highly characteristic of American theodicy: the Devil is waiting for you, in your neighborhood.

NOTE

1. See Gowan Dawson and Bernard Lightman, eds., *Victorian Scientific Naturalism: Community, Identity, Continuity* (University of Chicago Press, 2014).

Works Cited

Armstrong, Karen. *The Battle for God: Fundamentalism in Judaism, Christianity, and Islam.* HarperCollins, 2004.

Barkun, Michael. *Religion and the Racist Right: The Origins of the Christian Identity Movement.* University of North Carolina Press, 1997.

Benét, Stephen Vincent. *Selected Works of Stephen Vincent Benét, vol. 1: Poems.* Farrar and Rhinehart, 1942.

Selected Works of Stephen Vincent Benét, vol. 2: Prose. Farrar and Rhinehart, 1942.

Blatty, William Peter. *The Exorcist.* Corgi, 1972.

Burroughs, William S. *The Naked Lunch.* 1959. Grove Press, 1987.

The Charlie Daniels Band. "The Devil Went Down to Georgia." Epic Records, 1979.

Cowan, Douglas E. *America's Dark Theologian: The Religious Imagination of Stephen King.* New York University Press, 2018.

Sacred Terror: Religion and Horror on the Silver Screen. Baylor University Press, 2008.

Cuneo, Michael W. *American Exorcism: Expelling Demons in the Land of Plenty.* Bantam, 2001.
The Fear of God: 25 Years of "The Exorcist." BBC TV, 1998.
Fiedler, Leslie. *No! in Thunder: Essays on Myth and Literature.* Eyre and Spottiswoode, 1960.
Frazer, James George. *The Golden Bough*, ed. Robert Fraser. Oxford University Press, 1994.
Gates, David, with David J. Jefferson and Anne Underwood. "The Pop Prophets." *Newsweek*, US ed. (May 24, 2004).
Gosden, Chris. *The History of Magic: From Alchemy to Witchcraft, from the Ice Age to the Present.* Viking, 2020.
Hanegraaff, Wouter J. *Esotericism and the Academy: Rejected Knowledge in Western Culture.* Cambridge University Press, 2012.
Hawthorne, Nathaniel. *Tales and Sketches, Including Twice-Told Tales, Mosses from an Old Manse, and The Snow-Image; A Wonder Book for Girls and Boys; Tanglewood Tales for Girls and Boys; Being a Second Wonder Book.* Library of America, 1982.
Hofstadter, Richard. *Anti-Intellectualism in American Life.* Alfred A. Knopf, 1963.
"The Paranoid Style in American Politics." *Harper's Magazine* (November 1964). https://harpers.org/archive/1964/11/the-paranoid-style-in-american-politics/.
James, William. *Varieties of Religious Experience.* In *Writings 1902–1910.* Library of America, 1987.
Kermode, Mark. *The Exorcist*, 2nd ed. BFI, 1998.
King, Stephen. *IT.* Viking, 1986.
Needful Things. Viking, 1991.
Salem's Lot. New English Library, 1976.
LaHaye, Tim, and Jerry B. Jenkins. *Left Behind: A Novel of Earth's Last Days.* Tyndale House, 1995.
Lévi, Éliphas. *The History of Magic: Including a Clear and Precise Exposition of Its Procedure, Its Rites, and Its Mysterie.* Trans. A. E. Waite. William Rider & Son, 1922.
Lindsey, Hal, with C. C. Carlson. *The Late, Great Planet Earth.* Zondervsn, 1970.
Luck, Georg. *Arcana Mundi: Magic and the Occult in the Greek and Roman Worlds.* Baltimore, MD: Johns Hopkins University Press, 1985.
Melville, Herman. *The Letters of Herman Melville.* Ed. Merrill R. Davis and William H. Gilman. Yale University Press, 1960.
Redburn: His First Voyage, White-Jacket or, The World in a Man-of-War, Moby-Dick, or The Whale. Library of America, 1983.
Morone, James A. *Hellfire Nation: The Politics of Sin in American History.* Yale University Press, 2003.
Murphy, Bernice M. *The Rural Gothic in American Popular Culture: Backwoods Horror and Terror in the Wilderness.* Palgrave Macmillan, 2013.
O'Malley, John W. *What Happened at Vatican II.* Belknap Press of Harvard University Press, 2008.
Oldridge, Darren. *The Devil: A Very Short Introduction.* Oxford University Press, 2012.
Olson, Charles. *Call Me Ishmael.* Reynal and Hitchcock, 1947.
Partridge, Christopher, ed. *The Occult World.* Routledge, 2016.

Poole, W. Scott. *Satan in America: The Devil We Know*. Rowman & Littlefield, 2009.

Russell, Jeffrey Burton. *The Devil: Perceptions of Evil from Antiquity to Primitive Christianity*. Cornell University Press, 1977.

Mephistopheles: The Devil in the Modern World. Cornell University Press, 1986.

Sanborn, Geoffrey. "The Name of the Devil: Melville's Other 'Extracts' for *Moby-Dick*." *Nineteenth-Century Literature* 47, no. 2 (September 1992).

Stanford, Peter. *The Devil: A Biography*. Henry Holt & Company, 1996.

Stratton, Kimberley B. "Early Greco-Roman Antiquity." In *The Cambridge History of Magic and Witchcraft in the West: From Antiquity to the Present*, ed. David J. Collins. Cambridge University Press, 2015.

The Three Magical Books of Solomon: The Lesser Key of Solomon the King; The Greater Key of Solomon the King; and The Testament of Solomon, trans. Samuel Liddell MacGregor Mathers, Aleister Crowley, and F. C. Conybeare. Mockingbird Press, 2017.

Twain, Mark. No. 44, the Mysterious Stranger, *in* The Gilded Age, and Later Novels. Library of America, 2002.

Webb, James. *The Occult Underground*. Open Court, 1974.

Yates, Frances. *Shakespeare's Last Plays: A New Approach*. Routledge, 1975.

Zinn, Howard. *A People's History of the United States: 1492–Present*, 3rd ed. 1980. HarperCollins, 2005.

11

BETSY HUANG

SF and the Weird

This chapter examines the way two related genres, science fiction (SF) and the weird, deploy horror to critique the sources and expressions of "American horror" – namely, the dark side of American exceptionalism and the social and environmental consequences of its imperialist projects. Both SF and the weird have been platforms for colonialist and nationalist imaginations, but both have also been potent vehicles for revealing, resisting, and repairing the brutalities of such imaginations – exploitative and extractive practices that demonize, destroy, or oppress what humans seek to control or what they do not understand. The two genres share similar generic genealogies, but they diverge teleologically. SF is built on the assumptions of scientific rationalism and therefore follows an identifiable internal logic, relying on our implicit or explicit belief in the plausibility of the story. The weird, by contrast, is resolutely committed to the inexplicable. Both, however, use horror to disrupt our reliance on realist modes of representation that flatter our epistemological certainties.

Rooted in the Gothic, which ruptures the rational to confront forces humans cannot account for, horror's synergies with SF and the weird are best captured by Elisabeth Anker's description: "Horror is a genre form known for mobilizing and intensifying fear through narratives of terror and scenes of violence. Its conventions depict an ever-present threat of social disintegration through vivid images of gruesome monstrosity" (795). In the American scene, there is no shortage of historical violence and terror that unsettles our delusional ideations of the American Dream. The storming of the Capitol, the mass shootings, the land grabs of indigenous territories and Black-owned property, the inhumane treatment of "caravans" from south of the border, and, most dreadfully, the countless but continual assaults and murders of people of color – these are not just indicators of a particularly difficult moment in the present, but symptoms of monstrous doctrines that took root at the inception of "America." To correct course, we must first recognize their horror. Horror is thus fundamentally and ultimately disruptive, a negative affective state brought on by a triggering event that forces us to look underneath the illusions of the ideal and the normal. So are SF and the weird.

The Horror in/of SF

American science fiction came of age in the first part of the twentieth century amid social and environmental concerns brought on by the Industrial Revolution, settler colonialism, the eugenics movement, Jim Crow, and immigration from Europe and Asia. Its peddling of horror in service of validating racist, sexist, and xenophobic fears of the time is therefore no surprise. This is most emblematic of the work of H. P. Lovecraft, widely known and often celebrated as one of the progenitors of American horror, SF, and weird fiction. Early SF of the Lovecraftian ilk gave expression to the white supremacist views of the time and emerged within the same motivations as Cecil B. DeMille's post-Reconstruction nationalist romance, *Birth of a Nation*, a film that propagated anxieties of Black misrule and miscegenation as threats to the white Christian nation, a threat that justified the formation – and the brutality – of the Ku Klux Klan. Like so many cultural productions of that time, Lovecraft's early fiction set the stage for seeing racialized bodies as the material expression of monstrosity and the unhuman, spectacularizing "abnormal" bodies by feeding the fear of racialized bodies as both contaminant and the contaminated. His short story "Herbert West – Reanimator" (1921–22), an homage to and satire of Mary Shelley's *Frankenstein* (1818), puts on parade his revulsions of immigrant and racialized bodies as contaminated, "unfresh," bespoiled specimens of humankind. Lovecraft's work, notes Ezra Claverie, thus appeals most to the reader who "adopts the generic subject position of the European coloniser or the American white racist. For that subject, disproportionate violence against the brown and the Black, the 'hybrid' and the 'half-caste' is a self-evident necessity" (263–64). Indeed, the advancement of nonwhite people, and African Americans in particular, in the public sphere, along with the prospect of racial mixing such advancement brings, informed much of early SF on both sides of the Atlantic. The work of British writer H. G. Wells, who enjoys an even more unimpeachable canonical SF status, poses similar challenges to scholars who have had to confront his racist and classist representations of race and Blackness, most notably in *The Island of Dr. Moreau* (1896) and *The Time Machine* (1895). Even in the American scene, one does not need to be a white racist to deploy racist horror, as evidenced by conservative Black writer George S. Schuyler, whose novel *Black No More* (1931) expresses Lovecraftian unease with raciality, and with Blackness in particular, complicated by the toxicity of racial self-hatred.

SF's preoccupation with racialized bodies as pollutants and disease carried on into the mid-twentieth century. Richard Matheson's 1954 plague novel, *I Am Legend*, widely credited as the first modern vampire story after Bram Stoker's *Dracula* (1897), depicts the experience of a middle-class white man coming to terms with the reality that his place in society is no longer at the top as newly evolved vampires (coded as women and people of color) become the leaders of the new world order. The novel is a transparent expression of not only white patriarchal anxieties about the advancement of women and changing gender roles in the wake of World War II, but also the advancement of African Americans in the wake of Reconstruction and, later, the onset of the civil rights movement. The plague that infects and turns people into vampires can be read as a metaphor for the encroachment of people of color and other social "undesirables" into the white middle class and positions of social power. Neville's concession to the new vampire majority, and the dominance of its social rules and norms, conveys a sense of mournful horror for those who resist and fear this social prospect.

The camp horror of the 1950s science fiction B-movies channeled these same anxieties into popular horror films for mass consumption, which helped to secure the reactionary response as the only response to these societal changes. Films such as *Attack of the 50-Foot Woman* (1958), *Planet of the Apes* (1968), and countless alien abduction narratives not only amplify racist and sexist horror, but expiate it through either the destruction or domestication of the monsters in the end. The horror persists, however, well beyond the containment and neutralization of the threats that the endings of these films usually deliver. Susan Sontag identified the shared aesthetic and moralistic structures of SF and horror films in her caustic 1965 essay, "The Imagination of Disaster." Sontag describes the narratives of early and mid-century SF films as predictable scripts of threats and atrocities committed by the identified enemies, usually aliens of some kind, against the white male hero and his perpetually endangered white female love interest, who represent, respectively, the strength and vulnerability of the state. "Science fiction films are not about science," she declares, "they are about disaster" (1005), where disaster is the destruction of the bodies and landmarks valued by the state. She elaborates that SF and horror films that feature monstrosities overlap in the way both participate in "extreme moral simplification – that is to say, a morally acceptable fantasy where one can give outlet to cruel or at least amoral feelings" (1007). She links horror's supply of the "pleasure we derive from looking at freaks, beings excluded from the category of the human" with the same supply in SF films: "In the figure of the monster from outer space, the freakish, the ugly, and the predatory all converge – and provide a fantasy target for righteous bellicosity to discharge itself, and for the aesthetic enjoyment of suffering and disaster" (1007). In these scripts, the only way to address difference is to destroy it, and the destruction is simplistically and morally justified in order to preserve what Donna Haraway calls "the sacred image of the same" (67).

Dislodging the replicative aesthetics of the old guard requires the imaginations of marginalized writers who brought to the SF playground new rules forged from the perspectives of the putative monsters themselves. Samuel R. Delany, Octavia E. Butler, Ursula K. Le Guin, and Joanna Russ made critical interventions by leveraging the conventions of the genre as the very tools that shook the master's house. Le Guin stridently skewers SF's long history of racism, sexism, and xenophobia in her 1975 essay, "American SF and the Other":

> SF has either totally ignored women, or presented them as squeaking dolls subject to instant rape by monsters – or old-maid scientists de-sexed by hypertrophy of the intellectual organs – or, at best, loyal little wives or mistresses of accomplished heroes. Male elitism has run rampant in SF. But is it only male elitism? Isn't the "subjection of women" in SF merely a symptom of a whole which is authoritarian, power-worshiping, and intensely parochial? (208)

Sontag and Le Guin reveal the great irony of early SF: that as a form that aims to imagine new worlds, it was perpetually replicating the old, reproducing familiar fears, and engendering reactionary responses. As recently as 2015, Samuel Delany shares in an interview with *The Nation* his frustration with the recalcitrance of the old guard and the gatekeepers:

> Generally, black people do not struggle with racism. It's just a given. We combat it when possible. We accept it when we can't. Those are our choices and have always been. And as I wrote 17 years ago, when the combat, gentle or forceful, expands the minority presence notably beyond tokenism, that's when the hegemonic folks get upset. That's not prediction. That's part of the way the system functions.

Indigenous writers, too, have always understood SF as a genre that has habitually narrated "the atrocities of colonialism as 'adventure stories'" (Dillon, 2).

SF in the hands of minoritarian writers deploys horror to achieve effects very different from when they are in the hands of the "hegemonic folks." Indigenous writers discovered SF's critical capacity to move beyond the constraints of "reservation realism" to "envision Native futures, Indigenous hopes, and dreams recovered by rethinking the past in a new framework" (Dillon, 2). Butler, in particular, deploys horror as an intersectional, anticolonial aesthetic that disrupts SF's historical project of defining the "human" against racialized, gendered, differently abled, augmented, and hybrid bodies. Genetic mixing, inter-species sex, intra- and inter-generational metamorphoses – these are the horrors propagated by traditional SF that Butler confronts head-on in all of her writing. She routinely evokes the "horror" of racial mixing and miscegenation in theme, plot, and characterization as a way of normalizing hybridity. Her fully fleshed aliens such as the Oankali in the Xenogenesis series (published in 2000 under the new series title *Lilith's Brood*) and the T'lic in the short story "Bloodchild" (1984) detail not only scenes of human-alien mating rituals designed to evoke shock, but also equally detailed explanations of why such relationships are necessary for the survival and longevity of the species involved. Butler never presents death as an option to "stay human" and insists instead on survival at all costs, including a willingness to consider species transformation, as the only way to guarantee one's place in the future. Her "monsters" are not reducible to metaphors for the inhumanity of humans, but are to be taken in all their literality. The alien Oankali of the Xenogenesis series, for instance, have no clear analog in any human culture or population and are to be taken as they are described in the novel. Her worldview extends far beyond terrestrial notions of difference and prepares us for difference that cannot be understood via human lexica. "Perhaps someday we will have truly alien company," she prognosticates:

> Perhaps we will eventually communicate with other life elsewhere in the universe or at least become aware of other life, distant but real, existing with or without our belief, with or without our permission. How will we be able to endure such a slight? The universe has other children. There they are. Distant siblings that we've longed for. What will we feel? Hostility? Terror? Suspicion? Relief? ("The Monophobic Response," 415–16)

The postcolonial critic Peter Mason once asked the crucial question, "How are we to handle what is other without robbing it of its otherness?" Butler's answer would be that we merge with it, and let it change us as we change them, in an act of "fair trade" that reforms the historically asymmetrical power relationships of colonized states and subjectivities. Her Xenogenesis series, "Bloodchild," and "Amnesty" all share this core ethos; for Butler, the most powerful way to counteract the horror of the other is to imagine an incorporated future with it.

Anxieties of hybridity also prevail in stories featuring robots, androids, and artificial intelligence, narratives that dramatize the erosion of the clear distinctions we have drawn between the human and the machine. Anxieties of the distinction between the "real" – variously understood as the original, the organic, the natural, and the material – and its putative opposite, which includes constructs of the simulacrum such as the fake, the copy, the virtual, and the artificial, have long undergirded this body of literature. Narratives of artificial lifeforms that prove intellectually or physically superior to humans are particularly disarming because they compel us to confront the prospect of being outplayed, dominated, or replaced by replicable artificial versions of our bodies and minds, and therefore our obsolescence as a consequence of our own inventions. This fear is evident in early portrayals of robots, such as those in Czech playwright Karel Capek's 1920 play *R.U.R. (Rossum's Universal Robots)* and the robot Maria in Fritz Lang's 1927 SF film *Metropolis*, and extends to artificial intelligence narratives later in the century, such as the HAL 9000 computer in Stanley Kubrick's adaptation of Arthur C. Clarke's *2001: A Space Odyssey* (1968), the androids of Philip K. Dick's universe and Ridley Scott's *Blade Runner* (1982), the Cylons in the *Battlestar Galactica* universe, and, more recently, the AIs of Spike Jonze's *Her* (2013) and the recent HBO series *Westworld* (2016–20), a reboot of Michael Crichton's 1973 SF horror film.

A variation on this fear is the end of human existence in the hands of more technologically and evolutionarily advanced extraterrestrials. Extraterrestrials' lack of regard for human importance has been a longstanding theme in SF, one that first gained traction in H. G. Wells' 1897 novel *War of the Worlds* and disseminated into the popular consciousness through Orson Welles' panic-inducing radio broadcast adaptation in 1938. Unlike alien invasion narratives in which extraterrestrials take interest in humans and introduce benevolent interventions, such as in Clarke's 1953 novel *Childhood's End* or Robert Wise's film *The Day the Earth Stood Still* (1951), narratives that induce deep horror are those in which human agency and ontology are deemed insignificant or inconsequential by the aliens. In Ridley Scott's film *Alien* (1979), in which an alien creature mercilessly hunts the crew of the spaceship Nostromo, the android Ash's oft-quoted description of the alien as the "perfect organism" articulates what we would regard as a very unhuman sentiment; Ash calls the creature a "survivor ... unclouded by conscience, remorse, or delusions of morality," and expresses his deep admiration for its "structural perfection" as well as its "purity." Ash's observations induce horror in us because they reveal both the creature's and Ash's lack of regard for the core values of liberal humanism. Another notable instance is an exchange between Captain Jean-Luc Picard and the Borg in the television series *Star Trek: The Next Generation* (1987–94), in a tense moment when the Borg is on the verge of "assimilating" Picard's crew. When Picard tells the Borg that he will resist because human culture "is based on freedom and self-determination," the Borg tells him: "Freedom is irrelevant. Self-determination is irrelevant. You must comply." And when Picard responds defiantly that "we would rather die," the Borg affectlessly replies: "Death is irrelevant" – a proclamation that might as well be restated as "humans are irrelevant," an idea that perhaps strikes the deepest blow of all to our hitherto uncritical anthropocentrism ("The Best of Both Worlds").

The horror engendered by the Borg has its roots in the mechanization of human labor in the mass production economy of the Industrial Revolution. Robots in early SF were metaphors for oppressed workers, as evidenced in *Metropolis* and *R.U.R.* Depictions of robots took a brief turn for the positive in the mid-century alongside advances in robotics; robots in Isaac Asimov's sprawling Robot Series, for instance, are hard-wired with and bound by the Three Laws of Robotics and portrayed as loyal sidekicks, as tools that, despite their extra-human abilities (such as their computational capacities and a much longer lifespan), never threaten the authority of their (male) human masters. Figurations took a darker turn once again in the sixties in response to the cultural moment of the civil rights movement and anti-establishment countercultures. Critiques of the exploitative and dehumanizing practices of state institutions and multinational corporations in the early years of globalization informed much of Philip K. Dick's fiction, whose famed androids became signifiers of enslaved labor and human bioweapons.

Undergirding these familiar tropisms is the horror induced by the breach of clear definitional borders within the context of liberal humanism. Katherine Hayles sees the debate between the human and the not-human in Dick's android fiction as "boundary disputes between human and android" in "highly commercialized spaces in which the boundaries between autonomous individual and technological artifact have become increasingly permeable" (162). Indeed, the prime mover of Dick's fiction seems to be his desire to expose nefarious corporate or military plans for amassing large-scale biopower to feed capital growth, and he does so by dramatizing the way humans are altered, replicated, augmented, and weaponized in service of multinational corporate profiteering. The horror of corporate and governmental exploitation, weaponization, and commodification of human and artificial bodies was also taken up and made spectacular in big Hollywood box-office hits like Scott's *Alien*, James Cameron's *The Terminator*, Paul Verhoeven's *Robocop*, and the Wachowskis' *The Matrix* trilogy (1999–2003). Hayles explains:

> The interpellation of the individual into market relations so thoroughly defines the characters of these novels that it is impossible to think of the characters apart from the economic institutions into which they are incorporated, from

> small family firms to transnational operations. Moreover, the corporation is incorporated in multiple senses, employing people who frequently owe to the corporation not only their economic and social identities but also the very corporeal forms that define them as physical entities, from organ implants and hypertrophied brains to completely artificial bodies. Given this dynamic, it is no surprise that the struggle for freedom often expresses itself as an attempt to get "outside" this corporate encapsulation. (162)

Indeed, the value of a body in a market economy that reduces an individual to the embodiment of either capital or labor is the governing theme of postmodernist and late capitalist SF.

Robot and android narratives of this period thus reshaped the genre into powerful vehicles for uncovering the imperialist, white supremacist practices rationalized by the rhetoric of liberal humanism and the logic of capitalism. In essence, robots and androids in these works are built not in the likeness of humans but in the likeness of humans reduced to their labor – military grunts, sex workers, hired guns, domestic servants. This informs, too, the persistent gendering of the robot as female, an ongoing problem in a genre still grappling with the legacies of its heterosexist and heteronormative conventions in depictions of human/machine relations, where women and their labor – domestic, sexual, parental – are reconfigured as faithful artificial companions or servants. The female body, mind, and subjectivity have always served as the sites for the male experimental gaze, and this relationship continues to serve as the master script for Hollywood, as evidenced by Ira Levin's robot wives in *The Stepford Wives* (1975), Dick's Pris Stratton in his novels and in Ridley Scott's *Blade Runner*, or even *The Jetsons*' Rosie the Robot, and most recently in Alex Garland's 2014 *Ex Machina* and Spike Jonze's 2013 *Her*. And just as the real world of the politics of capital versus labor, the fantasy of the perfectly obedient and docile workers is always threatened by the fear of their revolt. Just as Hollywood serves up its familiar menu of feminized artificial intelligence or robots, it also delivers stories of their rebellion and emancipation in equal measure. Whether the audience feels horror or excitement at their capacity to exceed or reject their algorithmic scripts depends on with whom the audience identifies.

In real life, our increasing reliance on artificial technologies raises few flags. We acclimate easily to them through the introduction of endless small-scale new technologies into the practice of everyday life. In what Rob Nixon might call the slow violence of the culture of upgrades, SF and horror's cautionary impact is regularly blunted and domesticated by our daily grind and our uncritical embrace of quick solutions and creature comforts. In such a gradual and steady trickle, no tipping point will be easily identifiable, and large-scale human and environmental consequences will remain imperceptible until too late. New technologies are rarely carbon-neutral, as evidenced by the massive obsolescence they produce, the vast e-waste dumps in poor nations, and the massively distributed trash debris across the Great Pacific Garbage Patch. What greater ciphers of our own technologies turning against us than robots, spelling our eventual obsolescence and extinction at the hands of . . . ourselves?

The Horror in/of the Weird

Weird fiction is often described by writers and scholars of the genre as a close relation of SF by dint of their shared preoccupations with and deployments of monstrosity and other tropes of horror. But weird fiction also differs from SF by degree and by kind. The weird has a much more extensive history and genealogy than SF. Michael Moorcock traces weird fiction's origins to surrealist, absurdist, and supernatural fiction of the likes of Franz Kafka, Samuel Beckett, Angela Carter, and Jorge Luis Borges, whose work shares a narratological blueprint that typically involves a strange event that remains unexplainable ("Foreweird"). "The Weird," explain Ann and Jeff VanderMeer, "has eschewed fixed tropes of the supernatural like zombies, vampires, and werewolves, and the instant archetypal associations these tropes bring with them. The most unique examples of The Weird instead largely chose paths less trodden and went to places less visited, bringing back reports that still seem fresh and innovative today" (xvi). And lest we engage in that hackneyed pastime of trying to identify the "first" work of weird fiction, China Miéville effectively talks us out of it: "We're tempted to hunt Patient Zero. Is there a culprit in this library? Which book was first sick? (Of course they're all in terrible health)" (1115). Nevertheless, such exercises, both generative and reductive at times, have yielded a putative consensus: that the weird is any genre of literature that resolutely eschews explanations and answers. As such, the weird is a genre not of human conceit but of human humility. Its preoccupation with unexplainable events and phenomena that elude human comprehension is always already an acknowledgment of existences beyond our epistemological scope.

Early weird fiction is plagued with the same anxiety of Lovecraftian influences as early American SF: social anxieties and fears around race, gender, and class propagated by the white dominant culture of the time. Alison Sperling inveighs against Lovecraft's status in critical weird studies as a persistent symptom of the entrenchment of the old guard: "His racism and dismissive, discriminatory attitudes toward women do not just haunt his tales; they are central to his mythos" ("Acknowledgment"). Critical scholarship on the author has only recently begun to grapple with the tension between the philosophical implications of his work and its inherent xenophobia as contemporary writers and scholars engage in soul-searching about their "debt" to Lovecraft. But can weird fiction truly do critical and emancipatory work if the genre continues to fetishize the Lovecraftian mythos?

Lest we overplay Lovecraft's influence, Stefanie K. Dunning reminds us that racism and xenophobia in the weird long predate Lovecraft: "Even if the definition of Weird Literature was not consecrated until H. P. Lovecraft came along, the sense of supernatural dread that characterizes the Weird is present even as far back as Shakespeare's Caliban" (46). Contemporary writers of the weird thus either negotiate that legacy through ironic, critical homage or sidestep it altogether. For Black writers, this means reappropriating Lovecraftian tropes through retellings of his stories, as Victor LaValle's *The Ballad of Black Tom* (2016) demonstrates so compellingly, or resignifying Blackness not as the monstrosity but as the countermeasure to the atrocities of white supremacy. Dunning makes the case that "we can read blackness as the primal ground of the Weird" because "Blackness, in the white imagination, is the very uncanny that disrupts time/space" (47). Contemporary Black weird fiction such as Boots Riley's *Sorry to Bother You* and Jordan Peele's *Get Out*, Dunning explains, dramatize the appropriation and destruction of Black bodies for the maintenance of white power, squarely identify white supremacy as the true monster, and Blackness as both insight into systemic injustice and embodiment of truth. Black writers also imagine different relationships between putative humans and nonhuman "monsters" in weird fiction. Octavia E. Butler, for instance, consistently compels us to accommodate the difficult but often unavoidable reality of accepting alien "monsters," often coded as racial selves or others, as cocreators of the future. This means seeing the others as sexual partners, a prospect made more challenging by the radical asymmetries of not just bodies, but the power dynamics that already structure these relationships.

Writers less interested in Lovecraftian influences and more concerned with a different form of horror – the human footprint on our precarious terrestrial ecologies – have turned their attention to what David Thompkins identifies as "ecologically minded Weird fiction." "Eco-weird," for short, this growing body of literature depicts the accumulated horror from scores of destructive practices and disasters, distributed over extended time and space, that not only questions human ontology, but forecasts its end. Eco-weird combines the aesthetics of eco-fiction and the weird to dramatize what Amitav Ghosh would describe as our deranged self-harm on our environment, and what Timothy Clark calls "Anthropocene horror," a phrase he coined to "name a sense of horror about the changing environment globally, usually as mediated by news reports and expert predictions, giving a sense of threats that need not be anchored to any particular place, but which are both everywhere and anywhere" (61).

"Anthropocene horror" is a useful heuristic for understanding how weird fiction deploys horror to call urgent attention to the immensity of the problem. As Clark usefully describes, Anthropocene horror "is being lived as a pervasive affect in daily life, not as an easily compartmentalized emotion. It need not be a response to some obviously perceptible assault on the natural environment, but may even or perhaps especially affect someone living in and surrounded by a 'developed' infrastructure" (62). This horror is often expressed not through the figuration of metaphoric or literal monsters but through depictions of supernatural phenomena in our natural environments that cannot be represented, much less explained, by human systems of knowledge. The eco-weird also attempts to capture the vastness of the Anthropocene's "hyperobjects," Timothy Morton's term for ecological phenomena such as global warming, the accumulated effects of which are so "massively distributed over time and space relative to humans" that we are unable to fathom or represent its totality" (1). As such, the eco-weird aesthetic is often built on a slow-burn narrative structure in which phenomena that defy human explanation accrue imperceptibly but insistently, with no clear resolutions or effective mitigation strategies in sight. Jeff VanderMeer's fictional "Area X" of his Southern Reach trilogy (2014), widely recognized as a contemporary exemplar of eco-weird, is a place in which natural phenomena not of human making or intent appear to be erasing the land of the human footprint. Area X's unsolved mysteries make Lovecraftian monsters feel like quaint campfire tales, figments of the fabular limitations of the human imagination. The eco-weird reckons instead with the factual and material evidence of ecological phenomena not of human making. This underscores not only the very real prospect that humankind's dominance in the terrestrial ecosystem is coming to an end, but also the idea that our putative control of everything on our planet is not even ours to cede, but is merely being eroded and disregarded. Human agency, the cornerstone of liberal humanism, is irrelevant here. "In the books," Tompkins observes in his review of the novels, "Area X is not a channel into the primordial ooze where tentacled, bloblike Old Ones lurk (à la Lovecraft). Area X is frightening, yes, but what appears to be happening there is not a reversion to Chaos and Old Night but what we might see as the start of a comprehensive reversal of the Anthropocene Age" ("Weird Ecology"). The titles of the three novels that comprise the trilogy – *Annihilation*, *Authority*, and *Acceptance* – can be read as stages in the decentering of the anthropocentric lens in our narratological structures, epistemological systems, and ontological conceits.

Alongside Clark's Anthropocene horror as a useful heuristic for understanding the weird is what I would call an aesthetics of explanatory deferment. "One formal mark of the genre," John MacNeil Miller argues, is that "within the confines of the text itself, the weird tale resists description" (245). I would modify this to say that weird tales are actually steeped in description, interpretation, and evaluation. What they resist is definitive verification of the interpretive and evaluative efforts. As Miller observes, "Weird tales are identifiable by the way they linger too long over objects and settings in particular, affording these apparently ancillary elements of narrative a kind of interest and attention that unsettles expectations about who or what matters in the storyworld." This is evident in weird fiction both old and new, from Shirley Jackson's domestic gothic horror to Kelly Link's quirk horror to VanderMeer's perseverative repetitions of descriptive details and interpretive theories that lead to no verifiable explanation. "By exposing and disrupting the ossified patterns of attention that structure our storytelling," Miller elaborates, "weird fiction makes room for new attributions of agency and ethical significance to previously unrepresented or unrepresentable actors" (245). To capture the unrepresentable scale of the Anthropocene's harmful ecological impacts, explanatory deferment immerses the reader in thick descriptions of local phenomena – specific sites of the hyperobject that serve as case studies from which we are to extrapolate and to assemble the elusive "big picture" – and endless futile attempts at interpretation, theorization, and resolution, all of which reflect the limits of human epistemes. "We are always inside an object," Morton theorizes, and that hyperobject can feel more monstrous than the ones created by humans simply because, as Morton describes the hyperobject, "there is no center and we don't inhabit it," and, even more awe-fully, "there is no edge! We can't jump out of the universe" (17).

Futurity is an actuarial exercise, and it is a human one. The weird insists on the futility of that exercise. Prediction is a human strategy of containment and control, but the weird is also a human strategy of chastening our own conceits. In this sense, the weird is perhaps the most humble literary genre of all. It is entirely predicated on the knowledge of human limitation and fallibility. Stanislaw Lem's *Solaris* (1961), Clarke's *Rendezvous with Rama* (1973), Jeff VanderMeer's *Southern Reach* trilogy (2014), and the TV series *The Expanse* (2015–) – in which extraterrestrial forces that exceed and elude human understanding, much less management – are depicted to barely bat a proverbial alien eye at human activity. The diminishment of anthropocentrism in these stories reflects less our fear of our extinction and more our fear of our own insignificance. And given the deep colonial and masculinist footprints of the Anthropocene, it is not surprising that Anthropocene horror also tends to be expressed most strongly in works by male writers.

(In)Conclusion: The After-Effect of SF and the Weird

How do we free ourselves from paralyzing horror?

Clark points to an "intense ecological grief ... suffered by people who are the most vulnerable to environmental change for reasons of poverty, social status or mode of livelihood" (62). Along with that grief, Clark also points to "an emergent environmental remorse" that eco-weird fiction expresses, "an anxious awareness that significant nonhuman subjects have been left undervalued or unaccounted for in our anthropocentric representations of the world" (62). Remorse is good; it could lead to course correction, whereas fear leads to protectionist behavior that rationalizes destruction of the unknown. Remorse can move us to restorative action, as we are now seeing in environmental policy arenas where the rights of nonhuman subjects, such as rivers and forests, are being discussed and granted. Another response is the increasing pressure on what Clark sees as "a refreshingly specific human target – on central governments," because it is the authority of these institutions "that is increasingly felt as simulative, a shift both exciting and potentially dangerous" (76). This is precisely the target of VanderMeer's critique in the Southern Reach trilogy, and in *Authority*, the second novel of the series, in particular. For what is the Southern Reach Agency but a version of an arrogant central government, and the character "Control" the agency's human executor, whose arrogance and conceit, time and again rendered powerless by Area X's indifference, are exposed as the perpetrators and perpetuators of a never-ending horror?

The way out of American social and environmental horrors, then, is not grief, but a compelling combination of grievance and remorse that prompts reparative action. Horror may be paralytic, but SF and the weird can be catalytic toward a more just and sustainable future.

Works Cited

Anker, Elizabeth. "The Liberalism of Horror." *Social Research: An International Quarterly* 81, no. 4 (Winter 2014): 795–819.

"The Best of Both Worlds." *Star Trek: The Next Generation*, Season 3, Episode 26. June 18, 1990. Written by Michael Piller. Directed by Cliff Bole.

Butler, Octavia E. "Bloodchild." In *Bloodchild and Other Stories*. Seven Stories Press, 1995.

Lilith's Brood. 1987–89. Grand Central Publishing, 2000.

"The Monophobic Response." In *Dark Matter: A Century of Speculative Fiction from the African Diaspora*, ed. Sheree R. Thomas. New York: Warner Books, 2000. 415–16.

Carroll, Jordan S., and Alison Sperling. "Weird Temporalities: An Introduction." *Studies in the Fantastic* 9 (Summer–Fall 2020): 1–17.

Clark, Timothy. "Ecological Grief and Anthropocene Horror." *American Imago* 77, no. 1 (Spring 2020): 61–78.

Claverie, Ezra. "Weird Interpellation." *New Formations: A Journal of Culture/Theory/Politics* 84–85 (2015): 261–64.

Delany, Samuel R. "Samuel R. Delany Speaks." Interviewed by Cecelia D'Anastasio. *The Nation*, August 24, 2015.

Dillon, Grace. *Walking the Clouds: An Anthology of Indigenous Science Fiction.* University of Arizona Press, 2012.

Dunning, Stefanie K. "What Is the Future? Weirdness and Black Time in *Sorry to Bother You*." *Studies in the Fantastic* 9 (Summer–Fall 2020): 44–60.

Haraway, Donna. *Primate Visions: Gender, Race, and Nature in the World of Modern Science*. New York: Routledge, 1989.

Hayles, Katherine. *How We Became Posthuman: Virtual Bodies in Cybernetics, Literature, and Informatics*. Chicago: University of Chicago Press, 1999.

Le Guin, Ursula K. "American SF and the Other." *Science Fiction Studies* 2, no. 3 (1975): 208–10.

Miéville, China. "Afterweird." In *The Weird: A Compendium of Strange and Dark Stories*, ed. Ann VanderMeer and Jeff VanderMeer. New York: Tor, 2011.

Miller, John MacNeill. "Weird Beyond Description: Weird Fiction and the Suspicion of Scenery." *Victorian Studies* 62, no. 2 (Winter 2020): 244–51.

Moorcock, Michael. "Foreweird." In *The Weird: A Compendium of Strange and Dark Stories*, ed. Ann VanderMeer and Jeff VanderMeer. New York: Tor, 2011.

Morton, Timothy. *Hyberobjects: Philosophy and Ecology after the End of the World.* Minneapolis: University of Minnesota Press, 2013.

Roberts, Adam. *Science Fiction: The New Critical Idiom.* London: Routledge, 2005.

Sontag, Susan. "The Imagination of Disaster." In *Science Fiction: Stories and Contexts*, ed. Heather Masri. New York: Bedford, 2009. 1002–14.

Sperling, Alison. "Acknowledgment Is Not Enough." *Los Angeles Review of Books*, March 4, 2017. https://lareviewofbooks.org/article/acknowledgment-not-enough-coming-terms-lovecrafts-horrors/.

Tompkins, David. "Weird Ecology: On the Southern Reach Trilogy." *Los Angeles Review of Books*, September 30, 2014. https://lareviewofbooks.org/article/weird-ecology-southern-reach-trilogy/.

VanderMeer, Ann, and Jeff VanderMeer. "Introduction." In *The Weird: A Compendium of Strange and Dark Stories*, ed. Ann VanderMeer and Jeff VanderMeer. New York: Tor, 2011.

12

DAWN KEETLEY

Monsters and Monstrosity

American freedom was birthed with slave labor. What historian Edmund S. Morgan calls "the marriage of slavery and freedom" (6), of "irreconcilable opposites" (x), engendered what can only be called a "monstrous" birth – a nation deformed from its beginning.[1] In their Introduction to this collection, Mark Storey and Stephen Shapiro define horror as that which focuses on "the body in distress," that "lingers on the body turned inside out." Just as the "body" of horror is a monstrous body, America has been a monstrous body from the start: it has contained both Mr. Hyde and Dr. Jekyll, both the devil and what Abraham Lincoln in 1861 called the "better angels of our nature."

Monsters have also populated American literature from its beginnings – in religious pamphlets, journals, and sermons. Two "monstrous births" featured, for instance, in documents swirling around the Antinomian controversy of 1636–38. This was a religious conflict in which ministers of the Massachusetts Bay Colony, believing in the sanctification of works, clashed with those whom they held to be adherents to the heresy of God's grace. One of those heretics, Mary Dyer, gave birth in 1637 to an infant "so monstrous and misshapen, as the like hath scarce been heard of," wrote the governor of the Massachusetts Bay Colony, John Winthrop. He continued that its "eares (which were like an Apes) grew upon the shoulders"; the "brest and back was full of sharp prickles, like a Thornback [a fish]"; "in stead of toes, it had upon each foot three claws, with talons like a young fowle"; and above the eyes were "four hornes" (Hall, 280–81). The second monstrous birth was to Anne Hutchinson, who had already been banished and excommunicated from the Massachusetts Bay Colony.[2] Again, as Winthrop describes it, Hutchinson delivered "30. monstrous births or thereabouts, at once; some of them bigger, some lesser, some of one shape, some of another; few of any perfect shape, none at all of them (as farre as I could ever learne) of humane shape" (Hall, 214). Such "monsters," contemporaries averred, must be a sign of God's displeasure.[3]

Indeed, the births were interpreted as "divinely caused manifestations of their mothers' doctrinal errors," as historian Anne Jacobson Schutte puts it (103). Of Hutchinson, Winthrop wrote, "And see how the wisdom of God fitted this judgement to her sinne every way, for looke as she had vented misshapen opinions, so she must bring forth deformed monsters; and as about 30. Opinions in number, so many monsters" (Hall, 214). The theological errors and sins of both Dyer and Hutchinson were manifest, quite literally, in the hybrid and deformed "monsters" they birthed. Each woman's tragedy, moreover, was inextricable from the interwoven theological and political context through which they were understood. Monsters have been with America – and have been political – throughout its history. This chapter will describe the most important paradigms for conceptualizing the monsters of American horror, marking their entanglement with politics and moving toward identifying the principal forms of monstrosity in the early twenty-first century.

12.1 Impure Monsters

The "monstrous" births of Mary Dyer and Anne Hutchinson illustrate almost perfectly the definition of the monster offered by philosopher Noël Carroll in his discussion of "art-horror." Although Asa Simon Mittman has declared that Jeffrey Jerome Cohen's influential 1996 essay "Monster Theory (Seven Theses)" inaugurated the field of "Monster Studies" (2), Carroll in fact did so in 1990. He argues that the monster demarcates horror from other genres, and he devotes significant space to elucidating the monster's principal property: impurity. Relying on the work of anthropologist Mary Douglas, Carroll characterizes impurity as an object or being that "is categorically interstitial, categorically contradictory, incomplete, or formless" (32). He continues that, in their hybridity, their existence on borders, monsters "are not classifiable according to our standing categories" (33). He then usefully elucidates the forms of impurity that characterize monsters – "the mixture of what is normally distinct," categorical "incompleteness," and "formlessness" (34) – varieties of boundary-crossing that exist beyond what science knows.

Almost all subsequent writing on monsters has reinforced Carroll's essential characteristic of "impurity." In "Monster Culture (Seven Theses)," for instance, Cohen includes the thesis: "The Monster Is the Harbinger of Category Crisis," a section that begins with the claim that the monster "refuses easy categorization," continuing that monsters are "disturbing hybrids" and embody an "ontological liminality" (6). And Mittman writes that the monstrous asks us "to acknowledge the failures of our systems of categorization" (8). The dominance of this definition of the "monster" as impure is due to the fact that it describes so many of the monsters of American horror. The "poisonous" Beatrice Rappaccini from Nathaniel Hawthorne's "Rappaccini's Daughter" (1844) horrifies because she is interwoven with deadly plants – her breath a venomous miasma. Tod Browning's *Dracula* (1931), a landmark film in the American horror tradition, features a "categorically contradictory" monster that is both living and dead, originating a long tradition of vampire (and zombie) narratives. Indeed, so many of the monstrous bodies of horror are hybrids, unnatural conjoinings of opposites, formless blobs, massed collectives. And they all, as Carroll aptly insists, push beyond the boundaries of the known.[4]

A linchpin of Carroll's definition of the monster is specifically that it is *not known by science*: "'monster' refers to any being not believed to exist now according to contemporary science" (27; see also 37, 40, 41). But for something not to exist "according to contemporary science" does not mean that it is not "known" in a much broader sense. In fact, the monsters of horror exist to expand the very nature of the known *beyond* the boundaries of what "science" knows. In Stephen King's novel *The Outsider* (2018) and the HBO adaptation (2020), for example, the characters eventually come to accept that the murders they are trying to solve are committed by a shape-shifting monster, "El Cuco," of Spanish folklore. That this monster is denied by science is emphasized by the way in which the story veers, at first, toward the police procedural. After private investigator Holly Gibney (Cynthia Erivo) in the HBO adaptation explains her theory about El Cuco to the lead detective, Ralph Anderson (Ben Mendelsohn), he asserts, "I have no tolerance for the unexplainable" (ep. 3). The characters are eventually compelled to acknowledge the existence of El Cuco, however – thus accepting a being that is not "unknown" at all but has long been described in both folklore and art (ep. 4). As Holly tells the assembled investigative team, when confronted with "seemingly impossible" events," the "first step to seeing things clearly is not to find a way to dismiss those facts but to expand your sense of what reality might entail" (ep. 6). In all of their impurity, in their defiance of the categories of science, monsters perform exactly the expansion of reality that Holly advocates; monsters open up what is already "known" in myth, folklore, superstition, religion, and art. Indeed, narratives about monsters are narratives about the persistence of all that secular, rational society disavows. The more science tightens its grasp on "reality," the more monsters it creates – and the more we need them.

12.2 Monsters as Other

Along with the notion of the monster as "impure," a second influential conception of the monster is as incarnation of the "Other" – what Cohen aptly calls "difference made flesh, come to dwell among us" (7). Film critic Robin Wood famously articulated this conception of the monster in his discussion of 1970s horror films. Like Carroll, Wood positions the monster as a defining characteristic of horror, which he claims dramatizes the dictum, "normality is threatened by the Monster" (78). For Wood, the normality-shattering monster renders incarnate "all that our civilization represses or oppresses" (75). Wood thus characterizes the monster as an embodiment not of category transgression but of societal repression and oppression – and the horror film dramatizes the horrific return of both.

Wood's formulation allows for human monsters, which Carroll as good as rules out, arguing that no matter how psychologically disturbed they may be, humans are, in the end, "believed to exist now according to contemporary science" (27). Thus, he claims, Norman Bates (Anthony Perkins) from *Psycho* (dir. Alfred Hitchcock, 1960) is technically not a "monster" (and the film not "horror") because Bates is not an unclassifiable monster but a schizophrenic, "a type of being that science countenances" (38). Wood's theory, on the other hand, foregrounds human monsters since it is predominantly aspects of human nature and human groups that society represses and oppresses. For Wood, monsters most often emerge from those impulses and people who are "Othered" by society – not least women, the working classes, non-US cultures, ethnic and racial groups, children, and those who embrace "alternative" ideologies and "deviations" from the sexual norm (73–75). In Wood's view, monsters are always born in relation to a dominant worldview or ideology, bursting from the cracks in "dominant social norms" (73, 78). The horror film is, then, inevitably political, and its particular political meanings, according to Wood, depend on the monster, integrally bound to the dominant culture that created it. Progressive horror films represent the monster sympathetically, perhaps even allowing it to persist at the end of the narrative. Reactionary horror films, on the other hand, express more hostility toward the monster and ensure that it is expelled, shoring up normative values (77, 80). The monster is often the most visible sign, then, of a text's politics.

Multiple critics have developed Wood's theory of the monster as incarnation of the culturally repressed and oppressed. Or, as Cohen puts it: "for the most part monstrous difference tends to be cultural, political, racial, economic, sexual" (17).[5] Bernice Murphy has described how poor rural whites are transformed into (often inbred) monsters in backwoods horror

(133–77), and Jeffrey Weinstock has elaborated the long-standing "monsterizing of indigenous peoples" ("American Monsters," 42). Above all, perhaps, Black people have long served as America's monsters. Robin Means Coleman describes how Black characters are cast as the monster in American horror film through their connection to a "powerful and savage" Black religion (6) or to "deadly real estate," a dangerous and crime-ridden Black inner city (170). *Candyman* (dir. Bernard Rose, 1992), to take one example, embodies both: Candyman (Tony Todd) is a monstrous Black man at the center of an urban legend circulating in the urban housing project of Chicago's Cabrini-Green, sexually pursuing white women while brutally killing Black women (Means Coleman, 188–91).

The transformation of Black Americans into monsters preceded film; indeed, the very system of slavery depended on it, as did post-Emancipation Jim Crow and persistent systemic racism. In his 1904 short story, "The Lynching of Jube Benson," Paul Laurence Dunbar unveils the mechanism that turns Black people into monsters. After a white woman is found murdered, a white physician reflexively blames a Black man on the basis of no evidence at all. As he tells it, when he finds Jube Benson hiding in the woods, "I saw his black face glooming there in the half light, and I could only think of him as a monster" (236). At the same time, however, he recognizes that this visceral response to a man he previously called a friend has been thoroughly primed by "tradition" and a "false education" (236). It is the consequence of a false, pernicious ideology.

In Dunbar's "The Lynching of Jube Benson," the Black man is not born but "created" as a monster by American's dominant white supremacist structures of thought and institutions. Perhaps no story presents this Frankenstein-like creation of the Black monster more explicitly (and tragically) than Stephen Crane's "The Monster" (1898), a novella about a Black man, Henry Johnson, who cares for the horses of a wealthy New York man, Dr. Trescott. One fateful night, Johnson saves Trescott's son from a house fire and is horribly burned. Trescott cares for him and saves his life, although he is warned by the town's judge that it would be a mercy to let him die: "he will hereafter be a monster, a perfect monster." When Trescott declares that he has no choice but to save Johnson, the judge declares, "He will be your creation, you understand. He is purely your creation. Nature has very evidently given him up. He is dead. You are restoring him to life. You are making him, and he will be a monster" (473). Trescott's dedication to Johnson's humanity is anomalous in a town in which even an act of heroism is no defense against the powerful drive to turn a Black man into what another resident of the town thinks is "simply a thing, a dreadful thing" (489). A similar mechanism is evident as late as

1968 in George A. Romero's *Night of the Living Dead*, when a group of white police and military, moving across the state killing the newly risen dead, fire at the Black protagonist of the film, Ben (Duane Jones). Having survived the nighttime siege of the "ghouls," Ben is killed by humans whose propensity to see him as the "monster" is, as Crane and Dunbar diagnosed, born from centuries of "tradition" and "education." Whether a crime occurs adjacent to them, as in Dunbar's story, or whether Black men act heroically to save others and themselves, they are all subject, at any moment, to being reduced to monstrous versions of Frankenstein's creation, nonhuman, monstrous "things."

Women's sexuality has also long served to generate the monsters of American horror, from *Cat People* (dir. Jacques Tourneur, 1942) and Stephen King's *Carrie* (1974) to Karyn Kusama's *Jennifer's Body* (2009). Indeed, all kinds of nonnormative sexuality – beyond just women's sexuality – have been dramatized as monstrous in horror. "'Deviant' sexual identity," Cohen declares, "is similarly susceptible to monsterization" (9). Jack Halberstam has persuasively argued that the twentieth century saw a shift toward a primary focus on sexuality and gender in representations of monstrosity (26): *Psycho*, Brian De Palma's *Dressed to Kill* (1980), and Jonathan Demme's *The Silence of the Lambs* (1991) all feature monsters that appear to be transvestites (and are monstrous for that reason). *The Silence of the Lambs*, in particular, saw a significant backlash against what critics insisted was a homophobic portrayal of its principal "monster," Buffalo Bill. Many objected to the film, Halberstam writes, because its plot was driven by "gender confusion" as "the guilty secret of the madman in the basement" (166). Demme was not alone, however. In his representation of Buffalo Bill, he drew on a long tradition of horror films – crystallized in the slasher subgenre – that feature a killer who is, as Carol Clover puts it, a "male in gender distress," propelled by "psychosexual fury" (27). One could argue, in fact, that both "gender distress" and sexual distress have forged the most visible forms of monstrosity in twentieth-century American horror.

12.3 Monsters in the Mirror

What becomes strikingly evident if you pursue the monster as "other" very far, however, is that it rarely remains "other." It turns, offering a terrifying reflection of the self. In large part, this is because monsters make manifest what must be expelled in order for the self, or the society, to exist at all. Drawing on Julia Kristeva, Barbara Creed calls what must be expelled the "abject," which includes bodily waste, the corpse, and the maternal body – all of which threaten the notion of the self as singular and pure. Creed defines the horror plot as a confrontation with the abject "in order, finally, to eject the abject and redraw the boundaries between the human and the nonhuman" (46). The monster that embodies the abject is in many ways more threatening than the "other" because its existence threatens not only the self but also the border between self and other. As Margrit Shildrick puts it, the monster is not merely "an instance of otherness"; rather, it "reminds us of what must be abjected from the self's clean and proper body" (163). William Friedkin's *The Exorcist* (1973) exemplifies the horror film as confrontation with the abject "in order, finally," as Creed puts it, "to eject the abject and redraw the boundaries between the human and the nonhuman" (46). What appears on the surface to be about the exorcism of a possessed girl, Regan MacNeil, is in fact the confrontation between "the world of the symbolic, represented by the priest-as-father, and the world of the presymbolic, represented by the woman aligned with the devil." These two forces clash "head on in scenes where the abjection of the feminine is signified by her putrid, filthy body covered in blood, urine, excrement, and bile" (Creed, 44). Regan embodies the abject that must be expelled for the pure, singular subject to exist.

While the abject directs attention to parts of the self – bodily wastes, for example – that are expelled and that return as monstrous, much American horror has explored in more literal fashion the notion that the "other" is in truth the self. In his 1835 story "Young Goodman Brown," Nathaniel Hawthorne describes Brown racing through the New England forest at night, convinced it is inhabited by witches and wizards, Indians, and even the Devil himself. But the narrator undercuts Brown's fear: "In truth, all through the haunted forest, there could be nothing more frightful than the figure of Goodman Brown" (284). Brown's own superstition, judgmentalism, self-righteousness, and lack of faith become what is monstrous in the story. Foregrounding the reiterated discovery that the "other" is the self, mirrors have long been staples of horror narratives. H. P. Lovecraft's story "The Outsider" (1926) is a veritable exegesis of this paradigm of the monstrous self. The protagonist, who has lived his life in solitary confinement, explores a castle only to confront an "inconceivable, indescribable, and unmentionable monstrosity" – a "compound of all that is unclean, uncanny, unwelcome, abnormal, and detestable" (12–13). The protagonist, it turns out, is looking in a mirror (14). This tradition extends to twentieth-first-century film. In *Us* (2019), Jordan Peele uses a literal hall of mirrors to show the confused identities of two girls, one who kidnaps the other and imprisons her underground, taking her place in the above-ground world. While the film is seemingly structured by the sharply demarcated below- and above-ground dwellers, the former of whom seem to be the "monsters" as they slaughter their counterparts above, the film actually puts this certainty in question through its use of literal mirrors and mirrored selves (clones).

In cases from Young Goodman Brown to the protagonist of Peele's *Us*, Adelaide (Lupita Nyong'o) characters in horror remain steadfast in casting *others* as monsters. There is a strand of horror, however, in which (marginalized) protagonists consciously embrace the role of monster for themselves. In these texts, the values associated with both "normality" and the "monster" are flipped: the self-aware monster-hero revels in threatening the representatives of normality, now aligned as antagonistic, even expressly corrupt. Narratives of the voluntary monster constitute some of the most progressive kinds of horror – and they invite more or less wholehearted audience identification *with the monster*.[6] Natalie Wilson has named this "willful monstrosity," describing how the "other" embraces their difference and fights back against the social structure that defined them as other in the first place. As she puts it, the "crux" of "willful monstrosity" is "a monstrosity that resists assimilation, exploitation, and annihilation" (12).[7] In one of the most progressive horror films of the twenty-first century, the zombies of Romero's *Land of the Dead* (2005), led by a Black gas station owner (Eugene Clark), acquire enough sentience to revolt against and destroy the bastion of white privilege and exclusion ruled by Kaufman (Dennis Hopper). Together a Black and a Latino zombie (Jon Leguizamo) ensure, personally, that Kaufman dies – in an utter reversal of the white police/mob murdering the Black survivor at the end of *Night of the Living Dead*. And in Emil Ferris' 2017 graphic novel *My Favorite Thing Is Monsters*, the protagonist, Karen Reyes, adopts monstrosity (casting herself, for instance, as a werewolf) as a means not only to make herself visible as a Latinx lesbian in late 1960s Chicago but also to forge alliances with other outsiders. As Stephen Shapiro writes, Ferris "draws on a visual and textual history of cinematic gothic and horror as a slantwise syntax to convey the presence of queer desire" (129). Karen and her friends adopt monstrosity as a means to achieve both identity and affiliation, constituting what Shapiro calls a "crew of monsters" (131), a very useful phrase that aptly describes how adopting monstrosity can become a form of community building.

12.4 Monsters from Margin to Center

While willful monsters elicit sympathy, even identification, they are still outside mainstream society; the monster still threatens (and thus constitutes) "normality" (to return to Wood). Hence, Stephen King famously claimed, in 1981, that horror films necessarily appeal "to the conservative Republican in a three-piece suit who resides within all of us." We love monstrosity, he adds, "because it is a reaffirmation of the order we all crave as human beings" (39). Twenty-first-century horror, however, has upended the formula of "normality is threatened by the Monster." Now, normality *is* the monster. The monster *is* "the conservative Republican in a three-piece suit," avatar of a specifically dominant white, male normality – a trend that arguably began in 2000 with Mary Harron's scathing portrait of wealthy, privileged, yuppie monstrosity in *American Psycho*'s Patrick Bateman (Christian Bale). Kinitra Brooks has pointed out that Wood's formulation has always presumed that "normality" equates to "the normative experiences of white men." Therefore, she continues, "the anxiety examined in horror is continuously about the other sides of the white male binary" – notably the "monster" as Black man and/or white woman (8).[8] In the twenty-first century, though, horror is increasingly taking as "normative" the experiences of precisely those "other" groups – women, nonwhites, immigrants, queer folks, the poor – and showing that the "monsters" of *their* narratives are the incarnations of "normality" itself: they are the monsters *of* normality rather than the monstrous threats *to* normality. The monsters of normality are those who exploit their position of power and privilege to harm others, almost always in intentional ways. Twenty-first-century horror is replete with monsters that yearn to shore up inequitable systems of power, often harking back to a sense of order and tradition that is in the process of vanishing.

There are certainly important precedents for the recent trend of "monsterizing" hegemonic structures and white men in particular – most influentially, perhaps, Richard Connell's story "The Most Dangerous Game" (1924) and the 1932 film adaptation, in which a wealthy white man hunts people on his island. Much later, Wes Craven's *The People under the Stairs* (1991) depicted the monstrous "Mommy" and "Daddy," white stand-ins for Ronald and Nancy Reagan, who keep poor whites imprisoned in their basement and rob from and cannibalize their poor Black neighbors. And Rusty Cundieff's horror anthology *Tales from the Hood* (1995) imagines white police as monsters. Such narratives have exploded in the first two decades of the twenty-first century. As I have argued in an essay on the trope of the captive woman, since "around 2010, there have been growing numbers of horror films in which the 'monster' is just a white man" ("Lock Her Up!," 97). One of the most iconic monsters of the twenty-first century, for instance, is Jigsaw (Tobin Bell) from the Saw franchise (2004–21), a white man intent on punishing those who stray from conservative values. Reece Goodall has astutely written about how these films exemplify a rise in white authoritarianism that is linked to the "impending minority status of whites" (125). The same anxiety and compensatory white authoritarianism run through The Purge (2013–21) franchise, especially *The Purge: Election Year* (2016), released in the summer before the highly contentious presidential election that saw Donald Trump beat Hillary Rodham Clinton. And in Adam Cesare's 2020 retro-slasher novel, *Clown in a Cornfield*, the older generation in a rural Missouri town dons clown costumes to stalk and slaughter the young – a purportedly "blighted crop," their morality warped (the elders believe) from traditional social values, not least by social media (282).

The surge of monsters that embody dominant and regressive social structures and ideologies is in part evident in the proliferation of horror narratives in the twenty-first century that feature cults. Cults make visible the ways in which, as Stephen Asma aptly puts it, "[i]ndividual monsters are extensions of monstrous institutional systems" (244). Cults are "monstrous institutional systems" writ large and writ horrific. One of the foundational texts of the cults-as-monstrous-institutions narrative is Ira Levin's 1972 novel *The Stepford Wives* and Bryan Forbes' film adaptation (1975). The uncanny (and occasionally malfunctioning) housewife robots may appear to be the monsters of *The Stepford Wives*, but it is the group of Stepford men – "normal," mundane – who are the true monsters, preserving patriarchal privilege by replacing their fractious real wives with compliant simulacra. Jordan Peele indicts systemic racism in *Get Out* (2017) by making it clear it isn't only the Armitage family that is conspiring to implant white consciousness in Black bodies. They are part of a cult, the Coagula, a veritable religion that believes, as Dean Armitage (Bradley Whitford) puts it, that they "are the divine ones. We are the Gods who are trapped in cocoons," and Chris (Daniel Kaluuya) is the "sacrifice" who must lose himself so the members of the Coagula can take their "baptism" and shed their skin "to awake renewed and perfect" (Peele, 128). In *Get Out*, Black bodies are sacrificed for white apotheosis. In his 2016 novel *Lovecraft Country*, adapted by HBO in 2020, Matt Ruff weaves his plot around a centuries-old white sect, the Adamite Order of the Ancient Dawn (75), which functions as a synecdoche for America's endemic racism. Although there are certainly hideous creatures in the novel and the series – including the forest-dwelling shoggoths – *they* are not the truly terrifying monsters. Driving through a "sundown county," where African Americans risk being lynched if found there after dark, one character turns away from the woods "and [runs] back out to the road, which is where the real monster was waiting for him" – the county sheriff (21). Ruff's plot weaves the police into the cult, both parts of a seamless whole, a monstrous whole that is the edifice of bland and yet devastating "normality."

12.5 Monsters of Entangled Life

As the previous sections have made clear, monsters are increasingly visible as "us" in the twenty-first century: we look in the mirror and see ourselves, whether we recognize what we see or not. Monsters are more frequently the sympathetic protagonists of horror texts, resisting the structures of "normality" from their spaces of difference. And especially in the twenty-first century, the monsters *of* normality, which represent the violence of oppressive systemic structures, are moving to the forefront of horror plots that are intent on critiquing structures of power. There is one last way in which monstrosity is depicted as very close to home in the 2000s – a surge of monsters that disclose we have never been "human," that the border between human and monster has always been permeable.

Science is revealing the thoroughgoing entanglement of life, the ways in which the "human" is not singular, not exceptional, its boundaries not demarcated. As biologist Margaret McFall-Ngai declares, humans are "not what we thought"; "every 'I' is also a 'we,'" and we are "*more microbe than human*" (M51–M52). Biologist and mycologist Merlin Sheldrake concurs that developing knowledge in the microbial sciences shakes the very foundation of the idea that "we start where our bodies begin and stop where our bodies end." We are not individuals but ecosystems, Sheldrake continues, "composed of – and decomposed by – an ecology of microbes" (16–17). These definitions of the *human* return full circle, uncannily, to Carroll's definition of the *monster* – the "categorically interstitial, categorically contradictory" (32). However, twenty-first-century science reveals that to be an entangled hybrid of human and nonhuman life – to be "categorically interstitial" – is not monstrous but the human state. "Against the conceit of the individual, monsters highlight symbiosis, the enfolding of bodies within bodies in evolution and in every ecological niche" (Swanson et al., M3). Humans have always been monsters, symbiotically entwined with nonhuman life.

Horror has long exploited the entanglement of the nonhuman and the human. As the twenty-first century progresses, however, the presence within the human of the parasitic, the viral, the vegetal, and the fungal is depicted less as an alien takeover and more as a mundane state (albeit exaggerated, of course, for horrific effect). In *Alien* (dir. Ridley Scott, 1979) and *The Thing* (dir. John Carpenter, 1982), a literally alien entity is able to "hide" for a while in a human body, dissembling as human, but it eventually bursts out, making visible a distinction (human vs. alien) that had been present from the beginning. More recent narratives, though, show a more immanent, persistent, and synergetic relationship – and it is with the nonhuman life of *this* planet, not another.[9] Monsters are increasingly becoming "observable parts of the world" (Swanson et al., M3) and they are inextricable from us.

In her 2020 novel *Mexican Gothic*, Silvia Moreno-Garcia describes a house and a family (the Doyles) in a remote part of Mexico that are entangled with fungus. As one character explains, "Fungi can enter into symbiotic relationships with host plants. Mycorrhiza. Well, it turns out that it can also have a symbiotic relationship with humans" (211). The hybrid house-fungus captures and preserves the family's memories, inducing what seem to be nightmares in visitors to the house, as they too become infused with spores and drawn into the mycorrhizal network. The fungus has entwined itself not only with the house, though, but also with the Doyle family, making their bloodline immortal (212). As Francis Doyle tells the protagonist Noemí Taboada, some people are able to have "a symbiotic relationship with the fungus," while, for others, it "can burn out your own self" (212). Francis later likens the effect of the fungus on most people to the "cicada fungus. *Massospora cicadina*," which infests the cicada, consuming its body from within (232). The symbiotic relationship of the fungus with the Doyles has enabled this colonial English family, who came to Mexico to exploit the region's silver mines, to keep their stranglehold over the local economy and townspeople. Moreno-Garcia effectively employs the human-nonhuman symbiosis to dramatize the parasitic colonial relationship.

If "[m]onsters ask us to consider the wonders and terrors of symbiotic entanglement" (Swanson et al., M2), Moreno-Garcia depicts its terrors, focusing on how symbiosis signals a systemic, imperialistic predation. But in all their variegated incarnations, monsters can also offer potential "wonders" of future becoming (Cohen, 20). As Michael Hardt and Antonio Negri put it, "*The new world of monsters is where humanity has to grasp its future*" (196; emphasis in original). The possibilities of the monstrosity of entangled life are eminently visible, for instance, in *Annihilation* (dir. Alex Garland, 2018).[10] In the mysterious "Shimmer," a spreading tract of land into which people disappear never to return, all kinds of DNA combine and recombine, so the characters who venture in become mixed with animals, plants, lichen, and fungi. This can be horrific – as in the case of Cass (Tuva Novotny), who is dragged away by and becomes part of a bear. But it can also be seductive, a desired becoming, as in the case of Josie (Tessa Thompson), who chooses to mutate into a plant-human hybrid. Monsters are always horrifying; after all, they knock humans off their pedestal of exceptionality and show us that we are not singular, bounded, unique, and autonomous. But monsters can also be embraced as a means of becoming something new.

NOTES

1. Critics have elaborated the profound connection of the American Gothic to the nation's history of oppression. Goddu founds her study of American Gothic on the fact that it is "haunted by race" (7) – not least slavery (10). For a comprehensive survey of how American history has bred monsters, see Poole.
2. For a discussion of the births of both Dyer and Hutchinson, see Schutte and Winsser.
3. For a discussion of teratology – the study of monstrous births – as one of the three principal categories in the genealogy of monster theory, see Weinstock, "Introduction," 4–13.
4. Carroll is careful to distinguish "art-horror" from what he calls "*natural horror*" – real atrocities like genocide, nuclear war, or ecological disaster (12), but like everything having to do with the monstrous, this boundary does not hold. There is a significant literature on "real" monsters (both historical and contemporary) and the cultural purposes their being, and making, serves. See, for instance, Calafell; Ingebretsen; and Keetley, *Making a Monster*.
5. The collection edited by Grant, *The Dread of Difference*, is a landmark in exploring how gender and sexuality (and to a lesser degree race) have served as a fount of monstrous difference. See also Part II, "Monsterizing Difference," in Weinstock's *Monster Theory*, 173–286, which considers the "monsterizing" of race, Jews, the feminine, homosexuals, and nonnormative bodies.
6. The seeds of this inversion have long been inherent to the horror film, as Wood points out when he claims (of 1970s horror) that "[f]ew horror films have totally unsympathetic Monsters" and that we are also typically ambivalent about normality, enjoying horror films for the ways they "smash the norms that oppress us" (80).
7. Calafell examines "those moments in which I have been made monstrous as a queer woman of color in the academy" (7). As a "mestiza," she felt herself drawn to narratives of werewolves, vampires, and other shape-shifters, willfully embracing those who, like her, were "hybrid" and living "in a middle state" (2).
8. Brooks goes on to argue that the Black woman has been excluded from this binary formulation as the "non-Other, the Other of the white male's Others (black men and white women") (8).
9. In "Introduction: Six Theses on Plant Horror," I discuss at greater length how the "human harbors an uncanny constitutive vegetal" (16), which can be seen, for instance, in Scott Smith's 2006 novel *The Ruins* (16–19).
10. Luckhurst fleetingly references *Annihilation* to exemplify a new way of understanding monstrosity – beyond the concept of the border to a "volume" that "expands, enfolds and entwines identities in a wholly new way" (15).

Works Cited

Asma, Stephen T. *On Monsters: An Unnatural History of Our Worst Fears*. Oxford University Press, 2009.

Brooks, Kinitra D. *Searching for Sycorax: Black Women and Horror*. Rutgers University Press, 2017.

Calafell, Bernadette Marie. *Monstrosity, Performance, and Race in Contemporary Culture*. Peter Lang, 2015.

Carroll, Noël. *The Philosophy of Horror; or, Paradoxes of the Heart*. Routledge, 1990.

Cesare, Adam. *Clown in a Cornfield*. HarperCollins, 2020.

Clover, Carol J. *Men, Women, and Chain Saws: Gender in the Modern Horror Film*. Princeton University Press, 1992.

Cohen, Jeffrey Jerome. "Monster Culture (Seven Theses)." In *Monster Theory: Reading Culture*, ed. Jeffrey Jerome Cohen. University of Minnesota Press, 1996. 3–25.

Crane, Stephen. "The Monster." In *The Portable Stephen Crane*, ed. Joseph Katz. Penguin, 1969. 449–508.

Creed, Barbara. "Horror and the Monstrous-Feminine: An Imaginary Abjection." In *The Dread of Difference: Gender and the Horror Film*, ed. Barry Keith Grant. University of Texas Press, 1996. 35–65.

Dunbar, Paul Laurence. "The Lynching of Jube Benson." In *The Heart of Happy Hollow*. Dodd, Mead, and Co., 1904.

Ferris, Emil. *My Favorite Thing Is Monsters*. Fantagraphics Books, 2017.

Goddu, Teresa A. *Gothic America: Narrative, History, and Nation*. Columbia University Press, 1997.

Goodall, Reece. "John Kramer for President: The Rise of Authoritarian Horror." *Horror Studies* 11, no. 1 (2020): 123–40.

Grant, Barry Keith, ed. *The Dread of Difference: Gender and the Horror Film*. University of Texas Press, 1996.

Halberstam, Jack. *Skin Shows: Gothic Horror and the Technology of Monsters*. Duke University Press, 1995.

Hall, Donald D. *The Antinomian Controversy, 1636–1638: A Documentary History*. 1968. Duke University Press, 1990.

Hardt, Michael, and Antonio Negri. *Multitude: War and Democracy in the Age of Empire*. Penguin, 2004.

Hawthorne, Nathaniel. "Young Goodman Brown." 1935. In *Nathaniel Hawthorne: Tales and Sketches*. Library of America, 1996. 276–89.

Ingebretsen, Edward J. *At Stake: Monsters and the Rhetoric of Fear in Public Culture*. University of Chicago Press, 2001.

Keetley, Dawn. "Introduction: Six Theses on Plant Horror." In *Plant Horror: Approaches to the Monstrous Vegetal in Fiction and Film*, ed. Dawn Keetley and Angela Tenga. Palgrave, 2016. 1–30.

"Lock Her Up! Angry Men and the Captive Woman in Post-Recession Horror." In *Make America Hate Again: Trump-Era Horror and the Politics of Fear*, ed. Victoria McCollum. Routledge, 2019. 97–118.

Making a Monster: Jesse Pomeroy, the Boy Murderer of 1870s Boston. University of Massachusetts Press, 2017.

King, Stephen. *Danse Macabre*. Berkley, 1981.

Lincoln, Abraham. "First Inaugural Address." March 4, 1861. The Avalon Project, Yale Law School, https://avalon.law.yale.edu/19th_century/lincoln1.asp. Accessed September 24, 2020.

Lovecraft, H. P. "The Outsider." 1926. In *H. P. Lovecraft: Tales*. Library of America, 2005. 8–14.

Luckhurst, Roger. "After Monster Theory? Gareth Edwards' *Monsters*." *Science Fiction Film and Television* 13 (2020): 269–90.

McFall-Ngai, Margaret. "Noticing Microbial Worlds: The Postmodern Synthesis in Biology." In *Arts of Living on a Damaged Planet: Monsters of the Anthropocene*, ed. Anna Tsing et al. University of Minnesota Press, 2017. M51–M69.
Means Coleman, Robin R. *Horror Noire: Blacks in American Horror Films from the 1890s to Present*. Routledge, 2011.
Mittman, Asa Simon. "Introduction: The Impact of Monsters and Monster Studies." In *The Ashgate Research Companion to Monsters and the Monstrous*, ed. Asa Simon Mittman and Peter Dendle. Ashgate, 2012. 1–14.
Moreno-Garcia, Silvia. *Mexican Gothic*. Del Rey, 2020.
Morgan, Edmund S. *American Slavery, American Freedom*, 2nd ed. 1975. Norton, 2003.
Murphy, Bernice M. *The Rural Gothic in American Popular Culture: Backwoods Horror and Terror in the Wilderness*. Palgrave, 2013.
Peele, Jordan. *Get Out: The Complete Annotated Screenplay*. Inventory Press, 2019.
Poole, W. Scott. *Monsters in America: Our Historical Obsession with the Hideous and the Haunting*. Baylor University Press, 2011.
Ruff, Matt. *Lovecraft Country*. HarperCollins, 2016.
Schutte, Anne Jacobson. "'Such Monstrous Births': A Neglected Aspect of the Antinomian Controversy." *Renaissance Quarterly* 38, no. 1 (1985): 85–106.
Shapiro, Stephen. "Speculative Nostalgia and Media of the New Intersectional Left: *My Favorite Thing Is Monsters*." In *The Novel as Network: Forms, Ideas, Commodities*, ed. Tim Lanzendörfer and Corinna Norrick-Rühl. Palgrave, 2020. 119–36.
Sheldrake, Merlin. *Entangled Life: How Fungi Make Our Worlds, Change Our Minds and Shape Our Futures*. Random House, 2020.
Shildrick, Margrit. "You Are There, Like My Skin: Reconfiguring Relation Economies." In *Thinking through the Skin*, ed. Sara Ahmed and Jackie Stacey, Routledge, 2001. 160–73.
Swanson, Heather, et al. "Introduction: Bodies Tumbled into Bodies." In *Arts of Living on a Damaged Planet: Monsters of the Anthropocene*, ed. Anna Tsing et al. University of Minnesota Press, 2017. M1–M12.
Tsing, Anna, et al., eds. *Arts of Living on a Damaged Planet: Monsters of the Anthropocene*. University of Minnesota Press, 2017.
Weinstock, Jeffrey Andrew. "American Monsters." In *A Companion to American Gothic*, ed. Charles L. Crow. John Wiley, 2014. 41–55.
"Introduction: A Genealogy of Monster Theory." In *The Monster Theory Reader*, ed. Jeffrey Andrew Weinstock. University of Minnesota Press, 2020. 1–36.
Weinstock, Jeffrey Andrew, ed. *The Monster Theory Reader*. University of Minnesota Press, 2020.
Wilson, Natalie. *Willful Monstrosity: Gender and Race in 21st Century Horror*. McFarland, 2020.
Winsser, Johan. "Mary Dyer and the 'Monster' Story." *Quaker History* 79, no. 1 (1990): 20–34.
Wood, Robin. *Hollywood from Vietnam to Reagan*. Columbia University Press, 1986.

INDEX

Cambridge Companions To . . .

AUTHORS

Edward Albee edited by Stephen J. Bottoms
Margaret Atwood edited by Coral Ann Howells (second edition)
W. H. Auden edited by Stan Smith
Jane Austen edited by Edward Copeland and Juliet McMaster (second edition)
James Baldwin edited by Michele Elam
Balzac edited by Owen Heathcote and Andrew Watts
Beckett edited by John Pilling
Bede edited by Scott DeGregorio
Aphra Behn edited by Derek Hughes and Janet Todd
Saul Bellow edited by Victoria Aarons
Walter Benjamin edited by David S. Ferris
William Blake edited by Morris Eaves
Boccaccio edited by Guyda Armstrong, Rhiannon Daniels, and Stephen J. Milner
Jorge Luis Borges edited by Edwin Williamson
Brecht edited by Peter Thomson and Glendyr Sacks (second edition)
The Brontës edited by Heather Glen
Bunyan edited by Anne Dunan-Page
Frances Burney edited by Peter Sabor
Byron edited by Drummond Bone
Albert Camus edited by Edward J. Hughes
Willa Cather edited by Marilee Lindemann
Catullus edited by Ian Du Quesnay and Tony Woodman
Cervantes edited by Anthony J. Cascardi
Chaucer edited by Piero Boitani and Jill Mann (second edition)
Chekhov edited by Vera Gottlieb and Paul Allain
Kate Chopin edited by Janet Beer
Caryl Churchill edited by Elaine Aston and Elin Diamond
Cicero edited by Catherine Steel
J. M. Coetzee edited by Jarad Zimbler
Coleridge edited by Lucy Newlyn
Wilkie Collins edited by Jenny Bourne Taylor
Joseph Conrad edited by J. H. Stape
H. D. edited by Nephie J. Christodoulides and Polina Mackay
Dante edited by Rachel Jacoff (second edition)
Daniel Defoe edited by John Richetti
Don DeLillo edited by John N. Duvall
Charles Dickens edited by John O. Jordan
Emily Dickinson edited by Wendy Martin
John Donne edited by Achsah Guibbory
Dostoevskii edited by W. J. Leatherbarrow
Theodore Dreiser edited by Leonard Cassuto and Claire Virginia Eby
John Dryden edited by Steven N. Zwicker
W. E. B. Du Bois edited by Shamoon Zamir
George Eliot edited by George Levine and Nancy Henry (second edition)
T. S. Eliot edited by A. David Moody
Ralph Ellison edited by Ross Posnock
Ralph Waldo Emerson edited by Joel Porte and Saundra Morris
William Faulkner edited by Philip M. Weinstein
Henry Fielding edited by Claude Rawson
F. Scott Fitzgerald edited by Ruth Prigozy
Flaubert edited by Timothy Unwin
E. M. Forster edited by David Bradshaw
Benjamin Franklin edited by Carla Mulford
Brian Friel edited by Anthony Roche
Robert Frost edited by Robert Faggen
Gabriel García Márquez edited by Philip Swanson
Elizabeth Gaskell edited by Jill L. Matus
Edward Gibbon edited by Karen O'Brien and Brian Young
Goethe edited by Lesley Sharpe
Günter Grass edited by Stuart Taberner
Thomas Hardy edited by Dale Kramer
David Hare edited by Richard Boon
Nathaniel Hawthorne edited by Richard Millington
Seamus Heaney edited by Bernard O'Donoghue
Ernest Hemingway edited by Scott Donaldson
Hildegard of Bingen edited by Jennifer Bain
Homer edited by Robert Fowler
Horace edited by Stephen Harrison
Ted Hughes edited by Terry Gifford
Ibsen edited by James McFarlane
Henry James edited by Jonathan Freedman
Samuel Johnson edited by Greg Clingham

Ben Jonson edited by Richard Harp and Stanley Stewart

James Joyce edited by Derek Attridge (second edition)

Kafka edited by Julian Preece

Keats edited by Susan J. Wolfson

Rudyard Kipling edited by Howard J. Booth

Lacan edited by Jean-Michel Rabaté

D. H. Lawrence edited by Anne Fernihough

Primo Levi edited by Robert Gordon

Lucretius edited by Stuart Gillespie and Philip Hardie

Machiavelli edited by John M. Najemy

David Mamet edited by Christopher Bigsby

Thomas Mann edited by Ritchie Robertson

Christopher Marlowe edited by Patrick Cheney

Andrew Marvell edited by Derek Hirst and Steven N. Zwicker

Ian McEwan edited by Dominic Head

Herman Melville edited by Robert S. Levine

Arthur Miller edited by Christopher Bigsby (second edition)

Milton edited by Dennis Danielson (second edition)

Molière edited by David Bradby and Andrew Calder

Toni Morrison edited by Justine Tally

Alice Munro edited by David Staines

Nabokov edited by Julian W. Connolly

Eugene O'Neill edited by Michael Manheim

George Orwell edited by John Rodden

Ovid edited by Philip Hardie

Petrarch edited by Albert Russell Ascoli and Unn Falkeid

Harold Pinter edited by Peter Raby (second edition)

Sylvia Plath edited by Jo Gill

Edgar Allan Poe edited by Kevin J. Hayes

Alexander Pope edited by Pat Rogers

Ezra Pound edited by Ira B. Nadel

Proust edited by Richard Bales

Pushkin edited by Andrew Kahn

Thomas Pynchon edited by Inger H. Dalsgaard, Luc Herman and Brian McHale

Rabelais edited by John O'Brien

Rilke edited by Karen Leeder and Robert Vilain

Philip Roth edited by Timothy Parrish

Salman Rushdie edited by Abdulrazak Gurnah

John Ruskin edited by Francis O'Gorman

Sappho edited by P. J. Finglass and Adrian Kelly

Seneca edited by Shadi Bartsch and Alessandro Schiesaro

Shakespeare edited by Margareta de Grazia and Stanley Wells (second edition)

George Bernard Shaw edited by Christopher Innes

Shelley edited by Timothy Morton

Mary Shelley edited by Esther Schor

Sam Shepard edited by Matthew C. Roudané

Spenser edited by Andrew Hadfield

Laurence Sterne edited by Thomas Keymer

Wallace Stevens edited by John N. Serio

Tom Stoppard edited by Katherine E. Kelly

Harriet Beecher Stowe edited by Cindy Weinstein

August Strindberg edited by Michael Robinson

Jonathan Swift edited by Christopher Fox

J. M. Synge edited by P. J. Mathews

Tacitus edited by A. J. Woodman

Henry David Thoreau edited by Joel Myerson

Tolstoy edited by Donna Tussing Orwin

Anthony Trollope edited by Carolyn Dever and Lisa Niles

Mark Twain edited by Forrest G. Robinson

John Updike edited by Stacey Olster

Mario Vargas Llosa edited by Efrain Kristal and John King

Virgil edited by Fiachra Mac Góráin and Charles Martindale (second edition)

Voltaire edited by Nicholas Cronk

David Foster Wallace edited by Ralph Clare

Edith Wharton edited by Millicent Bell

Walt Whitman edited by Ezra Greenspan

Oscar Wilde edited by Peter Raby

Tennessee Williams edited by Matthew C. Roudané

William Carlos Williams edited by Christopher MacGowan

August Wilson edited by Christopher Bigsby

Mary Wollstonecraft edited by Claudia L. Johnson

Virginia Woolf edited by Susan Sellers (second edition)

Wordsworth edited by Stephen Gill

Richard Wright edited by Glenda R. Carpio

W. B. Yeats edited by Marjorie Howes and John Kelly

Xenophon edited by Michael A. Flower

Zola edited by Brian Nelson

TOPICS

The Actress edited by Maggie B. Gale and John Stokes

The African American Novel edited by Maryemma Graham

The African American Slave Narrative edited by Audrey A. Fisch

African American Theatre by Harvey Young

Allegory edited by Rita Copeland and Peter Struck

American Crime Fiction edited by Catherine Ross Nickerson

American Gothic edited by Jeffrey Andrew Weinstock

American Literature and the Body by Travis M. Foster

American Literature and the Environment edited by Sarah Ensor and Susan Scott Parrish

American Literature of the 1930s edited by William Solomon

American Modernism edited by Walter Kalaidjian

American Poetry since 1945 edited by Jennifer Ashton

American Realism and Naturalism edited by Donald Pizer

American Travel Writing edited by Alfred Bendixen and Judith Hamera

American Women Playwrights edited by Brenda Murphy

Ancient Rhetoric edited by Erik Gunderson

Arthurian Legend edited by Elizabeth Archibald and Ad Putter

Australian Literature edited by Elizabeth Webby

The Beats edited by Stephen Belletto

Boxing edited by Gerald Early

British Black and Asian Literature (1945–2010) edited by Deirdre Osborne

British Fiction: 1980–2018 edited by Peter Boxall

British Fiction since 1945 edited by David James

British Literature of the 1930s edited by James Smith

British Literature of the French Revolution edited by Pamela Clemit

British Romantic Poetry edited by James Chandler and Maureen N. McLane

British Romanticism edited by Stuart Curran (second edition)

British Romanticism and Religion edited by Jeffrey Barbeau

British Theatre, 1730–1830, edited by Jane Moody and Daniel O'Quinn

Canadian Literature edited by Eva-Marie Kröller (second edition)

The Canterbury Tales edited by Frank Grady

Children's Literature edited by M. O. Grenby and Andrea Immel

The Classic Russian Novel edited by Malcolm V. Jones and Robin Feuer Miller

Contemporary Irish Poetry edited by Matthew Campbell

Creative Writing edited by David Morley and Philip Neilsen

Crime Fiction edited by Martin Priestman

Dante's 'Commedia' edited by Zygmunt G. Barański and Simon Gilson

Dracula edited by Roger Luckhurst

Early American Literature edited by Bryce Traister

Early Modern Women's Writing edited by Laura Lunger Knoppers

The Eighteenth-Century Novel edited by John Richetti

Eighteenth-Century Poetry edited by John Sitter

Eighteenth-Century Thought edited by Frans De Bruyn

Emma edited by Peter Sabor

English Dictionaries edited by Sarah Ogilvie

English Literature, 1500–1600 edited by Arthur F. Kinney

English Literature, 1650–1740 edited by Steven N. Zwicker

English Literature, 1740–1830 edited by Thomas Keymer and Jon Mee

English Literature, 1830–1914 edited by Joanne Shattock

English Melodrama edited by Carolyn Williams

English Novelists edited by Adrian Poole

English Poetry, Donne to Marvell edited by Thomas N. Corns

English Poets edited by Claude Rawson

English Renaissance Drama edited by A. R. Braunmuller and Michael Hattaway, (second edition)

English Renaissance Tragedy edited by Emma Smith and Garrett A. Sullivan Jr.

English Restoration Theatre edited by Deborah C. Payne Fisk

Environmental Humanities edited by Jeffrey Cohen and Stephanie Foote

The Epic edited by Catherine Bates
Erotic Literature edited by Bradford Mudge
European Modernism edited by Pericles Lewis
European Novelists edited by Michael Bell
Fairy Tales edited by Maria Tatar
Fantasy Literature edited by Edward James and Farah Mendlesohn
Feminist Literary Theory edited by Ellen Rooney
Fiction in the Romantic Period edited by Richard Maxwell and Katie Trumpener
The Fin de Siècle edited by Gail Marshall
Frankenstein edited by Andrew Smith
The French Enlightenment edited by Daniel Brewer
French Literature edited by John D. Lyons
The French Novel: from 1800 to the Present edited by Timothy Unwin
Gay and Lesbian Writing edited by Hugh Stevens
German Romanticism edited by Nicholas Saul
Gothic Fiction edited by Jerrold E. Hogle
The Graphic Novel edited by Stephen Tabachnick
The Greek and Roman Novel edited by Tim Whitmarsh
Greek and Roman Theatre edited by Marianne McDonald and J. Michael Walton
Greek Comedy edited by Martin Revermann
Greek Lyric edited by Felix Budelmann
Greek Mythology edited by Roger D. Woodard
Greek Tragedy edited by P. E. Easterling
The Harlem Renaissance edited by George Hutchinson
The History of the Book edited by Leslie Howsam
Human Rights and Literature edited by Crystal Parikh
The Irish Novel edited by John Wilson Foster
Irish Poets edited by Gerald Dawe
The Italian Novel edited by Peter Bondanella and Andrea Ciccarelli
The Italian Renaissance edited by Michael Wyatt
Jewish American Literature edited by Hana Wirth-Nesher and Michael P. Kramer
The Latin American Novel edited by Efraín Kristal
Latin American Poetry edited by Stephen Hart
Latina/o American Literature edited by John Morán González
Latin Love Elegy edited by Thea S. Thorsen
Literature and the Anthropocene edited by John Parham
Literature and Climate edited by Adeline Johns-Putra and Kelly Sultzbach
Literature and Disability edited by Clare Barker and Stuart Murray
Literature and Food edited by J. Michelle Coghlan
Literature and the Posthuman edited by Bruce Clarke and Manuela Rossini
Literature and Religion edited by Susan M. Felch
Literature and Science edited by Steven Meyer
The Literature of the American Civil War and Reconstruction edited by Kathleen Diffley and Coleman Hutchison
The Literature of the American Renaissance edited by Christopher N. Phillips
The Literature of Berlin edited by Andrew J. Webber
The Literature of the Crusades edited by Anthony Bale
The Literature of the First World War edited by Vincent Sherry
The Literature of London edited by Lawrence Manley
The Literature of Los Angeles edited by Kevin R. McNamara
The Literature of New York edited by Cyrus Patell and Bryan Waterman
The Literature of Paris edited by Anna-Louise Milne
The Literature of World War II edited by Marina MacKay
Literature on Screen edited by Deborah Cartmell and Imelda Whelehan
Lyrical Ballads edited by Sally Bushell
Medieval British Manuscripts edited by Orietta Da Rold and Elaine Treharne
Medieval English Culture edited by Andrew Galloway
Medieval English Law and Literature edited by Candace Barrington and Sebastian Sobecki
Medieval English Literature edited by Larry Scanlon
Medieval English Mysticism edited by Samuel Fanous and Vincent Gillespie
Medieval English Theatre edited by Richard Beadle and Alan J. Fletcher (second edition)
Medieval French Literature edited by Simon Gaunt and Sarah Kay
Medieval Romance edited by Roberta L. Krueger

Medieval Women's Writing edited by Carolyn Dinshaw and David Wallace

Modern American Culture edited by Christopher Bigsby

Modern British Women Playwrights edited by Elaine Aston and Janelle Reinelt

Modern French Culture edited by Nicholas Hewitt

Modern German Culture edited by Eva Kolinsky and Wilfried van der Will

The Modern German Novel edited by Graham Bartram

The Modern Gothic edited by Jerrold E. Hogle

Modern Irish Culture edited by Joe Cleary and Claire Connolly

Modern Italian Culture edited by Zygmunt G. Baranski and Rebecca J. West

Modern Latin American Culture edited by John King

Modern Russian Culture edited by Nicholas Rzhevsky

Modern Spanish Culture edited by David T. Gies

Modernism edited by Michael Levenson (second edition)

The Modernist Novel edited by Morag Shiach

Modernist Poetry edited by Alex Davis and Lee M. Jenkins

Modernist Women Writers edited by Maren Tova Linett

Narrative edited by David Herman

Narrative Theory edited by Matthew Garrett

Native American Literature edited by Joy Porter and Kenneth M. Roemer

Nineteen Eighty-Four edited by Nathan Waddell

Nineteenth-Century American Poetry edited by Kerry Larson

Nineteenth-Century American Women's Writing edited by Dale M. Bauer and Philip Gould

Nineteenth-Century Thought edited by Gregory Claeys

The Novel edited by Eric Bulson

Old English Literature edited by Malcolm Godden and Michael Lapidge (second edition)

Performance Studies edited by Tracy C. Davis

Piers Plowman by Andrew Cole and Andrew Galloway

The Poetry of the First World War edited by Santanu Das

Popular Fiction edited by David Glover and Scott McCracken

Postcolonial Literary Studies edited by Neil Lazarus

Postcolonial Poetry edited by Jahan Ramazani

Postcolonial Travel Writing edited by Robert Clarke

Postmodern American Fiction edited by Paula Geyh

Postmodernism edited by Steven Connor

Prose edited by Daniel Tyler

The Pre-Raphaelites edited by Elizabeth Prettejohn

Pride and Prejudice edited by Janet Todd

Queer Studies edited by Siobhan B. Somerville

Renaissance Humanism edited by Jill Kraye

Robinson Crusoe edited by John Richetti

Roman Comedy edited by Martin T. Dinter

The Roman Historians edited by Andrew Feldherr

Roman Satire edited by Kirk Freudenburg

Science Fiction edited by Edward James and Farah Mendlesohn

Scottish Literature edited by Gerald Carruthers and Liam McIlvanney

Sensation Fiction edited by Andrew Mangham

Shakespeare and Contemporary Dramatists edited by Ton Hoenselaars

Shakespeare and Popular Culture edited by Robert Shaughnessy

Shakespeare and Race edited by Ayanna Thompson

Shakespeare and Religion edited by Hannibal Hamlin

Shakespeare and War edited by David Loewenstein and Paul Stevens

Shakespeare on Film edited by Russell Jackson (second edition)

Shakespeare on Screen edited by Russell Jackson

Shakespeare on Stage edited by Stanley Wells and Sarah Stanton

Shakespearean Comedy edited by Alexander Leggatt

Shakespearean Tragedy edited by Claire McEachern (second edition)

Shakespeare's First Folio edited by Emma Smith

Shakespeare's History Plays edited by Michael Hattaway

Shakespeare's Language edited by Lynne Magnusson with David Schalkwyk

Shakespeare's Last Plays edited by Catherine M. S. Alexander

Shakespeare's Poetry edited by Patrick Cheney

Sherlock Holmes edited by Janice M. Allan and Christopher Pittard

The Sonnet edited by A. D. Cousins and Peter Howarth

The Spanish Novel: From 1600 to the Present edited by Harriet Turner and Adelaida López de Martínez

Textual Scholarship edited by Neil Fraistat and Julia Flanders

Theatre and Science edited by Kristen E. Shepherd-Barr

Theatre History by David Wiles and Christine Dymkowski

Transnational American Literature edited by Yogita Goyal

Travel Writing edited by Peter Hulme and Tim Youngs

Twentieth-Century British and Irish Women's Poetry edited by Jane Dowson

The Twentieth-Century English Novel edited by Robert L. Caserio

Twentieth-Century English Poetry edited by Neil Corcoran

Twentieth-Century Irish Drama edited by Shaun Richards

Twentieth-Century Russian Literature edited by Marina Balina and Evgeny Dobrenko

Utopian Literature edited by Gregory Claeys

Victorian and Edwardian Theatre edited by Kerry Powell

The Victorian Novel edited by Deirdre David (second edition)

Victorian Poetry edited by Joseph Bristow

Victorian Women's Poetry edited by Linda K. Hughes

Victorian Women's Writing edited by Linda H. Peterson

War Writing edited by Kate McLoughlin

Women's Writing in Britain, 1660–1789 edited by Catherine Ingrassia

Women's Writing in the Romantic Period edited by Devoney Looser

World Literature edited by Ben Etherington and Jarad Zimbler

World Crime Fiction edited by Stewart King, Alistair Rolls and Jesper Gulddal

Writing of the English Revolution edited by N. H. Keeble

The Writings of Julius Caesar edited by Christopher Krebs and Luca Grillo